**Two brand-new stories in every volume...
twice a month!**

Duets Vol. #65

The holidays are almost here
and we have a delightful duo just for you.
Multipublished author Jacqueline Diamond returns
with a delicious doc and the unexpected twins the
heroine is *clearly* expecting! Making her Duets debut
this month is talented Stephanie Doyle with a
Fran Drescher look-alike character who's definitely
out of her element down on the farm!

Duets Vol. #66

The holiday fun continues with
Harlequin American Romance author Nikki Rivers,
who serves up a quirky, fast-paced romance.
"Ms. Rivers brings her characters to life with a fire
that is magic," says *Affaire de Coeur*. New author
Kathleen O'Reilly will tickle your funny bone with a
warm story about two best buds who suddenly see
each other in a different light at Chistmastime. Enjoy!

Be sure to pick up both Duets volumes today!

"I'm in a hurry," Rory explained.

"So am I! I have to get to Chicago and you're heading there and you've got the last rental car."

"No."

Sunny stopped short. "No? How can you say such a thing? I have to get there, the wedding I've been dreaming of is tomorrow!"

Darkness was beginning to creep over them. The slush was now turning into snow. She could feel the huge flakes gathering in her hair and on her lashes.

He advanced toward her and swept her into his arms. Immediately they were heading for the only car in the illuminated parking lot.

"What do you think you're doing?" she demanded.

"Look, if you're going to make your wedding and I'm going to have my business meeting and news conference, you'll have to pick up the pace."

My wedding. Did she dare? Could she, should she, correct his mistake? She took one look at his presumptuous grin and then looked toward the lonely vehicle waiting for them. *Not on your life, buster.*

Once Sunny was in the car, she made sure to fasten her seat belt tightly, because without question, it was going to be a bumpy ride.

For more, turn to page 9

A Christmas Carol

Alone. At last.

No relatives, no Autumn Hills residents, no Junior Leaguers.

"Carol, are you sure about this?" Mike didn't smile, his gaze intent upon her.

She studied him—the dark eyes, the smooth line of his jaw, the ridge that sat in the middle of his nose.

Sure? She wasn't sure what the hit toy of the season was, couldn't decide what she wanted to wear to work on Monday and didn't know if she was a Republican or a Democrat. But there was one fact she could absolutely, positively count on.

In the next three seconds she was going to start kissing this man, and she wasn't going to stop. Ever. Five years. Ten years. Yep, fifty years later, she was still going to be kissing him. Her mother could have a fit and it really didn't matter.

Not anymore.

Carol walked across her living room and pulled a little bow from her Christmas tree, turned and stuck it on her head. Then she smiled the sexiest smile she knew how.

"Merry Christmas, Mike."

For more, turn to page 197

HARLEQUIN DUETS

ISBN 0-373-44132-0

Copyright in the collection:
Copyright © 2001 by Harlequin Books S.A.

The publisher acknowledges the copyright holders
of the individual works as follows:

A SNOWBALL'S CHANCE
Copyright © 2001 by Sharon Edwin

A CHRISTMAS CAROL
Copyright © 2001 by Kathleen Panov

This edition published by arrangement with Harlequin Books S.A.

® and TM are trademarks of the publisher. Trademarks indicated with ® are registered in the United States Patent and Trademark Office, the Canadian Trade Marks Office and in other countries.

Visit us at www.eHarlequin.com

Printed in U.S.A.

A Snowball's Chance

Nikki Rivers

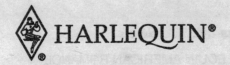

HARLEQUIN®

TORONTO • NEW YORK • LONDON
AMSTERDAM • PARIS • SYDNEY • HAMBURG
STOCKHOLM • ATHENS • TOKYO • MILAN • MADRID
PRAGUE • WARSAW • BUDAPEST • AUCKLAND

Dear Reader,

In this season of sleigh rides and jingle bells, what better way to celebrate than to go back home again? That's exactly what I did for my very first Duets novel. I grew up in Michigan's Upper Peninsula, where much of *A Snowball's Chance* takes place and where the weather is as unpredictable as—well, as unpredictable as love. As a child, I loved a good blizzard, even if it meant I had to shovel snow. It was such fun creating that kind of storm for *A Snowball's Chance*, then tossing into the whirlwind a man and woman who, but for the force of nature, never would have met. Fun-loving Sunny Morgan and no-nonsense Rory Temple are as different as winter is from summer, but in their mad dash against time and nature they prove to each other, and to themselves, that life is full of surprises.

I love writing romantic comedy because, like Sunny, I believe that knowing how to laugh just makes life's twists and turns that much easier to navigate. Sunny and Rory's blizzard is my holiday gift to you—and you don't even have to shovel!

May your holiday season be full of surprises!

Nikki Rivers

Books by Nikki Rivers

HARLEQUIN AMERICAN ROMANCE

For my mother, who still knows how to laugh.

For my mother, who still knows how to laugh.

1

Sunny Morgan reached up and adjusted the wide brim of the chiffon hat she was wearing so it shaded her face, sighed through a satisfied smile, and snuggled deeper into her airplane seat.

Life was good. Even if she did have to wear the hat all the way from San Francisco to Chicago. Her father's Aunt Tilly, the matriarch of the California Morgans, had made it especially for the wedding tomorrow. At five feet ten inches tall with size ten feet to match, Sunny was used to being visible. But nothing had ever made her feel as conspicuous as Great-Aunt Tilly's rendition of a wedding hat. Sunny couldn't even blame the gawkers and the gaspers. It was impossible not to react to a near Amazon of a woman in a crowded airport wearing something that looked like headgear from a Scarlett O'Hara tea party.

The quick trip she'd just taken through the Minneapolis airport while changing planes had been a test in patience. Every time someone nearly fell over their own feet from staring, Sunny flashed them a brilliant smile and reminded herself that the reason she had to wear the frothy confection with the spray of silk lilacs cascading across the brim was because her suitcase was stuffed with wonderful—well, stuff.

Sunny could definitely handle a stare or two in payment for just the Art Deco flower frog alone that she'd discovered in a ten-dollar box of junk at an estate sale in

San Francisco. And there was a tabletop cigarette lighter in the same box that looked promising, as well.

But those little items were far from the best of the finds. The best of the finds was going to pay for everything else. In fact, combining the trip to satiate Cordelia Gordon's Art Deco fixation with a visit to Great-Aunt Tilly was like an all-expenses paid vacation. Sunny had enjoyed Aunt Tilly's hearty roast beef dinners with mounds of mashed potatoes drizzled with gravy, her "who ever heard of fat grams" cream-filled doughnuts, and the wonderful view from the porch of her stately Pacific Heights house. Plus, she had found plenty of wonderful things to restock the display room of A Sunny Touch, the interior design studio Sunny ran in Chicago's River North area—who could ask for anything more?

Fattening, too, of course, she reminded herself as she tugged at the skirt of her simple black sheath dress. Sunny was tall, but far from skinny. Her curves belonged on a woman from an earlier time and they were directly responsible, Sunny thought as she wiggled her cramped toes, for her lousy choice in footwear. *The higher the heel, the thinner you'll look and feel,* she chanted in her head while she daydreamed about kicking the toeless pumps off as soon as she had claimed her car from the parking lot at O'Hare.

With a long finger, she lifted the brim of the hat enough to see the face of her watch. Two o'clock. In an hour she'd be landing at O'Hare airport. There would be plenty of time to pick up her car, deliver the contents of the carton she'd just gate-checked in Minneapolis to Cordelia in Lake Forest, and head into the city for the wedding rehearsal at seven that evening. The rehearsal would be followed by a dinner at her parents' favorite vegetarian restaurant in Wrigleyville—the section of Chicago where they lived above a flower shop, which they owned.

She yawned, let the brim of the hat fall over her eyes again and was asleep before the plane even left the gate.

RORY TEMPLE LOOKED impatiently at his watch. They should have taken off by now but they were still sitting at the gate.

"What's the holdup?" he asked the flight attendant who was once again counting heads as she strolled the aisle.

"It's snowing in Chicago, sir," she said as she placed a hand on the back of his seat and leaned forward. "We're waiting for word on conditions there before take-off."

"Oh, fine," Rory muttered. "Are you expecting a long delay?"

"Let me check with the pilot and get back to you on that, sir."

Rory watched the attendant head for the cockpit. She was an attractive woman but the thought barely registered with him. His mind was on Chicago. Two hours from now, he would be signing papers on a business deal that fulfilled a promise he'd made to a special woman. Someone who had not lived long enough to witness the moment. He was scheduled to announce this latest business venture at a live televised press conference right after the meeting.

"Well, Molly," he murmured to himself, "I always said the only thing to stop me from keeping my promise to you would be an act of God." *Yeah, a snowstorm at the end of April, that would qualify,* he thought as a small smile spread across his lips.

The attendant came back. "We're taking off momentarily, Mr. Temple," she said. He nodded his thanks before he flipped open his cell phone and punched out the number for his Chicago office. His assistant, Agnes, answered on the first ring.

"Everything set?"

Agnes chuckled. "For the fifth time today, and the twenty-fifth time this week, yes, boss. Everything is set."

Rory pressed his lips firmly together and narrowed his eyes, about to snap at Agnes's reply. But, as usual, where his assistant of five years was concerned, he easily let it go. Agnes was one of the few people in life who could get away with poking fun at Rory Temple.

Rory allowed the corners of his mouth to lift slightly. "So glad I can amuse," he commented dryly.

"So am I. Everyone needs to laugh now and then, especially at themselves."

"I'd be happy to howl like a hyena just as soon as this deal is done and announced."

"I'd pay good money to see that," Agnes said. "Where are you, anyway?"

Rory glanced impatiently out the window. "Still at the gate in Minneapolis. Something of a delay because of weather at O'Hare, apparently."

"Really?"

Now it was Rory's turn to chuckle. Agnes, efficient, loyal and no nonsense, probably wasn't even aware that it was snowing in Chicago. "Take a look out the window," he said.

"Now when on earth did that happen?" Agnes asked after a moment's silence.

"That's what I like about you, Agnes. Neither rain, nor sleet, nor black of night—"

"I believe you have me confused with the mail carrier."

Rory laughed again just as he felt the plane move beneath him. "We're finally backing out of the gate. I'll see you in an hour. Bring the file on the press conference with you to O'Hare so we can go over it in the limo. And—''

"And the market is closing soon so check the quotes again," Agnes finished for him.

"Watch it, Agnes. No one is irreplaceable."

"Want to bet?" Agnes said before hanging up the phone with a smart little click.

Rory switched off his cell phone and buckled his seat belt, knowing that she was absolutely right. No one could ever replace Agnes. She had that quality most prized by Rory in a woman. Practicality.

His grandmother, Molly Temple, had been like that. She did what needed to be done, such as working in a factory that made twine to support Rory when his widowed father wasn't up to the task. And Molly did it without self-pity, without complaint and with plenty of humor. Rory had yet to meet a woman who could hold a candle to Molly Temple. Unless, of course, he considered Agnes. If Agnes wasn't nearly sixty years old and still crazy about her husband of thirty years, he'd snatch her up for himself. At thirty-five, with real estate holdings worth millions, Rory was one of the most eligible bachelors in the Midwest. And, despite no lack of female attention, he was likely to remain so.

He gazed out the window as the plane taxied down the runway and rose into the air. Unless there was a woman out there who combined the traits of Molly Temple and Agnes Johnson along with the excitement he felt from putting his name on another building, there wasn't a snowball's chance in hell that Rory Temple was ever going to become a bridegroom.

THE PLANE SUDDENLY bucked and dipped and Sunny woke with a start.

"Huh?" she said aloud, forgetting for the moment

where she was. When her surroundings came into focus she blushed at her outburst. At least the seat next to her was still empty. She felt like she'd been sleeping deeply enough to drool—or even snore. Better not to have a witness for either, she thought, as she picked Great-Aunt Tilly's hat up off her feet where it had fallen when she'd woken so abruptly. It felt like she'd been sleeping for hours.

She checked her watch. Four o'clock.

She did a double take. That couldn't be right. Because, if her watch was right, it meant that she'd indeed been sleeping for hours. Two to be exact. Nice nap. The only problem was, the plane was supposed to have landed at O'Hare an hour ago.

She looked frantically around before spotting the flight attendant coming out of the cockpit.

"Excuse me," she said softly as the attendant passed by.

"Yes?"

"What time do you have?"

The young woman looked at her watch. "It's just after four."

"That's not possible," Sunny said. "We should have been in Chicago an hour ago."

The woman looked at her strangely. "Ma'am, you must have missed the pilot's announcement. We've been diverted because of a snowstorm."

Sunny frowned. "What?" Full of Great-Aunt Tilly's proteins and carbohydrates, Sunny had slept like a rock. Apparently her hearing had turned to stone as well, because she could have sworn the flight attendant said it was snowing. But that was impossible. It was nearly the end of April.

"Excuse me," she said, "I must have heard you wrong. I thought you said it was snowing."

The attendant smiled weakly. "More than just snowing, I'm afraid. O'Hare is closed because of a major blizzard."

Sunny blinked. "Well, then where are we landing?"

"We'll be landing in Escanaba, Michigan, in just a few minutes. Now, if you'll excuse me, there's a gentleman in back with a question."

"But—but," Sunny said to no one at all, "I can't land in Michigan!"

She got to her feet and went after the flight attendant. "How far is this Escanaba from Chicago," she asked.

"I'm told it's about six hours by car. Now could you please—"

Six hours! That would put her in Chicago around midnight. Way too late for the rehearsal, or the rehearsal dinner.

"Ma'am? Could you please take your seat and fasten your seat belt?"

"Oh! Yes. Of course."

Sunny made her way back to her seat and strapped herself in, distracted as she thought about the six-hour drive ahead of her. The rehearsal dinner was no great loss. No doubt her mother had ordered some sort of tofu and brown rice thing to serve. Personally, Sunny would rather have a rare burger smothered in cheese. And what did she really need with the rehearsal, anyway? She was perfectly capable of walking down the aisle carrying flowers without a lesson. The important thing was not to miss the wedding ceremony tomorrow at noon. She'd been waiting for this moment since she was a little girl. Nothing was going to keep her from it.

The plane bucked again and her teeth sank into her lower lip. "Ouch," she said, putting up her finger to rub the pain out. She looked out the window, squinting for any sign of snow. It sure felt like they were in for a bumpy landing.

Oh, goodness! A bumpy landing? They couldn't have a bumpy landing with the two vintage Cowan Pottery Jazz Age plates on board, which Sunny had found at the estate auction in San Francisco. Where did they put gate-checked items, anyway? Sunny plopped the chiffon hat back on her head, unbuckled her seat belt and struggled to her feet.

She started to weave her way up the aisle toward the flight attendant while the plane dipped and bucked. It wasn't an easy task given the three-inch heels she was wearing.

"Excuse me," she said to a woman whose eye she nearly poked out with a finger. "Oh—sorry," she muttered to the bald man when Tilly's wedding hat landed on his head.

The flight attendant turned to find out who was causing all the commotion.

"Ma'am! Please!" she said before Sunny had even reached her.

"I just wanted to ask you about the crate that I—"

"I really have to insist that you take a seat," the flight attendant said.

The plane jolted again and Sunny lost her balance and did, in fact, take a seat. Unfortunately, it was already occupied.

"Oh! Sorry! I was just trying to—"

Strong hands came out to tighten around her middle and stopped her struggle to get back to her feet.

"What I think you better do," said a masculine rumble near her ear, "is stay right where you are. We're about to land."

She shot a helpless glance at the attendant, but she was already hurrying off to strap herself into a seat.

Sunny was about to insist on being allowed to get free, when the captain's voice crackled over the loudspeaker.

"Ladies and gentleman," he said, "in just a few minutes we'll be landing in Escanaba, Michigan, where conditions are currently thirty-six degrees with freezing rain and with winds of thirty-five miles per hour. Tonight's forecast calls for falling temperatures and worsening conditions as the rain turns to snow and—"

With a sinking heart, Sunny listened to the pilot list the Midwest airports that were closing one by one as the storm, which had started just south of Chicago, moved steadily northward. By the time he reached the part where he assured them that the airline would do all it could to make up for the inconvenience, Sunny was beginning to think that they were lucky to land at all—even if they were landing in some little town in Michigan's upper peninsula.

The plane jerked again, causing Sunny to be pushed back against what felt like a very solid chest.

"Sorry," she said. As she tried to sit up straighter, it was hard to ignore the fact that her bottom was wiggling against a pair of equally solid thighs. The arms around her middle tightened.

"It would help if you sat still," came the rumble in her ear.

"Sorry," she said again, grimacing.

"Look, don't be sorry, just hold still," he ordered and she suddenly felt like a small child being allowed to sit at the adult's table, instead of a thirty-two-year-old grown woman.

"Tell you what," she retorted, "let go of me and I'll just go back to my seat and—" the plane dipped, then rose, dipped, then rose—like an elevator that couldn't decide which floor it wanted to stop on, and every time it dipped her body made contact with the man beneath her.

He flattened and tightened his palms against her midriff. "You're not going anywhere," he said in a voice that was crater deep and far too assured.

Sunny thrust her chin up stubbornly. "I beg your pardon?" she asked haughtily of the empty air.

Behind her, the man's laugh was brief, but she felt the rumble of it all the way through her body. "Don't worry," he said, "you're perfectly safe where you are. I have no use for frivolity. But the last thing we need during a rough landing is you hurtling about the cabin. That ridiculous concoction on your head is dangerous enough as it is."

"Frivolity?" Sunny could feel her patience waning. "Of all the nerve! What is this?" she demanded, as she tried unsuccessfully to turn around to look into the man's face, "A special flight for disagreeable men?"

"No," he answered in sonorous tones, his breath warm on the side of her neck, "it's a charter flight for women in very stupid shoes and ridiculous hats."

"Stupid shoes?" Sunny asked, affronted that anyone would find a thing wrong with the open-toed snakeskin pumps she was wearing. True, they had rather high heels but in them her size ten feet could pass for size eight and her legs looked long and shapely despite the few extra pounds she'd put on because of Great-Aunt Tilly's cooking. Sunny couldn't see anything stupid about that at all. "What's wrong with my shoes?" she asked with a frown.

"Well, if they weren't too high to walk in you wouldn't be sitting on my lap right now."

Sunny tried again to turn around so she could look him in the eye to tell him that an unexpected landing was what put her in his lap not her shoes. However, the plane's descent was an uneven jog that kept bouncing her around. There was a real danger of Sunny biting off her tongue every time she opened her mouth, so she reluctantly kept it closed until she heard a muffled cry from behind her.

"Are you all right?" she asked him.

"Just barely," came his voice, dry as expensive champagne. "Would you mind taking that thing off your head before I lose an eye? Surely the FAA has some kind of regulation against wearing a hat that size on an airplane."

"Well," Sunny replied defensively, as she reached up to remove it, "it's not like I wanted to wear it."

"I'm relieved to hear that," he replied.

"It's just that there wasn't enough room in my suitcase."

"Let me guess—because it is overflowing with additional pairs of stupid shoes."

Sunny's mouth flew open to correct him, but suddenly her mind had gone blank. It was just too disconcerting to have such constant bodily contact with a total stranger of the opposite sex. She couldn't seem to think clearly. She really should get up and get back to her seat, even if she had to crawl to do so. But before she could make a move another sudden dip, much deeper this time, had the passengers gasping in unison. Sunny sank her teeth into her lower lip, closed her eyes, and leaned back against that solid chest, all at once thankful that if these were the last moments of her life, she wasn't going to be spending them alone.

Her human seat belt might be a grouch, but at least he smelled good. His scent was drifting up to cradle her far more gently than his arms. He smelled like wind and water. Like waves hitting hot sand. She could feel the breath moving in and out of his chest against her back. The man she was sitting on might not be pleasant, but he sure was comfortable.

Well, okay, more than comfortable, Sunny admitted. There was something decidedly erotic about being sheltered in a strange man's arms as the plane struggled through the storm. A man whose face she had never seen. A man who was only a voice—but what a voice! Well, more than a voice, actually. He also seemed to be hard muscle, a hot scent, and—

The plane touched down on the runway with a hard thud and she felt the brush of what felt like a thumb on the underside of her breast.

It was an accident, of course. But her breast didn't seem to know it. And the feeling was only heightened by the plane's bumpy ride down the runway. She felt the heat of embarrassment flame on her cheeks. Surely, he couldn't *know*. Could he? Beneath her, he shifted in his seat and a shaft of awareness shot through her belly. My goodness! What was happening to her? Sunny had never been so embarrassed in her life.

As soon as the plane came to a stop, she jumped to her feet and shoved the hat back on her head. Other passengers in the aisle parted like the Red Sea; no doubt they were in fear of Aunt Tilly's work of art. Sunny grabbed her tote bag and hurried as fast as she could, as if deplaning was the most exciting thing she'd ever been allowed to do in her life. All the while, she was very careful not to look back.

Outside, the rain hit Sunny's face like icy needles as she battled the wind all the way down the metal staircase. She was beginning to wonder if her shoes might just be stupid after all. They certainly weren't designed for easy going in rugged weather. By the time she got to the cart that held the gate-checked luggage the small crowd around it was as ferocious as the wind. Sunny kept getting swept back by men in suits and women who didn't have to worry about trying to shield an enormous hat from the freezing rain. Great-Aunt Tilly wanted pictures of the wedding and she would be expecting Sunny to be wearing the hat she'd coaxed her arthritic fingers into making. Sunny, who'd spent more than one carefree summer in Pacific Heights hiding out from puberty and tofu overload, would rather break her own heart than disappoint Aunt Tilly.

"Excuse me," she repeated as she edged her way closer, taking a slight detour a couple of times when she thought she heard *the voice* just ahead. She had absolutely no desire to run into her landing partner ever again. The situation, now that she was soaking wet, could only get more embarrassing.

By the time she made it up to the cart, her hair was dripping, her dress was clinging to her, and Aunt Tilly's hat had lost most of its starch. But, there, on the cart, was one last small wooden crate. Sunny smiled as she reached out to claim it.

Inside the small terminal there were already lines formed in front of the only two car rental counters. Flinging her head back to get the sodden hair out of her face, Sunny glanced longingly at the sign for the women's rest room then got into the shortest line. There'd be time to dry off once she'd secured a car.

She was shaking out Great-Aunt Tilly's hat when a voice in front of her said, "I know. I can't believe it either, Agnes. We're going to have to reschedule—"

Her eyes popped wide. It was *him*. The *voice*. She whirled around and headed for the other rental counter.

The line was longer, and it seemed to be moving more slowly. The crate was getting heavy and she rested it on her hip, while she dug in her bag for a credit card. She heard someone further ahead complain that renting a subcompact wouldn't be acceptable. Sunny didn't care what kind of car she got, as long as it had a heater that worked.

By the time it was her turn, it felt as though all circulation to her arms had been cut off. Gratefully, she heaved the crate onto the counter.

"Sorry," the young woman behind it said, "we're out of cars."

"What?"

"We're out of cars," the woman repeated pleasantly.

"How can that be? I mean—"

"You might like to try across the room," the woman said, before putting up a Closed sign and turning away.

By the time Sunny gathered the crate back into her weary arms and made it over to the competition, they were out of cars, too.

"Just rented the last one to a man going to Chicago," said the young man at the counter.

"Chicago! But, that's where I need to go!" She looked frantically around. "Where is he?" she asked. "Which one is the man going to Chicago?"

"Over there." She followed the young man's pointing finger to a tall, dark suited man just pushing out of the doors to the parking lot.

"Wait!" Sunny called as she stumbled after him, still clutching the crate and the hat in her hands.

The door had shut behind him by the time Sunny reached it. She pushed through it and returned to the wet, windy afternoon.

"Excuse me!" she cried at the lone man striding across the parking lot. He didn't seem to hear her. She started after him. "Please! Could you stop? Can we talk?"

The man finally slowed to a stop. He waited until she had nearly reached him before he turned around.

When she saw his eyes, Sunny thought unaccountably of wolves. They were green, tilting upward slightly at the outer corners, glittering intensely while they looked down a sharply chiseled nose, and focused on her. Chiseled, too, were his jawline and the deep cleft in his chin.

She shifted her gaze to his mouth. It was well shaped and at the moment, molded into an expression of impatient disapproval.

"Is there something else I can do for you?" he asked.

Sunny's mouth dropped open. *Oh no! That voice! It was him!* The man who'd held her in his arms as the plane made its way back to earth. The man who'd called her frivolous! The man who, with a tiny, inadvertent brush of his thumb, made her feel like—made her feel like—

She wasn't going there. Best to leave that sentence unfinished—even in her mind. What mattered was that she would have to convince *this man* to take her with him to Chicago!

2

SHE TRIED FOR A SMILE, but it felt totally false on her lips. "Oh!" she said, trying to sound pleased. "It's you."

"Yes," he said in the voice that her ear already recognized, "your human seat belt."

With the freezing rain slashing his face, it was hard to tell if it was a glint of humor or a glint of anger in his deep green eyes.

"Thanks for the—um—the safe landing," she said rather lamely. Was there a socially correct way, she wondered, to extend gratitude to a stranger for using his lap for an airplane seat and his arms for a seat belt?

His arms. Her gaze flicked over them. The fine tailoring of the black suit jacket he wore couldn't hide the hard muscle underneath. She shifted her gaze to his shoulders. It was clear why she'd felt so secure despite the rough landing. His shoulders were broad in a way that had nothing at all to do with tailoring. Beneath the jacket he wore a shirt of fine black knit, open at the throat where the coarse hair from his chest was already showing. *Wolf,* she thought again, trying not to let the reaction shooting through her body show on her face.

"You're welcome," he said before turning away and starting toward the far side of the airport parking lot where one last, lone rental car waited in the rain that was starting to thicken into lazy, slushy drops.

"Wait!" she cried, with all the gusto of a cruise passenger calling out to the last lifeboat being lowered.

He swung around just long enough to say, "If you don't mind, I'm in a hurry."

She gripped the crate tighter, renewed her hold on Great-Aunt Tilly's hat, then went after him as fast as she could. Given the heels on her snakeskin shoes and the slick wetness of the pavement, she wasn't moving very fast at all. Damn her vanity. Right now she'd gladly swap the toe-cramping things for a pair of white size-ten sneakers—even if they would make her feet look like pontoons on a seaplane.

"Well, I'm in a hurry, too!" she cried against a sudden gust of wind. "That's the point!"

"What's the point?" he called over his shoulder.

She flicked her head back to clear her face of wet hair. "I have to get to Chicago and you've got the last rental car. The guy at the counter said you were heading for Chicago, too, so I thought—"

He finally stopped walking, turned around, looked her up and down like she was a cheap suit on a discount store rack and said, "No."

Sunny stopped short with her mouth dropping open. "No? How can you just say no like that? At least think it over."

He shook his head decisively. "Wouldn't be a good idea." With that, he turned and started walking away again.

"But—but—you can't leave me stranded up here in the north woods," Sunny stammered as she started after him. "I have to get back! The wedding is tomorrow! I've been dreaming of this wedding since I was eight years old!"

A howl of wind hit her, rocking her on her feet, and she started to lose her grip on the crate. She let go of the hat and caught the crate just as it started to slip from her grasp.

She closed her eyes for one moment's thankfulness, then opened them in time to see the hat twirling off into the wet, gloomy afternoon.

"My hat!" she cried and ran after it.

"Are you trying to kill yourself in those shoes?"

Teetering dangerously, Sunny turned to face him. He was coming toward her, his dark brows lowered over his glowering eyes. "No!" she cried over the wind. "But Great-Aunt Tilly made that hat! It's for the wedding tomorrow. I can't just leave it!"

"Sometimes I wish to hell my grandmother hadn't taught me manners," the man groaned as he shook his head. He put his black leather carry-on bag down next to her. "Stay where you are," he ordered. "I'll get the damn thing."

He stalked off into the storm and Sunny waited, shivering in the wind, trying to stay on her feet, trying to keep from dropping the crate that held the Jazz Age plates for Cordelia Gordon. Dropping the crate would cost her nearly four thousand dollars, and that wasn't counting the profit she intended to earn from Cordelia.

The slush was turning into snow now. She could feel the huge flakes gathering in her hair and on her lashes as she waited, while the simple black sheath that she'd paid a fortune for was starting to freeze on her body. Not only was Aunt Tilly's hat not going to be in the wedding photos, but if she stood here shivering much longer, Sunny would be headed for a hospital, not a wedding.

She shook her head like a dog to clear it of snow and through her bedraggled hair she glimpsed the wolf man striding out of the storm. The wind was whipping his dark hair back from his scowling face, and there was a dusting of snow on his broad, dark clad shoulders, and something lilac clutched in his—

"You found it!" she cried, grinning with joy to see

the chiffon and silk concoction hanging from one of his large hands. "How can I thank you?"

"You can buy one that ties under the chin next time," he stated firmly before plopping the sodden mess on her head and sweeping her up into his arms.

Sunny squealed. "What do you think you're doing?" she demanded once she'd overcome her surprise. After all, she was no small package. It wasn't every day she met a man up to the challenge of carrying her in his arms. She started to demand that he put her down, but he dipped to pick up his overnight bag and she had to use all her powers of concentration to keep a grip on the crate in her hands.

"Look," he said as he strode toward the only car sitting in the halo of lamplight illuminating the parking lot, "I told you I was in a hurry. If you're coming along, it'll be quicker to carry you. We'd waste an hour with you trying to totter over to the car."

"I do not totter," she insisted.

"In those heels, in this weather, you totter."

"Well, it's hardly my fault that it decided to snow in April, is it?"

"I wouldn't be surprised if it was," he said, before plopping her unceremoniously on her feet next to the car.

"Are you always so grouchy?" she asked him while he walked over to the driver's side.

He paused, then scowled at her over the roof of the rental car. "It is imperative that I get to Chicago by morning. I don't have time for frivolous women in stupid shoes and ridiculous hats. If it wasn't for the real possibility that you'd miss your own wedding without this ride, you'd be sitting in that terminal right now, waiting for the May thaw."

"My own wedding?" she croaked.

"Yes," he said, opening the driver's door. "I may be

a grouch, but I'm not heartless enough to make a woman miss the wedding she's been dreaming of since she was a little girl. But if you don't get in the car this instant so we can get out of here, I may just leave you here to let the snow finish ruining that absurdity on your head once and for all.''

Sunny opened her mouth to explain. But then she closed it—she could always set the record straight later. Right now the important thing was to get out of there before the roads became totally impassable.

She got into the car, placed the crate between her feet, tossed the sodden hat behind her, and buckled her seat belt.

RORY TRIED TO IGNORE HER, tried to focus on the two-lane highway that would get them out of there. But it was impossible. Two things in particular made it impossible. First, the scent of her. It had teased him during their cozy landing. Now, wet as she was, the scent that was like spring rain rose off of her richly enough to make his senses question the snow on the windshield.

Second, the simple fact that she was, indeed, wet. Wet and shivering. Rory was carefully keeping his eyes on the road, but it didn't really matter. He'd looked at her well enough back in the parking lot to forge the image of her into his brain forever. Her luxuriantly curved body under the clinging material of her dress, along with the fact that he already knew what her body felt like, was making him just a little crazy.

"Haven't you got a jacket or sweater or something?" he asked her gruffly.

She glanced in the back seat. "I—" she began.

But Rory was already steering with one hand while he struggled out of his jacket. "Here," he said roughly, handing it to her, "it's a little damp but it'll help. I've got a sweater in my bag back there that I can—"

She sneezed and he looked at her.

Her chin-length, chestnut hair hung damply about her face and her slightly swollen bottom lip was trembling with the cold. Her eyes were a deep hazel, her lashes wet and spiky. There was something damned appealing about her, something beyond the mere attraction her body seemed to hold for him. And he didn't like it. Didn't like it at all. But that wasn't her fault.

"Look, I'm sorry. I don't mean to be a grouch," he told her, giving her a quick smile as he used her word for him. "I've already had to reschedule a very important business meeting and cancel a press conference because of this storm. If I seem edgy because of it, I do apologize. Now, please, put the jacket on."

When she smiled, her mouth was as lush as her body. "All right, thanks," she said, as she struggled into his jacket. "What business are you in—um—" She laughed and the sound had a husky catch to it. "I'm afraid I don't know your name."

"Temple," he said. "Rory Temple."

"And I'm Sunny Morgan," she said.

Sunny. Rory fought a wicked grin as he let his glance move over her again. Her name said gingham, her body said satin. He felt his blood start to heat and decided that it was best to remember that Sunny Morgan was less than a day away from becoming another man's bride.

"What kind of business—" she started to ask, before she gasped, "Goodness! Rory Temple? *The* Rory Temple? The guy who owns all that real estate?"

"I own a building or two," he answered dryly.

"So I've heard," she said, grinning at him as she wrapped his jacket more closely around her body. The next time he put it on it would smell like her.

"We should stop soon so you can change out of that wet dress. You'll be sick at your own wedding."

She looked startled for a moment, then grinned again. "About the wedding," she said, then paused, lightly biting her full lower lip while she obviously thought over what to say next. While he waited, Rory thought over what he'd like to *do* next.

Taste that mouth.

She belonged to another man—and she wasn't the type he usually went for. But what he really wanted to do next was to taste her mouth.

He cleared his throat. "What about the wedding?" he asked, badly needing the dash of cold water she'd provide as soon as she started talking about flower arrangements.

"It's just that—" she began as she twisted around toward the back seat. "Oh no!"

Rory frowned. "What?"

"My luggage!"

"What about your luggage?" he asked.

"It's—um—" she paused, looking at him as if she was about to deliver bad news.

"It's what?" he asked carefully.

"It's back—um—there," she said, cocking her thumb at the road behind them, "at the airport."

Rory tightened his jaw and groaned. "Don't toy with me," he said.

"I wouldn't dream of it," she answered. "My luggage is still at the airport. We have to go back and get it."

"No," he said.

"No? What do you mean *no?* Stop the car and turn around. We're going back."

"Are you forgetting whose car this is?"

"But we've only gone thirty miles!"

"Yes. And it's taken us nearly an hour to do that. We're not turning back. Here," he said, handing her the map he'd been given when he'd rented the car, "find the location of the next town. We'll find someplace there to stop for warmer clothes."

"But I have a Waylande Gregory in my suitcase! And an original WPA—"

"Look, I know we're not likely to find a Lord & Taylor anyplace up here, but I've got to get back to Chicago before morning. And at the rate we're going, it just might take that long. I'm not taking another chance on having to cancel my activities in Chicago to go back for a few dresses with designer labels."

"Gregory isn't—"

"Save your breath. We're not going back."

Sunny's mouth dropped open. "And you call yourself a businessman?" she demanded.

He laughed without humor. "The entire country calls me a businessman, Miss Morgan."

"Really?" she asked, with slightly exaggerated wide-eyed innocence. "And as a businessman, Mr. Temple, would you do whatever you could to protect your investments?"

He spared her an impatient glance. "Of course."

"Well, I am merely trying to do the same thing."

He snorted. "Designer dresses are not a business investment, Miss Morgan."

"I couldn't agree more. I own an interior design studio called A Sunny Touch, Mr. Temple. I specialize in room accessories and I am returning from a buying trip in San Francisco, which is why I had to wear that ridiculous hat because my suitcases are filled with *investments*. And not," she added firmly, "stupid shoes."

He was staring grimly out the windshield, his hands gripping the wheel as if will alone would make a difference in their progress. He looked implacable, unmovable, carved of granite. And at the moment, he had power over whether or not she'd get to that wedding tomorrow. But she couldn't leave her precious finds without at least trying to persuade him. She took a deep breath and went on.

"Several of my clients are fans of Art Deco. Waylande Gregory is one of the better known designers of the period and the WPA I was referring to is an original art poster worth hundreds. You might find it difficult to believe, Mr. Temple, since the Waylande Gregory flower frog and the poster are small potatoes compared to owning half of Chicago's Loop, but the things in my suitcase are as valuable and important to me as your latest high-rise is to you."

There was tension in his jaw and thunder in his eyes when he glanced at her. She was bracing herself for some sort of eruption when she heard the rumble of laughter coming from his chest.

"A very persuasive argument, Miss Morgan," he said after the laughter. "And probably the only one that had a prayer of winning me over."

The car slowed and Sunny's eyes grew wide. "You're turning around?"

"Yes, Miss Morgan. I am turning around. Now don't belabor the point."

Sunny grinned. "I wouldn't dream of it."

While he found a place to turn the car around, she huddled into his jacket, pulling the lapels up around her neck. It smelled like him. Her eyes started to drift shut as the scent took her back to the landing, when she'd been sitting on his hard thighs, cradled in his strong arms—

Her eyes flew open at the sudden flutter in her lower belly. She risked a glance at him. He was too intent on turning the car safely around to notice her.

Goodness, she thought as she watched him, the man

was gorgeous. His profile was swoon-worthy. That thick dark hair flowing back from his strong face. That nose that looked like it belonged on an old Roman coin. No wonder he got so much press. Sunny wasn't a huge fan of the business section but even she had heard of Rory Temple.

He'd been one of those day-trader whiz kids of the late 1980s, working at some kind of muscle-building drudge job by night and playing the market by day. He'd made a killing in something to do with the Internet, then started buying up real estate like he was determined to be Chicago's version of Donald Trump before he hit forty.

He couldn't be much older than thirty-five now, she thought, and the Temple empire already included three hotels, several high-rise apartment buildings along Lake Shore Drive, and the recent acquisition of a very old department store that had long been the grand old lady of State Street.

That department store was one of Sunny's favorite things in Chicago. Its windows during the Christmas season had always fascinated her. They were the main reason Sunny became interested in design and decorating when she was barely twelve years old. She used to stand and gaze into them, snow falling around her unheeded, while she edited the contents of the windows. She'd move that teddy bear over there and put that doll in the rocker. And the red velvet dress should go on the dark-haired mannequin, while the blonde should be in the midnight blue.

Some of her fondest memories were of window shopping and browsing that department store. She'd heard that Temple was going to totally revamp the place. How she would love a part in it, no matter how small. What a kick it would be.

Yeah, and what a long shot, too, she reminded herself

as she shoved her hands into the pockets of Rory Temple's jacket. With all the trouble she was causing him, there wasn't a snowball's chance in hell that he was ever going to want to lay eyes on her again, much less do business with her.

"I'm really, really sorry about this," she said with true regret. "I'm usually not so careless or forgetful."

He kept his eyes on the road. "Prewedding jitters, I expect."

Sunny bit her lip and decided that maybe it was time to tell him the truth. The longer she kept it from him, the worse it would be when he found out. "About the wedding," she said. "I meant to tell you—"

He glanced swiftly her way. His tilted green eyes touched on her briefly but intently, the dark brows above them drawn low in question. "Yes?" he asked in a voice deep enough to put Red Riding Hood on the run.

It was a relief when he turned his attention back to the road. His profile in the darkening afternoon was stern, impatient. Maybe now was not the best time to tell him that it wasn't exactly her own wedding she was rushing home to. Perhaps she should wait until after they'd picked up her luggage.

"What about the wedding?" he asked again.

"The bridesmaids will be in yellow," she said with a falsely bright smile.

He looked at her, his eyes narrowed like he was sizing up prey. "One word about the flower arrangements," he growled, "and you're out in the snow."

Sunny slid further down in the seat and kept her mouth shut.

RORY SIPPED THE BITTER coffee from the coffee machine back at the Escanaba airport and waited for Sunny to come out of the women's rest room, confident that he could deal with her more safely now. She was talking wedding colors. It was more than enough to quell his suddenly overactive libido. She'd be out of that wet, clingy dress, too. That couldn't hurt. It was bad enough he was lusting after a woman he'd barely met—but to be lusting after someone else's blushing bride was making him feel like a jerk. He should be ashamed of himself for the wicked thoughts he'd been having ever since Sunny Morgan's sweet, round bottom landed in his lap.

He'd been alone too long, that was all. Because even if Sunny Morgan weren't about to wed, they were totally unsuitable in a thousand other ways.

He took another swallow of coffee and nearly choked on it when he looked over the rim of the paper cup to see her coming out of the rest room. She was struggling with her suitcase and the crate that she'd refused to leave in the car. Unsuitable was the word, all right. The outfit she had on couldn't have been less practical for a snow-storm.

Yes, she was wearing pants. But they were pink and snug and ended just above the ankle. Nice ankle, too, Rory noticed. His gaze moved up her long legs, over the abundant curve of hip, to the definition of her waist. Tucked into the pants was a simple white cotton shirt, open at the throat, and slung over her shoulders was a thin cashmere cardigan of pale, tender green. It enhanced the green flecks in her hazel eyes. It wouldn't do to look into them too long, Rory decided. It wouldn't do at all.

But it wasn't only her eyes that were causing him trou-ble. Her face, now scrubbed free of makeup, was sprin-kled with little brown freckles. Her hair, still damp, clung to her cheeks. Her lower lip was still tender looking. And he still wanted to taste it. He let his gaze run down her body to her feet. They were long, elegant feet—black flats, no socks.

He was thinking that he could encircle her ankle with his hand, but what he said was, "There's already a couple of inches of snow over a sheet of ice out there in that parking lot. You might want to rethink the shoes."

She looked down at her feet, then back up at him. "I wasn't exactly expecting a blizzard," she said.

"Obviously."

She put her suitcase down and placed one hand on her hip. "I thought you were in a hurry."

"I am," he said grimly.

"Then maybe you better skip the fashion review," she said, "before the two inches turn into four."

He suppressed a grin as she headed for the airport entrance, carrying the crate but leaving the suitcase for him to take care of. He picked it up and followed her. She had a point, he supposed. She also had a pretty incredible backside. She walked like a woman should walk. It made him wonder if—he cleared his throat. "Wait here," he said gruffly when he'd reached the door. "I'll put your bag in the trunk and bring the car closer."

He didn't turn back to see if she obeyed, just walked out into the falling snow hoping it would provide the cold shower that he needed.

SUNNY WAS FEEDING CHANGE into the pay phone when he came back.

"What do you think you're doing?"

"I have to call my mother to tell her I won't make it in time for the rehearsal tonight," she said, digging for more change in her purse.

"Nothing doing. We're getting out of here now—or there's a chance you won't make it for the wedding tomorrow. It's starting to really blow out there."

"It'll just take a minute."

"Right. You get on the phone with your mother the

night before your wedding and it will only take a minute.
I'm too old for fairy tales.''

"But—but—they'll be worried.''

"You can use my cell phone once we're on the road.''
He grabbed her hand. "Now come on.''

Her hand felt small in his as he pulled her toward the
door. She was nearly breathless when he pushed through
it and the cold air hit her lungs.

"More stupid shoes,'' he muttered grimly as he swung
her up into his arms.

She lost her breath again for one dizzying moment,
then he steadied her against his solid chest and there was
little she could do but wind her arms around his neck as
he strode through the snow to the car parked at the curb.

"Mr. Temple, must you go hauling me around like an
animal with its prey?''

"I'm merely trying to save you from frostbite, Miss
Morgan. Open the car door.''

She reached out and did as she was told and he ef-
fortlessly slid her into the passenger seat. He studied her
a moment, his face only inches from hers as he leaned
in the car door. "You've been in my arms three times
now, Sunny,'' he said. "Maybe you should start calling
me Rory.''

If he spoke the right words in that soft dangerous voice
his prey would lie down and willingly be devoured,
Sunny thought as she looked into his clear, green eyes.
He could have nibbled on her a little at that very moment
and all he'd done was to tell her to use his first name.

She had an urge to touch him—just the tip of her finger
to the sharp angle of his jaw, or maybe the deep cleft of
his chin. She was wondering if touching him would be
as dangerous as touching a wolf when he said, "Sunny?''

She nearly jumped. "Yes?''

"If you keep looking at me ???? ????, I'm going to forget that you're about to become another man's wife."

She blinked. "What?" she croaked, her mouth suddenly gone dry.

He ran a finger over her lower lip. "I've been working twelve-hour days on this deal, angel. You're nothing but trouble, believe me, I know that. But if you keep tempting me with those eyes I might have to show you how much of an animal I can really be." Watching her all the while, he moved his finger from her lower lip to brush a strand of hair from her cheek and tuck it behind her ear. "And, I don't think you're ready for that, angel." His finger lingered on her cheek while his green eyes continued to study her. "No," he said softly. "Not ready at all."

He drew back and closed the car door before she remembered to breathe again. What a predicament. The most eligible bachelor in the Midwest was calling her tempting! And there wasn't a darn thing she could do about it because he thought she was going to be married tomorrow!

Not that she wanted to do anything about it, of course. Did she?

Well, no. Of course not. She wasn't the type of woman who had flings with strangers. Not that Rory Temple was a stranger exactly. He came into her home with the morning paper on a pretty regular basis. And if a woman was going to have a fling with someone, Rory Temple would be perfect, wouldn't he? Not only was he gorgeous and rich, but he was a busy man. By all accounts, he put business before anything else in his life. One night of passion and she'd probably never see him again unless he was on the evening news.

He opened the driver's side door and slid in behind the wheel. One look at him and she knew how crazy the idea of a fling wa̲s̲ ̲ Rory Temple. He'd probably never had anyone other than a supermodel on his arm.

Still, she should really tell him the truth about tomorrow's wedding. Keeping up the charade was only making an awkward situation more uncomfortable. Best to tell him and get it over with.

"About the wedding," she began.

"Yes?" he said. And then his cell phone rang.

"Temple," he said. Then, "Yes, Agnes—"

He listened, his face growing stormy. "Then go to another station. I don't care that we promised Harrington an exclusive. If they can't preempt programming, then we'll go elsewhere—"

Whoever Harrington was, Sunny was happy not to be him. She wasn't exactly looking forward to being on the receiving end of any part of Rory Temple's temper. She bit her lip. Maybe she should rethink the whole idea of telling him the truth.

Rory ended the conversation on his cell phone and turned to her. "Sorry," he said, smoothly. "More problems. Now what were you saying about the wedding?"

His green eyes were just for her once again. That quickly. That smoothly. Oh, he was a dangerous man, was Rory Temple, she thought as his voice poured thickly over her. And not just because of his temper.

She'd face the temper if he learned the truth—and possibly lose her ride back to Chicago. And if he didn't get mad, she'd be facing something else. And maybe he was right. Maybe she wasn't ready to find out what an animal he could be.

He was waiting for her answer.

"The bridesmaids will be carrying daisies," she said.

He glared at her. "All right," he said in resigned tones. "You might as well tell me about the cake."

By the time she finished telling him about the chocolate wedding cake, an impatient look was back on his face and she was feeling a whole lot safer about everything.

3

"I KNOW MOM, it's a shame," Sunny was saying into the cell phone when Rory climbed back into the car. He'd been brushing the snow off the windows with his bare hands. "Of course I'll be there tomorrow." She stole a glance at him. He was busy settling himself in and she wasn't sure if he was listening or not. "I mean, how could I miss the wedding I've been waiting for since I was eight years old?" She smiled in Rory's direction, suddenly uncomfortable. Maybe she wasn't really lying to him, but she was certainly misleading him. "Yes, Mom. Great-Aunt Tilly's hat is safe and—" she twisted around to look in the back seat at the pile of limp, lavender chiffon "—well, it's safe," she finished. After saying goodbye to her mother, she ended the call and reached into the back seat to retrieve the hat.

"Poor thing. It's a mess."

"Count your blessings," Rory said grimly as he dried his cold wet hands on his sweater. "The hat is a monstrosity. I should think you'd be happy to go bareheaded down the aisle."

"Well, it was a lot less of a monstrosity before it got wet and I still have to wear it down the aisle."

"You're joking. Why?"

"Because I promised Great-Aunt Tilly I would."

"I take it Great-Aunt Tilly holds the strings to the family fortune?"

She looked at him in surprise. "Is money the only

reason to do anything? The way you talk, you'd think it was. It's got nothing to do with money." Sunny tried vainly to fluff the silk lilacs on the brim—or what used to be the brim. "She's just my favorite aunt, that's all."

"Don't tell me. She's the one who gave you your first diary with a lock and key."

"No, she's the one who gave me red meat."

Rory threw back his head and laughed. "I should have known it wouldn't be any of the usual reasons. So Great-Aunt Tilly bought your undying love with a hamburger?"

"Oh, not just hamburgers. Steaks. Roasts. Mounds of mashed potatoes and gravy."

He grinned at her and it did great things for his green eyes. They practically danced.

"The way to your heart, then, is with gravy, hmm? Not diamonds?"

"Hey, when a girl is on tofu overload, a rump roast is halfway to heaven."

"Tofu?"

"My parents are vegetarians. It fostered a guilty love of red meat from an early age. Give me a cheeseburger and I'll follow you anywhere."

He laughed again. The faint lines at the corners of his eyes deepened, and his lips parted to show a flash of strong white teeth. He was even more attractive this way. Quite devastating, she thought.

"Laughing becomes you," she said. "Too bad you don't do it more often."

He gave her an amused look. "So you've already decided that I don't laugh often enough? What do you base that on?"

She looked at her watch. "Two hours of observation."

He groaned. "That alone is one good reason not to laugh."

"What do you mean?"

"We landed at that excuse for an airport two hours ago and we're still trying to get out of the parking lot."

"But we have until tomorrow morning to get back to Chicago. It's impossible not to make it there in time, even given the snow. So why not enjoy the trip?"

"Driving through the wilderness during a snowstorm is not my idea of enjoyment."

"Maybe not. But the alternative is to not enjoy it and that," Sunny stated with sureness, "would be totally wasteful."

He looked at her. "Are you saying you decide on the spur of the moment what will or will not be enjoyable?"

She shrugged. "Sure. Why not? I mean there are plenty of places I'd rather be right now but as long as this is exactly where I am, why should I waste the experience wishing I were somewhere else?"

He scowled. "Swell. I'm trapped in a rental car with a Pollyanna. No wonder they call you Sunny."

"They call me Sunny because that's my name. Well, Sunshine, to be exact."

"Your parents, the vegetarians, named you Sunshine?"

She shrugged. "It was the late sixties. A lot of kids in the commune were—"

"Wait a minute," he interrupted. "Commune?"

She nodded. "We lived in one until I was eight."

"Hmm, that could explain your ability to circumvent reality," he said, nodding at the stormy landscape. "But your shoes—and you do seem a little capitalistic and acquisitive for someone who was raised in a commune."

"Call it rebellion," she said, and he laughed again.

In fact, Rory wasn't sure but he just might have grinned all the way out of the parking lot and onto the far-too-inadequate two-lane road.

What was it about her? The question never left his mind as he watched the windshield wipers try to keep up with the snowfall. When she wasn't irritating and exasperating him she was making him laugh. Just when he thought he had her figured out, like a diamond in candlelight she revealed a new color or sent sparks off into a different direction.

Rory wasn't often wrong about people. The ability to read people was part of the reason for his early success. But Sunny Morgan threw him. He'd had her pegged for a frivolous female. A spoiled, impractical, petulant woman. But here she was without socks with the temperature hovering around twenty degrees and the most she'd done was fiddle with the car's heater. She hadn't once complained. And she was even more concerned about the ridiculous hat an elderly aunt made than she was about the crate she'd barely let out of her sight. Rory had no idea what was in it. Given her more than thorough description of the wedding cake of her dreams, he was loath to ask her about it. It was probably some hugely overpriced trinket for a suburban matron's dining room table.

Rory wasn't exactly feeling generous toward designers lately. He'd been checking bids and interviewing them for the Simpson Twine condo project for weeks. As far as he was concerned, they were all under-talented and overpriced. One corner of his mouth lifted as he imagined Pollyanna Sunshine's righteous indignation if she knew what he was thinking.

They seemed to have the road to themselves, but he reminded himself to keep his eyes on it—and his mind. So far, his eyes kept straying to those wonderfully long legs in the snug, pink capri pants. He couldn't even begin to imagine them in a bathing suit.

Humph. Bathing suit. Fat chance. The snow was

blowing across the road with enough energy to completely hide the bay that was there according to the map. If there was a beach, it had been obliterated by snow and wind. Still, the idea of her sweet bottom in—

The weak glow of headlights started to emerge from the other direction, which got Rory's mind off Sunny's body and back on the road.

"Well, that's a relief," he said. "I was beginning to think we were the only people left on earth."

"You don't think that would be romantic?" she asked.

"Romantic?"

"Well, imagine it," she said, a little dreamily. "Two people alone in a winter wonderland—"

"It's April," he interjected.

She looked at him, smiling patiently. "Okay—two people alone in a snowy wonderland. Fluffy snow clinging to everything. The trees. The fences. The crocuses. The daffodils. The—"

The lights grew brighter and came with a plow, its blade up, its huge tires churning up a wave of snow that landed right on their windshield.

"—the windshield," he finished for her. "Don't forget the snow clinging to the windshield. Put there, I might add, by a snowplow that should have been plowing instead of spewing."

He reached out to thumb on the windshield washer. Nothing. He pushed the switch again. And again. Still nothing.

"Swell. We're out of windshield washer solvent. Terrific. Now if they ever do get around to salting the roads, we'll be flying totally blind."

"We'll just have to stop and buy some," Sunny said.

"Where do you suggest, Sunshine?" he said. "I can't see the strip mall for the trees, or is there an underground gas station on the map, perhaps?"

"Oh, stop being such a grouch." She unfolded the map again. "There are towns coming up. There's bound to be someplace to stop—a general store or something," she said, looking up from the map and peering through the cloudy windshield. "In fact, I think I see something ahead. On the right—"

"We are not in Oz, Dorothy. You can tap your heels together all you like, but—"

"Look! There it is!"

Sure enough. Rory peered through the snow and there it was. An old gas station, but with the lights off.

"Better keep tapping," he said dryly. "You found us a station, but it's closed."

"Turn in, anyway," she said.

"What on earth for?"

"You never know. Someone could still be there."

"Yeah, like a man of tin," he muttered, "badly rusting in the snow."

Just then more headlights crept out of the snowy road ahead. When the pickup passed them it spit more slush onto the windshield.

Rory swore.

"Worth a try," she said cheerfully.

Rory swore again and turned into the gas station.

He left the car running and got out.

The snow whipped him in the face as he rattled the doorknob of the old wood frame gas station. Locked. He rubbed a spot clear in the big window with Harry's One Stop scrawled across it in chipped red paint. The place was dark inside. No sign of life.

"Just as I thought," he said when he returned to the car. "Closed."

"You're sure no one is around?"

Rory looked at her, not knowing for sure whether he was amused or angry. This girl—woman, he amended in his mind, because surely with a body like that she qualified as a woman—questioned every damn thing he said. He was used to people following his orders. Men and women. But not Sunshine Morgan.

She unfolded her impressively long legs and got out of the car. Clutching the thin cashmere sweater to her, she picked her way gingerly through the snow and tried the door herself. Satisfied that it was locked, she started to pound on it.

Amused, Rory got out of the car, leaned back against it and watched her. Finally, she gave up and tiptoed her way back to the car.

"It's closed," she said.

"Humph," he said. "What a surprise."

"Well, you never know—"

"Ah, but I *did* know. I told you—"

He didn't get to savor his I told you so. A ramshackle panel truck, with the legend Clyde's Used Furniture painted on the side, pulled into the gas station.

The driver rolled down his window. "You folks got a problem?" he yelled over the uncertain sounding chug of the engine.

"Several," Rory muttered.

Sunny cast him a look as she walked on her tiptoes through the snow toward the truck. "We've got to get to Chicago by morning," she said to the driver. "And we're out of—" she paused and looked back at Rory "—we're out of gas," she finished as she turned back to Clyde.

Clyde looked from her to Rory, then back again. "Shame," he said, shaking his head sadly. "Generally, Harry stays open late on a Friday. Musta decided to close 'conna the storm." He suddenly brightened a little. "Bet I knowed where he is, though."

"Really?" Sunny asked as if Clyde had just claimed knowledge of something grand.

"Down the road a ways at Ethel's—same place he'd be an hour from now if he hadn'ta decided ta close. Yup, he'll most likely be sittin' on a stool at the counter, chewing down one of Ethel's doughnuts and complainin' about the day's take."

"Well, make sure you tell him that by closing early he missed a sale," Rory said. "A good businessman would know that today of all days—"

Sunny jabbed him in the side with an elbow and shot him a look. "Be quiet! I'll handle this," she hissed.

Rory opened his mouth to say something but damned if he knew whether to be amused or angry again. He'd put together deals that made the pages of the *Wall Street Journal,* but here was this woman who didn't have the sense to pack a warm sweater telling him to keep his mouth shut.

Well, that's exactly what he'd do, then. He stepped back, folded his arms across his chest, and prepared to watch Miss Sunshine fall on her face. The old rascal behind the wheel of the truck looked like he was used to dealing with lumberjacks, not women. Rory'd be willing to bet that he wasn't going to listen to a woman tiptoeing around nearly barefoot in the snow.

"How well do you know Harry, Clyde?" Sunny asked the driver.

"All my life, missy." His look narrowed suspiciously on her. "Why you askin'?"

"I was just wondering if you thought there might be a chance that if Harry knew for sure he was going to have a sale he'd open the place up for us?"

"Don't know about that," he said. "Harry's something of an ornery cuss. Never knowed him to go out of his way for anyone."

Sunny looked over her shoulder. Rory was standing there with his arms folded, snow collecting on him, look-

ing as if he had all the time in the world. He raised a
brow at her, and one side of his mouth lifted in amusement. Darn it! Didn't the man get cold? Sunny felt as if
she would never be warm again. There must be something that would speed things up with Clyde a little. She
swore she could actually feel cold germs starting to mi-
grate into her blood stream through the thin soles of her
shoes. Her eyes were starting to tear up and her nose was
starting to run. She sniffed and dashed at her cheeks.

"Aw, miss. You ain't gonna cry now, are ya?"

Sunny opened her mouth to explain, then decided that
she wasn't above using Clyde's mistake to her advantage.

"I'm sorry," she said. "I just don't know what I'm
going to do." She sniffed again. "I have to get back to
Chicago in time for the wedding tomorrow."

The man jerked his chin toward Rory. "You marryin'
him?"

"No! No, I'm not marrying him," Sunny said, shaking
her head vehemently. Suddenly, she noticed that she was
holding Great-Aunt Tilly's hat in her hand. "This is the
hat I'm wearing when I—um—walk down the aisle tomorrow. My Great-Aunt Tilly in San Francisco made it
especially for me," she added, as she plopped it on her
head.

Behind her she could hear Rory start to chuckle. Sunny
made up her mind to ignore him. This part, after all, was
the truth and nothing but. "She couldn't come to the
wedding because of her arthritis, so I promised to send
her pictures, with me wearing the hat she made." She
sighed tremulously. "Now, it looks like we just might
not get there at all."

She shrugged and sniffed, then slowly turned back toward Rory and the rental car. She made a face at him
when she saw the self-satisfied smile lifting the corner of
his mouth. It was only window washer solvent, but she

hated the thought of defeat when the wolf man was so obviously delighted by her unsuccessful theatrics.

"Miss!" the driver behind her called out.

She stopped. But before she turned around, she gave Rory a triumphant grin.

"Yes?" she called back.

"Hop up here, miss. I'll take you over to ask Harry yourself if he'd reopen. Even Harry ain't heartless enough to say no to that story."

"Come on!" she called to Rory as she ran around the truck, tugged the door open, and hopped into the cab.

Rory appeared in the doorway, scowling at her before climbing up beside her.

"Slightly devious, wouldn't you say?" he asked under his breath.

The question made her shiver. Or was it his warm breath on her earlobe when he spoke that was giving her goose bumps? Delicious as the feel of his breath was, she was pretty sure the word "devious" had something to do with it. But it didn't take a business genius to figure out that they'd have better luck getting someone to open up for a tank of gas than they would for a gallon of window washer solvent. Surely, Rory Temple could afford to tip the guy a twenty? So she wasn't really being devious. She was just being expedient.

Nor was she being devious about the wedding tomorrow. She never actually *said* that it was hers. She was just doing what she needed to do to assure that everything turned out okay.

"Hey, it's dangerous driving in this weather with a dirty windshield," she whispered back. "I'm only doing what I have to do."

"You folks musta been on that plane landed here this afternoon," Clyde said. "One that was supposed ta land in Chicago."

''That's right,'' Sunny said.

Clyde leaned forward a little and eyed Rory. When he settled back against the seat again he leaned his head nearer hers. ''Whatcha doin' with him?'' he whispered roughly.

''He got the last rental car,'' Sunny whispered back.

Clyde leaned forward to check out Rory again. This time Sunny took a look, too.

He was closer than she'd expected—just inches away when her gaze locked with his. He was scowling, of course. His black, arched brows drawn low over his narrowed green eyes. His jaw was set, his head cocked slightly as if he were listening, which, of course, he was.

''You think he's okay, miss?'' Clyde whispered. ''He looks like he could be dangerous, to me. You sure you're safe crossin' state lines with him?''

Oh, Sunny thought as she looked into that remarkable face, he could be dangerous, all right. Dangerous to a woman's peace of mind. Dangerous to a woman's self-control. Oh, boy, thought Sunny as the truck bounced along the road, would Clyde be shocked to know what Sunny was thinking with Rory's thigh crushed against hers, so that she could feel the heat of the friction between them as the truck hit a bump or slid a little on a patch of ice. The thin, fine fabric of his trousers, the smooth cotton of her capris. That's all there was between them.

Clyde turned a corner and she was jostled against Rory with enough force to cause her breasts to bounce slightly. The movement rekindled the fire his touch had started on the plane. Her breasts ached as if they knew what possibilities existed in the man pressed next to her.

Clyde slowed down for a bump but it still hit with enough force to cause her hands to leap up and settle down hard into her lap. Well, one of them settled hard into her lap. The other one settled into Rory's.

Hard was the word, all right, Sunny thought irreverently before catching herself. She looked in horror at her hand resting on Rory Temple. She snatched it away immediately, of course. It was only because it was so embarrassing that it seemed to have been lying there forever on his hardening—um—his—

He cleared his throat and her gaze shot to his face. He looked positively wicked. Lethally, gorgeously wicked. Like a wolf who knew that all he had to do was pounce and the prey would be his. She wouldn't at all be surprised to see the hint of fangs gleaming from behind that gorgeously chiseled mouth. She was actually waiting for him to growl.

But what he did was wink.

And what Sunny did was choke.

"You okay?" Clyde asked her as he pulled the truck to a stop and started to thump her on the back.

"Yes! Yes!" she said before good old Clyde could administer another blow. "I'm okay."

"Good. Here we are, then."

Ethel's turned out to be a diner whose parking lot was packed. As soon as Rory opened the truck door Sunny could smell the scent of frying fat. Her stomach rumbled. She hadn't had anything to eat since room service coffee and danish that morning. Even the vegetarian meal she was going to miss at the rehearsal dinner that night was starting to sound good.

She picked her way through the snow once again, following Clyde through the parking lot to the side entrance of Ethel's.

The first thing she noticed, when Clyde opened the door, was the rush of warm air that wrapped itself around her and drew her in. The second thing she noticed was the heavenly smell of hot coffee and fresh doughnuts.

"Hey, Harry!" Clyde called over the sound of Elvis Presley coming out of the jukebox. "Got a couple of stranded travelers with me here!"

"Yeah? And what do you want me to do with 'em? Cook 'em for Sunday dinner?" As Harry cackled, a couple of gaps in his teeth appeared that made his round face look like a jack-o'-lantern with a perpetually bad mood. In a pair of coveralls that must have had a grease stain on them from every job he ever did, Harry made Clyde look like a choirboy in his Sunday best. He eyed Sunny up and down while he opened his mouth and devoured half a doughnut. The missing teeth didn't seem to be a liability.

"Where you goin', little lady? A tea party?" he asked, cracking up at his own joke.

"Actually, I'm trying to get to a wedding in Chicago tomorrow but our plane got rerouted and the storm is slowing us down and now we're almost out of gas—"

Harry shoved the rest of the doughnut in his mouth. "Yeah? What's it got to do with me?"

"Well, we thought maybe you'd be willing to—"

Whatever chitchat had been going on in the diner suddenly came to a halt. Sunny nervously looked at Rory. He was standing in the doorway, hands shoved in his pants pockets, watching her. The darned amusement was back in his eyes.

"You wanted to handle it," he said.

She glared at him before turning back to Harry with wringing hands. "You're my only hope," she said in a rush. "Unless you open your gas station I'm going to miss the wedding I've been waiting for since I was eight years old," she recited, starting to feel like a little girl who was dragged out on a regular basis for the purpose of amusing mommy's guests at luncheon.

She decided that now was as good a time as any to blow her nose, maybe feign a tear or two. Who knew what it would take to melt the heart of a man like Harry?

"Ain't that just the saddest thing you've ever heard?" said the woman behind the counter.

"Aww, Ethel," Harry grumbled.

"Ya gotta admit, Harry," put in Clyde, "it could bring tears to yer eyes."

"You're too soft, Clyde. Always was."

Ethel slapped the coffeepot down in front of Harry. "And you're too damn hard, Harry."

"Aww, Ethel," Harry said again.

"I mean it, Harry. Any man who is too mean-spirited to open his gas station to help a bride-to-be make it to her own wedding isn't welcome in my diner."

"Ethel—do you know what you're sayin'? Tonight's Friday. Salmon loaf. I gotta have me my salmon loaf, Ethel."

The salmon loaf was starting to sound like a necessity to Sunny, too. Her stomach growled in agreement.

Ethel placed her hands on her substantial hips. "You want salmon loaf, Harry Palmer, then you know what you gotta do."

Harry scratched his head and screwed up his face. He was obviously distressed at the idea of missing the Friday night special. Finally he heaved a sigh. "Aww, okay. But at least put a couple of them fresh doughnuts in a bag fer me, Ethel," he said as he slid off his stool.

"I'll have a few, too," Sunny added, while her stomach did a couple of hopeful handsprings.

"No time for doughnuts," Rory said, grabbing her hand. "We've got to get going."

She wiggled her hand out of his grasp. "It'll just take a minute to get a couple of doughnuts."

"No," he said in that unyielding way that made her want to ignore him.

She watched Ethel hand a small brown bag over to Harry. "See? It only took a minute," she said.

"Well, actually, hun," Ethel said, "Harry got the last of them. But the next batch'll be up in ten minutes."

She looked hopefully at Rory. "It's only ten minutes."

"Absolutely not."

"In fact," she said, her mouth watering as she watched a waitress carry a platter of fried chicken over to a booth, "maybe we should stay here and eat dinner." She plucked a menu from the counter and opened it. "Who knows when we'll find some place to stop again."

"You order off that menu and I leave without you," Rory pronounced in his best doom-to-the-masses voice.

She looked at him, and was about to argue, but he held up the keys to the rental. "My car. Remember?" he said.

"Ohh, you got yourself a tiger there, girl," Ethel said.

Sunny sighed. "I see him as more of a wolf," she said as she handed Ethel the menu.

"Either way, hun, he's an animal."

"That's what I'm afraid of," she mumbled as she followed the three men out the door. When he found out the truth, he was going to devour her for sure.

"DOES YOUR FIANCÉ know what he's in for?" Rory asked her as they waited inside Harry's One Stop for Harry himself to put the windshield washer solvent into the rental.

"What do you mean?"

"Come on. You've got those two northern boys," he nodded out the window to where Clyde seemed to be supervising the job, "eating out of your hand like a couple of tame yearlings despite the fact that you told them a lie.''

"Well, they understood. People generally do, you know," she added pointedly, hoping he'd remember this conversation when the time came, "if you explain things to them. It's just that sometimes for the sake of expediency you have to sort of—"

"Lie," he finished for her.

She grimaced. "I'd prefer to think of it as sort of sliding into the truth. Look, how about if I buy something to make up for the gas we aren't buying? Will that make you feel better?"

"Humph." He scowled. "I'm sure the place is simply brimming with things that a Chicago interior designer on her way home from a buying trip in San Francisco would want."

"Well, you never know," she said as she started off down an aisle. "The place does have a sort of rustic charm."

"Pollyanna strikes again," she heard Rory mutter.

Ignoring him, she rummaged among the shelves. "Goodness!" she suddenly cried. "Monkey socks!"

"Monkey socks?"

"Yes!" she said, shoving her hand inside a tweedy sock as she came toward him. "Don't you remember?" she asked, wiggling her fingers inside the sock. "They used to make stuffed monkeys out of these."

"No," he said grimly. "I don't remember."

"No? Well, I suppose your father had you playing the market at the age of three," she said as she brushed past him on her way to the checkout counter.

After a moment, he followed. "Are you planning on an arts and crafts session between here and Chicago?"

"Nope. I'm going to wear them."

"Wear them?" Rory boomed just as Clyde and Harry came back into the store.

"Yes," Sunny said. "My feet are freezing. I think I'm in danger of getting pneumonia by osmosis. You don't happen to have any other kind of wearing apparel, do you, Harry?"

"Wearing apparel?" Harry grumbled, his gap-toothed face scrunched up as if he was hearing Greek.

"Yes, Harry," Rory said caustically. "The little lady is looking for some designer ski wear."

Sunny gave him a dirty look.

Harry snarled, "This here is a gas station. You were supposed to buy gas."

"I know," Sunny said with real regret, "but I'll be glad to buy something else, okay? Like these socks and anything else you have around here that would keep me warm."

"This ain't no boutique," Harry grumbled.

Sunny smiled sweetly. "I know that, Harry. But you have so many interesting—er—things," she said, picking up a can opener in one hand and a fish scaler in the other. "I was just kind of hoping—"

"Well," Harry said, looking a little prideful, "I do got a couple of hunting parkas in the back someplace."

"Hunting parkas?" Sunny asked, her heart starting to beat faster.

"Yeah, I guess I could try to dig 'em up if yer interested."

"I am definitely interested," Sunny said enthusiastically.

"I didn't think that blaze orange was your color," Rory said.

"I don't look so great in blue, either. But that's the color I'm gonna turn if I don't get something warmer to wear," she said as she followed Harry to the back of the cluttered store.

"I generally keep some bits and pieces of hunting gear on hand. You know," he stopped and looked at Rory, "in case some city slicker comes up here not knowin' nothin' 'bout what ta wear."

"Harry's One Stop fashion consulting service," Rory murmured gloomily, wondering why he wanted Sunny to show disdain for anything she might find in Harry's One Stop. He was not happy at all with her cheerful enthusiasm for a blaze orange hunting jacket. He'd feel a lot better if she pitched a temperamental fit about the snow, about the clothes, about his attitude.

"It fits!" she cried as she wrapped the parka around herself.

And damned if she didn't happen to look good in blaze orange.

Her hair, nearly dry, hung in a shimmering fall to her chin. The orange of the jacket turned the chestnut to auburn when she turned this way and that. From the look of happiness on her face you'd have thought she was trying on a mink coat.

"What have you got for feet, Harry?" she asked. "I'm never going to be able to fit my flats over these monkey socks."

"Oh, I got nothin' for women's feet here," Harry said gruffly, clearly a little insulted at the notion.

"Harry," Sunny said, holding out a foot for his inspection, "I take a size ten shoe."

Harry looked down at her feet. "Damn you got big feet," he blurted out indelicately.

Rory waited for Sunny to explode. Now, he thought, she will show her true temperament. Because surely a woman who'd worn those three-inch snakeskin heels had some sort of vanity about her feet.

But to Rory's chagrin, when she opened her mouth it was to laugh. "And for once," she said, "having big feet is going to work to my advantage." Harry was actually cackling as he sorted through some boxes and pulled out a pair of men's rubber boots.

"Fetching," Rory said dryly when Sunny tried them on.

"Maybe you'd like a pair," she said, grinning at him as she walked up and down the aisle like a runway model.

She had the infectious enthusiasm of a child and the seductive body of a wanton woman. He was finding the combination irresistible in the extreme. Even in men's hunting clothes she was seductively feminine. Good thing he planned on driving all night. The bride-to-be was far too tempting to be sleeping on the other side of a hotel room door.

She turned at the end of the aisle and started back toward him. She was prancing as if she was wearing heels instead of clodhoppers, and was giggling so hard that she didn't notice the stack of shoeboxes in the middle of the aisle. She crashed into them, lost her balance, and started to fall. Rory rushed forward, sending boxes flying, and put out his arms. Sunny fell right into them.

His arms went around her and her full breasts were crushed against his chest. She was all soft woman under his hands and they itched to roam, to discover. Quickly, he righted her, set her away from him and kicked a few shoe boxes aside to put even more distance between them.

"I think I'll pass on the boots," he said to Harry, deciding he'd be safer once they were on the road and his hands were occupied with the steering wheel. "I will take an orange parka, however."

Harry cackled again. "This is gonna be my biggest

sale of the season,'' he said as he pawed through sizes to find an extra large for Rory.

"Quite possibly," Rory said without humor. "What else have you got in this little magic kingdom, Harry? We could use some gloves, hats and a window scraper."

"YOU KNOW WHAT THE BEST thing is about these boots?" Sunny asked him fifteen minutes later when they were brushing snow off the rental with the two window scrapers Harry had thrown into the deal.

"What?"

"You can no longer accuse me of wearing stupid shoes," she said.

"No. Now I can just accuse you of looking stupid in your shoes," he said, unable to resist baiting her even though he knew he was playing with fire.

Her mouth dropped open as she gasped in indignation. "You'll be sorry for that, Mr. Temple," she said as she bent to gather up snow in her hands.

"You wouldn't dare," he growled.

"Want to bet?" she said as she came after him.

He dodged out of her way then grabbed her by the waist and swung her into his arms. But she still had her hand full of snow and while he was trying to keep his face out of reach his foot hit a patch of ice. When he landed, she was on top of him.

"That's what you get for being such an animal," she said through sputters of laughter.

Her eyes were shining, her checks red with the cold, her lashes dusted with snowflakes. And suddenly he didn't care that she was going to be another man's wife. In a flash, he reversed their positions, straddling her and pinning her arms at the wrists.

She was still laughing. "Let me up!"

"No," he said.

"Mr. Temple, you seem to be overly fond of that word."

"Right now," he said softly, knowing he shouldn't, knowing he was just asking for trouble, "I'm overly fond of the way the snowflakes are melting on your warm lips."

She stopped laughing. "What do you think you're doing?" she asked him breathlessly as he lowered his head to hers.

"I'm kissing the bride," he said. And then he did.

4

THERE WAS SUCH HEAT IN his mouth. She knew she should push him away, put a stop to it. But the heat from his mouth seemed to be pouring into her bloodstream, setting her heart to beating with such vigor she wondered for one wild second if it had ever beaten before. His hands were hard on her wrists, his body tight against hers. He was holding her captive in the frigid snow.

Like prey.

And just as she'd thought earlier, when he'd been bending so close as he slid her into the car, she was willing to lie down and be devoured.

Oh sure, her mind was screaming, *Push him away!* But her body was screaming back, *More!*

Yes. *More.*

Boldly she tasted his lower lip with her tongue. With a low, fierce noise from his throat, his tongue joined hers. If his mouth was heat, this was fire. With a will of its own, her body bucked against his like it didn't care if it got burned.

And maybe Sunny didn't care, either.

Her back arched, her soul yearned. Ten seconds more of his mouth and she'd be incapable of rational thought. Then, just as she was about to surrender to her irrational side, she felt the cold wind back on her lips.

She struggled to open her eyes. Rory Temple was staring down at her. His breath was coming shallow and quick, while his eyes narrowed dangerously.

"What kind of woman is it, Sunshine," he asked, his eyes glittering, "who reacts like that to a kiss on the eve of her wedding to another man?"

For a big man he was surprisingly agile as he got to his feet. She remained lying there panting in a puddle of melted snow, until the shame of how much she wanted his body against hers again catapulted her to her feet.

"Look—" she started. "It's not what you think."

"Get in the car," he demanded. His hand was already on the driver's door handle.

"I can explain," she insisted.

"Save it for the groom," he said, not even bothering to look at her. "I have a feeling he'll be needing plenty of explanations once he's walked down that aisle with you tomorrow."

Sunny gasped. "What's that supposed to mean?"

Hand still on the door handle, he did turn to look at her then. "You're not a naïve girl, Sunshine," he said, his gaze running over her, "despite your name. I think you can figure it out."

Her bottom lip started to tremble—and Sunny had an awful suspicion it wasn't the cold causing it. "Are you trying to say that I'm—" She couldn't seem to come up with a polite word for it, so she left the obvious question hanging in the air.

He waited until he'd opened the car door before he answered her. "You're getting married in the morning, Sunshine. You had no business kissing me back that way. And," he added in a huff, "you have no business looking at me as you are right now. Now, get in the car before I decide to take you up on your offer of ravishment."

Sunny's bottom lip stopped trembling and nearly hit the slush at her feet.

"Of all the nerve," she managed to sputter. A moment

too late because Rory had already gotten into the car and shut the door.

Her olive drab boots made squishing noises as she plodded through the slushy snow to the passenger door, flung it open, got in and slammed it shut.

"You've got a lot of nerve," she said, "judging me. What were you doing kissing an engaged woman that way?"

"You wanted it," he said with simple arrogance, his gorgeous mouth moving ever so slightly into a satisfied little smile. She started to fume. She could practically feel the steam rising out of the top of her head.

"Oh, so Rory Temple is into good works, is he?" she asked testily. "Taking pity on sexually starved women across the country?"

"Not true, Sunshine," he said. "You're my first damsel."

"I'm a damsel in need of a ride! Not one in need of being devoured!"

"You could have fooled me," he said as he started the car.

"Of all the arrogance! You think you're irresistible, don't you?"

"Well, if I'm not, then I'm right about you, aren't I?" He paused to maneuver the car back out onto the highway. "You're as fickle as a stray cat looking for a saucer of milk."

"In other words, you think I'm going to cheat on my husband."

"If the—" he glanced toward her feet "—galoshes fit—"

That did it, the steam building in her head was boiling to a whistle. "Of all the arrogant, judgmental—and what about you, Rory Temple! What were you doing kissing a woman who is about to marry another man?"

He glanced at her with one brow raised mockingly. "If he doesn't do it for you in the bedroom, Sunshine, maybe you should think twice about walking down that aisle tomorrow."

"Who said he doesn't do it for me in the bedroom? How dare you make that assumption! Why there is absolutely nothing wrong with him in the bedroom!"

Sunny took in a breath so she could continue with her defense then suddenly realized what she'd just said. Him? *Who* him? There *was* no him! The situation was getting way too bizarre. Here she was practically rating the lovemaking prowess of a man who didn't even exist! If she kept this up much longer, the fine line between reality and fantasy was going to get as blurred as the visibility out there in the storm.

She absolutely had to tell him the truth. Now.

She chewed on her lower lip and looked anxiously out the windshield. If only it wasn't snowing so thickly. If only the road wasn't so narrow. If only it wasn't starting to get dark. If only Rory Temple weren't so—so—difficult.

She glanced at him out of the corner of her eye. He was looking attractively grim as he concentrated on the road ahead. If she told him would he immediately toss her out of the car? Could she chance it?

Could she *not?* Wasn't death preferable to dishonor? Better to risk frostbite and hypothermia than to be thought a woman loose enough to be willingly devoured on the eve of her own wedding.

And she did feel rather devoured, she mused as she stole another glance at him in the weak light of an oncoming car. She looked at his hands on the steering wheel. Large, hard hands. Her wrists tingled at the memory of being held by them. She moved her gaze up to his face.

He was incredibly handsome, really. And rugged, slightly weathered, but elegant and graceful, as well. Was it possible that a man like this could actually be attracted to her? Despite her blaze orange hunting jacket? Despite her feet looking every inch a size ten in the olive drab rubber boots? If there was any chance at all, it was absolutely imperative that Sunny tell him the truth immediately.

Maybe it would be easier if she wasn't looking at him, she thought, returning her concentration to the road ahead. She tried to focus on the snowflakes whipping at the windshield. Maybe the repetition would calm her. She took in a breath. "About the wedding—" she began but what she saw in the road ahead made her choke on the words in her throat. "Oh—oh—oh!" she managed to sputter shrilly. A family of deer had materialized not four yards away. They stood in the road, calmly watching the car approach as if they hadn't a care in the world. "Move!" Sunny screamed at them. They ignored her, of course.

"Hold on!" Rory shouted as he pulled the wheel hard right.

For just a second, Sunny's eyes locked with the wide doe eyes of what must have been the mother deer. Then Sunny slammed on the imaginary brake at her feet and braced her hands against the dashboard with enough pressure to stop the world. Unfortunately, it did nothing to stop the car.

For one brief moment, she thought she could feel the antilock brakes start to grip. But just as quickly, they lost their tenuous hold.

She yelped and Rory replied, in that maddeningly assured voice, "Hang on, angel."

The deer were a blur as the car skidded past them. Rory started to pump the brakes as the trees on the side of the road seemed to leap at the car from out of the snow. Rory whipped the wheel to the left, then corrected, and the car slid sideways, spun when it hit the shoulder and finally jerked to a halt with the rear tires hanging over the ditch that separated the forest from the road.

Her arms still braced against the dashboard, Sunny felt the jolt run up her wrists and shoulders and whip her head back and forth like a rag doll.

"Are they okay?" she asked, her voice nearly a whisper.

"Take a look," he said.

Little by little she opened her eyes, and from her position, strained to see that there were no dead deer in the middle of the road.

She had trouble drawing in a breath. "I—I feel shaky. I have to get out."

Sunny was unbuckling her seat belt when the rear of the car suddenly dipped and groaned. Without thinking, she launched herself at Rory, throwing her arms around his neck, burying her face in his shoulder, until the car was still again.

"Will we be able to get out?" she asked.

She felt his chuckle deep in his chest under the softness of his jacket. "Yes, angel. I think so."

"Are you sure?"

"Fairly sure. All the same we should probably get out and take a look."

She nodded against his shoulder, but made no effort to move from the warmth of his arms. "I was so afraid you'd hit them."

With his fingers under her chin he raised her face so that she was looking up at him. "Look," he whispered gently before turning his head toward the driver's side window. Her gaze followed.

Two feet away stood the doe, peering into the car as if checking to see if they were all right.

Neither of them said a word as they watched her, her ears now and then flickering to clear the snow from them, her eyes huge and warm—and so alive. Suddenly she blinked, swished her white tail and bounded off into the forest.

"I think she was thanking you," Sunny said, looking up into his face.

His fingers were still under her chin and her head was lying back in the crook of his other arm.

Like a lover, she thought.

Oh, if only he would kiss her again! It surprised her how much she wanted that. For a moment she was sure that he wanted it too. Something flickered in his eyes and his mouth moved closer, so close that she could feel his warm breath on her cold lips.

And then he pulled back.

"I better check the car. Make sure we can get it back on the road," he said as he disengaged himself and opened the car door to get out. "Stay put," he told her.

Disappointed, she thought well, why *would* he kiss her again? He still thought she was getting married tomorrow. She absolutely had to tell him the truth. Now. She glanced around. This was the perfect place to break it to him. So quiet. So peaceful. After they'd just shared the beautiful moment of the doe how could he get really mad?

Maybe he'd even be happy to know she was free.

She dipped her head so she could see him out the window on the driver's side. He was standing alongside the car, and flipped the collar of the hunting jacket up against his neck. Wow, he'd look better in a Ralph Lauren ad than Ralph Lauren himself! He'd managed to transform the coat into something dashing, where on her—she looked down at herself, her mouth twisting ruefully. On her it just looked like a really ill-fitting blaze orange hunting jacket.

Her gaze followed him as he rounded the back of the car to survey the damage. With the wind and snow in his dark hair and the scowl on his extraordinary face, he looked exactly like what he was, even without the tailoring. And what he was, was a wildly sexy, outrageously successful businessman.

"Oh, why bother dreaming?" she muttered to herself. Rory Temple was probably used to women that came in a size four. The same women who wore expensive perfume and even more expensive jewelry. In fact, the same women who would never, ever find themselves in the kind of predicament where they'd end up in drab green rubber boots, men's size nine!

Well, at least her size would be good for something, she thought as she slid over to the passenger door and carefully opened it. But she didn't see Great-Aunt Tilly's wedding hat float to the ground when she got out of the car.

"You steer, I'll push," she called to him across the top of the car.

"I can handle it," he said emphatically. "Get back in the car."

"Don't be silly. Two bodies are always better than one."

With a raised brow, he glared at her. "It might surprise you to know, Sunshine, that dozens of employees follow my orders every day."

"Well, lucky for you I'm ignoring your orders. We'll have this car out of here in a jiffy."

His mouth quirked. "I take it you've done this before."

"Everybody in the commune had junkers. We pushed

regularly. My father taught me how to pop a clutch at a very early age.''

"And I bet you never obeyed him, either."

She grinned. "He always says I'm as stubborn as a blind mule."

"And no doubt the apple of his eye."

She laughed. "Guilty."

"Thought so," he muttered. "He'll no doubt be proudly giving away the bride tomorrow."

Sunny stopped laughing and gulped. Rory had just handed her the perfect opening. Was this the time to tell him? Or maybe, she thought, her heart lifting a little at the thought of a slight reprieve, she should wait until the car wasn't hovering over a ditch.

"Well—um—he'll certainly be walking down that aisle, same as me," she said, marveling at how quickly that little distortion of the truth came to her. "I'm sure your father is very proud of you, too," she added, neatly trying to change the subject.

He grunted. "Don't bet the commune on that one, Sunshine."

She frowned at him. "What does that mean?"

"Look," he said, his dark eyes suddenly glaring again, "are you going to help me get this car back on the road or not?"

"Grouch," she muttered as she plodded around to the back of the car, placed the flat of her hands on it, planted her feet apart, and leaned into it.

"Say when," she called.

Rory took the position at the side of the car, one hand to the open door frame and the other on the steering wheel. "Now!" he yelled.

With their combined weights pushing it, the rear end of the car easily bucked up and rolled away from the precipice of the ditch. Rory turned the steering wheel to guide the car back onto the road. "That's it!" he hollered. Sunny stopped pushing. The car continued to roll forward slowly until Rory jumped into the front seat and pumped the brakes. He then started the car and edged it over to the shoulder of the road.

She knew he was waiting for her to get into the car, but she was wary of doing so before she told him the truth. Out of the car, the snow didn't seem to be so threatening. It was softer, blanketing the earth and clinging to the trees. Once they were back on the road, the storm would be against them again and Rory would look increasingly forbidding as he did battle with it. Here, she might have a chance of making him see reason.

She pulled back the hood of her parka, shook her hair out, fixed a hopeful little smile on her face and plodded over to the car, motioning for Rory to roll down the window.

"What's wrong?" he asked.

"Do we have to leave already?"

"Leave already?" He looked at her like she'd just suggested something not quite sane. "Sunshine, this isn't exactly a scheduled stop on the White April tour. We are on a mission, are we not?"

His use of the royal we, in her opinion, wasn't a good sign. "Well, I know," she said, trying to sound all sweet and innocent, "but it's so beautiful here. So peaceful."

She held out her hands and tilted her head back, sticking out her tongue to catch snowflakes.

"Why do I get the feeling that any minute now you're going to ask if we can build a snowman?" Rory grumbled.

She laughed, laying it on a little thick, like he was just sooo funny. "Silly. I was thinking more of a tiny little walk in the woods?"

"No."

She dropped the useless snow-bunny charm. "There you go again, saying that word."

He got out of the car, went to the passenger side, and opened the door. "In," he said.

"What am I? Some kind of dog? Sit! Stay! No! In!"

"At the moment you're acting like some kind of two-year-old. Even if we both didn't have places to go to, it's going to be dark soon. And we don't know these woods. I'm a man who likes an adventure, angel, but that's one risk I'm not going to take."

Well, it wasn't as if his argument lacked sense. The forest around them was an enchantment with the snow falling and dusk settling, but in less than an hour it would be so black in those trees that anything human would lose his or her way.

She was just considering what might be around after dark that *wasn't* human when she heard the flapping of wings coming from something that sounded too big to be anything of this earth.

She shivered and grabbed his arm. "What was that?"

"A bird," he said, sounding altogether exasperated. Well, she supposed she was acting sort of nervous. But she figured she had a right, considering that Rory Temple was about to find out that it wasn't the flap of a bird's wings that was really causing her nervousness.

"I need to tell you something," she said, looking up at him.

"Well, tell me in the car. We need to get out of here."

She tightened her grip on his arm. "I'd rather tell you here."

"All right," he said, a little too quietly for Sunny's peace of mind. "Tell me and get it over with."

"There's something about the wedding—"

He made that growling sound in his throat, shook off her hand, and started to storm off toward the car. "I'm sick of hearing about this wedding of yours—and about your perfect groom.''

She had already started to follow him, but his words nearly tripped her up. ''What? When did I ever say—''

He turned around to face her. It brought them too close together, as far as Sunny was concerned.

''Let's not discuss it,'' he said, in that dangerously quiet voice that was so effective. ''And,'' he added, looking her up and down in a way that was making her sweat inside her blaze orange jacket, ''let's make an effort to never forget that you're getting married in the morning.''

''But that's just it!'' she cried.

''What's just it?''

''I'm not—'' before she could go on, there was a loud squawk from behind her.

She whirled around.

The biggest crow she ever saw stood by the side of the road, with a wet, drooping mass of lavender chiffon trailing from its beak.

''That bird has Aunt Tilly's hat!'' she yelled, pointing at it accusingly. The bird just stared out of inky-colored eyes.

''This wouldn't have happened if you'd stayed in the car like I told you to,'' Rory grumbled.

''Don't just stand there saying I told you so! What are we going to do?''

''*We* are going to get in the car and get out of here before it gets completely dark.''

''I can't leave Aunt Tilly's hat!''

''What do you intend to do? Wait here until the crow's taste improves?''

She resisted the urge to stick out her tongue at him. ''Do you think you could quit cracking jokes and help me out here?''

"What do you suggest? That I offer him money for Aunt Tilly's hat?"

"Not everyone can be bought, Mr. Temple. But that does give me an idea. Open the trunk."

"If we're going to offer him a ride to Chicago, perhaps he'd prefer the back seat."

She gave him a look. "Very funny. Now would you stop wasting time and open the trunk?"

He scowled at her, preparing to demand that she get in the car at once. But he knew there wasn't a snowball's chance in hell of her doing it without an argument. For time's sake, he decided to open the trunk.

She dipped her head inside and unzipped her case then started to rummage around, tossing small, silky looking things here and there. Rory tried not to wonder what they might be—or how she might look in them. It was a losing battle. Even the blaze orange parka couldn't hide the lush femininity of her body. He had just started to wonder if Sunny had the same little freckles all over that she had on her face, when she pulled out a long, red scarf.

"Here it is," she said triumphantly.

"That's what you've been looking for?"

"Yes!" she answered, as she started toward the crow.

"What are you doing," he asked dryly, "helping him accessorize?"

She gave him a look. "Don't be silly. I'd never advise anyone to wear this color of red and lavender together. I'm going to try to make a trade."

"With a crow? You're going to try to make a deal with a bird?"

"Well, it's worth a try. Now be quiet," she said over her shoulder as she approached the bird. Rory crossed his arms and settled back against the car, preparing to be amused.

Sunny started talking to the bird in soothing tones, all

the while holding out the length of crimson like an offering.

"So you see, Mr. Crow," she said, as her story wound down, "it's very important that I take Aunt Tilly's hat to Chicago with me."

The crow blinked, then spread his huge wings and flapped a few feet closer to the woods.

"Hmm, your wiles aren't working," Rory said sardonically. "Must be a female crow."

Sunny threw him a look then proceeded to move closer to the bird, jiggling the silk ever so gently. "See?" she said. "Isn't it pretty?"

"Take the deal, bird," Rory called, "the hat went out of style more than a century ago."

"Will you hush up?" Sunny hissed at him. "Save your stand-up routine for the press conference tomorrow."

Rory looked at his watch then up at the sky. Almost seven. It would be dark soon. "You've got five minutes, Sunshine, and we're out of here."

"Shh!" was her only answer.

He stalked over to the car and started shoving things back into the suitcase so he could close the trunk. Something cool and smooth caught on his fingers. He raised his hand. Peach silk. A jolt of raw energy hit him low, stirring him enough to make him raise the silk to his nostrils, just to see if the scent of her skin was there.

It was. The scent of spring here amid the snow. It made him ache and harden.

Angry at himself, he tossed the scrap of silk into the suitcase. "Still lusting after the bride-to-be," he muttered in disgust as he zipped the case closed. Other men ached over the kind of women Rory had, not the other way around. Aching over another man's woman was foreign to him. Just as women like Sunny Morgan were foreign to him.

With his hand on the trunk, ready to shut it, he looked back over his shoulder at her. There she was, crouching in the snow, holding out a crimson scarf to the huge black bird. No, none of the many women he escorted around Chicago would try to barter with a crow for a hat that should have been put to rest miles ago.

Hell, none of the women he knew would be taking that particular kind of hat to their wedding in the first place—no matter who had made it. The thought made him think of his grandmother Molly and how hard she'd tried to instill some sort of tradition in him despite their limited resources. Even during his typical teen years, she insisted that he eat Thanksgiving dinner with her and her assortment of friends—usually people who had no where else to go—and that he go with her to pick out a Christmas tree. Year after year, he'd drag home the cheapest tree on the lot and help her decorate it with the glass ornaments that had come over from Ireland with his great-grandmother.

Yes, Molly would have kept her promise about the hat. Just the same way that Sunny was trying to.

Jeez, the last thing he needed was to start comparing the bride to be to his grandmother! He looked at his watch. "Time's up, Sunny," he called as he slammed the trunk shut.

"Oh no! There he goes!"

The huge black bird spread its wings and took off, climbing a good twenty feet before heading into the forest, with Great-Aunt Tilly's hat still hanging from its beak. Sunny headed toward the woods.

"Where do you think you're going?" he shouted.

She turned. "I can't leave Aunt Tilly's hat. I have to try to get it back."

"Are you crazy? Aside from the fact that you can't

fly, it will be dark in less than half an hour. You're not going into those woods!"

He could see that she was hesitating. Just as his chest swelled with the idea of winning there was a caw from the trees. Sunny looked up.

"There it is!" she cried as she started to run. Rory started after her and then the cell phone in his pocket began to ring.

"What?" he barked into it.

"I see you're being your usual pleasant traveling companion."

"Look, Agnes, I don't have time for pleasantries. At present I'm chasing a woman who is on the trail of a big black bird that stole her Great-Aunt Tilly's hat."

"Have you been watching Bogart movies again, boss?"

"I think I'm experiencing something slightly more Felliniesque, Agnes. I'll get back to you during intermission. Meanwhile, do me a favor. See what you can find on the name Sunshine Morgan."

"Sunshine?"

"She was raised on a commune."

"Not your usual type, boss."

"You're telling me. Now excuse me while I search the enchanted forest for the damsel and the crow."

He ended the call before Agnes could ask any more questions.

It was easy to follow Sunny's trail in the forest since they appeared to be the only two people crazy enough to be out in such weather. At least among the trees the wind was low. The snow fell more sedately to the ground, but it was also darker. Where had Miss Sunshine Morgan gotten to with that bird?

He looked skyward, hoping to spot the spread of black wings. But it was blaze orange that caught his eye.

There, halfway up a maple tree, clung Sunny, her hand outstretched toward the limp lavender chiffon hat caught on a branch just out of her reach.

"Will you get down from there?" Rory yelled as he raced forward. "You're risking life and limb—not to mention hypothermia."

"I'm not leaving without that hat!"

"Of all the stubborn—" Rory muttered as he took up a stance under the tree. "I have never met a woman who is as single-minded as you are," he called up to her.

"Haven't you ever wanted to keep a promise?" she yelled down to him as she tried to attain some sort of footing further up on the branch.

Oh, he knew all about the quest to keep a promise. That's why he was in this situation to begin with. He was about to tell her so when her foot slipped and she started to fall.

"Sunny!" he yelled, his heart nearly stopping as he danced around under the tree, arms outstretched, hoping she'd fall into them. There was the snap of wood, the tear of clothing—and then she stopped falling and started dangling—like a huge, orange Christmas ornament—from a branch of the spreading maple.

"Are you all right?" he called as she swung past him just above his reach.

"I got the hat!" she said on her next swing by.

And sure enough, there it was, hanging limp and slightly soiled from her hand. And there Sunny was, hanging from a tear on the back of her blaze orange jacket, swinging perpendicular above the snowy ground, with the kind of smile on her face that might just make her the most beautiful woman Rory had ever seen.

"Try to hold still!" he called up to her. "I'm coming up after you!"

Rory easily climbed up to the branch Sunny was

swinging from. Reaching out, he grabbed her jacket and pulled her closer. There was the sound of fabric tearing again and then she was in his arms, clinging to him.

"You scared me, angel," he said into her still smiling face.

"I'm sorry, Rory," she said. "But—"

"Yes, I know. You couldn't leave without the hat."

She laughed and the sound of it stung him in the heart for some reason. She was so full of joy. And over a homemade hat. It was nearly impossible not to be affected by it.

But it was also nearly impossible to not be affected by her ripe body clinging to his. The sooner he got them out of that tree and onto safer ground, the better.

"Hang on, angel," he said. "We're going down."

"Together?" she gasped.

"Together," he answered.

She wound her arms more tightly around his neck.

"Wrap your legs around me," he demanded.

Oh my, she thought, as she did so. And then he was carrying her down the tree, like a wolf carrying his live prey back to his lair. She felt the warmth of him against her, felt his hard muscles working. When they touched the earth again, he didn't immediately let her go, but held her against the trunk of the tree, staring down at her with an unnerving scrutiny.

He's going to kiss me again, she thought, her breath quickening, her lips parting, her body turning liquid where it was pressed against his. And then he let go of her and her feet touched the ground.

"I thought I told you to never let me forget again that you're about to become another man's wife," he said while he stared down at her.

"But—" she said as he turned away.

"Just get into the car," he threw over his shoulder.

"If I have to cancel my meeting again tomorrow, you're going to wish you'd stayed with the crow."

"Rory, please! Wait!"

"One more word, Sunshine, and I drop you off at the next town and you find your own way back to Chicago."

Sunny pressed her lips together and got into the car.

RORY WAS BROODING AGAIN. Sunny sneaked a look at his face and had to admit that no one brooded more attractively than Rory Temple. What was he thinking, with his mouth set so sternly and his brow so furrowed? No doubt he was forming a worse opinion of her since the incident at the foot of the maple tree. Why, oh, why did she have to make it so blatantly obvious that she'd wanted him to kiss her again?

Sunny stole another look at him in the dim light. Why? Silly question. He was gorgeous, powerful—and she wasn't talking about his business acumen here—and highly provocative, what with the way he was forever sending out mixed signals. Although, she supposed she was sending out some mixed signals of her own.

She wasn't about to set the record straight right now, though. Not with another town coming up soon. If she had any hope of getting to Chicago by morning, she was going to have to continue to keep her secret for the time being.

Aunt Tilly's hat was still in her lap. Not that it any longer looked like a hat, she thought as she held it up. It was beginning to look more like something to use to scrub the kitchen floor. She sighed. Maybe she should have let the crow have it, after all. At least it would have made a good story. Aunt Tilly probably would have gotten a good laugh out of it. But since she'd rescued the hat, she might as well see what she could do to salvage it.

She unbuckled her seat belt, twisted around and got to her knees.

"What are you doing?" Rory asked suspiciously.

"I'm going to smooth Aunt Tilly's hat out on the back seat. Maybe it'll look better after it dries," she said.

"Do you ever stop being overly optimistic?"

"Any reason I should?"

He grunted. "It somehow doesn't fit with your penchant for throwing yourself into the arms of men other than your intended."

Sunny stopped fiddling with the ruined lilacs on the brim of the hat, and was about to fume at the audacity of the remark. Especially since his were the only arms she was throwing herself into! She was about to tell him so when she thought better of it. Unless she was going to tell him the truth, the subject of her faithfulness was taboo.

Without saying a word, she turned around and sat down, fetching the small wooden crate from the floor at her feet before buckling up again.

"I think I'll have a look at how Cordelia Gordon's plates are doing," she said.

He grunted again. "Good luck getting into the crate."

"Do you ever stop being overly pessimistic?" she asked as she rummaged through her voluminous shoulder bag.

"Forget it, Sunshine. It's going to take more than a nail file to get into that crate."

"Luckily," she pulled out a compact pink plastic case with a flourish, "I have more than a nail file."

She popped open the lid of the case and brandished it toward him. "Compact tool kit. A girl should never leave home without one."

"Nice tools," he said, sardonically. "Lovely shade of pink."

"Thank you." She took out the small battery-operated screwdriver, selected the proper head, inserted it, then turned it on, easily unscrewing the Phillips screws at all four corners. She gently lifted the lid and set it next to her on the seat of the car. Carefully, she pushed aside the shredded material to find the first of the plates nestled comfortably in place. She sighed, both in relief and because, even in the dashboard light, the Jazz Age plate with its deep-blue glaze was beautiful. Almost reverently, she lifted it from its nest, turned it this way and that, running her fingers over the rim, then across the back.

"Still perfect," she said.

"You say that with the reverence of a connoisseur."

"I've become a fan of Art Deco since hunting down pieces for clients. Cowan Pottery turned out some wonderful pieces in the period. These Jazz Age plates are very rare. A real find."

"All right. Let's have a look at them, then." Rory flipped on the dome light in the car. "Show me what makes them Jazz Age."

Sunny squinted for a moment against the sudden light, then carefully held up the earthenware plate for him to see. "It's the etchings. See? They're all symbolic of the Jazz Age. Cocktail glasses, martini shakers, skyscrapers."

"Bring it closer," Rory said. "Turn it more toward me."

He was scowling hard enough at the plate to make it crack. "Are you trying to scare it?" she asked.

"Hmm?" he mumbled, clearly preoccupied.

"That scowl on your face is enough to crack crystal."

"It's just that it looks familiar."

"Really?"

"I've seen it somewhere before. Or something like it, at least."

"The plates are extremely rare. They were made to go with a bowl that Eleanor Roosevelt had designed as a gift for FDR."

"Oh?"

He seemed interested so Sunny told him about the designer and other pieces he made. She was just about to launch into a discourse about another designer who was more prolific when Rory interrupted.

"Bowls, you say?"

"Yes. The original was commissioned by Eleanor Roosevelt but there were fifty made in all."

"How big were they?"

"Well, it was intended for use as a punch bowl. I'd say it was maybe sixteen inches across."

"My grandmother had one."

Sunny looked from the plate to Rory and back again. "Seriously. Are you sure? I mean, one of the bowls sold at auction at Christie's for over fifteen thousand dollars."

"I'm sure. She kept it in her china cabinet, along with a picture of my mother and my bronzed baby shoes."

"But I thought—I mean, I thought I read somewhere that you came from—"

He laughed shortly. "Humble beginnings?"

"Well—yes."

"I did. Molly, my grandmother, raised me after my mother died. She worked in a factory, making twine."

"Then how—"

"How did she get the bowl?" He shook his head. "I don't know. All I know is that anything that meant anything to her was kept in that cabinet."

"Where is it now?"

He shrugged. "One day it was just gone. I think it was around the year I graduated from high school. When I asked her about it she said something about it being one less thing to dust.''

Sunny lowered the plate back into the crate then started to replace the screws. She heard Rory's rumble of laughter over the faint whir of the screwdriver and looked up.

"What?" she asked.

"The lady carries tools."

She grinned. "In my line of work you never know when you're going to need them."

"And to think that just a few hours ago I thought of you as a frivolous woman."

"Teach you to judge a woman by her shoes."

He laughed again. She liked the sound. He didn't let it out that often, which made it all the more special, she supposed. His face seemed much more relaxed suddenly. The harsh lines softened.

She wiggled around to face him as much as her seat belt would allow so that she could watch him while he talked. "Tell me about Molly," she said.

Rory took the chance of looking at her. She was curled up like a little girl waiting for her bedtime story. The hood of her parka was pushed back. Her cheek rested on the back of the seat. Her thick chestnut hair had dried full and shiny. She was biting on her lower lip, gazing up at him, looking expectant.

Luckily he had to turn his attention back to the road, because suddenly there was nothing childish about that full lower lip, at all. And he knew that if he allowed himself to run his gaze over her like he wanted to, he'd be all too aware of what a woman she really was. All in all, Rory figured it was safer to talk about Molly.

"Molly was an original. She was a good Catholic who went to movies on Saturday nights, went to church Sunday mornings, and spent the rest of the week standing behind a machine watching twine spin onto a spool. Her saving graces were her humor and her sense of duty. She knew how to laugh, and she knew how to be tough when she needed to be.''

"Did she have to be tough with you?''

He glanced over at her again. People didn't ask him such questions. Didn't she know? Rory Temple was the worst interview in the Midwest. He was private about everything but his business dealings. He resented small talk and prying minds. Yet, somehow, with her, he didn't feel angry at the intrusion.

In fact, the memories her question invoked made him chuckle. "It would be safe to say that she didn't stop boxing my ears until I was seventeen years old.''

She laughed and it was like a reward. He wanted more of it.

"She met me at the curb one night when I was out past curfew. Pulled me right out of Steve Kramer's Chevy by the ear, told Steve he better get his backside home because she'd already called his mother, and generally made us feel about twelve years old. We were sixteen at the time.''

Sunny laughed again. "You have a great laugh,'' he said. "So did Molly.'' She glanced down when he made the remark and he fancied he could see a blush on her cheek. Sweet.

"Did she laugh a lot?'' Sunny finally asked.

He grinned. "All the time.''

"Except when she was boxing your ears,'' Sunny said.

"Except then. But she never stayed mad for long. The house was usually filled with people. All kinds of people. With Molly there was always time for a friend or neighbor with a problem. Always room at the table for one more.'' He shook his head at the memory. "She knew some real characters. The neighborhood was a melting pot. There was a butcher who used to bring her soup

bones every week, an Italian guy who owned a bakery—
we always had plenty of day-old bread and soggy cannoli
to eat—the spinster sisters from down the street. And
then there was the professor.''

''The professor?''

''That's what everyone called him. Apparently, or so
Molly believed, he really had been a professor at the
University of Chicago. But he got into some sort of trouble. Couldn't get another teaching job. He clerked at a
bookstore downtown, but rented a room from the two
spinster sisters. He was a great talker. Molly would always say, 'Hear that, Rory? That's how smart people
talk.' I would sit on the floor and listen to him, trying to
remember the words he used so I could look them up
later. He's the one who taught me how to handle myself
in the world.''

''Did Molly live long enough to see what a success
you'd become?''

He shook his head. ''No. I'd just graduated from college when she died. But she always knew I'd make it.
She willed me to become successful—to make something
of myself.'' He paused, remembering how she'd sat with
him looking over college catalogs, listening to him end-
lessly discuss the pros and cons and costs of different
schools. The cost—

''You know something? I think I just figured out what
happened to my grandmother's bowl.''

She sat up straighter. ''What?''

''I think it helped pay for those first few years of college. I always wondered where she'd gotten the kind of
money those first few years took. I'd won grants and
scholarships based on my academic performance after
those years, but I never would have made it to my junior
year without her help. And she sure didn't make that kind
of money in the factory.''

"What a wonderful legacy for one of those bowls. Eleanor would have been pleased, I'm sure."

Rory hadn't expected that kind of reaction from a woman who was an acquirer of material possessions. But then, Sunny was a continual surprise. He had no doubt at all that he'd be smiling for weeks every time he thought of her following that crow up a tree to rescue a ruined hat.

"She obviously loved you very much," Sunny said. "And you loved her just as much."

It wasn't a question, but he felt compelled to respond. "I owe her everything. The deal I'm trying to get back to Chicago to settle is a promise I made to her when I was barely out of high school. I told her one day that I would buy that big, ugly factory across the street from our house and that I would turn it into something beautiful and that she'd never have to work in it again."

She was silent while the windshield wipers made their whumping sound and the snow built up on the hood. What had made him say so much? He never discussed his grandmother with anyone. He'd learned very early on that to show weakness in the business world was the first step to failure. The thought of Molly, with her callused hands, her sassy mouth and tender heart, could still bring tears to his eyes.

He still missed her. After all these years.

Sunny was glad it was so dark outside because she felt like crying. It was such a sweet promise. Rory was obviously capable of great tenderness and sensitivity. Too bad he was so reluctant to let it show.

She snuggled deeper into the seat. "Tell me what you're going to do with the factory," she implored dreamily, more than ready to be dazzled by something philanthropic and civic-minded.

"I'm going to build the most luxurious condominiums Chicago has ever seen."

She blinked, certain she'd heard him wrong. "Excuse me?"

"Luxury condos," he repeated. "Nothing under a million and a half."

She sat bolt upright. "You're joking, right?"

"I never joke about money, angel."

"But—a million and a half? That'll change the whole neighborhood!"

"That's exactly the point."

"But, what about the spinster sisters? The Italian baker? The professor?"

He threw her an impatient look. "What are you talking about? Those people have been gone for years."

"But people like them still exist in that neighborhood, Rory! After my parents left the commune, they bought a flower shop in this wonderful old neighborhood in the Wrigleyville section of Chicago where there was a lot of diversity. We lived in the apartment upstairs. If it weren't for so many different kinds of people surrounding me while I grew up, I would have felt like more of a misfit than ever after living on a commune until I was eight. Don't you see that something like that wouldn't be possible if you go ahead with your plans? Your luxury condos will kill the essence of the neighborhood."

"The essence of the neighborhood is a lot of run-down wood frame houses that can only benefit by either being torn down or restored."

"You mean gentrified."

"Oh, no, don't tell me I'm trapped in a car with a preservationist. I should have known by the way you've been hanging on to that hat."

"And what do you think Molly would have thought of your million-dollar condos?"

"Million and half. And Molly wanted me to be a success."

"Which you are. So it wouldn't ruin you to make some of the condos affordable or rent-subsidized. Or even use part of the building as a community center where—"

"Your heart is bleeding all over your two-thousand-dollar plates, Pollyanna," he said dryly. "Aren't you forgetting that it's only the wealthy who can afford your services?"

"That's not true. I've worked with people of all socioeconomic backgrounds."

He snorted derisively. "I wasn't aware that people in the projects were into Art Deco."

"As a matter of fact, Rory Temple, I have worked with people in low income housing, providing low-cost decorating ideas and workshops."

"And did having ruffled curtains solve their problems?"

"No, of course not. But caring about your surroundings is vital to any kind of success. Didn't your grandmother hang curtains? If she owned a china cabinet and the Jazz Age bowl, she must have cared about her surroundings!"

"My grandmother made a wonderful home for me." He gave a short bark of laughter, but somehow it didn't sound all that amusing. "I didn't even know we were poor when I was a kid. It wasn't until I got older that I hated how hard she had to work. I hated that I didn't have the power to give her things. I wanted things for her. I wanted things for myself. There's nothing wrong with that."

"No, of course there isn't. But I would think you'd want the project to reflect Molly in some way."

"You didn't even know her. How can your presume to know what would or would not reflect her?"

He was back in his haughty, I'm-big-shot Rory Temple mode. Listening to him, looking at him, it was hard to believe that he was the same man who'd been talking so lovingly about his grandmother just moments ago.

"Well, I know enough to know that if she were alive today she wouldn't be wearing fur and living in a condo worth a couple of million."

His jaw was starting to work. Well, so what? Her jaw was doing some working, too. It was ridiculous to think that he couldn't see the validity of her argument. The man who'd just been talking about the butcher, the baker and the professor, the man who taught him how to talk like big-shot Rory Temple, would know better than to price people like that out of their homes.

"I did not get in the position to be able to buy that factory by wearing a bleeding heart on my sleeve."

"Obviously. The only thing you've ever worn on your sleeve was the badge of a mercenary."

He glared at her, then reached out to flip the radio on. "Do you think you can suspend the lecture on ethics long enough for me to hear the weather report?"

Sunny glared right back at him, wishing Molly was still around to box his ears. She would have loved to have seen that.

THE WEATHER REPORT wasn't pretty. The storm was moving northward. At some point, they were going to run straight into the worst of it. Rory reached out and fiddled with the radio, trying to get the station to come in clearer, then glanced over at Sunny. She'd been silent for the past thirty miles, leaving him to listen to the thump of the windshield wipers and the static of the radio every time it lost the station, which was about every half a mile. No doubt Sunny was thinking of all the throngs of homeless his condos would be creating. Humph. It would take years and years for the entire area to become gentrified enough to price the lower middle class out of the neighborhood.

He frowned. She did have a point, though—much as he hated to admit it. It might take years, but there was no denying that his project was going to get the ball rolling for change in the old neighborhood. There would undoubtedly be gentrification. But Chicago would be the winner in the end.

Wouldn't it?

What *would* Molly think of his condo project? Would she want the kind of people who would own the units as neighbors? Doctors, lawyers, stockbrokers? Somehow he couldn't see any of them sitting around Molly's old kitchen table, eating day-old cannoli.

He was getting damned irritated with himself. Not only was he lusting after Sunny, but now the bride-to-be was making him rethink things he thought he'd sorted through long ago. The Simpson Twine factory project had been his goal in life up to now. Was he going to let a woman who talked to crows make him start second-guessing himself?

More importantly at the moment—and this surprised and irritated him as well—was she ever going to talk to him again?

The radio spit out a few lines of a country tune before sputtering and crackling again. He reached out and switched it off.

The silence was deafening.

Rory burst out in frustration. "Are you going to give me the cold shoulder the rest of the way to Chicago? You might as well get it over with. Tell me what else you're thinking!"

"I'm thinking that if we don't stop real soon, we're

going to find out how waterproof this blaze orange coat really is.''

"What?"

"I have to go to the bathroom."

Rory threw back his head and laughed. "Well, why didn't you say so?"

"It's not like there's been anywhere to stop, anyway."

"We'll find someplace," he said. "And I think we can both use some food, too."

Suddenly, he was feeling a lot better.

He slowed the car so he could read a sign at the side of the road. Welcome To Menominee, Michigan, it said. A short while later they came to a stoplight, blinking red through the thick, wet snowfall. Theirs was the only car at the intersection. The road ahead was drifted with pristine snow. No tire tracks. No footprints. The only thing that seemed to be moving was the snow. And that was falling faster than ever.

"Where's the map we bought at Harry's?"

She pulled it out of her shoulder bag and opened it. "We're nearly to the Wisconsin border. Looks like it's just a couple of miles."

"Good. Hopefully we'll find a place open soon."

Sunny sighed. "It seems a shame in a way."

"What does?"

"To have to drive down that road. I mean, it looks like a deserted planet—a ghost planet—and our tire tracks will be the first in hundreds of years."

"You have a rather fanciful mind, don't you? I bet you spent your summers barefoot, making daisy chains." He got a sudden image of her, barefoot in a field of flowers, filmy dress gently moving against her long legs, chestnut hair tossed by the wind. Only she wasn't a child. And there was absolutely nothing childlike at all about what the image was doing to him.

"Barefoot, yes. But we didn't make daisy chains on the commune, we made strawberry preserves and pickles. We grew our own food."

"Food," he repeated, gladly seizing a change of subject. "Let's start exploring this planet. See if the natives have ever heard of a thing called a hamburger."

She laughed. "Onward, Captain Temple."

"Hmm, you're willing to mar the landscape for a hamburger?"

"Nothing is sacred when it comes to red meat," Sunny answered. "Full speed ahead."

Full speed on the deserted, snow-covered streets amounted to about twenty-five miles an hour. When the car turned onto the long bridge that spanned the Menominee River between Michigan and Wisconsin, the wind buffeted the car violently enough to make it an adventure. When they reached the town of Marinette on the other side, the square of its downtown was asleep under a blanket of white. The old library looked like it belonged in a Christmas movie. There were a few restaurants, but they were dark and closed.

As they turned onto the highway that headed out of town, Sunny's stomach growled.

"Did you hear that?" Rory asked. "Was that the engine?"

"Um—no."

"You sure? That's all we need is car trouble."

Sunny held her breath and willed her tummy to be quiet. It didn't listen.

"There it is again," Rory said. "If this car breaks down," he grumbled darkly, "I'm suing the rental company."

"The car isn't going to break down."

"How can you possibly know that? Were you into fortune-telling at that commune, too?"

"No. If you must know, the noise isn't coming from the car's engine, it's coming from mine."

He gave her a puzzled look.

"Haven't you ever heard a girl's stomach growl before?"

He threw back his head and laughed. It was a gesture she was becoming inordinately fond of. "I guess we better find some food on this planet soon," he said.

She bit her lower lip. Those size fours he was used to probably never got hungry enough for their stomachs to growl. They were too used to starving themselves. Well, if they ever did find a restaurant that was open, he was going to find out that her appetite was as uncouth as the jacket she was wearing. It'd been a long time since Aunt Tilly's roast beef.

Suddenly she saw a dim light up ahead.

"Slow down! I think I see something." She peered through the windshield. "Is there such a thing as a snow mirage? Because I could almost swear there are huge letters in the sky ahead that spell the word 'eat.'"

"I certainly hope it's no mirage, angel," he said, "because I think the beast in your stomach is about to get nasty."

Sunny rolled her eyes. She supposed that if a gorgeous, virile man is going to talk about your tummy it was good that he called you angel. Still, she wished her darned tummy would shut up.

Just as it let loose with another growl, a huge, flying-saucer-sized hamburger materialized next to the three-letter word.

"Either I'm hallucinating," she said, afraid to take her eyes off the apparition on a bun, "or there is a diner up ahead."

"Unless we're having the same hallucination, Sunshine, there is a diner up ahead."

"Hamburgers!" Sunny gushed.

"Mickey-Lu's Bar-B-Q. Hang on, angel, I think we've found you a bathroom and a meal."

Those weren't exactly the words she would have wanted to hear if she was ever alone with a man like Rory Temple, but at the moment they were more thrilling than anything else could possibly be.

Rory switched on the turn signal and slowly pulled into the parking lot that surrounded the small, flat-roofed building. There was one lone semi parked nearby.

Sunny was out of the car by the time he came around to open the door.

"Oh my God! Smell that! It's heaven on a bun."

Rory laughed and held out his arm. "Shall we check their wine list?" he asked.

"Wine? Forget that. Let's see if they have fried onions!"

"Not only a connoisseur of fine haberdashery but also of gourmet food, I see."

"If they toast the hamburger buns, I'm going to swoon." She started to take his arm, then remembered the plates. "Oh, wait a second!"

"What are you doing?"

"The plates. I'm not leaving them in the car alone."

"Leave them," Rory said. "We'll lock the car. They'll be fine."

"Maybe so, but the way my luck is running today, I'm not letting them out of my sight."

She lifted the crate out of the car, tucked it under her arm, then took Rory's arm with her other hand. They slogged through the snow together, the night silent around them. The building was squat—brick painted white, red awnings catching the snow over its low windows. The green door advertised soda pop in a red tin. Rory held it open for her and she went inside.

Heat and light hit her snow-chilled face with as much force as the music from the jukebox and the sound of waitresses joking and counting tips. There was one man slumped on a stool at the counter, but the tiny booths against the wall and the few small tables in the middle of the floor were empty. Sunny's gaze glanced off all of this on its way to the brick barbecue pit set in the wall behind the counter. Her mouth started to water.

When the door slammed behind them, everyone looked up from what they were doing.

"Sorry, people, but we're closed," a middle-aged woman wearing a name tag that read Mildred, assistant manager, called over the music.

Sunny's heart sank. The scent of char-grilled burgers was heavy in the air. To deny her the taste of one was just too cruel.

"Oh, please!" she said. "We only want a couple of burgers. For the road. We'll take them with us so we won't even dirty a table."

"We're closed," Mildred said again.

"But it's taken us hours to drive from Escanaba and there hasn't been a single place open the entire way. We're starving!"

"And we're closed," the woman said flatly, totally untouched, it would seem, by Sunny's lament.

"Come on, Mildred. Make the kid a burger," said the truck driver. "You know the grill is still hot enough."

"This isn't any of your business, Fred. You think those measly tips you leave buys you stock in the place or something?"

"Woman," Fred said, "you are colder than that snow out there."

Mildred gave him a sour look. "And where would it all end, Fred? I make an exception for one, where do I draw the line? Suppose the entire Green Bay Packers football team came walking through those doors right after I put this lady's burger on? Then I gotta feed them, too.''

"Oh, like you're going to turn down that cute quarterback for the Packers," said one of the waitresses. "You know darn well, Mildred, that you'd fall all over yourself trying to cook that man something."

Mildred started to blush, but it wasn't enough to make her relent about the burgers. "Tell you what," she said grudgingly, "I'll sell you a couple of pieces of pie and some coffee for the road."

Sunny's stomach growled its disappointment, but Mildred seemed unmovable. She walked over to Rory, who was leaning against the door. "What do you think? I guess pie and coffee is better than nothing."

"Looks like your powers of persuasion don't work on the female gender," he said. "If the manager had been a man, we'd be eating burgers by now."

She put her hands on her hips. "Oh, you think so, huh?"

"Absolutely," he nodded.

He was stunningly handsome, even in the hokey hunting jacket, leaning there with his mouth twisted into a wry grin and one flared, dark eyebrow raised. He loved to bait her—and she, like a starving perch, snapped up the bait every time. It left the air charged between them with an energy that was close to sexual, as if their antagonism were a form of foreplay.

"Tell you what," she told him, stuffing her hands into her pockets, "since it's a woman, why don't you try getting us what we need for a change. Use your male wiles."

"Male wiles?" he asked "Is there such a thing?"

"Let's find out, shall we? I've heard you've talked your way into many a boardroom—and many a bedroom—Rory Temple. Surely you can talk us into a couple of burgers.''

He came away from the wall and she appreciated how wide his shoulders looked in the blaze orange jacket when he straightened to his full height. ''Think I can't?'' he asked her, his dark eyes challenging her.

She shrugged. ''Mildred doesn't look easy. She was totally unmoved by Fred. Maybe you can do better,'' she said, shrugging. ''Maybe you can't.''

''Sunshine, the day I can't do better than Fred is the day I shave my head.''

''Hmm. Shame to see all the nice thick hair go.''

''Get ready to eat some burgers,'' Rory said as he headed toward Mildred.

He leaned on the counter, bending his upper body very close to Mildred. Whatever he was saying, he was saying in a voice too low and soft for her to hear so Sunny gave up and headed for the ladies' room.

When she came out, Rory was sitting at a booth drinking coffee.

''Well?'' she asked, sliding in next to him and taking the cup of coffee he held out to her.

''Our burgers will be ready in a few minutes,'' he said with the air of a man who hadn't seen any other outcome.

She laughed with delight, and was more than willing to concede victory to him if it meant she'd be eating soon. ''Sorry I missed the show,'' she said.

''Speaking of shows, will you take a look at this place? It could be a movie set.''

Sunny looked around. ''Wow. It's like a time warp.'' There was an abundance of aqua Formica and chrome. The café curtains had little geometric shapes on them in aqua and shrimp and the jukebox looked like an original. ''Look at the old-fashioned malt mixer behind the counter. I bet this is the place kids came to after football games.''

''Yeah,'' Rory said, ''back when the curtains were new.''

Sunny laughed. ''Boys in letter sweaters and girls in full skirts jitterbugging by the jukebox over there.''

''And every Saturday night someone's father would come rushing in the door to see if his daughter was here past curfew.''

''The cheerleaders would hold court at one table—''

''And the greaser babes would hang out in a booth.''

''Greaser babes?''

''Yeah. Mildred over there was one of them.''

Sunny nearly choked on her coffee. ''You think so?''

He looked over at Mildred and winked. ''Oh, she's definitely got an edge to her.''

''Hmm. Just how far did Mildred fall?''

''All the way. We're eloping tomorrow,'' he told her, grinning.

She grinned back but all of a sudden the look on his face sobered. He put his hand up and swept her hair back behind her ear. His fingers lingered on her cheek. ''Are you really getting married in the morning, angel?'' he asked her softly.

He was so close, there in the tiny booth next to her. She could feel his thigh gently resting against hers. The look in his eyes made her think that maybe he would be happy to hear the truth. ''I—I—'' she began.

''Burgers are up!'' called Mildred, sliding a white bag along the counter. ''Now get out of here so I can close.''

6

"THIS IS THE BEST BURGER I've ever tasted."

Rory watched Sunny pop the last bite of her burger into her mouth. "The buns are toasted. Are you swooning?"

"I'm too busy devouring," she said with her mouth full. "How many did you get?"

"Six."

"Great!" she said, wiping her mouth with a paper napkin then holding out her hand, palm up. "I'll have another."

Rory chuckled. He wasn't used to women with appetites. Most of the women who sat across a restaurant table from him acted as if they had absolutely no interest in the overpriced, diminutive entrée before them—or the expensive ambiance surrounding them. Yet here was Sunny Morgan, sitting in a rented car in a truck-stop parking lot, relishing a burger wrapped in white paper like it was a gift from the Gods. He dug in the bag and brought out another one of the burgers, placing it in her waiting palm. The paper crackled as she unwrapped it and took a huge bite.

"Do you always eat like a lumberjack or is that jacket having an effect on you?"

She laughed. "I'm afraid I'm disgustingly carnivorous whenever I get around a burger. Growing up on lentils and tofu will do that to a girl."

"You never ate red meat as a child?"

She shook her head. "Only at Aunt Tilly's."

"And when the other kids went for fast food?"

"But the other kids I knew didn't eat fast food. The commune was like its own little world. We were home-schooled and seldom went into town for anything. All my friends were children of the commune. And none of us ate meat."

"An unconventional childhood."

She twisted her mouth. "I didn't know how unconventional until we moved into Chicago and I started going to public school."

"Difficult transition?"

About to take a bite of her burger, she paused and lowered it. "Yes, it was," she answered thoughtfully. "Especially when I found out that my parents weren't—"

He waited for her to go on, but she didn't.

"Weren't what?" he prompted.

"Well—they just weren't like the other parents, that's all."

She kept her head lowered, fiddling with the paper on her burger. He was betting that there was more to it than the fact that her parents wore Birkenstock sandals and didn't eat meat. Whatever it was was obviously not something that she normally talked about. Rory wasn't the kind of man who made a habit of drawing anyone out when it came to personal details, yet he felt compelled to with Sunny.

"You were hurt somehow," he prompted.

She looked up with surprise in her eyes. "Oh—no. No, I wasn't. My parents are wonderful, loving people. I'm still close to them. It's just that, well—"

When she hesitated, he said softly, "It's just that to a child punishment is sometimes preferable to being different."

She stared at him for a moment before a small smile lifted her luscious mouth. "Yes, that's exactly how I felt sometimes. How did you know?"

"Are you serious? My grandmother raised me after my mother died and my father took off. I wore secondhand shirts and my winter jackets were always too short in the sleeve. I know all about being different."

"Is that what drove you to become so successful? You wanted to show them?"

"Partly. And you? Is that what makes you want to do something as conventional as a wedding in April?"

She looked a little taken aback by his question. She turned away from him to stare out the front windshield, he watched her and wondered at her spirit. When she'd hit that brick wall of conformity known as public school, it must have hurt like hell, yet she was still so vibrant and open, still so full of childlike delight. She was...Rory actually had to grope for the word, he was so unused to using it. And the word was *fun.* Sunshine Morgan knew how to have *fun*—something Rory was beginning to fear he'd forgotten. They'd had nothing but trouble on the trip so far, and yet Sunny always managed to find something to laugh at. It was like she carried her good time with her.

"Enough about my childhood," she said suddenly, looking at him with a new glint of mischief in her dark eyes. "Why don't you tell me what you said to Mildred back there to get us these burgers."

"I just used my irresistible charm."

She eyed him suspiciously, her full mouth twisted to one side. "Mildred didn't exactly look easy to charm, Rory."

"That's only because she had never come under the influence of the Temple charm before."

"Really? Hmm. Then tell me what you said to her."

"You want specifics?"

"Yes, I want specifics. Tell me what seductive words you used to win her over."

"Sorry," he said, fishing in the bag for another burger. "It's all copyrighted material."

Quickly, she lunged at him and grabbed the burger out of his hand.

"Hey, that's stealing!"

She shook her head. "I'm merely holding it hostage until you tell me what I want to know."

He laughed and tried to grab it back. She giggled and held it further away from him.

"Tell or it goes out the window."

"Heartless wench! You'd keep a cold, starving man away from the best burger in the Midwest?"

She looked thoughtful for a moment, then said, "Yup."

"Okay, okay. What I said to her was—"

Sunny leaned forward eagerly. "Yes?"

"I said, if you'll make us some burgers I'll give you—"

Sunny gasped and he wondered if she had visions of something carnal instead of carnivorous in her mind. Rory certainly did. He wasn't given to teasing. Not since he was in high school, anyway. Yet he found himself wanting to tease her, wanting to see those eyes grow big, wanting to see a blush stain her cheeks.

"What—um—did you promise to give her?" Sunny asked in a voice that caught in her throat.

Oh, Rory knew where her mind was, all right, because his was in exactly the same place. He knew he should, but he couldn't seem to stay away from the fire. In fact, he wanted to stoke it. Dipping his head closer to hers, he lowered his voice. "I promised to give her—"

"Yes?" she asked, the word coming out in a hoarse whisper.

He dipped his head further still until his forehead was resting lightly against hers. He heard the soft intake of her breath and his body relished her reaction.

"I promised," he whispered, "to give Mildred—" he paused and brought up his hand so he could brush his thumb across her lower lip. He felt her mouth tremble against the pad of his thumb.

"Y-yes?"

"A hundred bucks," he finally said.

Sunny's mouth dropped open. "What?"

"I slipped her a hundred. Now give me back my burger!"

He lunged for it, but Sunny wasn't going to give it up without a fight. She held it just out of his reach. But then, Rory wasn't exactly trying hard to reach it. He was enjoying being close to her too much to want it to end soon. Like a lovesick kid he was using their tussle over the burger as an excuse to touch her, to press his thigh into hers, his chest against her breasts.

Her body hardened his. Her scent filled his nostrils. Her laugh filled his head. It was hunger of the kind that had nothing to do with eating a burger.

"I guess that means," she said between sputters of laughter, "that you aren't irresistible, after all."

Her face was turned up to his, her big dark eyes laughing along with her full mouth. His body was suddenly hungrier than it had been for anything in a long, long time.

"Not irresistible?" he murmured, slipping his arm around her and pulling her tight up against him. "Then try resisting this."

Before she could protest he took her mouth with his. She struggled for one instant more, and then there was the sound of the burger falling to the floor, and the feel of her hand thrusting through his hair, and the taste of her mouth, eager as his, hungry as his.

That quickly.

Outside the car, the snow fell thickly. Inside the car, the windows steamed up from the boiling of his blood, wrapping them in frosted silence, shutting out the world.

Shutting out the fact that she belonged to someone else.

He ended the kiss only because he needed to look into her eyes, to kiss her nose, her cheek, her throat. Only because he needed to bury his face in her hair.

But his mouth couldn't stay away from hers for long. Her lips were soft and moist, her tongue wet and hot. He devoured it like a beast who hadn't eaten in years.

Needing to feel the warmth of her blood, he unzipped her jacket and slipped his hands inside, praying that she wouldn't stop him. Knowing that she should.

She didn't and he couldn't. Couldn't because he hadn't felt this way since he was a kid making out for the first time. Couldn't because this is what he'd wanted ever since he'd first had his hands on her when she fell into his lap on the plane.

He skimmed his hands up her sides. He wanted her breasts against his palms. He wanted to hear what she would sound like when he touched them.

When he brushed his thumbs along the sides of her breasts, he felt her stiffen and hold her breath, like she was waiting. When he moved his hands to cover her breasts she gasped into his mouth and it was like she'd come to life again. Her nipples hardened beneath his touch, her fingers dug into his scalp, her mouth moved wildly on his.

He had never, ever felt anything like it.

His fingertips found her nipples and she moaned as

they grew harder. He needed to feel them against his tongue. He pulled his mouth from hers and tore at the buttons of her shirt while he trailed his mouth along her jawbone, her chin, her throat. And lower still to taste the valley of her cleavage, to feel her heart beating under his lips.

His mouth had just touched the lace edge of her bra when there was a loud knock on the window.

Sunny pushed him away so abruptly that his forehead banged into her chin.

"Ouch!" she said.

"Sorry," he said, trying to smooth his hair and straighten his clothes.

She couldn't look at him while she fumbled with the buttons of her shirt and pulled the hunting parka around her.

Whoever was outside knocked on the window again.

Rory turned the key on and hit the button to open the window. It was Mildred.

"Just wanted to tell you folks that the radio says things are getting worse around Green Bay. If you're heading south, you better quit fooling around and skedaddle."

"Fooling around!" Sunny tried for indignant but her voice cracked, spoiling the effect. "We were—um—just eating."

Mildred looked at the burger on the floor, looked back up at Sunny's face, which she was sure looked as hot as it felt, and said, "Uh-huh. I make a damn good burger, and your man paid enough for them, but they still aren't enough to make you breathe as heavy as you two are breathing."

Sunny opened her mouth to say something and Mildred shook her head and laughed.

"Thanks for the information, Mildred," Rory offered.

"That was a big tip you left. I figured you had extra service coming."

Sunny watched Mildred walk away and felt mortified. She'd never wanted a man's hands on her so much in her life. Even now, after being caught like a teenager, all she wanted was to fill his arms again. Totally mortifying.

And now she supposed Rory was going to launch into one of his lectures on her unbridelike behavior. Bad enough to be caught with her hormones raging like a high school junior on prom night, now she was going to have to once again face deciding whether or not to tell Rory the truth.

And she was going to have to make the decision while her body still throbbed for his touch, while her head still spun from his mouth.

She just could not face it. Not yet.

She flung open the door and stepped out of the car. Furiously, she started to sweep the snow off the front windshield with the sleeve of her jacket. She heard the driver-side door open so she shuffled through the snow to the back of the car and started clearing the rear windshield.

"Sunny?"

She ignored him and started to hum "White Christmas." Never mind that it was April. If the weather wasn't going to pay any attention, why should she?

Rory appeared on the other side of the trunk, across from her. He started brushing at his side of the windshield. Their hands collided while hers were on the upswing. She snatched it back, heat flaring through her body and into her face.

"Look, Sunny, I—"

The cell phone in his pocket started to ring. He made an impatient sound low in his throat, then answered the call.

Sunny took the opportunity to get into the driver's seat and start the engine. The windows were still steamed, probably from the heat pumping off her cheeks. Zero visibility. She turned on the defroster and the windshield wipers then took off her gloves and pressed her palms to her cheeks.

Mercy. Her body was humming like it'd just been plugged in for the first time.

Was she ever going to cool down? She pushed a button and let the car window glide down a few inches. Flurries of snowflakes whipped in, stinging as they melted on her hot cheeks.

"What are you doing?"

Sunny jumped at the sound of his voice coming through the open window. She resisted the impulse to answer, *"Lusting after you,"* and said instead, "I thought I'd drive for a while."

He glared at her for a moment, then said, "Look—" His pocket started to ring again.

"Damn," he said, then answered it.

Saved by the bell—she thought with no originality at all. While he talked into the phone he rounded the car and got in.

She pulled out of the parking lot, hoping that his phone call lasted a good long time.

It did. And when he finally hung up, Rory was looking grimmer than ever.

"Trouble?" she asked, certain from what she heard of his side of the conversation that he had bigger trouble than her, and what he referred to as her penchant for throwing herself into his arms, at the moment.

"It seems my absence has been noticed."

"Excuse me?" she asked.

"There's a rumor going around that I've left town because I can't swing the deal."

"Who would believe that?" she asked, slightly aghast.

"No one, I hope. But someone is trying to make Josiah Simpson, the man who owns the building, believe it."

"Who would do that?" If this kept up she was going to start to sound like an owl. But she figured anything was preferable to rehashing her role as the fallen fiancée.

"An enemy."

She gave him a quick look. Well, he did look like the kind of man who made enemies. Too successful. Too arrogant. Too handsome. And he certainly didn't seem like the kind of man given to melodrama, despite his rather gothic, lupine appearance.

"It seems," he went on, "that a competitor is spreading the rumor that I canceled the meeting because the financing fell through."

"But you've got a legitimate reason for having to cancel."

"I know. And hopefully, old Josiah will also know— just as soon as I get a hold of him."

His phone rang again. Agnes had the number he needed. He dialed and Sunny listened to the conversation, which turned out to be better than anything she'd ever heard on talk radio.

"You have my word on it, Simpson," Rory said after several minutes of fast talking. "Nine o'clock tomorrow morning."

"Whew!" she gasped, when he ended the call. "That had me at the edge of my seat."

He pocketed the phone. "Josiah Simpson is a tough old guy. Took him awhile to let go of the fact that I was the kid who soaped his car windows every Halloween and threw rocks at the lights in the parking lot at Simpson Twine just to hear the sound of the breaking glass."

She laughed. "So Rory Temple was a bad boy."

"Did you ever doubt it?" he said in a wicked voice.

Sunny tried to ignore what that voice did to her insides. "Sounds like he still doesn't quite trust you."

"He's had help," Rory said sardonically.

"Who from?" she asked, wincing when she realized she was sounding like an owl again.

Rory told her about his competitor and the rivalry that had existed between them since Rory bested him in a real estate deal years ago. As she listened to him she was amazed anew at how much this project meant to him. How much his grandmother Molly meant to him.

By the time he'd finished, she'd worked up a fine sense of indignation. "It would be a damn shame, Rory, if you don't get that building."

Rory laughed. "So you're on my side again, angel?"

"Absolutely!"

A shiver ran through her when she felt his fingers tucking the hair behind her ear again. "Thank you, angel," he said, as his fingers trailed down the side of her throat. "I like having you on my side."

She gulped. What was he doing? Trying to make her forget that she was engaged again?

Well, not that she was. But he didn't know that.

"What would the other guy do with the building if he got it?" she asked in a rush, eager to get his mind back on business.

"He'll turn it into a parking structure."

"That's horrible! We can't let that happen!"

Sunny looked down at the speedometer. They were only going forty. She squinted out the windshield. Could the conditions bear anything faster?

She started to edge the speed up.

"Whoa, angel!"

"I just want to see that you make it to that meeting in the morning."

"I'll make it. We've got all night."

Oh, how she wished he was saying that for another reason. She liked listening to him talk with such passion about his work, but even more she wanted to be back in his arms. To finish what they'd started back there in the parking lot of Mickey-Lu's Bar-B-Q.

She was shocked at just how much she wanted it.

Luckily, Rory's phone rang again and Sunny turned her full attention to the road ahead.

IT TOOK THEM AN HOUR and a half to cover the sixty miles to Green Bay. Sunny leaned forward in the driver's seat and squinted through the windshield. It was blowing so hard that all she could see was snow swirling all around them.

"Look for signs for the Tower Bridge," she told him.

"I think I see something ahead. Lights."

Sunny slowed the car, although they were only going about thirty miles an hour. Suddenly, there was a car ahead of them. And another. And another.

"I was beginning to think we were the only ones out here," Sunny said, as she stopped the car behind a van.

"There are two flashing yellow lights on the side of the road ahead," Rory said.

Sunny craned her neck, but visibility was next to nothing. "Accident?"

"I can't quite see."

Sunny hit the button to roll down the windows. Rory stuck his head out. When he came back in, his scowl was covered in snow.

"And I thought things couldn't get worse," he grumbled.

"What?"

"The lights are illuminating a sign that says the bridge is closed."

"No! I don't believe it!"

"Well, apparently the cars ahead of us do because we're going nowhere," he said grimly. "You better pull over so I can take a look at the map."

Sunny eased the car to the side of the road and put on the flashers while Rory turned on the dome light so that he could read the map.

"I think if we go back the way we came, we'll be able to hook up with Highway 57. It's a two-lane road, but it looks like it's all we've got. As long as we're pulled over, let's switch places and I'll take over the driving again."

Sunny had no intention of arguing with him.

AN HOUR LATER, visibility was down to a few feet and they were still looking for Highway 57.

"A little more to the right!" Sunny, who was leaning as far as she could out the passenger-side window, called over her shoulder. "No!" she yelled, spitting snow out of her mouth. "Too far! You're heading for the ditch!"

"This is impossible," Rory growled. "We've got to find a place to stop for the night."

Sunny pulled her upper torso back into the car. "No! We can't give up yet! You have a deal to make and I have a wedding to get to. If we stop now we'll never make it in time."

"And if we don't stop, angel, they are going to find our stiff, dead bodies with the thaw." Humor quirked at the corner of his grim mouth. "You're already starting to resemble a snowman."

Sunny shook her head to clear off some of the snow. "But what are we going to do?"

"Look for a place to stop, then hope that the storm clears and we can get an early start in the morning."

"But, what if—"

"Sunny, we have no choice."

She knew he was right but she hated the idea of giving

up. She wiped her face on her glove, then thrust her upper body out the window again, hoping she'd spot a motel before frostbite claimed her nose.

After calling instructions over her shoulder to Rory for another mile or so, she thought she saw a dim glow up ahead.

"Wait!" she shouted. "I think I see lights!"

Rory slowed the already crawling car. "What is it?"

Sunny ducked back in but before she could answer him, Rory burst out laughing. "Angel, if you could see yourself. All you need is a black top hat and a carrot for a nose."

"Never mind that! I think it's a farm! And it's all lit up, which means someone must be home!"

Rory reached into the back seat and grabbed his sweater, then handed it to her. "Here, use this to dry your face."

"But—but this is cashmere! I can't use it as if it was a towel!"

"Yes, you can angel, because you've got to go back out there and guide me to that farmhouse. Otherwise we're going to end up in the ditch. And then what good will a cashmere sweater do me?"

Sunny laughed. "Interesting logic," she said as she wiped her face with the cashmere. It was soft and warm—and it smelled like him. She wanted to keep her face buried in it.

"You okay, angel?"

She jerked her head out of the sweater. "Yes! Of course!" she said too brightly, then thrust her upper body out the window again before she could make a bigger fool of herself.

A few minutes of shouting instructions at Rory and he managed to pull into a small area in front of the farmhouse that had already been plowed. There were already two cars parked there.

"Looks like they've got a full house," Sunny murmured unhappily.

"Well, they better find room for two more because there is no way we're going any further tonight. Wait here, I'll check it out."

Sunny decided not to complain about the order this time. Instead, she watched as the snow swallowed Rory, then she buried her face in his sweater again.

She jumped guiltily a few minutes later when he opened the door.

"They've already got a house full," he yelled above the wind. "But there's a room above the garage they said we can use for the night. It's not heated but there's a wood-burning stove. They gave me a flashlight," he said as he switched it on. "Come on, let's go."

Sunny shoved the leftover burgers into her shoulder bag, gathered up the crate, and started to get out of the car.

"Leave that!" Rory yelled. "The wind out here is brutal."

"It goes where I go," she yelled back. "Now quit wasting time!"

He grumbled something she couldn't hear, then gave in and helped her out of the car. She stuck close behind him while they battled the wind and snow to the garage.

"The stairs are inside!" Rory called before putting his shoulder to the door and forcing it open.

The garage was dark and smelled damp. The glow of the flashlight revealed a set of dusty, cobwebbed stairs.

"The old guy who owns this place said his hired hand used to live up there. Hasn't been used for a while, but he says there's dry firewood."

Sunny peered up the stairs, visions of bats flying in her head. "Um—why don't you go first?"

"Afraid of things that go bump in the night?"

"No, afraid of things that fly into my hair in the night."

Rory laughed. "You're not afraid of wolves but a few bats scare you?"

Sunny's heart stumbled. How did he know that she thought of him as wolflike? She was just about to say something when she realized that he was referring to the woods where they'd almost been caught in the dark.

"The enchanted forest was populated with crows, Mr. Temple. Not wolves."

"Yes. Crows with bad taste in hats."

"Oh! Aunt Tilly's hat! I'd forgotten—"

She was already on her way to the door when he grabbed her by the shoulders and swung her around.

"Look, I'm willing to concede that their could be a thief with the same taste as Eleanor Roosevelt skulking in a snowdrift, but I really don't think any self-respecting thief would venture out on a night like this to steal Aunt Tilly's hat."

Sunny wasn't sure if it was his logic, or the feel of his big hands on her shoulders that made her loath to argue the point. Either way, when he turned away from her she followed him up the stairs and into the farmhand's room.

The place was surprisingly charming—and fairly clean. A handmade quilt covered a high feather bed with a tarnished brass headboard. Another quilt lay folded at the foot of the bed. There was a night table with a reading lamp. An old wooden rocker sat off to the other side of the table. An oval braided rug covered the bare plank floor. There was a long, low oak dresser against the wall next to the rocker. A few books and a small stack of magazines had been left behind on top of it. And on the wall opposite the bed was a large, black Franklin stove and a crude wooden box piled with firewood.

Very charming, thought Sunny. And then her eyes flew back to the bed. It was a double. And the only one in the room.

If he suggested they share it, would she be able to resist? And if she couldn't resist, wouldn't she have to tell him the truth?

She was cold. She was wet. She was exhausted. And she was confused about how she could be even considering the possibility of crawling into bed with a man she'd known for less than a day. What she needed to do was to sleep on it all.

Well, sleep on everything but Rory, that is.

"Um, I guess we could flip for the bed," she said in a rush. "Loser gets the floor or the rocker."

"Ladies always get the bed," Rory said.

"But, that's not fair," she protested. "Maybe we could sleep in shifts," she suggested, until the idea of Rory sitting in that rocker watching her sleep made her start to sweat inside her damp clothes. She shivered.

"I insist you take the bed. I'll be on the my cell phone half the night, anyway."

She was feeling chilled and tired enough to be greedy. "If you're sure," she said, moving gratefully toward the feather bed.

"I insist. I also insist that you get out of those wet clothes."

She spun around, the vision of stripping while he watched her with those dark, predatory eyes shot flames through her lower belly. But he was squatting down, his back to her. The only fire he was trying to light was in the Franklin stove.

Embarrassed, she stammered, "I—I don't have anything to put on. Our suitcases are back in the car."

He looked over his shoulder at her. "What's that you're holding?"

Sunny looked down. Along with the wooden crate, she was still hugging Rory's sweater to her chest.

"My sweater," he said when she appeared to have been struck dumb. "That's got to be dryer than your clothes. Change into it and we can drape your stuff on the rocker and move it closer to the fire to dry."

He turned back to building the fire. He was all business as usual. Meanwhile her excitement grew at just the idea of taking her clothes off in the same room with him. Even if he wasn't watching.

He looked over his shoulder again and gave an impatient grunt. "Well?" he asked.

"I—I—"

A wicked gleam came into his eye. "Did you think I meant to watch?"

"Well, no—I mean, of course not."

His mouth twisted. "Unless you want me to."

The thought that she did want him to swept through her brain like the storm rushing past the window. It startled her into bursting out, "No!" She swallowed and forced herself to appear calm. "I mean—no, of course not."

He gave a short laugh. "The farmer said there's a bathroom up here." He nodded toward the other side of the room. "That's probably it over there."

She turned to look. Sure enough. A bathroom. She felt so relieved she nearly ran to it and shut the door firmly behind her.

It still felt strange to undress knowing he was just on the other side of the door, especially since she'd just fantasized about stripping in front of him. She had never been the exhibitionist type, but something about Rory was striking a match far too close to her libido. She was shivering with the cold, yet her body felt infused with heat. When she slipped his sweater over her head and its softness floated down her body, enfolding her in his scent, she nearly moaned out loud.

How on earth was she going to go back out there and face him feeling like this? She looked down at herself. Would he be able to see the excitement her body betrayed under the sweater? Her nipples were so hard they ached. Luckily, she'd brought the crate in with her. Camouflage. She picked it up and hugged it to her chest with one arm, while she gathered her damp clothes in the other. Slowly, carefully, she opened the bathroom door a crack.

Rory was hunkered down in front of the stove with his back to her. The fire had caught and it danced off his dark hair and silhouetted his broad shoulders and strong back. She was relieved to see that he'd made a bed on the floor with the extra quilt and one of the pillows from the bed. There was a loud crack as a piece of kindling sparked and tumbled. She used the sound as cover to quietly hang her clothes on the back of the rocker, then to slip into the feather bed and draw the quilt up to her chin.

He stood and turned around.

"All tucked in safe and sound?" he asked, as wry amusement danced in his dark eyes.

"All tucked in," she said, feeling neither safe, nor sound.

He'd taken off his hunting jacket. The fine gauge knit of his black shirt clung to hard muscle as she watched him walk over to the rocker, pick it up and move it closer to the fire. She wished she'd grabbed one of those books off the dresser before she got into bed so she could bury her face in it. If she kept watching him like this she was going to explode into flames hotter than the ones in the Franklin stove.

She could not recall, she thought with astonishment, ever being so preoccupied with sex before. Was Rory right? Was she throwing herself into his arms with every chance she got?

She scooted further down in the bed, burying herself up to her forehead in the covers. It was no use. She kept peeking.

Maybe closing her eyes would work.

"Are you cold?"

Her eyes flew open to find him leaning over her. Cold? She'd never been so hot in her life.

"Um—no, I'm fine," she mumbled from her cocoon.

"You're sure? Because I could give you my shirt—"

"Yes! I mean, no! I mean, leave your shirt on. Please." The last thing she needed was a look at his bare chest.

He shrugged and held up his cell phone. "I've got some calls to make. I'll be as quiet as I can."

She had to wet her lips with her tongue before she could speak.

"Don't worry about it. I'm tired enough to sleep through anything," she lied, because she knew there wasn't a snowball's chance in hell she was closing her eyes with Rory Temple lying on the floor at the foot of her bed.

7

SUNNY SIGHED AND stirred in her sleep. Rory groaned, punched his pillow again, and rolled onto his back. Sleepless, he lay with his hands behind his head, staring at the patterns the flames from the fire made on the ceiling.

Maybe that was the problem. The fire. It was too damn hot to sleep in his clothes. Raising himself up on his elbow, he peered through the firelight at the figure on the bed. She was quiet enough to be asleep. To make sure, he got up and walked on bare feet over to the bed.

Sunny was lying on her back, her head turned to one side, one hand curled up near her full, luscious mouth, the other tangled in the thick chestnut hair spilling across the pillow. He put his hand out to touch her, but his fingers stopped just short of her cheek. If he touched her now, it wouldn't end with her cheek.

He turned away from the bed, stripped off his clothes and lowered himself again to the quilt on the floor. He rolled on his side, his back to the sleeping bride-to-be. The less he thought of her, the better. What he needed was sleep.

The phone call to Josiah Simpson, convincing him to reschedule the meeting one more time, had been a long, tiring one. Old Josiah, who still insisted on calling Rory a young whippersnapper when his ire was up, had taken some convincing. Rory had won out in the end, but Simpson had issued an ultimatum: if Rory didn't show up at the rescheduled meeting at noon tomorrow, the deal was off. It was imperative that they get an early start in the morning. He drew the quilt up further and closed his eyes.

Fifteen minutes later, he flipped over on his back again, still wide awake. But it wasn't the conversation with Josiah that was keeping him awake. Nor was it the blizzard that still raged outside or the hardness of the floor beneath him.

It was the bride-to-be, breathing softly across the room and wearing nothing but his sweater, who kept his mind—and his blood—churning far too fast for sleep.

First he kept going over and over her reaction to his plans for the Simpson Twine building. There was validity to Sunny's argument. And from the beginning, the project had never been about making money. That's why it had taken him years to be able to undertake it. Now he was successful enough to take a chance on the project—take a chance on making it a proper shrine to Molly.

He frowned up at the ceiling. *Shrine.* He turned the word over in his brain. Maybe that was the problem. Would a woman who made stuffed monkeys out of socks for her grandson want a shrine? His frown turned into a grin. Yes, he remembered monkey socks—but not until after Sunny had found them at Harry's One Stop back in Escanaba.

It was the Christmas he'd been seven, which was the same year his father left. There was little money, but there were presents under the tree. Among them, a gray tweed monkey with red button eyes. When he'd opened it, he'd scoffed that he was too old for stuffed toys, but he'd slept with that monkey every night until the fear of abandonment went away.

Maybe Molly deserved a shrine, but it was exactly what she wouldn't have wanted.

A fitting tribute. Those were the words Rory should be

concentrating on. A fitting tribute to Molly's warmth, laughter and tenacity. A fitting tribute to her humanity and generosity.

How could he possibly have ever thought that luxury condos were the answer?

Sunny had known immediately that they weren't the answer and she'd taken him to task for it. There were others older than Sunny who wouldn't have taken him so readily to task. He grinned at the memory of her dark eyes flashing and the earnestness of her full, soft mouth.

He thought of that mouth smiling.

Then he thought of how it looked just before he kissed it.

He groaned again, stirring restlessly on his hard, lonely makeshift bed.

And the bed wasn't the only thing that was hard.

How he wanted her. How he wanted to know what her soft, full breasts felt like under his sweater. How he wanted to draw the sweater up her body and over her head. How he wanted to—

"Eeeek!"

Rory sprang to his feet at the sound of Sunny's scream. "What—?"

"Something's in the bed with me!" Sunny screeched again, leapt from the bed, and pointed at the disheveled quilt.

Two small field mice scurried out from under the covers. There was a tiny sound as they jumped to the floor on the other side of the bed, then the scurrying of little feet again, then silence.

"Are they gone?" Sunny asked.

Rory squatted down to see if there was anything under the bed, then nodded. "They're gone. There's probably a hole somewhere in the baseboards. I'm sure you scared them enough that they won't be back." He stood. "Are you all right?" he asked, turning toward her.

There she stood, in nothing but his cashmere sweater, her long legs bare to the thigh, her hair tousled from sleep, her eyes bright and startled. She was beautiful. More beautiful than she'd been in his fantasy. And, if possible, he wanted her even more.

"You're—you're naked!" Sunny gasped, wishing she could pull the words back into her mouth as soon as she'd spit them out. Talk about stating the obvious. He was spectacularly naked. The light from the fire glowed across the flesh covering his hard muscles. Covering his hard—

"Oh, my!" she said.

Rory chuckled low in his throat. "I could say the same thing, angel," he said. "You are a sight."

"Um—so are you," she stammered, squeezing her eyes shut when she heard the words come out of her mouth.

"Open your eyes, angel," he said softly.

She did. He was coming toward her, slowly but surely.

"If you've ever doubted how very desirable you are, just remember how I look at this moment." He stopped just in front of her and brought up his hand to sweep the hair behind her ear. When the tips of his fingers brushed her ear she shivered.

"Do you know why I'm in this condition?" he asked in a voice that made the word *intimacy* somehow lacking.

"Um—well—I—"

He laughed softly again. "It's because I've been lying over there, sleepless, wondering what it would be like to feel you through the softness of my sweater."

She sucked in a breath when he reached out and pressed his hard hands against her breasts. The soft cashmere slid beneath his fingertips as they moved over her.

Her nipples started to tighten and throb with gentle anxiety.

He stepped closer, lowering his head close to hers so that she could feel the soft brush of his lips when he whispered, "I've been lying there wondering what it would be like to put my hands under it and touch your skin."

Her lips parted, her breath quickened. But when she actually felt his hands inch under the sweater, actually felt them on the bare flesh of her midriff, her body jerked like it had been shocked.

She heard him groan and then he pressed his mouth to her throat while his hands skimmed up to her breasts. Her nipples throbbed for more. She cried out in pleasure when he gave it to her. When he rolled her nipples in his fingers, when he tormented them with his thumbs, when he rubbed them with his palms. She cried out every time. The sensations came so fast, so hard, it left her reeling on her feet. She gripped his shoulders, afraid of sliding to the floor.

"Rory—Rory," she moaned, feeling that added thrill of just hearing her own voice say his name out loud. "Rory," she said again.

He took her mouth with his then, plundered it, whipping new sensations into her blood. She drew in a sharp breath when one hand left her breast and skimmed down her body to cup the mound between her legs through the silk of her panties.

Liquid. She turned into liquid fire.

He pulled his mouth away from hers and it was like losing her lifeline in a sea of sensation.

"Angel," he commanded in a voice raspy and urgent, "look at me."

She opened her eyes.

He was the wolf again. His green eyes were focused

intently on her, while his powerful chest rose and fell as if he'd been pursuing his prey.

"Are you going to stop me?" he asked, in that same rough voice.

A log fell in the fire, but she barely heard it above her own heart. Above his.

"No," she whispered. "I'm not going to stop you."

With swift grace, he reached out and pulled the sweater over her head, tossed it aside, then swept her into his arms.

His body was hard, hot, as needy as hers. She opened her mouth to his and shoved her hands into his hair, holding him there, determined to take as much from his mouth as she wanted this time. His hands were on her back, on the curve of her waist, on her buttocks, drawing her closer to him, lifting her up and onto him so that his hard length pressed into her, pushing her to another plateau of need.

"I want to be inside of you," he said roughly against her mouth.

"Yes," she whispered urgently.

He tore her panties aside, then lifted her against him until her feet no longer touched the floor. She wrapped her legs around him, and as smooth as silk flowing against silk, he was inside of her.

"Promise me that you'll never forget what I feel like inside of you," he whispered.

"Never," she whispered back, and knew she was speaking the truth.

He lowered her to the bed and started to move slowly inside of her. It was sweet agony. The tension building, the need spiraling. When she greedily thrust her hips up and tightened herself around him, his thrusting became as impatient as hers, as greedy as hers. She flung her arms above her head, feeling wanton, feeling beautiful.

Feeling like a woman.

She arched her back, offering her breasts, and he took one in his mouth, dragged his teeth over the throbbing nipple, lathered it with his tongue, sucked it with his lips.

She moaned and thrashed under him, drowning in need and want. And then it came. Tide after tide of pulsing sensation as her body exploded. It was too much. It was more than she could take—yet she knew she'd never get enough. Not now. Not ever.

"Sunny," Rory gasped roughly. And then she felt him explode inside of her. Hot lava flowing over swollen flesh. The sensation pushed her further, higher than she'd ever been. She wrapped her arms around him and rode with him the rest of the way.

"TELL ME ABOUT YOUR first building."

They were lying on the braided rug in front of the Franklin stove, facing each other, the quilt loosely covering their naked bodies. Sunny's hair gleamed in the firelight and Rory reached out to touch it. It felt like silk beneath his fingers. They'd just shared the last of the leftover hamburgers and he was more in the mood to have Sunny back in his arms than he was to talk business.

"Why?" he asked.

"Because I want to know," Sunny answered.

"It was a theater," he said absently, intent on tracing the tips of his fingers along her cheek.

"Really? Why a theater?"

"Because," he murmured, leaning forward and pressing a kiss to her throat, "it was the theater where I'd gone to Saturday matinees as a kid and they were going to tear it down."

"So Rory Temple, ruthless tycoon, was once a sentimental, romantic young man?"

He smiled softly. "I think the word is naïve, Sunshine.

A college buddy and I found some investors, did a little restoration and started showing artsy stuff." He pressed a kiss to her collarbone. "It was a total disaster."

"How come?"

His lips found the curve of her shoulder. "We'd neglected to take into consideration," he said, between placing kisses down her arm, "that the people in that neighborhood weren't exactly into art house films. And the people who were," he added, placing a kiss on the inside of her elbow, "didn't hang out in that neighborhood."

He felt a small tremor under her skin. He pressed the advantage by kissing the inside of her elbow again.

"Oh," she said, her voice all breathy huskiness. "Um—so what happened?"

He started working his way back up her arm again, planting little kisses in between words. "We lost every dime and just managed to avoid bankruptcy by the skin of our teeth. I learned not to be so sentimental after that."

"But," she burst out, pulling away from him, "isn't that kind of what you're doing with the condos? Not taking your audience into consideration?"

Rory sighed. "You know, angel, I'd rather make love to you again than argue business."

He reached for her but she wiggled out of his grasp.

"I mean it, Rory. You're going to have millionaires living across the street from mill workers."

Rory looked heavenward. Unfortunately, all he saw was the blank ceiling of the room above the garage. He shook his head, knowing he was going to surrender and have this conversation. He'd already learned that with Sunny, the best way around a subject was through it. With any luck, he'd answer her questions and be making love to her again before the night was over. "The location is good," he began. "Our feasibility studies showed that—"

Sunny didn't wait for him to finish. "And where did your feasibility studies show the people already in that neighborhood moving to?"

Rory sighed again. "Look, Sunny, your idea of ear-marking some of the units for lower income residents is wonderfully altruistic. But how are you going to convince my millionaires to want to live next to the guy with five-and-dime curtains in his windows and a Salvation Army sofa in his living room?"

He watched her start to worry over that one. She started to chew lightly on her bottom lip in a way that was making his body start to stir anew. Just as he was about to try reaching for her again, her eyes grew big and she exclaimed, "I know! You can hire a designer to help the low income residents learn how to use and decorate their space cheaply, efficiently and tastefully!"

He laughed softly. "Are you trying to maintain the neighborhood's diversity or are you applying for a job?"

She grinned at him and gave him a playful slap on the arm. "No, seriously. Taste doesn't have to come with a huge price tag. You could have someone on retainer. Design consultant services could be part of the purchasing package."

"And what kind of services do you see this designer supplying?"

He watched her while she talked. Such animation in her face. Such enthusiasm. Such hope and faith. And much of what she said made sense.

"And just how would you get buyers to cooperate?" he was interested enough to ask.

"By making all of it fun," she answered.

Fun. He should have known. And if anyone could

make it fun, it would be Sunny. She'd be perfect for the job.

And if he created such a job and gave it to her, he'd have to see her again—and again.

He liked the idea of that.

He was caught up in watching her face when he started to wonder if he would still like the idea of that if she was with another man?

The idea was preposterous. How could she ever belong to another man after what they'd shared together in the short time they'd known each other? How could she ever be with another man when Rory was falling in love with her?

Falling hard.

He had to tell her. "Sunny—" he began.

"Yes?"

There was so much he needed to say, but how could he when his heart was in his throat from just looking at her? All he could think about was how her pale skin glowed in the firelight, how it set her chestnut hair aflame, how it made her dark eyes glitter—and how very much he wanted her mouth again.

This time when he reached for her, she came willingly into his arms.

He kissed her slowly, gently, and explored her mouth while his hands explored her body. He trailed his fingertips over her breasts and felt the quickening of her heart when she tore her mouth away from his to let out her gasp of pleasure.

"Does this mean," she said breathlessly, "that you no longer want to talk business?"

"It strikes me at the moment, Miss Morgan," he murmured as his fingers trailed along the curve of her hip, "that perhaps some things are more important than business."

Her laughter was like bubbles floating to the ceiling. "Mr. Temple! I'm shocked! What could be more important than business?"

"Making love to you," he answered, feeling drunk on her. "At the moment, making love to you is all that matters in the world."

She stopped laughing and her gaze became serious as she smoothed the palm of her hand up his cheek and threaded her fingers into his hair. "Then," she said, her gaze steady on his, "make love to me."

And he did. While the storm shook the thin walls of the little room above the garage that belonged to someone they didn't know, he touched her in all the places he wanted to. Tasted her in all the ways he needed to. There wasn't a sound she made that he would ever forget. There wasn't an inch of her that wouldn't be a part of him come morning. By the time he was inside of her again, he knew there was no turning back.

Long after she fell asleep in his arms, Rory Temple silently promised himself that Sunny Morgan wasn't walking down that aisle tomorrow.

SUNNY STIRRED UNDER the quilt, snuggling deeper into its warmth. She was awake, but reluctant to open her eyes yet. She didn't think she'd ever felt so relaxed, so snug, so satisfied, so—so in love.

Her eyes popped open. "Oh, my!" she gasped to the ceiling before clasping her hand over her mouth and looking wildly over at Rory. Well, except Rory wasn't there beside her on the floor where she'd left him when she'd finally succumbed to exhausted slumber a few hours ago. She sat up and peered around the room. He didn't seem to be anywhere in the room at all.

She gathered the quilt about her, got to her feet, and headed toward one of the windows. Dawn hadn't yet broken, but the pale light in the early sky reflecting off the snow made it easy for her to see him. He was just below her, in his cashmere sweater, helping the farmer shovel his truck out of a snowdrift.

She bit her lip as she watched his muscles working under the soft fabric. She knew what his body felt like when it moved. She knew what his skin felt like when it was warm with passion. She smiled at the memory of all she'd learned about Rory Temple in the last twenty-four hours—of all that she'd learned about herself. Most importantly—oh, by far most importantly—she'd learned that she was in love with Rory Temple.

And because she was in love with him, she thought as she looked down on his dark head, just now being touched by the yellow glow of an April sunrise, it was time for her to tell him the truth about the wedding.

Below her, Rory thrust the blade of his shovel into a snow bank, turned and started for the door of the garage that led to the stairs. Sunny swung away from the window and started gathering up her clothes. It was going to be enough of an ordeal facing him with the truth, she had no intention of doing it naked.

She was still buttoning her shirt when he burst in the door.

"You wouldn't believe how warm it is out there already! The snow is already melting and the sun isn't even fully up yet!"

He was big and handsome, his dark hair tossed from the wind, his breathing labored from the exertion of shoveling. His enthusiasm spread through the room like a wave of life. Sunny wanted to jump into it, ride it the rest of the way to Chicago. But first, he had to know.

"Rory, there's something I have to tell you."

He grabbed her in a quick embrace and kissed her hard on the mouth. "And there are things I have to tell you,

too, angel,'' he said. "But not now.'' He let go of her
and started to gather up the few things he'd scattered
about the room. "We've got to hit the road. We can talk
as soon as we—''

"No, Rory. I—I think I better tell you now. It's about
the wedding.''

He stopped gathering his things and spun around to
face her. "You're joking.''

She shook her head. "No, there's something you need
to know before—''

He threw down his orange hunting jacket and in two
long strides he was in front of her. "No, there's something *you* need to know. There will be no wedding today,
because there is no way that I am letting you marry another man. And that's final.''

She gaped at him as he went back to gathering his
things. "Excuse me?'' she said, feeling her temper starting to rise.

"I said there isn't going to be a wedding today,'' he
repeated with that calmness that infuriated her.

She put her hands on her hips. "Of all the tyrannical,
egomaniacal, autocratic nerve! You can't just go around
telling people who they can and cannot marry, Rory
Temple!''

"Oh, no?'' he said, barely sparing her a look. "Well,
just watch me! Because I am telling you right now, Sunshine, you're not walking down that aisle today!''

"I'll walk down that aisle if I want to! If you think
you can make me cancel my own wedding—''

Sunny stumbled on the words. What was she saying?
Cancel her own wedding? What wedding? The wedding
she was rushing home to wasn't hers! It never had been!

"Rory, this is crazy!'' she exclaimed, her heart suddenly lifted at the idea of him knowing the truth. He was
going to be so happy and relieved when he heard it.

He glared at her while he shoved things into his pockets. "What's crazy is the idea that you could still plan on marrying another man after last night."

"But that's just it! I'm not planning on marrying another man!"

"Good!" he agreed, as he picked up his blaze orange hunting jacket again and swung it over his shoulder. "Then the first thing you're going to do when we get out on the road is to make a phone call to cancel that wedding! Now let's get out of here."

He headed for the door and she stepped in front of him, then placed her palms against his chest. "Rory, listen to me! There's no need to cancel the wedding today because I'm not the bride. I never was."

Rory looked down at her. "Sunshine, what are you talking about?"

"The wedding I'm rushing home for isn't mine."

"Not yours? Of course it's yours. You said you've been waiting for this wedding since you were eight years old."

"I have. But it's not *my* wedding."

Rory looked exasperated, impatient. "And whose wedding would a girl be dreaming of since she was little if not her own?"

"It's my parents' wedding."

Rory frowned. His dark brows hung low over his eyes. "Your parents?"

"Yes! My parents are finally getting married!"

He turned from her and walked to the window. He stared out at the day for a few moments before he turned back to her. The frown on his face had deepened into a glare. "And Aunt Tilly's hat?" he asked. "I suppose you're going to tell me that you'll be wearing it as one of your own mother's bridesmaids?" he asked derisively.

She swallowed hard. "Well, no. Not exactly." Why

wasn't this going well? Shouldn't Rory be looking happy and relieved?

"Then what—exactly?" he asked her carefully.

"I'm—um—I'm going to be wearing Aunt Tilly's hat as the flower girl."

Rory threw back his head and laughed, in that same abandoned way she'd come to love. Only, this time, she had a feeling that it had nothing at all to do with being amused.

He shook his head when he'd finished, and looked at her with an ironic twist to his mouth. "You'll say anything to get what you want, won't you?"

"Rory, I—"

"And you usually get what you want, don't you, angel? When there's a man involved, I bet you almost always get what you want."

"It wasn't like that!"

"No? Then why did you tell me that you were getting married today?"

"I didn't tell you! You—um—assumed."

"And you let me go right on assuming."

"Well, it seemed as if it was the only way you'd take me with you."

He thought her words over, then asked, "And once we were on the road, why didn't you set the record straight?"

"I wanted to, Rory," she said miserably. "I really did. But every time I tried to you'd get mad about something and I'd—"

"And you'd let me go on thinking you were the blushing bride-to-be to get your own way," he finished for her.

She shook her head. "No!"

He raised a brow. "No?"

"Well, okay, yes," she grudgingly conceded. "But—"

"And now you expect me to believe in thirty-something flower girls who dream of their parents' weddings and not their own?"

"But it's the truth. When we moved into Chicago and I started public school I found out that other kids' parents were married. Mine weren't. It was painful at first. I didn't understand it. I wanted to be like—"

"Save it, angel. I've seen you tell a sob story to get a man to do your bidding once too often. I'm not falling for it again."

"But it's true! To make me feel like I was special—you know, put a positive spin on it—my parents promised me that if they ever got married, I could be the flower girl."

"Right. And I suppose Peter Pan is going to be the ring bearer."

"Come on, Rory, why would I lie about this?"

He had already started for the door. He stopped to glare at her. "Do you really want me to answer that question? For nearly twenty-four hours, you've let me think you're rushing home to marry the man of your dreams. What's another little lie for the sake of expediency?"

Would it do any good for her to tell him that *he* was the man of her dreams? That he'd been absolutely right? After spending nearly twenty-four hours with him there was no way she could ever marry another man.

Unfortunately, the man standing at the door was the last man on earth who would ever ask her.

"Now, if you don't mind," he said, "I've got an important meeting to get to."

He went out the door, but Sunny wasn't ready to give up yet. She went after him. "Rory!"

He was already halfway down the stairs. He stopped

and turned. "I've had enough fairy tales, Sunshine. If
you want a ride the rest of the way to Chicago, I suggest
you get moving."

Sunny looked into the face of the big bad wolf and
decided to get moving.

8

OUTSIDE, THE APRIL SUN was melting the crazy snowfall, but inside the car the air was chilly enough for Frosty the Snowman to hitch a ride. Sunny had given up trying to talk to Rory a hundred miles ago. He refused to see reason when the whole thing seemed perfectly reasonable to her. Clear as an icicle melting in the sun, she'd say. Besides, wasn't it silly for him to be so angry that she wasn't getting married considering that he'd demanded that she call off the wedding? She'd been judged and sentenced for a victimless crime.

They passed a fast-food place and her stomach growled as if it'd been standing lookout. It seemed that Rory wasn't going to be content to give her the silent treatment—he was also planning on starving her to death. She was feeling more than slightly hollow. It had been a long time since the leftover burgers they'd shared after they'd made love.

She sighed and stole a look at Rory. His surly countenance bore little resemblance to the romantic, passionate man with whom she'd spent most of last night. His mouth was set in a disapproving line and his eyes had disappeared behind dark glasses. She looked beyond his classic, steely profile to a pair of golden arches on the other side of the road. Even a condemned person was allowed to eat a last meal. He already thought she was Mata Hari and Scarlett O'Hara rolled into one, so what was the harm in just asking if they could stop and eat?

"We're making good time," she ventured. "Do you think we could stop to eat?"

He didn't even look at her. "Watch for someplace."

"Preferably some place with bread and water on the menu," she muttered under her breath. Apparently, not far enough under, however. It seemed the wolf had big ears.

"Interesting to see that you find the higher moral ground so amusing."

She started to count to ten, then decided that she wasn't about to let him get away with the superior attitude. "An hour ago you were begging me to stand a guy up at the altar. Seems like you took a little tumble off that high moral ground yourself, Mr. Temple."

He shot her a look that was pretty withering despite the sunglasses. "The two situations couldn't be less alike," he said. "You deliberately misled me."

"No," she said reasonably, deciding not to wither, "you misunderstood."

"And you took advantage of the situation."

"That's true," she said, once again sounding perfectly reasonable. "But—"

"But what?" he cut in.

"It was for a good cause," she finished, satisfied that the statement was true.

"Right. The cause of the overaged flower girl," he said disdainfully.

His tone made her want to goad him. "I'm sure Molly would be amused if she knew how conventional you've become."

He spared her a quick look. "Leave Molly out of this."

"Why? I have a feeling that Aunt Tilly and Molly would have been great friends."

"Aunt Tilly—huh! How do I know she isn't just another one of your fabrications?"

"If there is no Aunt Tilly," Sunny said, holding up the limp chiffon hat, "then who fabricated this?"

He snorted. "Who knows?"

"And if there really were no wedding at all," she went on, ignoring him, "why would I carry a hat like this halfway across the country? Not to mention risk life and limb for it."

"Yours weren't the only limbs risked for that monstrosity. When I think that I actually climbed a tree for the sake of something you probably picked up as a prop at a flea market—"

"And why would I do that? For the chance to dupe an unsuspecting traveler in case there's a blizzard in the middle of April and my flight gets diverted to the middle of nowhere and the airport runs out of rental cars?" Sunny asked in a rush of indignation. "I assure you I do not run around making up such scenarios in my head just in case disaster falls," she added emphatically.

He was silent for a few moments and she started to wonder if maybe she'd gotten through to him.

He glanced at her, then back at the road. "But if it was your parents' wedding, why not just say so? Why let me go on believing that it was yours?"

"It just seemed easier and more—more expedient—than trying to explain the situation at the time," she answered quickly, grabbing on to the small thread of hope his question held out. "I mean, there you were, glowering at me through the snow, refusing to take me with you. And then as soon as you thought I'd be missing my own wedding if you left me there, you relented. I kept meaning to tell you, but every time I tried to—"

"Yes, I know," he said ruefully. "Every time you tried to do the right thing I turned into the big bad wolf, forcing you to go on lying for several more miles through the forest.''

Sunny laughed. She couldn't help it.

"What's so funny?" Rory demanded gruffly.

"The image of you as the big bad wolf. It's exactly how I see you sometimes."

He shot her a look that she couldn't read behind his dark glasses, but she thought it was safe to assume that he wasn't pleased. "Well, you certainly didn't turn out to be Little Red Riding Hood, did you?" he asked.

"But don't you understand?" she tried again, "I've waited practically my whole life for my parents to get married! I couldn't let a thing like an April blizzard keep me from getting there. I thought I'd never see you again. I thought you'd drop me off and keep going and that would be the end of that. No harm done because you'd never need to know the truth. How was I to know that—'' She faltered on the words. "How was I to know that—'' How on earth could she say the words aloud now, with his anger like a sheet of ice between them?

"How were you to know what?" he demanded.

On the other hand, what did she have to lose? Could things get any worse between them? "How was I to know that I was going to fall in love with you!" she burst out on one quick breath.

His gaze left the road and she could feel the intensity of it even through the dark lenses. Suddenly, she was pretty sure she didn't want to know what his reaction was going to be. A diversion, that's what was needed— immediately. She frantically looked for one and found it in the form of a giant picture of bacon and eggs looming along side of the interstate like a beacon of cholesterol for the hungry traveler.

"There!" she burst out, pointing across the road. "Danny's Diner! Let's eat!"

"THE SNOW IS MELTING faster than it fell, Agnes," Rory said into his cell phone from a booth in Danny's Diner. "We're making good time. We're in a place called Kenosha, Wisconsin. It's close to the Illinois border." He looked at his watch. Nine in the morning. They had three hours. "We should make it with time to spare. Old Josiah Simpson will have no reason to box my ears come noon."

"A shame really. I'd pay well to see that show," Agnes said. "And by the way, who is this *we* you keep referring to? Does your use of the pronoun have anything to do with that interior designer you asked me to find out about, boss?"

Rory rubbed his forehead and glanced over at the door to the ladies' room that Sunny had disappeared behind as soon as she'd taken off her hunting jacket. "Unfortunately, yes. Though I suspect she's not so much a designer as she is a disaster. She's certainly wreaked havoc on this trip," he muttered, more to himself than to Agnes.

He wasn't about to let his assistant know that Sunny had wreaked havoc on more than the trip. She'd done a fair job of messing up his head, as well. From the moment she'd fallen into his lap, he'd been captivated. It was one of the reasons he'd turned her down flat when she'd asked for a ride in the first place. Then when he'd discovered that she was about to be married, he figured he was safe and agreed to take her along. But he hadn't been safe at all. He'd fallen for her like he'd never fallen before—only trouble was, he'd actually fallen flat on his face.

Rory Temple, who'd gone up against some of the shrewdest businessmen in the country, had been bested by a wacky woman with bad taste in hats. And what was he to make of that wild, sudden declaration of love?

Well, maybe not so sudden. He would have sworn last

night that Sunny had been feeling exactly what he had been feeling. And if what he'd been feeling last night wasn't love, it was the closest he'd ever come to it. But last night he hadn't known that she'd made up everything about herself, including the fact that—

Rory let the thought hang for a moment. What was Agnes saying?

"—it's right off State."

"What's right off State?" Rory asked, frowning.

"The offices she designed," Agnes said. "The architectural firm. Haven't you been listening, boss?"

"Agnes, you know I hang on every word," Rory replied dryly. "What else has she done?"

"An art gallery in River North and—"

Rory listened to Agnes rattle off a short, but impressive, list of projects. When she started on the residential clients, Rory recognized some of the names. He'd recently attended a party at one particular loft.

So, A Sunny Touch really existed, he thought as he ended the call with Agnes. Not only existed, but apparently thrived. Young as she was, Sunny Morgan had already garnered professional respect. It shouldn't surprise him at all. There had been evidence of her business sense from the start.

But even if she hadn't lied about A Sunny Touch, she had lied to him about the wedding. And that lie had made him put the Simpson Twine project in jeopardy. He'd never let a woman come between him and a business deal before. He wasn't about to start with one who played the kind of games Sunny Morgan did.

The door to the ladies' room at the back of the diner opened and Sunny came out. He watched her walk toward him and, despite himself, something in him started to stir.

He picked up the menu and scanned it for anything

that cooked quickly. The sooner he dropped her off in Chicago, and dropped her out of his life, the better.

SUNNY EYED RORY SITTING across the booth from her, glowering into his coffee cup instead of gazing into her eyes. Having breakfast with the man you love after a night of incredible passion wasn't supposed to turn out like this. Shouldn't there be angels singing instead of country music whining out of a chrome jukebox? Shouldn't there be the scent of flowers instead of the aroma of bacon frying? Shouldn't the man you so recently declared your love for be at least speaking to you? It was hard to believe that just hours ago there had been enough heat between them to steam up every window in Danny's Diner.

The waitress came over and set a small plate of toast in front of Rory and a large oval platter of eggs, bacon and fried potatoes in front of Sunny.

"I see subterfuge hasn't spoiled your appetite," Rory observed dryly.

"Being rigid and disapproving seems to have spoiled yours, though," she said, nodding at his toast.

He stopped pawing through a bowl of little packets of fruit preserves to look at her with a raised brow. "So now it's rigid to expect honesty?"

She bit into a piece of bacon. "No," she said as she chewed, "but it might improve your appetite to give a person a chance to explain."

"You *did* explain, as I recall. The overage flower girl defense," he added with disdain.

She almost choked on her bacon. "That wasn't a defense! That was the truth!"

Rory finally chose one of the packets. "Then why," he said, as he struggled to break through the space-age polymers, "didn't you just say so in the first place?"

"And why," she said, grabbing the packet from him, "didn't you just say yes when I asked you for a ride?" She easily ripped the packet open and handed it back to him.

He stared down at it for a moment, then took it from her. "I didn't say yes at first," he said, once again glaring at her, "because you looked as if you were nothing but trouble. And I was right," he added, dropping the packet of strawberry preserves to his plate, unused. "Ever since you landed in my lap you've been nothing but trouble."

"And you," she said, biting rather viciously into another piece of bacon, "have been nothing but disagreeable and surly."

"And you think you deserved better?" he bit out.

"Yes!" she exclaimed, rather too loudly. Heads around Danny's Diner were turning their way. She leaned forward and lowered her voice. "I mean, you didn't even know I was lying at the time."

"Which proves my point exactly," he said stubbornly.

"You have a point?" she asked mockingly.

"Well, at least my point wasn't to drive one man insane because he thought you were engaged to another man!"

"Well, that wasn't *my* point, either!" she said defensively before she realized what he'd just said. "Um—did you just say that it drove you insane when you thought I was engaged to another man?" she asked, her voice suddenly sounding a lot smaller.

He opened his mouth as if to shoot back a verbal attack, then closed it again. His stare was hard, totally unreadable, and she saw what sort of opponent he must make across a conference table. He looked handsomely dangerous. But she'd had a glimpse of what was under that hard, outer layer. The loyalty, the courage—the passion. If there was any chance at all—

She swallowed. "Rory, last night when we made love—"

"Made love?" he scoffed "For all I know, you're mercenary enough to have had sex with me in order to get that designer's job you cooked up."

She gasped and jumped to her feet. "Why you—you—you're impossible! How could you even think such a thing?" she yelled, oblivious to the fact that every trucker and traveling salesman in the place was now wondering exactly what terrible thing Rory had been thinking.

Equally oblivious, Rory got to his feet. "Maybe I could think it because I've seen what you're capable of," he yelled back.

"What *I'm* capable of? Oh, and I suppose your motives for taking off your clothes last night were perfectly innocent?" There was a gasp from a woman shepherding her daughter to the ladies' room and a chuckle from a big guy in a John Deere hat at the counter.

"I was naked," Rory clipped out in his most arrogant manner, "because I was hot."

The guy in the John Deere hat spit out a mouthful of coffee.

Rory shot him a look. "From the fire in the Franklin stove," he said loud enough for any interested onlookers to hear. "You're the one," he said in only a slightly lower tone, "who was wearing nothing but my sweater."

"Because you suggested it!"

"If she were my woman, I'd suggest it, too," said the guy at the counter.

"I'm not his woman!" Sunny told him forcefully.

"And we'd thank you to mind your own business," Rory added just as forcefully.

"Well, ordinarily, I do," the guy said. "But there's a question I just gotta ask."

"What?" they both yelled at him at the same time.

He nodded toward the window next to their booth. "Isn't that your car?"

They both turned in time to see the rental car leave its parking place.

"Oh my goodness!" Sunny cried. "Someone's stealing our car!"

"Call the police," Rory yelled as he headed for the door.

"Where are you going?" Sunny called after him.

"I'm going to try to stop them!"

"Not without me, you're not! Call 911!" she said to the guy in the John Deere hat as she ran past him. "Please!" she shouted over her shoulder just as she pushed open the door.

She hit the blacktop parking lot on a run. Rory was yards ahead of her as she splashed through the puddles of melted snow and tried to catch up. He had nearly reached the rental where it waited for a break in traffic before pulling out onto the highway. Not two feet away from the rear bumper, he leapt, his arms out in front of him. As his feet left the ground, the rental pulled ahead and filled in a gap between a semi and a station wagon and Rory did a belly flop onto the wet cement.

"Rory!" Sunny screamed as she raced the rest of the way across the lot. When she reached him, he was lying, immobile, facedown in a puddle of slush. She squatted down next to him. Was she supposed to stabilize his neck or something? Maybe roll him over and do CPR? Get a blanket to cover him? Why hadn't she paid more attention in health class? "Rory?" she pleaded with the back of his head. "Rory? Can you hear me?"

Finally he stirred, slowly lifting his face out of the puddle.

"Thank goodness! Is anything hurt?"

"Only my pride," he said in a voice much dryer than

his face was at the moment. A drop of water dripped off the end of his nose as he got to his knees.

"But you almost had them!" she cried, relief that Rory wasn't hurt fueling her enthusiasm. "A couple of more inches and—"

Rory flung a shock of wet hair back from his grim face. "I bet the glass is always half full to you, isn't it, Sunshine?"

She grinned. "Half full is always better than half empty."

"Either way," he said, wiping his face with his sleeve, "it's a gray area."

"Haven't you ever taken a chance on a gray area, Rory?" she asked him softly.

He became still, gazing at her through the water dripping off his hair, watching her intently as she raised her fingers to brush a drop from his cheek. She was surprised at how tender she felt toward him, at how much she wanted to smooth the lines from his brow, at how much she wished she could go back and tell him the truth from the beginning. And she was surprised at how much she hoped his answer would be his willingness to take a chance on the gray for her.

But she never got to hear his answer because as soon as he opened his mouth the wail of a police siren split the air.

Other people lost their moments by the ring of a bell. Leave it to her to have hers interrupted by the wail of a police siren.

Rory got to his feet then held out his hand to help her up. He let go of it as soon as she was standing upright again. "Come on," he said. "Let's get this over with. I've got a meeting to get to."

"SO THAT'S WHY IT'S SO important for me to get home in time for this wedding," Sunny told the trucker in the

John Deere hat. His name was Matt and Sunny had spent the past twenty minutes drinking coffee with him at the counter while Rory was back in the booth racking up a huge cell phone bill.

Matt nodded. "Seems a damn shame you might not make it after all those years of waiting. I'd take you myself, 'cept, as I explained, I'm headed north and I've already lost time."

Sunny smiled at him and told him she understood completely. He was a lot like a huge puppy—eager, friendly and cute, with dimples in his cheeks where they belonged, not in his chin where they could drive a girl crazy. He'd thought it was sweet that she was going to be the flower girl at her parents' wedding. Not like some land developing tycoon she could name, she thought, looking pointedly over at Rory. Big mistake. Looking at him only made her remember how she felt about him. He was rigid, unreasonable, arrogant and impossible— but she was in love with him.

Before Rory could catch her looking at him, she swiveled her stool back toward Matt. Why couldn't Rory be more like him? Matt would have understood her lie. But, then, with Matt she wouldn't have had to lie because he wouldn't have said no when she'd asked for a ride in the first place.

Someone touched her shoulder.

"If you can tear yourself away, the new rental is here," Rory said.

"I'll be right with you," she said dismissively, turning another smile on Matt.

"I'll be in the car," Rory said. "Don't keep me waiting."

Sunny waited until Rory had stalked out before she said, "Thanks so much for the coffee, Matt. And thanks for listening."

"Hey, no problem. Hope you get to the church on time. Your daddy will be proud to see you wearin' his Aunt Tilly's hat."

She opened her mouth to say goodbye, then closed it again. Aunt Tilly's hat? Where was it?

She looked at the floor under the stool.

No hat.

She hurried over to the booth where she and Rory had been sitting.

It wasn't on the seat. It wasn't under the booth. It wasn't anywhere.

"Something wrong?" Matt asked.

"I'll be right back," she mumbled, then fled to the ladies' room.

She pushed through the door and startled a little old lady applying pink lipstick to her withered mouth.

"Did you see a hat in here?" she asked as she ducked down to check each stall.

"A hat?" the woman asked.

"Yes! About so big," Sunny said, spreading her arms, "limp lavender chiffon, with a wilted cascade of silk lilacs across the brim. Oh—and it might have one or two holes in it."

"Holes?" the woman repeated.

"From the crow's beak," Sunny said as she started to rummage through the used paper towels in the waste bin.

The little old lady gave up on her lipstick and left the rest room at a speed she probably hadn't achieved for more than ten years. Sunny gave up on the waste bin and finished checking the rest of the room. Nothing. Could she have dropped it out in the parking lot? Maybe someone turned it in.

It wasn't until she'd reached the counter again that she remembered that it wasn't just Aunt Tilly's hat that was missing. She hadn't seen the Cowan Pottery Jazz Age plates in quite a while, either.

"Oh, my God!" she gasped, suddenly remembering. "I left them in the car this time! Aunt Tilly's hat! The Jazz Age plates! They're gone!"

"What kind of plates?" Matt asked. His cute little nose wrinkled in consternation.

"They're Art Deco," she told him. "They were in the car that was stolen—along with Aunt Tilly's hat!"

The door to the diner burst open and the entire place turned to see what had practically blown it off its hinges. Rory stood there, looking every inch the big bad wolf. He strode up to her.

"Miss Morgan," he said through a clenched jaw, "would you be so kind as to join me in the car so we can get the hell out of here?"

"I—I can't," she stammered.

He gritted his teeth. "You can't," he repeated grimly.

"No. When someone took the car, Aunt Tilly's hat went with it and—"

Rory didn't wait for her to finish. She'd worn his patience much too thin. Whatever was left of it would be gone any second now.

"Miss Morgan, some of us live in the grown-up world. We can't afford to abandon our responsibilities to go chasing after fairy tales and wedding hats. If you want a ride the rest of the way to Chicago, I suggest you abandon that infernal hat and get in the car."

She shook her head. "You don't understand, Rory. I can't leave—"

"Then I go without you," he stated, not at all easy with the notion of doing so.

She made a little movement of her shoulders. "Then go," she said, while looking altogether miserable.

He pressed his lips together as he eyed her. Was this some new ploy she was trying? Was she just being stubborn, banking on getting her own way in the end? The thought made him even angrier. "Fine," he said, turning on his heel and heading out of Danny's Diner for what would be, he promised himself as he let the door slam behind him, the last time.

When he hit the fresh, crisp air outside he stood listening for a few seconds, hoping to hear her call after him. When he reached the new rental car, he stood listening for a few seconds more before opening the door, hoping to hear the sound of her running after him. He opened the door. Still no sound of her.

"Damn it," he muttered to himself, slamming the car door shut again and striding back to the diner. Much as he knew he should hit the road as fast as he could and forget all about her, he just couldn't seem to do it.

He pushed open Danny's door again, almost used to the smell of frying fat that hit like a wall when he entered. At first he didn't see her. But that was only because the blond mountain in the John Deere hat had gathered her to him in his big, beefy arms. The sight of Sunny crushed against his plaid flannel chest did it. The last of his patience went like the snow after an April storm.

"All right, that's it!" he said, striding over to them and yanking Sunny out of the trucker's arms. "The least you can do is stick to one victim per trip! Now forget the hat and get into the car! You're coming back to Chicago with me!"

"Now, buddy," the trucker said, pointing his finger at Rory, "you wait just a minute—"

"You stay out of this!" Rory roared.

"I'll stay out of it when she tells me to!" the blond giant roared back as he started toward Rory.

"Matt!" Sunny cried.

"What, darlin'?" the trucker asked and Rory wanted to rip his all-American baby face off at the sound of the endearment.

"I can handle this," she said.

The blond mountain backed off like an obedient dog.

"Didn't take you long to train him," Rory muttered. He drew her over to the area near the rest rooms for some privacy.

"He's a nice guy," she said, avoiding looking at him. "Perhaps you're not familiar with the breed?"

"I don't keep pets," Rory retorted before he realized that his behavior wasn't going to get her to come with him. He put his hands on her shoulders and tried to get her to look at him. "Sunny, please. Forget the hat. Surely, your parents would rather have you show up hatless than not at all."

Sunny looked up at him. "Does that mean you believe me about the wedding?" she asked.

That's when he saw the tears rising in her huge, dark eyes. He could see by the trembling of her mouth just what it cost her to keep them from falling.

He raised a hand to touch her cheek. "Sunshine. What is it? Can the hat mean that much to you?"

"Oh, Rory," she said miserably. "It's not just the hat. It's the Cowan plates. For once, I didn't take them with me—I left them in the car—and now they're gone, too." She drew in a shaky breath before going on. "I got them from a dealer I've done business with before for a very small deposit. If I don't deliver the plates, I don't collect the money from the buyer, but I—I—"

"You still have to pay the dealer," Rory quietly finished for her when she stopped to sniff.

She drew another shaky breath. "Exactly," she said.

She looked away from him and he could see that she was trying desperately to blink back the tears. He had the insane longing, one he'd never had before in his life, to take her into his arms and tell her he'd make it all go away.

"So you see," she continued, once she'd regained control, "it's not just that I'm being childish about a promise made to an aunt I love dearly. It's more than that. I stand to lose both a customer and a source. Most of my capital is tied up in another project right now. I don't work with the kind of margins you do, Rory—"

"No, no—of course not," he said gently, feeling like all kinds of a heel to have yelled at her the way he had; to have, once again, made assumptions about her that had nothing to do with reality. Was he so afraid of how he felt about her that he refused to see the truth?

Afraid? Damn right he was afraid. He was close to blowing the most important deal of his life. He should be gone from this place, barreling down the interstate with nothing on his mind but what he was going to say to the press once the Simpson Twine condo deal was signed. But all he wanted to do was take Sunny into his arms and tell her everything would be okay. He was about to do so when a big, beefy hand landed on her shoulder. Rory watched the trucker draw her protectively into the crook of his over-muscled arm and wanted to twist it behind his back.

"I've got an idea, Sunshine, that just might—"

"Look, do you mind, Tarzan," Rory said. "We're having a private discussion here."

"Rory!" Sunny admonished him. "What's your idea, Matt?" Sunny asked the trucker, giving him an encouraging little smile.

The smile dug at Rory. It'd been too long since Sunny had given him any kind of smile at all. Not that he'd done anything to deserve it lately, he reminded himself.

"How about I get on my CB and send out a description of the car that was stolen?" Matt suggested.

Rory snorted. "That's your idea? I think the police are probably ahead of you on that one, Tarzan."

Sunny gave him the kind of look he deserved but he couldn't seem to help himself. And if Tarzan didn't remove his arm from Sunny soon he was going to do a lot more than use words to offend him.

"But they don't have the network we truckers have," Matt said, beaming, obviously taking no offense at all. And why should he? He had Sunny glued to his side. "I get Sunny's story out to all those fellas out there," he went on, "and—"

"No," Rory interrupted, coming to his senses at last. "You don't have to explain it to me." He turned to her. "*Fellas* love to help Sunny."

"Rory, it's not what—"

"You don't have to explain, Sunshine. It looks like Tarzan here is your best bet," he said cavalierly, telling himself he'd be glad to be rid of her.

Still, to just leave. To walk away with no word about tomorrow, or the day after, or— He took out his wallet and extracted a business card, holding it out to her. "Good luck getting the plates back," he said. "If you need any information for insurance purposes or anything—"

She didn't touch the card. "I'll just call Temple Enterprises and talk to Agnes," she said, thrusting her chin up stubbornly.

He stared at her for a moment. "All right," he finally said, ripping the card in half and shoving the pieces into his pocket. "If that's the way you want it."

"I think it'll be better that way. I've caused you enough trouble already. Now, you have a meeting to get to and I have a business to save."

She started to turn away from him.

"What about the wedding?" he asked her.

She looked back at him and shrugged carelessly. "If I don't make the wedding, the world won't end. Like you said, Rory, it's time I stopped chasing fairy tales. Thanks for all you've done," she said before turning away. This time he let her.

He could hear her talking to Matt, but he couldn't really focus on what they were saying to each other. He knew he had to move. But he couldn't. His feet seemed frozen to the cracked linoleum floor of Danny's Diner. She'd been nothing but trouble, but he didn't want to leave her. He forced himself to look at his watch. Forced himself to calculate the time he had to make it to Chicago. Forced himself to remember how she'd lied to him. Forced himself to remember that she was no longer his problem.

And then he forced himself to turn away and walk out the door.

RORY HAD BEEN GONE LESS than twenty minutes and Sunny missed him already. She was sitting in the cab of Matt's semi, listening to him talk with other truckers on his CB.

Someone named Rooster had spotted a car similar to the stolen rental but didn't get the license number. Someone named Cheesehead had seen a couple of kids driving crazy near the exit for Milwaukee, forty miles back, but the car was the wrong color. They were currently waiting for word from a woman trucker with the handle of Mad Traveler who was rumored to know something.

Matt seemed even more excited than she was at the prospect of a solid lead. In fact, Sunny had had a hard time getting enthusiastic about anything since Rory left. It was terrible. Here Matt was, eager as a puppy, while Rory had had no trouble at all walking away from her.

Next to Rory, Matt was as sweet as Aunt Tilly's old-fashioned fudge. But just as Sunny had outgrown the fudge in favor of Tilly's rhubarb crumble, she found herself craving dark-visaged, black-humored Rory Temple. How could he have walked out of Danny's Diner—and out of her life—for good? After last night? After—

"Darlin'? Did you hear me?"

Sunny jumped. "What? Oh, no. I'm sorry, Matt, I guess I was, um, thinking. What did you say?"

"I said that if any of these sightings turn out to be

real, then maybe you'll make it to that wedding, after all.''

Sunny looked at her watch and sighed. Two hours until the wedding. They weren't that far from the Wisconsin/Illinois border, with two hours and decent traffic, she could make it in time. *If* she had a car and *if* she didn't have to worry about the Jazz Age plates. She sighed again. ''Seeing my parents get married seems like an impossible dream right now, Matt.'' Almost, she mused, as much of an impossible dream as having Rory Temple forget his important meeting and come back to rescue her again.

She looked out of the truck's window. The sun was shining. The sky was blue. The snow that had changed her life forever was dwindling by the minute, being reduced to rivulets of water that would eventually make their way to a storm drain. Everything looked so different than it had yesterday. Would she remember it all as a dream years from now?

Rory was right. It was time she started living in the real world—the grown-up world. The last thing she should be thinking about right now was Rory Temple. If she didn't get those plates back, she might lose her business. At the very least, her professional reputation would be damaged.

She looked at her watch again. It was time to make a decision. Even if Mad Traveler gave them a solid lead on the stolen rental, by the time the police recovered the car and she went through the paperwork to get the plates back, it would be too late to make it to the wedding.

''Much as I want to see my parents say *I do,* right now I'd settle for getting those plates back and getting home before the wedding cake gets stale,'' she said sadly. ''I better go call my parents and let them know I'm not going to make it to the wedding.''

She started to open the heavy door to the semi cab when someone pulled it open from the outside. She lost her balance and tumbled out of the cab—and straight into the waiting arms of Rory Temple.

"Just where do you think you're going?" Rory asked.

"Put me down!" Sunny demanded, trying to wiggle out of his arms.

"Not until you tell me where you're going," Rory insisted.

"If you must know, I'm about to call my parents to tell them I'm not going to make the wedding."

"What?" he asked with mock horror. "Pollyanna giving up?"

"Pollyanna is coming to her senses and taking your advice. It's time I started living in the real world. Now, will you please put me down so I can get to a phone?"

He seemed to be considering it. Then he said, "No, I don't think so."

She wiggled some more. "That's not fair! You promised me if I told you where I was going, you'd put me down!"

"I changed my mind because I didn't like your answer. In fact, I'm damn disappointed in it."

"But why?"

"You still have almost two hours till flower girl time, angel. Plenty of time for one more rescue."

She became still and wondered if the hammering of her heart had impaired her hearing. "But, but, I thought you said—"

"Forget what I said." Suddenly sober, he looked into her face, his green gaze examined her features thoroughly. "Promise me something, angel," he said softly.

"What?" she asked him.

"Promise me you'll never stop chasing fairy tales."

"Rory," she whispered, then touched his cheek with her fingertips.

"Promise?" he asked again.

She nodded and sniffed back a tear. "I promise," she said. "But what about *your* dream, Rory? Why did you risk coming back here when your deadline is only two hours away, too?"

His eyes were tender—more tender than she'd ever seen them. His arms were tight around her, holding her, keeping her from falling. His beautiful mouth was only inches from her own. It was so close that when he opened it to answer her, she could feel the sigh of his breath on her face.

"I came back because—"

"Yahoo!" yelled Matt as he jumped down from the cab. "Mad Traveler came through, Sunshine. She spotted the car in the parking lot of a liquor store in Kenosha. The license number checks out."

Rory put Sunny down abruptly. "Where is it?" he asked Matt.

"Not far from here," Matt answered. "Hop in the cab, Sunshine, I'll take you there."

"She's coming with me," Rory said. "I'll take her where she needs to go."

Sunny spun around to look at him. "Are you sure, Rory? What about your meeting?"

There was the glitter of a smile in his green eyes. "Maybe some things are more important than Temple Enterprises, after all." He reached out and touched her cheek with a fingertip, so softly and swiftly that she might have imagined it. "You get the directions, I'll get the car," he told her, and then he turned to go.

She watched him striding toward the car, but she was too stunned to move at first. Then she shook herself, turned back to Matt and said, "Tell me how to get there."

Matt gave her directions while Rory started the car and pulled it up alongside of them. Aware of Rory's eyes on her, she gave Matt a quick hug. "Thanks Matt. I won't forget this."

Matt grinned. "Me neither."

She opened the car door and got in. "Get back out on the interstate, going south," she told Rory.

Without a word, Rory did as he was told. Once they were back on Interstate 94, Sunny's attention left the road and fastened back onto Rory. The clock was ticking even faster for him than it had been when they'd landed in Escanaba yesterday. Yet, here Rory was, coming to her rescue again and looking like he was enjoying every minute of it!

"Rory? What are you going to do about Josiah Simpson and his ultimatum?" she asked.

Rory laughed shortly, but kept his eyes on the road. "Maybe I'll let you handle him for me this time, angel. You seem to have a way with men."

"If you're talking about Matt, I didn't do any—"

Taking his gaze from the road for a moment, Rory reached out and put a finger to her lips. "I know, angel," he said softly. She didn't have to do anything, he told himself as he turned his attention to the road again. Her eagerness, her enthusiasm, her utter aliveness is what drew people to her. Sunshine Morgan was about as devious as a collie puppy. It wasn't that she expected men to help her, it was that men just loved to rescue her. He was already on his second round playing white knight and he'd known her less than twenty-four hours. "We have things to talk about, Sunny," he told her. "But for now, let's concentrate on getting those plates back, angel, okay?"

He glanced at her and she gave him a small smile and nodded. "Take the next exit, then turn right."

The area just off the interstate was a hodgepodge of strip malls and franchise restaurants. The liquor store, with its garish primary-colored neon sign, was easy to spot.

As soon as they turned into the parking lot alongside of it, Sunny hissed, "There it is!" then threw herself on the floor of the front seat.

Rory tried not to laugh. "What are you doing, Sunshine?"

"I don't want them to see us," Sunny whispered.

Rory grinned. "But *they* don't know who *we* are," he said in a stage whisper.

"Oh, that's right," Sunny said, grinning back at him, the faint tint of pink blushing her cheeks.

She started to get up and Rory said, "No. It's too late. You'll have to stay down there. If they see you climbing back up from the floor now they might get suspicious."

"Then tell me what you see."

The car in question was parked near the back of the lot. Rory drove slowly past it, turned up the next aisle, pulled into a parking spot halfway up the other side and cut the engine.

"Well?" Sunny hissed impatiently.

"There's a boy behind the wheel. Looks like he's alone," he said, adjusting the rearview mirror so he could keep an eye on the car.

"A boy?"

"Maybe sixteen years old. Teenager of the young punk variety," Rory added dryly.

"What is he doing?"

"Nothing so far. He seems to be waiting."

After a few minutes, a girl came out of the liquor store and strolled up to the stolen rental.

"Hmm, our boy is no longer alone," Rory murmured absently.

"Who's with him? What's happening?"

To Rory the girl didn't look old enough to buy any alcohol. Maybe she'd gone in to buy gum. She was chewing like she had to generate enough power to make the car run without gasoline.

"Well?" Sunny shook his knee.

"Hey!" Rory exclaimed. "Didn't they teach you that patience is a virtue at that commune?"

"We were into instant gratification. Now tell me what you see or I'm going to inflict some real damage."

She was about to sink two fingernails into his thigh when he decided to relent. "Okay, okay," he said, grabbing her hand. He liked how it felt in his so he decided to hold on to it. "Romeo has been joined by his Juliet. I think we can safely say we have motive."

"What do you mean?"

"Well, they're making out like the bandits they are, so I'd say our boy stole the car because he was in serious need of a love machine."

Sunny gave a delicate snort of derision. "Some love machine. A midsize with no sound system."

Rory shrugged. "A sixteen-year-old with raging hormones and an unexpected snow day away from school is desperate enough to drive a sedan."

Sunny burst out laughing and he found himself caught up in her face. Her dark eyes were sparkling, her lush mouth was wide with delight, her skin was glowing. There was a chance she'd never see those Jazz Age plates again. There was an even bigger chance that she was going to miss the wedding of her girlhood dreams. Yet there she was, curled up on the floor of a rental car, laughing, shining, making an adventure out of a bad situation.

Which reminded him. He tore his gaze away from Sunny and checked out the area. No police as far as he could see. "I think we better call the cops again," he said. He fished his cell phone out of his jacket pocket and handed it to her. "Tell the police what's happening now and where we are."

Sunny made the call while Rory checked the rearview mirror again. They were still in the car. He looked at his watch, filing the time away in his mind, cataloguing things to tell the police. When he caught himself at it, he grinned and shook his head. None of his business connections would believe this even if they saw it. Rory Temple, risking an important meeting to stake out an amateur kissing bandit for the sake of a woman he'd known less than twenty-four hours.

Sunny's voice relaying the information to the police drew his gaze back to her. How had he ever thought he could leave her behind? Was this what they wrote about? What they sang about? What they acted out in films?

Was this what love was? The absolute inability to do without the other person? No matter what the stakes? No matter what the obstacles? Being with them just felt right. Being without them just felt wrong. He hadn't gotten far from Danny's Diner before he realized just how wrong leaving Sunny felt. It took him a few more miles to decide that he was a fool if he didn't turn around. There was every possibility that he was going to lose Simpson Twine, but at the moment he'd rather be sitting in this parking lot with the wackiest, most wonderful woman he'd ever met hiding on the floor of this car than anywhere else on earth.

Sunny ended the call. "Sit tight, Kenosha's finest said. They're on their way."

Rory laughed. "Did you tell them just how tight you're sitting?"

Sunny looked down at herself scrunched up on the floor and smiled. "No. But now that you mention it, is it safe for me to get up?"

Rory reached down and tucked her hair behind her ear. It amazed him how familiar the texture of it felt on his fingers. "You can get up," he murmured. "But I don't know how safe it is."

The light in her eyes changed subtly. From warmth to smolder. She wasn't the only one who wouldn't be safe. She dipped her head, but it was too late, he'd already seen that, despite the fact that he'd acted like—what had she said? A tyrannical, autocratic egomaniac. Despite all that, she still wanted him.

He traced a finger over her full mouth. "Get up here, angel," he murmured.

She looked up at him. Then, her eyes never leaving his, she rose from the floor like a goddess in olive drab boots and glided into his arms.

Just as he was about to touch his mouth to hers, he caught a glimpse of the stolen rental out of the corner of his eye. It was starting to pull out of its parking place.

"They're leaving," he murmured against Sunny's mouth.

It wasn't exactly what she'd been hoping for. She'd been hoping for the feel of his firm, gorgeous mouth on hers. Instead she got—

She pulled away from him. "What did you say?"

"They're leaving. Where are those cops?"

Sunny swiveled around so she could see out the passenger window. "Oh my goodness! What are we going to do? They're going to get away!"

And the Jazz Age plates and Aunt Tilly's hat were going to go right along with them. She couldn't let it happen.

She opened the door.

"Where do you think you're going?"

"To stop them!" She started to get out of the car.

"Sunny, it's too dangerous, don't you dare get out of this car!" Rory said firmly.

Sunny got out of the car. She had absolutely no idea what she was going to do. All she knew was she just couldn't sit by and watch the Jazz Age plates and Aunt Tilly's hat roll out of her life.

The stolen rental car was coming toward her. She didn't know what else to do so she stepped into its path, took up a wide-legged stance and put out her hand. "Stop!" she ordered.

The car, which had only been going about five miles an hour, came to a sedate stop a good two yards away from her and Sunny found herself feeling a little disappointed that there had been no dramatic squeal of tires.

A head with hair that looked like it'd been cut with manicure scissors popped out of the driver's window. "Lady, are you nuts?"

"Lady?" she squealed while trotting over to the window as gracefully as she could in her rubber boots. "Lady? Why, how dare you act like you've never seen me before!"

The boy curled his lip and gave her a lazy look up and down. "I haven't."

Sunny, trying for the injured lover look, gasped and clutched her blaze orange jacket somewhere in the vicinity of her heart. "How can you not remember me?"

The blond girl sitting next to the driver looked over toward Sunny. After a half-dozen or so chews of her gum, she asked, "Who is this psycho, Timmy?"

Sunny thrust up her chin. "Tell her who I am, Timmy," Sunny demanded, her hands on her hips.

"You dating senior citizens now, Timmy?" the girl

asked snidely. Timmy started to guffaw and Sunny felt highly insulted.

"Look, lady," Timmy said when he'd stopped laughing at her expense, "I don't know who you are."

Sunny bent down so she could direct her next words to the girlfriend. "Ask him to tell you where he was last Friday night," she said, taking a chance that maybe Timmy had been missing last Friday night.

The blonde gasped. "You told me you couldn't get your daddy's car!"

Timmy rolled his eyes. "Holly, come on. This lady's nuts. I ain't never seen her before."

"If that's true, Timmy," Sunny drawled, "then how do I know about that mole on your back?"

Holly gasped, slammed Timmy over the head with her purse and opened the passenger door.

"Where are you going?" Timmy asked as Holly struggled to get out of the car.

"Nobody cheats on me!" Holly screamed. "Especially not with someone who has such bad taste in shoes!"

Sunny looked down at her hunting boots in surprise. She was becoming quite fond of them.

"Holly, come on," Timmy whined. "Get in the car. We gotta get out of here."

For her part, Sunny hoped that Holly would stay out of the car as long as possible. At least until the police arrived. Holly seemed to be gearing up for what Aunt Tilly would call a real hissy fit when Sunny caught Rory out of the corner of her eye. He was heading their way.

Sunny groaned. Rory would start yelling at her for not staying in the car and spoil everything.

Sure enough, the closer he got the more she could see how mad he was. His brows were low over eyes that were shooting sparks of fury, his mouth was set in a grim line, his dark hair blowing back from his formidable fore-head.

He stalked up to her. "Is this the man?" he demanded.

Sunny blinked. "Huh?"

He gave her a disgusted grunt, then turned to the boy. "So you're the man who's been seeing my wife."

Sunny had to clamp her hand over her mouth to keep from bursting out laughing. Rory Temple as the wronged husband? And he was playing it to the hilt.

"I swear, mister," Timmy said, holding up a hand, "I ain't never seen your wife before in my life."

"He's lying," Holly yelled, tottering over to the driver's side of the car and pointing a finger at Sunny. "He was with *her* Friday night!"

Timmy stuck his head out the window again. "Hey!" he yelled. "Whose side are you on?"

"I can't believe you'd cheat on me!" Holly wailed as huge tears slipped out of her over-mascaraed eyes.

Timmy rolled his eyes impatiently. "Holly, don't have a cow, can't you see the broad must be twenty-five years old?"

"Huh! She's thirty if she's a day!" Holly sputtered.

"I think you better get out of the car and we'll settle this like men," Rory stated quite reasonably.

Timmy started to look worried. Sunny didn't blame him. Rory was looking broad and menacing in his hunting jacket and unruly hair. "Holly, get your butt in here or I leave without you," he demanded.

"Don't you talk to me that way, you pig. I'll get back in the car when I'm good and ready."

"Then you better be good and ready, 'cause I am outta here."

Timmy made a pathetic attempt to rev the engine but something was lost in the translation to a four-cylinder, four-door sedan. This time, Rory stepped in front of the car.

Timmy stuck his head out of the window again. "Who do you think you are, some dumb superhero?" he yelled.

"No," Rory answered. "That's why I've called for reinforcements."

Sunny hadn't noticed them and apparently neither had Timmy or Holly. But Rory had. Police sirens. And they sounded like they were just around the corner. Timmy looked panicked and revved the engine again.

"Move!" he yelled at Rory.

Rory just shook his head. "You picked the wrong car to steal, Timmy. You should have found one that didn't have Great-Aunt Tilly's hat in the back seat."

"Huh?" Timmy said, screwing up his face and craning his neck around to take a look.

And those few seconds were all it took for the squad cars to sweep into the parking lot and surround the stolen rental.

RORY LEANED AGAINST the rental car, and watched Sunny trying to talk the policeman out of Aunt Tilly's hat and the Jazz Age plates. She'd started to tell her story as soon as she'd found out that the hat and plates were considered evidence and would be impounded along with the stolen rental car. Rory could see the cop starting to weaken. And why not? he thought, chuckling to himself. It was a damn good story.

The other police car passed on its way out of the parking lot and he saluted at Timmy in the back seat who did his best to shoot him an obscene finger gesture despite the handcuffs. Holly's parents had been called and she'd been carted away in an expensive SUV just moments earlier by a woman who hadn't paused for breath since she had started scolding the young girl. Getting caught with Timmy while he was joyriding with a stolen car, Rory thought, was probably going to turn out to be one of the best things that ever happened to her.

Rory looked at his watch. Just after ten-thirty. There was still a chance he could make his meeting, unless he had to find the local jail to bail Sunny out for assaulting a police officer. She looked like she was getting agitated, her arms waving around while the cop frowned. He didn't fancy the idea of having to fight one of Kenosha, Wisconsin's finest for Aunt Tilly's hat. Maybe it was time he joined the negotiations.

He pushed himself away from the rental and headed over to the squad car.

"So you see, Pete," Sunny was saying, "if I have to be late for my parents' wedding, it will help to make up for it if I walk in wearing Great-Aunt Tilly's hat."

Pete. She was already on a first name basis with the cop. He shook his head. Big surprise. She probably already knew the names of his children, as well.

Pete looked at the report he was writing up. "Well, the hat hasn't been listed yet as property found in the car—"

Sunny plopped it on her head. The oversize brim drooped enough to cover her eyes. With a fingertip she lifted it so she could peak out. "As far as anyone has to know, Pete, it was on my head the whole time."

And why not? Rory thought, looking Sunny over. She was wearing pink capri pants with olive drab rubber boots and a blaze orange hunting jacket. The addition of Great-Aunt Tilly's ruined masterpiece didn't seem that far-fetched at all.

Officer Pete tried to suppress a smile. "All right, miss. But the crate—"

"I know—I know! You have to keep the crate!"

Sunny cried before throwing her arms around Pete and giving him a kiss on the cheek.

Red crawled up Pete's neck and into his face. "Aw, miss," he said, embarrassed as a schoolboy caught under the mistletoe. "You better get a move on or you'll miss that wedding altogether."

Rory held out his hand. "He's right, angel. Let's go."

THEY CROSSED THE BORDER into Illinois with forty-five minutes to go. For once, fate was on their side and the Saturday traffic was lighter than usual. Not long after they hit the Edens Expressway, Sunny glimpsed the skyline of Chicago in the distance. It looked every bit as beautiful as the Emerald City rising out of Oz.

"I have never been so happy to see the Sears Tower in my life," Rory murmured.

"I'm never leaving Chicago again," Sunny vowed.

"I'd wager you'd change your mind if one of Eleanor's punch bowls showed up somewhere."

Sunny laughed. "Okay, maybe," she conceded, her mind automatically calculating what she could charge for such a piece. She was just about to tell Rory that her exit was up next when the car lurched to the left.

"What could be wrong, now?" Rory muttered through a tight jaw.

"Ju-just pray that it's something easy to fix," Sunny sputtered as she was jostled left and right despite her seat belt.

"Start with the basics, Pollyanna, and just pray that we don't crash," Rory said grimly as he battled the wheel and tried to slow the car down at the same time.

The steering wheel started to vibrate and Sunny's gaze flew to Rory's hands. His knuckles were white with the effort of trying to control the car. There was the blare of a horn and Sunny whipped her head around in time to see another vehicle, coming up fast in the rear, swerve around them. A van was barreling down on them from behind when the car finally hit the shoulder of the road. Seconds later, Rory had the car under control again and Sunny heard the sound of rubber hitting pavement.

Whop, whop, whop.

They looked at each other. Sunny grinned. "Just a blowout from the sound of it," she said.

"*Just* a blowout?" Rory asked in amazement.

"At least it's something we can easily fix, that's something to be thankful for," Sunny said. Rory brought the car to a stop. "From the sound of it, I'd say half of the tread that used to be on our front left tire is now strewn across the highway behind us." She craned her neck around to take a look. "Yup. Peeled like an apple."

"Your enthusiasm at the moment seems as out of place as the April blizzard," Rory commented dryly. "I absolutely refuse to be thankful for a flat tire."

"Well, then, be thankful that I know how to change one. Come on," she said as she opened the door to get out, "I'll do most of the work."

Wind whipped her hair into her eyes and mouth when she got out of the car. The sound of traffic was deafening and exhaust fumes stung her throat, but she was only miles from home now. She was going to make it.

Rory was already surveying the damage when Sunny joined him at the front of the car.

"There's your lucky shot, Sunshine," he said, thrusting his chin toward the mangled tire. "Any more luck like that and neither of us will make our deadlines."

"Cheer up, Rory. We're within sight of the city. In less than ten minutes we'll be on our way again. Nothing else can possibly go wrong!"

"Humph!" Rory snorted as he went to the rear of the

car. Sunny followed. He unlocked the trunk and they both stood there staring.

There was something about the way the trunk looked that Sunny didn't like at all. "Why does it look so empty?" she asked.

"Your forgot, Sunshine. Our luggage was impounded by—" Rory stopped midsentence and she could see by the look on his face that he was starting to see what she saw.

Or, more accurately, starting to see what she *didn't* see.

"Tell me you see a spare," Rory said woodenly.

"I can't," Sunny answered with just as little animation. "I promised myself I'd never mislead you again."

"No spare," Rory said.

"No spare," Sunny agreed.

Rory closed the trunk and Sunny resisted the urge to sit down alongside of Edens Expressway and bawl like a baby. Instead, she walked around to the front of the car again, turned her back to it, and used her palms to hoist herself up on the hood. It was something of a task since her body suddenly seemed to have turned leaden. But it beat standing, because her legs were so weak with defeat she didn't think they'd hold her up.

She shoved a hand into her hair to hold it back from her face. There it was. Chicago. To the right, the top of the Sears Tower disappeared into a puff of white cloud. To the left, the crisscross braces of the John Hancock Center were just visible. So close. Closer still was the neighborhood in Wrigleyville where her parents had moved when they'd left the commune. In a few minutes, they would be exchanging their wedding vows in the little courtyard behind the flower shop on Belmont Street. And she wasn't going to be there. Despite all they'd gone through, she was going to miss her parents' wedding.

There was only one thing left to do as far as Sunny was concerned. Still sitting on the hood of the car, she threw her hands up into the sky and cried, "Uncle!"

10

"DON'T TELL ME you're giving up, Sunshine?" Rory asked as he came up alongside of her.

"Do I have a choice?"

Rory shook his head slowly and leaned back against the hood of the car. "You surprise me, Sunshine. I can't believe you would give up this easily."

"Easily?" she repeated incredulously. She'd never given up easily on anything in her life. "There has been absolutely nothing easy about this trip so far. First our plane was diverted to the relative wilds of the north woods because of a freak April blizzard. Then we nearly accompanied a herd of deer to the Promised Land. After which, we had to chase down a crow who wanted to accessorize, nearly breaking our necks in the process. Whiteout closes a bridge and we have to find shelter for the night. Then before we can even eat breakfast the next day, our car was stolen, nearly leaving me thousands of dollars in debt and ruining my professional reputation. We could have been in danger just now when our tire blew out. And now we discover that our replacement rental doesn't have a spare. The only thing that should surprise you is that I didn't give up a long time ago!"

By the time she finished her tirade, Rory was standing in front of her, his arms spread, his chiseled mouth smiling widely, his dark hair blowing back from his face, his green eyes glittering. "But we survived all that, Sunshine!'' he pronounced grandly, like he was the conqueror of the Midwest.

She slid off the hood of the car to poke a finger in his chest. "Exactly!" she said triumphantly. "And for what? To let something as simple as a flat tire end the race with the finish line in sight? For the sake of a little rubber, you're about to break a promise to your late grandmother and I'm about to miss my parents' wedding! Don't you think it's about time I gave up?''

Rory put his hands on his hips. "As Grandmother Molly used to say *hogwash*.''

Sunny tossed her head to get the windblown hair out of her eyes. "That's the very same thing Aunt Tilly always says. But I don't see what that has to do with—''

"Giving up?" Rory finished for her. "You're right. Aunt Tilly and Grandma Molly have absolutely nothing at all to do with giving up. And neither should you.''

He took her by the shoulders and gave her a little shake. "You're going to make that wedding, Sunny,'' he told her emphatically.

She stared at him. "I don't get it,'' she said, throwing up her arms. "This morning you didn't even believe that the wedding existed. For the entire trip, you've been acting like I'm this silly Pollyanna, living inside a bubble, dreaming up fairy tales, and now when I'm finally seeing how futile the reality of the situation is, you suddenly do an about-face and—''

"Not suddenly, Sunny. That's what I came back to Danny's Diner to tell you. I believe in the wedding, Sunny. And I don't want you to miss it. I don't want that little girl or this beautiful woman to lose her dream. I want you to make it to that wedding, Sunny!''

If she had heard those words from him anywhere else but by the side of the Edens Expressway, she would have been the happiest woman alive. But it was too late for dreams to come true.

"Thank you for that, Rory," she said with a sad little smile. "But even if you got on that cell phone of yours and ordered a cab to pick us up, we'd never make it in time."

"No, Sunshine, but there's another way."

Sunny spread her arms in a gesture of futility. "How?" she asked.

Rory ran ahead a few feet, turned around and stuck out his thumb. "This is how, Sunshine!" he called to her.

Cars whizzed by as if he were invisible. "Are you crazy?" Sunny shouted over the din of traffic.

"And here I thought you were a half-full kind of woman," Rory shouted back.

She put her hands on her hips. "And I thought you were a half-empty kind of man."

"Molly used to have this saying. Something about putting two very different people in a bag and shaking them up—"

The corner of Sunny's mouth quirked. "Aunt Tilly has the same saying—shake 'em up and they'd come out even."

"That's the one," Rory yelled.

Sunny heaved a sigh and plopped Great-Aunt Tilly's hat on her head. Who was she to argue with a land-developing tycoon spouting old-fashioned wisdom from the side of the Edens Expressway?

"You know," she yelled as she joined him, "I've only hitchhiked one other time in my life. It was in California and when Aunt Tilly found out she sent me to bed without supper." Sunny rubbed her empty belly at the memory. "She made pot roast that night, too. With mashed potatoes."

"Will you stop thinking of your stomach and get to work."

"I can't help it. I'm hungry. It's not like we got to eat much of our breakfast."

"Stick out your thumb, Sunshine, and you could be feasting on wedding cake before you know it."

"Fat chance," Sunny mumbled, but as soon as her thumb was out there catching a breeze, a dilapidated pickup truck slowed down to take a look.

"That truck is stopping!" Sunny gasped in surprise.

"Of course it is, Sunshine. There's a man driving. Come on before he changes his mind!"

Rory grabbed her hand and they ran for the pickup. They were almost there when Sunny felt her foot start to slip out of her boot. She looked down. The lace had come untied. She should stop to tie it, but the truck was so close, and the ceremony was about to start—

Suddenly her ankle folded to the side and she cried out in pain.

Rory assessed the situation at a glance, and without a word, scooped her up into his arms and continued running toward the truck.

The driver was just leaning over to roll down the window when they reached the pickup. A huge sad-eyed, floppy-eared dog the color of dirty putty stuck his head out and panted at them. "Something I can do for you folks?" the driver asked around the head of the dog.

"We need a ride!" both Rory and Sunny said at the same time.

The driver looked back at the rental. "Looks like it. Where to?"

"The Loop," answered Sunny.

"Wrigleyville," said Rory.

The farmer looked from one to the other of them. "So you two aren't together?"

"No!" Sunny said.

"Yes!" Rory answered.

The dog's enormous ears swung back and forth as he tried to follow the conversation.

"This woman has to get to—"

"This man has to get to—"

The dog, going a bit cross-eyed trying to keep up, threw back his head and let out a mournful howl.

"Rebel is right," the driver said. "You folks need to pick a designated talker."

Rory opened his mouth to grab the floor, or more accurately, the concrete, so Sunny quickly put her fingers to his mouth to quiet him. "This man," she said to the driver, "is Rory Temple and he needs to get to a meeting taking place in the Loop. It's very important."

Rory took her hand away from his mouth. "Sunny—no."

She sniffed back a tear and nodded. "It's too late for the wedding, anyway. It'll be over by the time we get there. But there's a chance that Josiah Simpson is still at your offices." She turned back to the driver. "Can you get him to the Loop?"

"Well, I'm headed that way myself." The driver jerked his head toward the back of the truck. "Gotta deliver a load of free-range chickens to a health food store, but I don't know," he said, looking skeptical. "I'm usually cautious when it comes to hitchhikers." He squinted at Rory. "And I don't really see what kind of business a man dressed in a hunting jacket might have in the Loop." He turned his squint on Sunny. "And, while I know that a lot of women hunt these days, I've never seen a female hunter wear a hat quite like that."

"Look," Rory said impatiently, "we're wasting time. Forget the Loop. This is Sunshine Morgan and she needs to get to Wrigleyville immediately or miss the wedding of her childhood dreams.''

The driver looked at the hat with new eyes. Eyes that twinkled. "A wedding?" he asked, giving them a smile for the first time. "Well why didn't you say so? Hop in.''

"No!" Sunny shouted. All eyes, including the dog's, fixed on her. "I can't let you do this," she said to Rory calmly. "You promised Molly.''

"Molly would understand. She'd want me to pay back the woman who made me remember monkey socks.''

Sunny's heart filled so suddenly she thought it might burst just like the tire had. "You remembered?''

Rory nodded. "Molly knew how to make those stuffed monkeys, Sunshine. She made me one. I'd forgotten. You made me remember—that, and a lot of other things. Like there are some things more important than business.''

"Rory," she whispered raggedly around the tears clogging her throat. She tightened her arms around his neck and pulled him closer to touch her mouth to his.

"You folks comin' or not?" the driver asked.

"We're coming," Rory answered against her mouth.

With his mouth still on hers, he reached for the door handle. Rebel let out another mournful howl and they pulled apart, both swinging their heads in the dog's direction.

"Sorry, folks," the driver said when he could get a word in. "Old Rebel here likes to ride shotgun. You'll have to ride in back with the chickens.''

RORY BLEW ANOTHER feather out of his mouth. "Yes, Agnes, those are chickens you hear," he said into his cell phone. "I'll tell you all about it later. Just tell old man Simpson that I'll give him a thousand dollars for every minute I'm late. That should get the old skinflint to think twice about stalking out of Temple Enterprises.''

While Agnes made notes, Rory watched Sunny try to carry on a conversation with a chicken. The wind was whipping her hair back from her face. Her cheeks were bright with color, her eyes sparkling, her lips laughing. The glass was half full again.

"What about the media?" Agnes asked.

"Tell them," he said, "that if they stick around a little longer, they're going to get a scoop more than worth the wait."

"Which is?" Agnes asked.

"You'll have to wait, Agnes, just like everyone else."

"It's Saturday, boss. I'm waiting at time and a half."

Rory laughed. "And worth every penny. Now put me through to the legal department."

"Like I said, boss, it's Saturday."

"We've got the best lawyers in the city. Someone will be there."

Agnes laughed and put him through.

By the time he finished with the legal department, the pickup was pulling up in front of a small redbrick building with striped awnings and colorful flower arrangements in the large front window. Rory looked up at the second floor. There were lace curtains in the windows. He pictured Sunny as a little girl, chestnut hair tangled from the adventures of the day, her nose in a book at the kitchen table while her mother fixed dinner and her father worked in the flower shop below.

He wanted to see that kitchen. And he wanted to see the bedroom where she dreamed her girlhood dreams and learned to chase fairy tales. But the clock was still ticking. He vaulted over the gate of the truck. "Put on Aunt Tilly's hat, Sunshine. You're about to go to a wedding," he called to her as he went around to talk to the driver.

"Want to earn five hundred bucks?" Rory asked him.

The driver squinted. "Is it legal?"

"Entirely," Rory told him with a wry grin. "Just wait here until we come out again then get us to the Loop as fast as possible."

"Just that and I get five hundred?"

"Just that," Rory said.

The driver thought for a moment. "Well, I guess those chickens aren't in any hurry."

"Good man," Rory said and gave him the address.

He went around to the rear of the truck. Sunny, Aunt Tilly's hat hanging forlornly on her head, was limping around the chicken crates.

"You'll never make it for the I do's if you walk, angel," he said, holding out his arms.

After only a second's hesitation, Sunny dropped into them and Rory started up the sidewalk to the flower shop.

"No—around back. The wedding's in the courtyard."

Rory veered off to a little cobblestone path that wound around the corner of the building. Next to a lilac bush, its spring blooms bursting through the snow, an arched gate led to the courtyard. Rory burst through it with Sunny in his arms.

Surrounded by dozens of baskets full of flowers, the guests stood in the courtyard amid the melting snow, all in spring finery with winter boots on their feet. Everyone turned at the sound of the gate. There was a collective gasp of pleasure, which caused the couple standing in front of a minister at the far end of the courtyard to turn.

"Sunny!" the woman exclaimed, a warm smile coming to her mouth and huge tears filling her eyes.

"Mom—Dad!" Sunny cried triumphantly. "I made it!"

"We knew you would," said the man.

Sunny beamed at her parents while Rory carried her through the gathering. He placed her gently on her feet then stepped aside, leaving her standing alone with her parents but staying close enough to watch her.

Great-Aunt Tilly would be so proud, he knew, because Sunny was wearing the hat. It had a few holes in it and its brim hung longer than Rebel's ears, but Sunny was wearing it with as much pride as Great-Aunt Tilly had made it with.

Dimly, Rory heard Sunny's parents reciting their vows, but he couldn't take his eyes off Sunny. She was amazing—like no other woman he'd ever known. There were chicken feathers tangled in her hair and sticking out of her blaze orange hunting jacket. One of her rubber boots was untied and she had a smudge of dirt across her cheek. Yet Sunny was oblivious to it all. All her attention was focused on her parents. Rory let his gaze drift over to them.

Sunny's mother, wearing a pale yellow lace dress, daisies tangled in her long, braided hair, was a plumper, more down-home version of Sunny. Her father still sported long hair and a beard—and still had a besotted look in his eye for the woman he'd been with all those years.

The couple completed their vows and Rory waited patiently in the background while someone snapped a picture to send to Aunt Tilly. Then he shouldered his way through the well-wishers.

"That's enough," he stated, swinging Sunny back up into his arms.

"Wh-what do you think you're doing?" Sunny gasped.

"We've got a meeting to get to, remember Sunshine?"

"*We?* Since when is it *we?* Put me down right now! I won't stand for this!"

"Was she always so strong-willed?" Rory asked Sunny's father.

"Always," he said, sounding well resigned to the fact. "Stubborn as a blind mule. Just like her mother."

"Dear," her mother said, "don't you think you should introduce us to your date?"

"Mother, he's not my date!"

"Actually, I am," Rory said. "Rory Temple," he added, awkwardly extending his hand from below Sunny's backside.

Mr. Morgan shook it as best he could.

Mrs. Morgan stood there with her mouth open. "*The* Rory Temple?" she asked, when she'd recovered.

"Can't you tell?" Sunny asked peevishly. "He's just as difficult and autocratic as they say."

Mrs. Morgan just smiled. "Well, how nice of you to come to our wedding, Mr. Temple."

"He's not staying," Sunny said.

"Neither is she," Rory added.

"Oh, yes I am! That was the whole point of this impossible journey. To make it to my parents' wedding. I'm here. I'm staying."

"Afraid not, Sunshine," Rory told her before turning to her parents. "I've rescued Aunt Tilly's hat twice," Rory said. "Now all I'm asking is that your daughter return the favor and help me rescue a business deal worth millions."

"Sounds fair," Mr. Morgan said reasonably.

"Daddy!" Sunny exclaimed.

"You will be back in time for cake, won't you?" Mrs. Morgan asked. "It's chocolate, Sunny's favorite."

"Wouldn't miss it for the world," Rory said as he strode back through the gathering, with Sunny struggling in his arms all the way.

THE OLD PICKUP PULLED up in front of the John Hancock Center in Chicago's Loop. Sunny slumped further down amid the chicken crates. "You didn't tell me your offices were in the John Hancock Center."

"You didn't ask," Rory said.

"I'm not getting out of this truck," Sunny insisted.

"Oh, yes you are, Sunshine."

"I don't see why you need me anyway. You're already paying Josiah Simpson to wait."

"To wait—but not to listen. I still have to convince him that I had a good reason to be late for the meeting or he's going to call the whole deal off."

"And you think he's going to listen to a strange woman wearing a lilac chiffon hat and an orange hunting jacket?"

"Why not?" Rory asked, smiling. "Everyone else has."

"Come on, Rory, at least let me take off the jacket and hat."

"Nothing doing, Sunshine. I want Josiah Simpson to get the full effect."

Sunny groaned and watched him vault over the gate of the pickup. She wished she could be as cheerful at the prospect of meeting Josiah Simpson and the media dressed as they were as he seemed to be.

While he went up front to say something to the driver, Sunny risked peeking around a crate. Pedestrian traffic from nearby Water Tower Place was brisk. There seemed to be a lot of well-dressed women carrying impressive shopping bags. As far as she could tell, no one else was wearing blaze orange and wilted chiffon.

She was startled by the clang of the pickup's gate being let down. She looked over to find Rory standing there. "Let's go, Sunshine," he said.

Sunny stood up. How could she not? She owed him. Not only had he rescued Aunt Tilly's hat more than once, he'd put business aside long enough for her to see her parents exchange their wedding vows. He'd put his own dream in jeopardy to make hers come true. But more than that, he was the man she loved. So what difference did it make if she had rubber boots on her feet? She might never see him again after today, but right now, right here, he needed her.

Using the chicken crates for support, she limped over to the tailgate. Rory held out his arms and it felt only natural to be in them again.

Rory strode up to the entrance to the building with the kind of majesty most men couldn't muster wearing a blaze orange hunting jacket, let alone carrying a woman also wearing one. Like the emperor in his new clothes, Rory's demeanor defied anyone in the lobby or on the elevator to mention the fact that they were leaving a trail of chicken feathers in their wake.

The elevator doors swished open on a floor high enough to make Sunny's nose twitch. Temple Enterprises was written on the wall opposite in huge, bronze letters. A short, plump, gray-haired woman in a very expensive looking suit stood waiting.

"Welcome back, boss," said the woman.

"Thank you, Agnes. It's good to be home. This is Sunshine Morgan," he said.

"Nice to meet you, Ms. Morgan," Agnes replied, as if there were nothing at all unusual about the situation. "The media are waiting just around the bend, boss."

"Then let's not keep them waiting any longer, Agnes," Rory said.

The hallway curved into a spiral then suddenly opened into a large reception area. As soon as they entered, cameras flashed and microphones were shoved in their faces.

"Mr. Temple, is it true—"

"Tell us, Rory, what happened—"

"Give us the scoop, Temple—"

Rory pushed his way to the front of the small crowd and turned.

"You promised us a scoop if we waited, Temple," someone yelled. "How about it?"

"Ladies and gentleman," he said formally as a white feather tumbled from his hair into Sunny's face, "if you'll follow me to the conference room, I think you'll find it worth the wait."

He turned and strode down the hall again, the media entourage following in his wake, and stopped in front of a pair of enormous doors. Agnes grabbed the twin ornate doorknobs and opened the doors with a flourish. They all swept in.

The bent old man standing at the window turned. He stared at Rory with a wizened, disapproving eye. "Still an irresponsible whippersnapper, aren't you, boy?"

"Not at all, sir. I think once you've heard the story of why I'm so late, you'll understand."

The man snorted. "Huh! And what makes you think I'll listen?"

Sunny's indignation immediately rose. "Not listen?" she piped up. "But that wouldn't be fair! You *have* to listen!"

Like a turtle coming out of his shell to snap, Simpson poked his head toward her. "Says who? You?"

Sunny wasn't sure how much authority she could wield given the wardrobe, not to mention the fact that she wasn't even standing on her own two feet, but she didn't care at all for the way this man was talking to Rory.

"Yes, says me!" she answered.

Simpson moved closer, his attention now drawn to Sunny's head.

"That hat—" he said.

"My Aunt Tilly made it," Sunny stated proudly.

"Looks like it's been caught in a rainstorm."

"Actually, sir, it was a blizzard."

Simpson chortled, his lined face cracked into a crooked smile. "My wife had one like it. We were at a picnic once when we were courting. Got caught in the rain. Damn thing looked just like that afterward," he said. He stared at it for a long moment and Sunny had the feeling that he was no longer in that conference room with them. He was back at that picnic, caught in the rain with his wife.

"Rory," she whispered. "Put me down."

Agnes pulled a chair out from the conference table and Rory slid Sunny into it.

"Mr. Simpson? Won't you sit down," she asked gently, indicating the chair next to her, "and let me explain why Rory is so late?"

Simpson hesitated, then pulled out the chair and sat down. There was a murmur of approval from the entourage.

And, once again, Sunny told the story of the wedding she'd been waiting for most of her life and of the plane that got diverted and the rental car they had to share and the bridge that was closed because of whiteout. She told him of the deer and the crow and the chickens. She told him everything. Well, everything except how she and Rory had spent the night they'd been marooned in the blizzard. Everything except how she felt about Rory Temple.

When she stopped talking, a hush had fallen over the conference room. The reporters and photographers seemed to be in a state of suspended animation. All eyes were on the old man, waiting to see what he would make of it.

"Remarkable," Josiah Simpson finally said and it was hard for even the most seasoned reporter in the room to tell whether he was referring to the story or the woman.

"And you're in love with this whippersnapper?" Josiah asked while he still studied her.

Sunny gulped. What was she supposed to answer to that? What else *could* she answer?

"Yes," she said. "I'm in love with him."

Josiah snorted, pushed his chair back, and stood up. "And you?" he asked Rory, who was standing across the conference table. "I don't suppose you've got sense enough to love her back?"

Sunny swung her gaze up to Rory, expecting to see thunder on his face and fire in his eyes at the spot Josiah Simpson just put him in.

Instead, he was smiling. At her.

"Yes, sir," he answered, his gaze never leaving her face, "I've got sense enough to love her back."

"Then let's make a deal," the old man said.

The room exploded with sound. One or two reporters started to run for the door, anxious to file the scoop. Sunny saw spots before her eyes as cameras flashed.

Suddenly Rory's voice, sure and strong, cut through the din.

"If everyone will just stay where they are—I have an announcement to make."

The noise in the room immediately quieted.

"The Simpson Twine Condo Project is dead!" Rory pronounced.

There was another collective gasp and Josiah Simpson pointed a long, wrinkled finger at Rory. "Are you telling me that after all this hoopla, Temple, you don't want my building after all?"

"Quite the contrary, Mr. Simpson. I want your building more than ever. But it's no longer going to be known as the Simpson Twine Condo Project." He looked at Sunny and smiled gently. "From this day forward it will be known as the Molly Temple Community Center."

Sunny's mouth dropped open and her heart leapt in her chest.

"Don't look so surprised, angel," Rory said in a voice laden with enough intimacy to make her forget for a moment that they weren't the only two people in the room. "You're used to getting your own way."

She laughed softly through the tears clogging her throat. "Molly would be so proud," she told him.

"Thanks to you," Rory said.

While Sunny sniffed and dabbed at her eyes with a knuckle, Rory turned his attention to the rest of the room again. They were staring as if they were watching a play, waiting for the next lines.

"I'd also like to announce that I've chosen the design consultant for the project. Sunshine Morgan of A Sunny Touch will be doing the interior design." The room started to explode again and Rory held up his hands for order. "And given how well I know Miss Morgan, I'm sure she'll generously agree to donate her time to heading a series of workshops in her field once the center is open."

Sunny was so pleased with this new way in which he planned to honor his grandmother that she enthusiastically nodded her approval.

"I'm sure," Rory went on, "that with Miss Morgan's help we'll have no problem getting other talented and skilled people in the Chicago community to volunteer their time, as well. I'm also sure," he added, his eyes glittering as he turned to the old man, "that Mr. Simpson would like to be the first to make a donation toward any equipment or supplies needed."

With a disgruntled look in his eyes, Josiah opened his mouth to protest. Sunny quickly shot him a dazzling smile and mouthed a thank-you. The storm in the old man's eyes turned into a twinkle. "I'd be happy to, you young whippersnapper," he said to Rory. "Just as long as you throw in two dollars for my every one."

Rory chuckled and inclined his head to acknowledge being bested by the old rascal. "I'd be honored," he said.

Cameras started to whir and snap again, hands were shaken, papers were signed and microphones were stuck into her face. She wasn't sure what she said or how she said it. The next half hour was a blur. Her mind was still spinning when, finally, the room cleared.

"I'll be at my desk, boss, if there's anything you want," Agnes said before going out and shutting the door quietly behind her.

"What just happened?" Sunny asked in a daze.

"I believe you just signed the biggest contract of your career," Rory answered.

Sunny picked up the sheaf of papers on the conference table in front of her. Sure enough, it was a contract and there was her name on it and the name of her business.

"But, when?"

"Temple has its own legal department. I had a phone conference with them while you were talking to the chickens."

"You mean you knew you were going to announce this?"

"Of course."

"You knew and you didn't warn me! Do you realize that the news that I've been chosen for the biggest project of my career is going to be accompanied by a picture of me in a blaze orange hunting jacket?"

His eyes glittered. "Don't forget the chicken feathers in your hair."

Sunny gasped and put a hand to her hair. Chicken feathers drifted down around her face. She shot to her feet.

"I don't believe it! How, how could you?" she demanded.

Rory grinned. "I knew the woman who tried to accessorize a crow could handle it."

"Of all the autocratic, domineering, exasperating—"

"Tell you what, angel, I'll make it up to you when we announce our engagement. You can dress any way you want for that."

"Well, I should hope so!" Sunny exclaimed, picking up the contract for a second look. "A woman should at least be able to pick what she wears at her own—" Her head shot up and the papers drifted to the floor. "What did you say?"

"I said," Rory repeated, his grin positively wicked now, "that you can wear anything you like when we announce our engagement."

Her heart pounded. "But, we're not engaged," she said.

Rory raised a brow. "Didn't I tell you that we're getting married?"

Sunny raised a brow right back. "Mr. Temple, I think we're going to have to do something about those autocratic tendencies of yours."

"You think so?"

Sunny slipped her hunting jacket off and let it fall to the floor. "I think so," she said.

"And when do you propose to start?"

"How about now?" she asked, taking off Aunt Tilly's hat and tossing it onto the conference table. "Any chance I could talk you into it?"

Rory took his hunting jacket off. "Every chance in the world," he said, tossing it into a corner. "As long as you promise that I'm the only man you try to talk into anything ever again."

"I think we can make that deal," she said.

"Then let's begin negotiating, shall we?" Rory suggested, swinging Sunny into his arms once more.

"Does it seem to you, Mr. Temple," Sunny asked, "that I spend an awful lot of time in your arms?"

"There's a reason for that," Rory said, lowering her to the conference table. "It's exactly where you belong."

She put her arms around his neck and pulled him down to her.

"I love you, Rory," she said.

"And I love you, Sunny," he said. "Now let's start negotiating," he added, lowering his mouth to hers.

"Uh-uh, Mr. Temple," she said, putting a finger to his lips to stop the kiss. "First I'd like to make it clear that I want in on that department store you're redoing."

Rory's mouth twisted. "And you said you weren't mercenary."

"Well?" she said.

"Done," he said. "Now kiss me."

She did. Thoroughly and well.

"One other thing," she murmured against his mouth.

"Hmm?" he asked. "What now?"

"I don't want to rush negotiations, but we have to get back to Wrigleyville in time for the chocolate cake."

Rory laughed softly. "Don't worry, Sunshine," he said. "We've got a whole lifetime ahead of us."

A Christmas Carol

Kathleen
O'Reilly

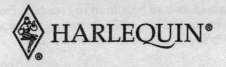

HARLEQUIN®

TORONTO • NEW YORK • LONDON
AMSTERDAM • PARIS • SYDNEY • HAMBURG
STOCKHOLM • ATHENS • TOKYO • MILAN • MADRID
PRAGUE • WARSAW • BUDAPEST • AUCKLAND

Dear Reader,

A Christmas Carol was so much fun to write! There's something about families and holidays that can bring out the very best and the very worst in people and it seemed the perfect time of year to torment Carol and Mike.

Carol was the culmination of a lot of female confusion and, yes, delusion that I've seen in myself and others. That bit of us that is completely unaware of who we really are, before we finally have that big V-8 moment in life. As for Mike, well, I gotta admit that I'm a sucker for superintelligent guys who can sometimes be clueless when it comes to matters of the heart. I truly believe that best friends do make the best lovers and I'm lucky enough to be married to my very best friend.

Oh, and I do have a goldfish named Pat (she's very fat), and my mom resembles Carol's in only two respects: she's always loved me and always wanted me to be happy. And as my kids get older, I only hope they think the same of me.

Best wishes,

Kathleen O'Reilly

P.S. I would love to hear from my readers. Please e-mail me at kathleenoreilly@earthlink.net or visit my Web site at www.kathleenoreilly.com

1

On the first day of Christmas, my mother gave to me—a stud with a laptop PC.

"THAT BOY DOESN'T have anything between his legs but air. Don't know why you call him Rock, he's soft as a marshmallow." The elderly woman was speaking in a quiet tone now, but that was subject to change at any moment.

Carol Martin cocked her head frantically toward the man in question. She wanted to sink into the tile floor at the Autumn Hills Home for the Elderly. "Brock, not Rock, Aunt Eleanor."

Of course her great-aunt paid no attention, continuing right along, her voice rising as she continued. "You need to find a man with substance. Someone that can satisfy your needs, give into those animal urges. That Rock's a cold fish, I tell you."

Carol lowered her voice to a whisper. "He's not a fish, he's a very nice person." She cast a worried glance toward the tall, handsome man industriously working in the corner of her aunt's room. Thankfully, he was too busy peering at the screen of his laptop to pay any attention to an old lady questioning the girth of his appendages.

"Toss him back and find yourself a real keeper. Now where did I put that thing?" Aunt Eleanor fumbled through the plaid throw in her lap and finally pulled a television remote control off her bedside table. "Here it is. And don't start thinking about contradicting your elders. Bad manners. When you get to be my age you can say whatever you want. Half the time nobody listens anyway."

"Aunt Eleanor—" Carol tried once more, but her aunt shushed her, pointing her remote at the large television on the far wall with the precision of a sharpshooter.

"Now be quiet, it's almost time for the news." The sound of trumpets blaring to the rhythm of a teletype flowed through the room and Aunt Eleanor fixed her eyes on the screen. "Take that Hurricane Dan. Had my eye on him for twenty-seven years. He just looks better every day. Substance, that's the key. Much better than that Rock of yours."

"Brock. Brock. It's Brock, not Rock, and he can hear you."

Brock, hearing his name, responded immediately. "Yeah?"

Carol shook her head, and Brock smiled before losing interest, his long fingers resuming their tap-tap on the keyboard.

Her aunt held a hand up to her ear, failing at an attempt

to look confused and feeble. "What are you talking about? There's nothing wrong with my hearing."

There was nothing wrong with her hearing, and there was no mistaking the wheels turning behind the faded blue eyes. Not wanting to face the disapproval lurking there, Carol turned to look at her new beau. For long moments she stared, waiting for a spark, a flame of passion. She let out a long breath. Nothing. Obviously she was deficient in some fashion if even Brock couldn't rotate her world.

As if sensing the desperate, woman-made vibes beaming his way, Brock lifted his well-formed head, the afternoon sun glinting off the golden strands of his hair. His azure blue eyes crinkled at the corners as he caught her looking at him. "Hey, sugar, you ready to go yet?" He checked the thin, gold watch on his wrist. "I need to be home by six to do my five miles." He patted his trim waist. "Can't afford to let myself slide."

No, even at Aunt Eleanor's age, Brock would still be watching his figure. He'd probably wear a girdle if he thought it was necessary—something chic and stylish. Carol squashed the giggle that rose in her throat. "Give me five more minutes, and then we can leave."

"You should come with me, Carol. A couple of weeks, and we'd have your thighs rock-hard."

Carol smiled, adding a pair of painful support hose to his imaginary wardrobe. Her legs weren't too bad; maybe she had one mini-dimple, or two. But on a good day, it certainly wasn't *that* noticeable. Truth was, she'd rather clean toilets than jog. As sweetly as possible, she wiggled her nose. "Someday."

Brock buried his head back in his computer, nodding absently.

Aunt Eleanor snorted, not taking her eyes off the last week's Dow Jones report. Saturday was a slow news day, after all. "Not a thing going for him, just those pretty-boy looks."

"And a nice car, a steady career, a mastery of California wines and a tailored wardrobe direct from London. Mother loves him."

Aunt Eleanor looked up, taking in Carol's jeans and Texas Rangers T-shirt. "It's not what they look like in clothes, it's what they can do out of them that will keep a smile on your face."

"Aunt El—"

An ear-splitting wolf whistle drowned out her plea. "Hey there, good-looking."

Carol knew that voice, and that cheerful greeting.

And it meant trouble with a capital T.

Mike Fitzgerald poked his head through the open doorway, surveying the three occupants. "No need to bunch your bloomers, Carol, I happened to be in the neighborhood and stopped by to flirt with your aunt, not you."

And what an amazing transformation a little flirting could make. Her favorite aunt patted her blue-rinsed hair, tucked the soft, plaid blanket neatly around the maroon recliner and muted the news.

"Ah, my boy. Come inside and keep an old woman

happy. Things just perk up so nicely when you come to visit. This nursing home has a shortage of young men. At least young men with substance.'' Aunt Eleanor turned her head in Brock's direction and nodded knowingly.

Mike wandered in, dropping on the bed in the corner, completely ignoring Brock. Carol knew the two men had to meet at some point, but this was not her idea of a controlled environment. And Mike was always the wild card. He grabbed Aunt Eleanor's hand and planted a gallant kiss on it. ''Anytime, you wicked temptress, you, anytime.''

Brock stood and strode forward, thrusting his hand toward Mike like a dog staking his territory. ''Brock Gregerson. Nice to meet you.''

''Mike Fitzgerald.''

Brock turned toward Carol, making a perfect golden arch with his eyebrows. ''This is Mike? Your friend, Mike?''

Ah, Mike. How to explain a whirlwind like Mike? The first time she met him was in second grade when he took the seat behind her in school and spent the entire morning batting her ponytail. She returned the favor at recess, smacking him on the head with her brand-new Scooby-Doo lunch box. It had been the start of a long-running friendship, a source of never-ending entertainment, and a constant irritant to her mother. Two out of three wasn't too bad.

''Rock, Rock.'' Mike shook his head. ''You think I'm

threatening your turf, huh? Trying to put the moves on your little woman? Did you know I've seen Carol naked fourteen times already?''

Oh no, he was starting already. She tried to regain control. ''Mike!''

He nodded in her direction, his brown eyes twinkling like the devil. ''You're absolutely right. It was fifteen.'' He turned to Brock. ''No need for panic, old man. Our days of playing doctor are long gone.''

Carol intruded, glaring at Mike before he got even rowdier. ''Mike, behave. Brock, calm down, Mike is only teasing. He does that so well. Aunt Eleanor, stop laughing.''

Mike actually looked offended. ''I'm not teasing. I was dead serious about the naked thing. Fifteen, if you count the Tenth Annual Girls' Gym Class Shower Raid. Vicky Lewis was giving you some serious competition back then, but when all the votes were counted, well, the boys awarded you first place.'' His dark eyes raked over her, and to her amazement she felt a blush coming on. What was with him today?

Brock moved to sit on the bed next to Mike, looking confused. ''First place for what?'' That sent Aunt Eleanor off into gales of laughter.

No. He wasn't going to do this to her. Not in front of Brock. Carol looked down her nose, straight into Mike's laughing eyes. ''Forget about naked, buster.''

''Well, you sure know how to hold a grudge. That was

eighteen years ago. You were older, more mature, and I wasn't ready to play doctor.''

Carol shook her head, amazed at Mike's ability to render her speechless. But she knew how he worked, and she recovered quickly. "Mike," she replied warningly, "I'm only three months older than you." She sniffed. "Besides, I got over it."

"You sure?" He sounded almost serious.

She had to look twice to make sure he was joking. Mike was always joking. "Of course." She cleared her throat, filling an awkward silence. "It doesn't matter, anyway. I'm sure you didn't come here to talk about sex."

Mike started to answer, but Aunt Eleanor interrupted. "Don't stop on my account."

Mike grinned, sensing a partner in crime. "I came to find out what I should get Eleanor for Christmas."

"She's my aunt, not yours," Carol replied defensively.

"Don't be such a Scrooge. It's Christmastime. And I like your aunt, you know that. Besides, she loaned me the money for my first Mustang."

Carol turned to look at Aunt Eleanor. "You did?"

Aunt Eleanor beamed. "Yep, got eighteen percent interest on the deal."

Mike shook a finger at Aunt Eleanor. "I got taken."

Aunt Eleanor just smiled.

"Carol, it's been ten minutes already…" Brock didn't seem interested in Mike's automotive history.

Carol could have sworn that Mike rolled his eyes.

"Cool your jets, Brock. You're undermining the societal aspects of family values, here. I bet you came from a broken home, didn't you?"

"Carol, we really need to go."

Carol watched, touched as Brock stood his ground, bless his buffed and polished little heart. And Aunt Eleanor thought he didn't have substance. Hah!

Mike's grin grew sly. Great, just great.

"Hey look, why don't you take off and I'll take Carol home. It's not like it would be out of my way."

"Y'all are neighbors?" Brock sounded almost jealous. Jealous of Mike? Carol looked at the guy who had tormented and teased her for most of her life. Brown hair, brown eyes, good shoulders. Mike.

He caught her watching him. His grin disappeared for just a moment before he shook his head, and then turned his attention to Brock. "Yeah. I'm right across the stairs from her." He shrugged. "What can I say, the rent's cheap, it's close to work, and Carol got a new grill for referring a friend."

Brock folded his arms across his chest, assessing Mike, who only stared blandly.

"Well." Carol deflated as she watched Brock cave. "If you're sure it's no trouble."

"None at all."

"Thanks, that's really nice of you." Brock planted a kiss on Carol's cheek, and strode toward the door, laptop secured firmly under his arm. "I'll call you later, sugar."

"Sure thing."

Aunt Eleanor punched her arm, pointing at Brock's retreating back. "Look at that, I've seen rump roasts that look better walking away. I'm telling you, Carol—"

"Tell her what?" Mike asked.

"Don't say a word, or I'll shut up Dapper Dan permanently." Carol poked her aunt with the remote to underscore the threat. The last thing Carol wanted was for Mike to join in on the gluteus maximus analysis.

"I was just telling Carol that we need someone to organize the Christmas pageant for the residents and I had volunteered her," Aunt Eleanor said.

Hello? Carol spun her head toward Aunt Eleanor in disbelief. "You did what?"

"Surely you wouldn't turn your back on all these lonely senior citizens with nothing to do all day but play shuffleboard and watch TV?" Her aunt's hands fluttered like a deadly moth.

"I would love to help, but I can't do it all by myself," Carol protested, but she sensed the rope tightening around her neck.

"Well, Mike can pitch in, can't you boy?"

"No problem. I'm on vacation 'til after the first."

Aunt Eleanor beamed proudly. "See there, the boy's got substance. And I bet he's got it where it counts most. Where did I put those pills?" She poked about her chair and table, before fixing a calculating gaze on Mike. "Mike, be a dear and check on that bottom bookshelf will you?"

"Where?"

Aunt Eleanor's finger wavered, pointing toward the low shelves underneath the window. Carol noticed the steadiness in Aunt Eleanor's arm, the consistent rhythm to the wobble. Oh, her aunt was good. Even Mike was no match.

"Just over there."

As soon as Mike bent down to begin a search for the mysterious bottle of pills, Aunt Eleanor turned and whispered to Carol. "Look at that butt, girl. They don't build tighter curves than that at Indy. You should be doing time with this one, not those Nancy-boys you're always mooning after."

Like a driver fascinated with the carnage in a traffic accident, she followed the line of her aunt's arm, focusing on the soft, faded denim around Mike's slim hips and muscular thighs. Levi's. Why did it have to be Levi's? Helplessly she felt herself consumed by prurient rubbernecking. Oh baby, come to momma. She closed her eyes for a moment, weak with despair. Oh please, let it be bad tuna fish.

And as fate will often do, choosing the exact moment of supreme weakness, Mike turned around and met Carol's eyes. Eyes that she knew contained more lust than a boat full of sailors after six months at sea.

It was her worst nightmare. Aunt Eleanor's trill of laughter faded away, as did the five-day weather forecast. Mike's eyes widened with surprise and Carol's stomach lurched in response. That warm front wasn't moving in from the Gulf, it was moving in right between Carol's thighs.

She looked down to count the floor tiles and had just reached fourteen when she felt it.

High humidity.

MIKE DROVE Carol back to her apartment in silence. She rummaged through her purse, adjusted the radio, and played with the reclining seats. Anything to avoid thinking about, well, that.

And Mike seemed just as uncomfortable. She watched as he fiddled with the air conditioning, tapped his fingers against the steering wheel with a quick, allegro beat, and tilted the rear view mirror at least seven times—not that she was counting.

The stifling December heat was making her sweat, or maybe it was the tension in the car, which seemed about as thick as curdled milk.

Finally, she knew she would have to speak or scream. She opted for conversation.

"So, you taking Linda the human vacuum to your company's Christmas party?" Smooth, very smooth.

"Who? Oh, sorry." Mike pulled a hand from the wheel, and rubbed it over his neck. "No, that's pretty much over."

"Sucked you dry, huh?"

He threw her a quick smile. "Be glad you're not a guy, Carol. This conversation would be taking a whole different turn." Mike turned up the air conditioner one more notch. "Linda's been seeing another guy at work. Some marketing dweeb."

"Hey, I resent that remark. I'd rather be a marketing dweeb than a geek."

"You are a marketing dweeb."

"Marketing research professional. It is very important to understand what gets people to buy a product—packaging, pricing, advertising. It could be any of a number—oh, no you don't."

"Don't what?"

"Spill it, Mike. Is your heart broken? Are you pining away? Going to go alone to your party and moon over the Queen of Darkness?"

"I'm not taking anybody to the party." Mike scanned through the radio stations, finally settling on a Bruce Springsteen classic. "It's this Tuesday night. Why don't you come with me?"

"Me?" she croaked and began to cough uncontrollably.

"Should I pull over? I didn't mean to get you all choked up." Mike waited until her coughing spasm subsided. "Why couldn't you go? The guys at work have never met you. Could be fun."

He knew. The evil man had sensed her dip in the whirlpool of desire and wanted to take further advantage. She would call his bluff.

Carol met his eyes, trying for a sexy, vixenish style. "You asking me out on a date, big boy?" She stretched, laying an arm across the top of his seat and flicked the soft, brown waves that brushed the nape of his neck. Her fingers tickled, daring her to bury them in his hair. She flexed her hand, barely managing to conquer the urge.

"A date? You mean a real, honest-to-goodness, man-woman date? And who do you think your mother would shoot first, me or you?" The muscles in his neck tensed under her touch, but his voice seemed perfectly calm.

She searched his gaze, looking for answers. But the brown, grinning eyes held no answers, not even a clue. "Nah. Just joking."

He wiped the back of his hand over his brow. "Whew. I think I could take Brock, but your mother? That woman scares me. Just friends, kiddo. Strictly buds. You want to go?"

Carol moved her arm, folded her hands in her lap, and studied the short, stubbles of her fingernails. "I don't know. Might have to wash my hair that night."

"Very funny. Come on, Carol. Be a pal."

Somehow she was going to regret this, but she had always been a sucker for Mike. When they were in junior high, she had covered for him when he put the firecrackers in the music room pianos. Did she ever get a thanks? Nope. Just a cheeky wink as if he knew he could count on her. Finally, she nodded her head. "Sure."

He winked. "It's black-tie. Your kind of shindig. Be sure to wear something nice. I, however, might need advice in the wardrobe department."

"Try shoes. With pants. It's a 90s thing."

"Paint-on latex, that's a 90s thing. But that's not

black-tie.'' He stroked his chin in a meditative manner. ''You know, you might want to try it. Women can get away with so much more.''

How to be serious with the joker? She didn't have the energy.

It would take more than a tight pair of Levi's to deviate her from her ideal man. And more than a contagious grin, even more than silky brown hair.

Darn.

What mischievous twist of fate had descended over Dallas today? It was almost Christmas. Didn't that count for anything anymore? Brock, Brock, Brock. That's what she wanted under her Christmas tree.

She thumbed through the calendar in her planner and noted the time of the month. It could be hormones. She was four years from thirty. Women reach their sexual peak near thirty. Maybe it had nothing to do with Mike, maybe she was just peaking early. She pulled a pen from her purse and made a quick notation on the square containing today's date.

Peaking.

2

On the second day of Christmas, my best friend gave to me—two primates peaking.

"THANKS FOR GETTING here so fast, my boy."

Mike saw her face light up as he entered the room. "Came as soon as I got your message. What's up, Eleanor, need someone to beat off all the old men? By the way, you didn't tell me what you wanted for Christmas yesterday. I'm not going to forget again today."

He collapsed into the chair, squinting as the late afternoon sun poked through the plastic blinds. The surroundings were nice, comfortable, but Eleanor didn't get out all that often and he tried to visit as often as he could. His paper route hadn't covered the vintage Mustang he wanted when he was sixteen, but Aunt Eleanor had. What a shark. He loved her ever since, just couldn't help it. If he were forty years older, he'd be chasing her himself.

Eleanor pulled out her hand lotion and began rubbing the cream over her wrinkled hands. The scent of raspberries obliterated the antiseptic smell in her room. She put the bottle of lotion away, then turned and smiled.

"They let you take a break from those gizmos you draw?"

Surprised, he looked at her carefully. "It's Sunday. I didn't work today."

She covered her eyes with her hands. "I just lose track of time. It's awful. Tell me again what you do?"

Mike wasn't fooled at all. "It's a chip manufacturer, Eleanor. Computer chips."

"Computer chips, cow chips, it's all the same to me. At least you make yourself a good living."

"Good enough to put you in diamonds and minks."

"Stock options? That's nothing more than legalized gambling."

Mike had seen Eleanor watch *Wall Street Week* enough to see through the old fraud. "Up forty-seven percent for the year."

She winked. "I bought their stock when you joined the company. You haven't let me down yet."

He couldn't help but smile. "So what do you want for Christmas, Eleanor? You're dodging the issue."

"Surprise me, my boy. Like surprises. But that's not what I wanted to talk to you about. I know you're a busy man, and it touches my heart that you have time to visit a lonely old lady like me. I just wanted to sit and chat. Catch up on how your family is doing."

Mike leaned forward, as his internal radar was flashing a warning. Eleanor wasn't one for chitchat. She was a cut-to-the-chase kind of dame. "Sure."

Eleanor stared out the window at the trees that had

long since lost their leaves. "You know, I'm not getting any younger. Time just flies when you get to be my age." She turned back toward him, and reached over to pat his knee. Her hand was shaking. "Don't you realize sometimes things are catching up with you, Mike? How old are you now, boy?"

"Twenty-six."

"And you haven't found someone to settle down with yet?"

Ah, there it was. She wanted to set him up with someone. Must be a grandniece of somebody from her wing, or the daughter of one of the nurses. "Not yet. I thought I had, but things didn't work out."

"Oh, who was that?"

"Just a girl from work. Nobody special." Thoughts of the three months he had dated Linda crept into his mind. He had been so sure she was the one, but their nights together had all the passion of a station wagon fresh off the Detroit assembly line.

"Doesn't sound like there was any sparking going on in that relationship."

"No, the sparks were definitely missing." The only thing left from that relationship was a bruised ego and a closet full of turtlenecks. He rubbed his neck, remembering Linda's more vampirish tendencies.

Eleanor patted her hair, a smug smile curving her mouth. "You know, I've found myself a boyfriend here. Thinking about getting married again."

"You? That's great."

"Yup, he's a keeper. Fred Waring, spelled just like the blender. Got to tell you, I wouldn't have given him the time of day a few months ago, but then God sent a miracle."

"Oh?"

"Pills. Magic pills. The man turns from a gelding into a stallion with the help of medical science. I even bought stock in that company. Never seen anything like it. Guess if scientists can send a man to the moon in my lifetime, they can figure out a way for us women to get up there, too. Figuratively speaking." Eleanor fanned herself with the newspaper. "Gets me flushed just thinking about it."

She fixed Mike with a pointed stare. "You need a girl that can raise your temperature. Someone with substance, spunk. Like my Fred. Know anybody like that?"

"Spunk and substance? Uh, no."

"Sure you do! Think harder, my boy. I'm sure you'll find somebody right under your nose. I gave this same lecture to Carol yesterday. Taking up with men named Rock! Silliest thing I ever heard. She's been spending too much time at the marketing firm where she works."

"I think it's Brock, not Rock, Eleanor."

"Brock, Rock, who cares anyway? Carol needs to find somebody better than that stiff-necked pretty-boy. I worry about my favorite grandniece. She needs someone special." She spotted her reading glasses and reached for them. After a few moments of fiddling with the black cord that held them in place, she speared him with an owlish stare. "Got any friends to fix her up with?"

"I don't think Carol wants to go out on a blind date with any of my friends. She's a breed apart from most of the guys I know."

"What do you mean by that?"

"She's got this thing about image—"

"Got that from her mother, bless her heart. Meredith spends more time with her head in the clouds. But she's got a good heart, and she does love my nephew, so I guess that makes up for it." She waved a hand. "I'm rambling. Tell me more about Carol's image problem."

"It's not an image problem. She just likes her men to have certain, uh, qualities."

"Like?"

"Class. A schmoozer."

Eleanor nodded. "Oh. Those." She examined him over the rim of her glasses. "But that's not what she needs. What kind of man do you think she needs, Mike?"

He shrugged absently. "I don't know. Haven't thought too much about Carol's love life." At least, since that one flash yesterday. Carol's mother had made her opinion of him abundantly clear, and Carol had always let her mother run over her. Mike certainly wasn't about to intervene. "Somebody that knows wine, likes culture. Stuff like that."

Eleanor snorted. "Wines. What good does that do anybody? She needs to find someone with a big heart, someone that will appreciate that strange sense of humor she has. Someone to take charge."

"I don't think Carol really wants someone to take charge of her life. She's done okay by herself."

"Well of course she has. She's a Martin. But I tell you, every now and then a woman needs a man to make his presence known. That Rock, he's not the man for her. Nope, not at all."

Eleanor picked up her hand lotion and rubbed some cream into her palms. "Love this stuff. Takes those liver spots right out. You ever had those kind of thoughts about Carol?"

Oh, no.

Mike gulped and stalled to put his brain back in gear. "Liver spots? I don't think she has any." Please, please, don't go there. The forbidden zone.

"Sex! Birds and the bees. Adam and Eve. Husker-doo. Thought about sleeping with her, my boy?"

Mike choked, and looked around desperately for an escape. Sleeping with Carol? His brain started working furiously—listing all the reasons he would not have such ideas about her.

They had known each other too long. People who know each other for more than one decade should not become romantically involved.

Carol could flush a man right out of her life when they were done dating. If—no, when—things didn't work out, he would have lost his best friend.

He wasn't attracted to Carol. She was cute, perky, just like a sister to him.

And the most important thing. Her mother would track

him down and shoot him like the stray dog she thought he was.

Murder, blood, death. Three very important reasons not to have those thoughts.

Sleeping with Carol? He'd have to be an idiot and if there was one thing Mike wasn't, it was an idiot.

Aunt Eleanor jerked him back to reality. "You're getting flushed, my boy." She laughed, rubbing her hands together. "I can see ideas running through your head right now."

Mike swallowed four times before replying, "No ideas, Eleanor. None at all."

He didn't want to think of ideas. He didn't want to think of smooth skin, soft hair, inviting eyes. But there they were, popping into his head with megawatt clarity. Ten million detailed images ran through his mind like Saturday night on the Playboy Channel. Damn.

A misguided fantasy began to take root in places it had no business being, and he stood up to leave. Having a testosterone moment over a girl he had known since second grade was not the smartest thing he'd ever done.

"Looks like you swallowed a watermelon, boy. Think about what I said. Aren't many men I think deserve my Carol." She fixed him with that glare he was quickly learning to recognize. "But I can see the two of you together."

Mike tried one last time. "Eleanor, I don't think about Carol that way. I've known her forever. She's just a friend."

"Bull-honky! You remember every time you saw her buck-naked. That's not friendship, you're getting humpy." She pulled her glasses off, and let them dangle around her neck. She leaned in closer. "Think what that sixteenth time will be like. Sparks, boy. Definitely, sparks."

THAT SAME EVENING Carol delicately sipped her California Merlot and curled up on her couch to watch the mating habits of the silver-backed gorillas on PBS. *Wine Connoisseur* magazine had given the Merlot its Best Red of the Year award and Carol was determined to speak fluent Wine-ese. The diet cola chaser stood nearby because the appeal for Merlot had always escaped her. But Brock seemed to enjoy it.

The antique Louis XVI clock said five to midnight, she now knew everything she needed to know about gorilla reproduction, and all she felt was horny. Pitiful. Even jungle primates were getting luckier than she was.

She eyed the telephone, knowing she could call Brock. Their relationship hadn't progressed to that next important step—sex—but he was a guy. One late-night phone call and they'd be rocketing to the next plateau. But she didn't want that plateau.

Not with Brock.

She punched her Ethan Allen sofa cushion without a twinge of guilt. This was all Mike's fault. Overnight, well, really during the last twenty years, he'd morphed from Goofball Mike into Sexy Mike.

But, Mike wouldn't know Merlot from cream soda. She wasn't sure if he owned a tie. And he wouldn't be caught dead watching PBS. No-siree, Mike didn't have any of the qualities she wanted in a man.

So why these sudden images of Mike with no shirt, Mike with an invitation in his eyes, Mike in the shower…

Aaaaggghhhhh!!!

The phone rang and she rushed over to answer it, praying to hear Brock's deep, dulcet voice.

"Hello?"

"Carol?" She was having a dream, a bad dream. An underused libido had conjured up Mike on the phone and now she was losing her sanity. His voice did sound a little wooly though. Must have been asleep before he called.

"Mike? You okay?"

"Fine, peachy, no problems here." He paused. "Do I sound different?"

"A little fuzzy."

"Damn. I've been thinking…. Never mind."

"You're acting really weird, you know that?"

"I'm not surprised. Anyway, I wanted to talk to you about the Christmas party."

Of all the nerve. He couldn't do this to her. "You're wimping out on me, aren't you? I knew it, I just knew it. God forbid that you would want to help me with something as mundane as organizing a Christmas pageant for a nursing home. I can't count on—"

"Carol, be quiet for a minute. I'm fine with Eleanor's

party. More than fine. I'm talking about the other Christmas party. The one at work. I've got a favor to ask."

"Like?"

"I was wondering if you could do a little acting. You were right about Linda."

"You're still pining for her, aren't you?"

"You could say that. I just don't think I'm ready to face her alone. Well, not technically alone, but seeing her going out with Jerry."

"Is Jerry the marketing dweeb?"

"Yeah."

"So what kind of acting are you envisioning here?"

"Pretending to be my date. A real date. I hate to ask, but…"

He sounded so miserable, she was tempted to just go hike across the stairwell and see what was wrong. Two exceptionally friendly gorillas filled the television screen and she thought better of it. "Of course I'll do it." Her heart started to melt a little. She could be mature about this. It might be a little awkward, but she could control her hormonal imbalance.

A real date. With Mike. Holding her close, looking deep into her eyes, pressing his body next to hers. And all the time the rat would be aching for Linda, the Hoover Professional upright model. The grunting sounds of primates in love broke the quiet of the room.

She was turning into a basket case. Peaking. Had to be.

"Thanks, Carol. You don't know what this means to

me." The phone went silent and Carol stared at the receiver in her hand.

The male gorilla picked a tick off the female gorilla, nuzzling her fur and Carol reached for her box of tissue as she felt the moisture welling at the corner of her eye.

You'd never see that kind of true love in the movies.

MIKE HUNG UP THE phone and fell back against the pillows. Stupid. He should've just told her the truth. Carol, I suddenly find myself lusting after your body. I wouldn't have Linda if she showed up naked at my door. Now, if you showed up naked, well…

Oh, yeah, that sounded good. Carol would leap into his arms and they'd live happily ever after. Right. If he even stood a chance with her. He was about a three on her Chic-Chic-O-Matic scale.

Even if the moon was aligned correctly, and the sparks were there, they'd have sex and then regret it for the rest of their lives. Awkward, embarrassing, and worst of all, what if they had bad sex? A perfectly good friendship shot down the tubes. Forever. Hang-'Em-High-And-Dry Martin could eradicate men faster than Dirty Harry. Another trait she had inherited from her mother. She'd dated every single, solitary, privileged frat boy in college. Four dates, every time. Just four. He could have set a clock by her dating record.

Maybe he was just getting a little crazy. Maybe the breakup with Linda had affected him more than he thought.

Maybe, maybe, maybe.

Nope, nope, nope.

Who was he kidding?

He wasn't the kind of man to fit into the Martin's lifestyle. A guy needed to pass the "Does Your Man Have Class And Cash?" quiz to go out with Carol. Wine, suits, hot car. Guys named Brock.

Mike didn't drink wine, except out of a paper box at parties. And then only when the beer ran out. He did have one suit, and a couple of pairs of khakis for when he had a presentation with upper management. And ten pairs of Levi's.

As for his car, well, his car was pretty hot. Even Carol liked his restored Thunderbird. But one day she'd wake up and realize she needed more from Mike than a souped-up 429 engine. He would have to wear a tie that cut off his circulation and take her to cultural events. Hell. He wouldn't last two weeks.

And then the inevitable breakup. Every reminder of Mike pitched from her apartment in some primitive female ejection ritual.

He sighed, knowing he'd be headed for Heartbreak City. No, he would keep his baser urgings a secret. The party would be a test. A scientific experiment. Aunt Eleanor was wrong, and he could prove it. What looked like lust was only stress, a little emotional instability. Carol would never know a thing.

He settled back in his bed and started flipping through

the channels. He settled on a gorilla documentary and went to sleep dreaming of swinging through the jungle trees in a loincloth, with Carol splashing naked in a nearby lagoon.

3

On the third day of Christmas, my mother gave to me—
three migraine headaches.

CREATIVE MEDIA WAS a good job, as far as jobs went.
Carol knew she was never going to take over the world,
but as she looked at the smirking faces around the conference table, she thought, did she really want to? She
took a sip of diet cola and shook her head. Nah, leave
that world-taking-over thing to gals named Helen of Troy
and Joan of Arc. Who ever heard of Carol of Martin
conquering the world?

She pulled out her notes for the meeting and glanced
over the numbers, just as her boss, Matilda Reinhart,
strode in. Matilda believed red was a power color, and
had seventeen suits in varying shades of scarlet in addition to the one set of crimson-rimmed glasses that she
wore everyday. Today she'd added a jingle bells pin to
her lapel, trying to get a little of that Christmas spirit—
it was in short supply within the hallowed walls of Creative Media.

"Okay, team. All your proverbial butts are on the line

this time. Ten days before Christmas and we need to have a straw man for the campaign done before anybody goes anywhere for vacation.'' Matilda's voice held the nicotine-induced rasp that came from too much time in the smoking lounge.

This is our chance. The proverbial brass ring. Yada, yada, yada. Carol had heard the words so many times, she knew them by heart.

Matilda grabbed a marker from the whiteboard and began to write as she talked. ''This is our chance. The proverbial brass ring...''

Everyone looked as excited as Carol felt. Early morning meetings made for a tough crowd. ''Team'' seemed like such an optimistic word to describe their group. Willard was a two-faced weasel and Harold was his evil twin. Barbara was the number cruncher, and Courtney and Lyle worked for the art department. Carol was the support person. Statistics, projections, charts. That's what she did best. All in all, these folks were a real fun bunch.

Carol reached for a doughnut, remembered Brock's crack about her thighs, and ate it anyway.

''...Stoneware Blue Jeans. Something zippy. Okay, what do you have for me today?'' Matilda looked around the room.

Silence.

Carol shuffled her papers, avoiding Matilda's eagle-eyed gaze. Big mistake.

''Carol?''

Darn. She was the support person; they weren't supposed to call on her. She dabbed at the chocolate remains on her mouth and swallowed. "Well, the target market is men, although statistically men seem to defer the buying habits of most clothing to women. Also, over the past six years, apparel has undergone a market transformation. It's much more unisex. I don't think that's where Stoneware is going, though, judging by the market breakdown. Most of their customers are over thirty and very much into the he-man theme. I think we should focus the campaign on a man's appeal to women. Men see jeans as a utilitarian item, whereas women see them as…" she trailed off for a moment, thinking of Mike, "…art."

Matilda scribbled the word "art" on the board. "Willard? What do you think?"

"I don't know. I think Carol may be right. We could target the campaign toward women, or alternatively, we might want to consider targeting it toward something new, ground-breaking, maybe men?"

"Ground-breaking" was Matilda's favorite word, guaranteed to elicit immeasurable praise. "Brilliant!" Matilda pounded the table.

Carol stared at her watch. Eight hours and forty-five minutes to freedom. One of these days she was going to break out of this joint. Break out and go shopping. She had a dress to buy and a Christmas party to go to. What kind of dress, though? Mike had said to wear something nice. Nice. What a mild-mannered word. She'd show him *nice*. He'd never seen her sexy. Even at their prom, she'd worn some lacy, frilly Victorian thing that her mom had picked out. All the other girls had been strapless and backless. But no, not Carol. Mike probably didn't even think she could do sexy.

Matilda went over to the whiteboard. "What would appeal to a man?"

Carol's thoughts drifted to her own malnourished wardrobe. "Definitely, sexy." Lots of skin.

"Well, that's a big duh," Harold chimed in.

Carol handed him a napkin and pointed to his upper lip. She took fiendish pleasure in having him dab at an imaginary speck of powdered sugar in his moustache. When he finished and mouthed a silent thanks, she wiggled her nose.

Matilda leapt to Carol's defense. "No, Carol's right to get it out there on the table. Sex is always good. So what is sexy? Power?"

"Money," answered Barbara, chewing on her pencil.

"Naked women." Willard grinned.

Many snickers followed and Matilda tried to look stern. "Willard, do you want to hear the sexual harassment lecture, *again?*"

The ultimate punishment. Willard knew he was whipped. He shrank in his seat.

"Okay, what is sexy? One word." Matilda began to write on the board.

"Muscles." Courtney sighed.

Carol thought of sexy. Thought of Brock in blue jeans. Erased that thought. Thought of Mike in blue jeans. Yeah, that worked better. "Unkempt."

Matilda turned around and raised her glasses. "Unkempt?"

She smoothed her skirt. "You know. Messy."

Heads turned, eyes goggled, and Carol made notes for her shopping list in her planner, trying to maintain a calm, professional facade.

"Messy." Matilda thought it over for a minute and smiled. "I like that. What else?"

"Worldly." That from Lyle. Who knew?

Carol went back to her list while the others continued. Black. Sophisticated. She laughed, an evil laugh. Sexy. Her hormones cheered. Yeah, Mike was going to remember tomorrow night for a long time to come.

THE MALL WAS decorated in its god-awful Christmas best, a kid's choir singing an off-key version of "Deck the Halls." Somewhere in the distance a baby howled. And then another. And soon they had all joined in, doing a good imitation of the fa-la-la's.

Nothing like Christmas in Dallas.

Carol had thought it'd be fun to go shopping with her mother. Of course that meant donning the Martin women's uniform of heels, hose and pearls, and as they trudged through the crowds, she was beginning to wilt. Her mother, immaculate in green silk, showed absolutely no sign of discomfort or wrinkles. Carol shook her head. Meredith Martin had tons of friends, thousands more than Carol could ever dream about having. A heavy sigh escaped her. She was never going to measure up, and one of these days she was going to stop trying.

"Hon, stop chewing on your nails. I should make an appointment for us to see the manicurist. The holidays are just so busy, though. You have such elegant hands. You need to take better care of them."

Carol pulled her finger out of her mouth and stared at the offensive digit.

"Sorry."

"What did you say you needed this dress for?" Her mother waved politely at a few Junior Leaguers on the other side of the walkway.

"A Christmas party."

"Brock's?"

"No, uh, Mike's."

Carol's mom fingered her pearl-drop earrings, a frown forming feather lines in her Pink Mist lipstick. "Why on earth are you going to Mike's Christmas party?"

"I'm just doing him a favor." Carol stopped in front of a window display at a shoe store. Tennis shoes would be nice about now. Her feet were killing her.

"Is this a date?" Her mom sounded appalled.

"No. Don't panic. And no need for the whole Mike and hell freezing over speech." She adjusted the load of packages in her arms.

"Maybe we should go get some coffee."

"No, I just need to find my dress and then head back home." Carol wasn't up to enduring caffeine-induced diatribes.

"He seems to be such a hooligan when compared to Brock."

"Yes, Mother. I know, Mother." Meredith seemed to overlook the fact that her daughter was a hooligan, too.

They walked in silence to the department store, and Carol ditched her mom in the Designer Women's Wear section. She wandered to the sale racks looking for a dress. She opened her planner, looking at her list of attributes, and checked it twice. *Nice.* That was a low blow. She marched through the aisles, determined to show Mike exactly what nice could mean.

The teenage salesgirl looked up from the cash register and then returned to doing her nails, Frosty the Snowman hanging cock-eyed over her head.

And then Carol saw it.

The Perfect Black Dress.

Classic, tailored, and a neckline down to there. Daring, yet understated. Carol studied her cleavage potential under her Ann Taylor button-down. Maybe a 7.0. She could hit 8.5 with the right combination of lift and separate. The dress beckoned, calling her name.

Conditioned by years of mall experience, she drifted over.

She ran a hand over the fabric, letting the soft, silky material run through her fingers. Delicious. Now for the moment of truth. She felt for the price tag.

And then the salesgirl, her name tag read Kirsten, decided to make her move. Ah, a commission-based system.

Kirsten popped her gum and leaned an arm over the rack. "So, ya looking for a party dress? Something special?"

"Yeah. For an office party. But a nice office party."

Kirsten raised her brows. "Lady, this is wasted on a bunch of office-schmos. This dress—well, this is a man's-man kind of dress. Unless, maybe you're looking for a piece of the action. This is definitely above and beyond Dress for Success. This is If-You're-Lucky-I-Might-Let-You-Think-About-Touching-My—"

Carol held up a hand to interrupt, not wanting to hear this from a girl who was nine years her junior. Kids. They were getting older every day. No, it was just Carol getting older every day. Turning into an old hooligan. Pitiful. "I like the dress. Let me try it on."

"You got a date for this thing, or are you going to," Kirsten wiggled her brows, "mingle?"

Carol thought of Mike. A date? Nope, he had nuked that idea right in the bud. "Neither."

Still, she would look good, sexy. About as far away from nice as she could get. It might not be a date, but it wouldn't hurt to make him sweat some. And it would do wonders for her ego.

She lifted the dress off the rack and went to try it on. "Hon? Are you in here?"

"Yeah. I'm in the last room on the right."

As she looked at the almost-sex-goddess in the mirror, she smiled. That was her, the one with the short blond curls, the wide blue eyes. She spun around, liking the swishy feel of the material against her legs. She stood up straight and poked out her chest. Definite help needed there, but with the right equipment, she would fill out nicely.

Ah, Christmas. She was beginning to catch a little holiday spirit. Mike was going to be in serious, serious trouble.

"Carol, why don't you come out and let me see?"

Her mother brought her crashing back to reality. Good old Mom. This was just a fluke, a passing whim. The kind of attitude that would lead to trouble. Mike was like a brother to her and Texas laws frowned on those kinds of relationships.

But the little devil sitting on her shoulder wouldn't quit. "He's not a brother to you. No blood relationship, not even fourteenth cousins. No reason in the world you couldn't dip your little toe in the water. You've always wanted to know, haven't you?"

Carol walked out of the dressing room and her mother stared.

"It's very pretty, but maybe it's a little too—trampy?" She held up a designer number in fuchsia. "What about this one?"

If her mother wanted to ensure that Mike didn't touch her at all, that dress would be the thing to do it.

Carol felt a wicked thrill course through her at the thought of Mike's touch. She flipped the price tag on the fuchsia nightmare. "Sorry, Mom, can't afford it. Trampy it is."

4

On the fourth day of Christmas, my best girl, uh, friend gave to me—four extra inches.

CAROL SPENT THREE hours getting ready for Mike's Christmas party. Now she had showered, bubbled, loofahed, waxed and gooped herself all over. Not one inch of her wasn't silky smooth and smelling of wild raspberries. She took The Dress out of the closet and pulled it over her head.

She pouted in the mirror as she applied the shiny, red lipstick. "Hello, Michael. I've been looking forward to tonight." Nah. She held up a single hand like an old Indian greeting. "Hi ya, bud. Long time no see. Ready to paint the town red?" Ugh.

The garter belt holding up her hose scratched against her thigh, and she adjusted it, trying to get used to the feel of it. There was no way he was going to see *that*, but just in case she was prepared. Besides, she had read in *Cosmo* that women had more confidence when they wore fancy underwear. With underwear like this, she should be able to buy and sell every guy in the joint.

She shook her head. No way. This was silly. She un-hooked the single button at her neck and pulled the halter dress down to her waist. She'd just find her interview suit.

The sound of the front door opening interrupted her indecision. "Hey, Carol, you ready to go?"

Oh, God. "Uh, I'll be right out." Show time. Her stomach was whirling like the teacup ride at Disney World and she pulled her dress back up, her fingers fumbling with the button.

"Hurry up, will you? I've got the car running down-stairs. It looks like it might rain. You got an umbrella here?"

That sounded like the Mike she knew and she felt a little better.

"Yeah, there's some in the stand behind the door. Just take one."

"Let's see. Picasso, Georgia O'Keeffe, Monet. Don't you just have a plain black one? I'd even settle for stripes."

She looked back at herself in the mirror and smiled. Suddenly, the night didn't seem so forbidding. The Dress was completely wasted on him. She practiced breathing and stood up straight. Mike wouldn't notice a thing.

The black heels were just the right finishing touch, and she spritzed a little more perfume between her breasts.

Perfect.

She opened the door to the living room and the world started to spin right along with her stomach.

This couldn't be Mike. Dressed in a black tux, his hair no longer waving in a haphazard manner, no faded Levi's. Sophisticated, worldly. Oh, God. Handsome. Goose bumps appeared out of nowhere, and there went her stomach again. She put a hand to her belly to keep it in place.

It took a moment for her mouth to work, her brain to function, and her heart to stop thumping like a scared rabbit. Even then she wasn't actually coherent. "Hell-How-Yeah."

Friends, they were just friends. She repeated the word over in her head like a Gregorian chant and pasted a smile on her face.

He looked at her and smiled back. A little crooked. At least that looked right.

"You look good."

She gulped. "Thanks."

"If you're ready, we should leave."

"Yes."

If he noticed she was acting like an idiot, he hid it well. She followed him out the door, would have followed him anywhere. Her eyes trailed over the broad lines of his shoulders under the black jacket and she wiped the corner of her mouth. The last thing she needed was for him to notice she was drooling.

MIKE PUNCHED THE up button in the lobby of the downtown bank building and stared at the lights above the bank of elevators. Anywhere but at Carol.

She had breasts. She'd never had breasts before. Why tonight? This was a test, only a test. And there she stood, smiling, humming, totally clueless she was blowing the curve.

Lovely.

With breasts.

The ding of the elevator startled him and he put a hand to her back to get her inside. He jerked away as he touched the warm, bare, silky flesh. Geez, no front, no back, she might as well be naked.

The entire board of directors from somewhere trotted in after them, laden with Christmas presents and bottles of wine. The old man next to him was wearing reindeer antlers and a ruddy, one-hundred-and-one-proof nose. Great, everybody in Dallas was in the elevator, and he was trapped.

Carol stood pressed against him and he bit back a groan. Just as the doors were closing, they opened again and more people filed inside, until they all stood there, packed like sardines with a red-and-green bow. Ho-Ho-Ho.

Fifty-one floors. Fifty-one floors of hell. The curves of her rear jostled between his legs and when she finally stopped the torture treatment, he was hard as a California redwood.

Maybe she wouldn't notice. Like how he didn't notice she was wearing a garter belt underneath that dress. Hell.

She looked back, calm as you please, her voice completely normal. "Uh, Mike. Can you move the umbrella, please? Just to the side, it's poking me."

The old man with the reindeer antlers moved a little before looking down and gave him a conspiratorial wink. Mike moved the other way, anything to escape that luscious rear. For two floors they were fine, but on seventeen the doors opened, and a stockbroker with a fruitcake the size of Rhode Island stepped into the elevator.

Carol moved back to where she was before. He started to sweat and prayed she would keep her mouth shut.

He should've known better. This was Carol, after all.

"Mike. You're doing it again. Fix it, please."

Mike felt his cheeks go hot and Rudolf started to snicker. There was nowhere to go.

"Shut up, Carol."

"Mike! You don't need to be rude."

He gritted his teeth and whispered against her ear, "Leave it alone, Carol. I can't do anything about it right now. Okay?" Raspberries. Ah, man, she smelled like raspberries.

She huffed and that perky little butt rubbed against him. At the fortieth floor, the Santa Claus convention departed, but not before the old man patted him on the back, his antlers bobbing. "Have a nice evening, son."

Mike scuttled to the farthest corner of the elevator. As far away from Carol as he could. When they finally reached the fifty-first floor, he felt as if he had just climbed Mount Everest. But the night was still young.

He followed her out of the elevator and as soon as

they were alone, Carol rounded on him, parts of her jiggling that had never jiggled before. Of course she wouldn't let it go.

"Mike, what is wrong with you? All I wanted was for you to move the stupid umbrella. But, *noooo*. You couldn't do that." She glanced down and for the first time noticed he wasn't holding an umbrella. Nope, the little hussy didn't miss a thing. Her cheeks grew amazingly pink and her mouth formed a little "o."

This was not how he had imagined this moment.

"Mike?" He heard wonder, amazement, and yeah, a little fear in her voice.

"Don't jump to conclusions. There's a logical explanation for this."

Those blue eyes of hers searched his, and he could almost hear the gears whirring in her brain. No way he was going to let her have this kind of advantage over him. Not yet. His experiment had barely started.

She didn't smile, and thankfully, she didn't laugh either. Her blue eyes were wide and staring at him as if he was some sort of laboratory rat. "What is it?"

The husky tickle in her voice was probably shock. He clenched his fists, feeling the sweat start to trickle under his jacket. Somebody had cranked up the heat.

The heavy bass beat of the music filtered in from the ballroom. He could face her, tell her she was turning him into a sex-crazed zombie. And what if she laughed? Or worse, what if she launched into a "you're a really nice guy, but…" speech?

It was too soon. He needed to say something, but what?

He found his voice, and fixed his gaze on the chandeliers above them. "It's my medication."

"Medication?"

"Yeah, it has some side effects."

"Medication for what?"

"Allergies."

"What are you allergic to Mike?"

You. I'm allergic to you in black dresses with no front, and you in a garter belt, and you naked, smooth and silky, and smelling of raspberries. "Dogs. Just up and developed an allergy to dogs. They have a new medicine they're testing, but it makes men kind of—sensitive. Don't take it personally, kid. I think Queen Elizabeth could have been in that elevator, and I would've reacted." He shrugged casually and risked a quick look in her direction.

Was that disappointment in her eyes? As soon as it appeared, it was gone and she laughed. Just like the old days.

"You know, I bet a lot of guys would pay money for a drug like that. I could think of all sorts of marketing campaigns."

He closed his eyes for a moment, opening them again, trying desperately not to look at her cleavage. "Yeah, I bet you could. Let's go inside. I need some water."

CAROL WATCHED THE dance floor and giggled. Marketing dweebs would never be able to party like computer geeks.

Rock and roll blared on the loudspeakers and a comedian from L.A. had been flown in to roast the CEO. Except for the bow tie that he tugged at every few minutes, Mike was in his element.

He introduced her to Tom and his wife, a pregnant redhead who looked ready to go into labor at any moment. Tom pumped her hand several times. "I've heard a lot about you, Carol. It's great to finally meet you. You work in marketing?"

"Yeah, I do research, surveys for laundry detergents, that kind of stuff."

Tom's wife patted Carol on the arm and measured her up for Mike-Wife prospect material. "I've got an idea. Maybe the two of you could come over for dinner some night?"

Mike coughed roughly and spoke before Carol had a chance. "We'll see. Carol, come on, you look like you need a drink."

Mike steered her toward the bar and went to retrieve some beverages. She took advantage of his absence to scan the crowd, looking for the woman she knew only as Linda. The one who had captured his interest longer than any other female ever had. Three months. For Mike, that was a lifetime.

In high school, he'd had one girlfriend their sophomore year. Amber Dyson. She'd been a cheerleader. Carol, who was not a cheerleader, hated her. The feeling had been mutual.

In college, he'd barely dated at all, but then, in college he had never had time for anything but school and work.

And then came Linda.

There'd been a ritual Carol and Mike had practiced during the Linda era. Every Saturday night he would go out with Linda, and every Sunday morning he and Carol went out for breakfast. One hot August morning Mike had shown up dressed in a turtleneck. She never brought it up, but he made some comment about the restaurant being too cold. Right, like she didn't know what was going on.

He never spent the night with Linda, instead driving home at three in the morning, parking in the same spot underneath Carol's window. Whenever she had suffered from Saturday night insomnia, the purring sound of his car engine had lulled her back to sleep.

The rhythmical beat of a samba brought Carol back to the present and she found Mike coming toward her, holding a glass of wine and a beer. As he walked through the crowd, Carol noticed the female heads turning when he passed by. He smiled and winked at a few, even doing a couple of quick dance steps for one girl, never spilling a drop.

When had he turned into such a flirt? The easygoing smile, the lighthearted teasing, Carol always assumed he was only that way with her. A twinge of disappointment fell over her. It had nothing to do with her. That was only Mike.

She found her best social-occasion smile and plastered it on as he handed her the wine.

She took a sip. Not too bad. "How're you doing? Is *she* here?"

The grin he'd been sporting faded away and Carol hated herself for bringing it up. He motioned Carol closer just as the music turned soft and dreamy.

"She's over there, in front of the stage. The brunette."

"Where?" Carol thought about mentioning there were fourteen brunettes in the general direction he pointed, but then, the auditorium was packed with people and she didn't want to seem petty.

He took the glass out of her hand, and put them on an empty corner of a table. "Here, take my hand, okay? Do you mind if we dance?"

His brown eyes looked so earnest, so nervous, that she grabbed his hand expecting sweaty palms. Instead, his hand was dry, warm, and felt amazingly right.

He gathered her into his arms and held her close. They swayed back and forth, not really dancing as much as just shuffling their feet every now and then. Her head fit right underneath his shoulder, and the steady rhythm of his heartbeat thumped under her hand.

It should've been strange to be in this situation with Mike, but nothing felt strange at all. He sighed heavily and she remembered why she was there.

"Are you okay?"

"Heaven, uh, yeah, uh, Carol?"

"Mmm?"

"Thanks for doing this. You're a trooper, did you know that?"

A trooper. She was getting about as mushy as a greeting card and he calls her a trooper.

"Mike?"

"Hmm?"

"Be quiet. I used to like this song."

"Sure."

She buried her face into his neck, closing her eyes and trying to forget who she was dancing with. He was wearing some heady cologne and it took all her willpower not to brush her nose against him like a kitten on the trail of catnip. Aw, what would a little neck rubbing hurt? "Is she watching?"

"Who?"

"Linda."

"Yeah, like a hawk."

"Okay, you're going to owe me big for tonight, Michael Fitzgerald." That sounded good. Like she really meant it. She rubbed her cheek into his neck, and knew it wasn't the wine that was making her woozy. She started to nuzzle the warm skin beneath his ear.

"Oh, God." His tortured exclamation broke through the murky haze.

"Should I stop? Is this too much?" What if he guessed?

"No, no, that's great. Absolutely perfect. You don't know how good it makes me feel—to be able to show her up tonight."

She didn't give a flying fig whether Linda was watching. She didn't care if the whole U.S. of A. was watching. Right now nothing mattered except that dangerous cologne of his and the way his arms were holding her close. No wonder he ended up wearing turtlenecks.

"Carol, I know this is going to sound weird, but I'm going to kiss you, okay?"

Weird? She was getting all sticky and gooey and he thought a kiss would be weird?

"Just hurry up and get on with it, will you?" Her voice might have cracked a little, but the words were effective.

He stopped moving and planted one on her, right there in the middle of the dance floor. His mouth was wonderful, moving, nibbling, doing things that would bring back the dead. She groaned and wrapped her arms around his neck, determined to win him an award for this performance. Before she could control herself, her hips rubbed against him, liking the feel of his medical side effect pressing between her thighs.

His lips touched the side of her neck and she struggled to breathe, peeking between her lashes. He looked intent, his eyes closed, concentrating on her neck with a studious intensity. She tilted her head to give him further access. "Is it working?"

"Gawd, yes. Like a giant sequoia."

"What?"

"Never mind. She's still watching. Go with me on this."

His eyes were still closed, but she sure as hell wasn't

going to call him on it. Then his mouth returned to hers, his tongue demanding entrance, and her brain shorted out anyway.

She forgot her earlier intentions and let her tongue mingle with his, her hands moving lower down the hard length of his back, nestling themselves underneath his jacket. He moved his hands to cradle her face as if to keep her firmly in place. A nuclear blast couldn't have shifted her from this spot.

And when he had done his damage, when he had thrown all her good intentions out the window, when he changed forever the way she would think of Mike Fitzgerald, he lifted his head and gave her a heart-stopping smile.

"Thanks Carol. Excuse me for a minute, will you? I think I need a beer."

MIKE SKIPPED THE beer and went directly to the men's room. It took eight splashes of cold water to the face before Mike felt his body temperature cool to something below two hundred and twelve. He had created this test and now he was the one who was flunking. This couldn't be real.

Of course there was an explanation. There had to be, didn't there? He looked in the mirror, one answer staring him in the face. Carol, the friend who'd been through algebra, acne and Duran Duran with him, was becoming something more. Becoming? He was such a liar. How many times had he thought about tasting those luscious lips? How many times had he imagined that he should be the one to put the stars in her eyes? And how many times had he realized that her mother treated him like the underbelly of society.

The creak of the door interrupted any further arguments that he could have with himself. He looked up to see Daniel, the closest thing to a geek Casanova that the company had. Noting the smug smile that covered his friend's face, there was no doubt that some young lady was appreciating Daniel's greatest talent, his encyclopedic repertoire of come-on lines.

"So. That's Carol. No wonder you kept her hidden all this time. Mike, you've been holding out on us, dude."

Mike closed his eyes, wanting for Daniel to disappear in a puff of smoke. He opened them again, but his friend still stood there, waiting for an answer. And Mike wasn't about to give him one, because he didn't have one himself. "How are the ladies treating you tonight?"

"Not as well as your lady is treating you." Daniel grinned knowingly. "Geez, I thought we were going to have to turn on the sprinkler system."

Mike gave up pretending to be polite. "I'm not in the mood for this, Daniel. Not tonight."

"Sorry to offend, Mr. Sensitivity."

"No, I'm sorry. I'm not feeling very good."

"Too bad Linda's not here to see all the fireworks. Did you notice she and Jerry missed the entertainment?"

"I looked for her early on, but then I lost track."

Daniel snickered and turned to leave. "Yeah. I could see how well you were getting off…track. Well, I got a hot redhead from HR waiting for me. Wish me luck. And holler if there's anything I can do."

Mike waved halfheartedly as Daniel left. There was nothing anybody could do.

He hit the button on the dryer above the sink and pointed the blast of hot air toward his face. He couldn't hide in the bathroom all night. He had to return. To Carol.

This was ridiculous. She didn't deserve for him to turn into a jerk. She deserved better. He wouldn't touch her again. No matter how tempting it was. She was doing this as a favor. As a friend. But could she ever kiss, completely un-friendlike. What if…?

He shook his head and straightened out his hair with his fingers. No way, Fitzgerald. No matter what foolish ideas he'd had when he created this test, the fact remained that Carol wasn't interested in him *that way*. They were too different. She liked restaurants with white tablecloths, he liked restaurants that served you in a greasy, white paper bag. She bought her clothes at Saks, he bought his off the Internet.

No, she fantasized about lawyers and doctors and guys who hung out in three-piece suits. The all-important image that her mother had pounded into her brain. Not a computer geek who played Nintendo.

He wasn't willing to gamble their friendship on a what-if. Nope, from now on, he was only Mr. Friend.

CAROL COULD'VE HIT Mike. Really hard, too. She didn't care if he was going through a traumatic experience with his ex. That didn't excuse bad manners. Her mother was right, he was a hooligan, and she was going to give him a good piece of her mind when he came back.

She looked down at her watch. If he came back.

"Carol, sorry it took so long." She felt a hand brush against her back and she jumped, her head bumping against something hard.

She turned around. Ah, Mike's chin.

He grinned, giving her that I-know-you'll-forgive-anything look and she felt her lips curve in an answering smile. Weak, very weak.

"No problem."

"Want some food? There's some buffalo wings that look pretty good. Maybe mushrooms? It's not caviar and truffles, but it's the best we plebeian computer types can do."

"I don't know...."

"Come on. Linda's gone, the night is young. Be a pal."

Ah, yes. Linda. How easy it was to forget. Now she was gone and Carol had been relegated to pal status. Better to pack it in now and go home. Now that she had finally experienced her first taste of unbridled passion, she didn't think she could go back to bear hugs and sex jokes. "If there's no reason to stick around, do you think we could leave?"

Maybe disappointment flashed in his eyes, but most

likely her fantasies were starting to affect her version of reality. "Sure. Let's go."

The ride home was quiet, thankfully. Mike didn't say a word, and she didn't feel like trying to come up with mindless chitchat.

He held open the car door, and she slid out of the warm, leather interior into the chilly December night.

"Cold?"

"Maybe a little."

He shrugged out of his tux jacket and wrapped it around her shoulders.

"You should have worn a jacket over that dress. There's not much of it to cover you up."

"It's only sixty degrees out and I didn't think we'd be spending a lot of time outdoors." She looked up at the clear night sky. "At least it didn't rain."

"Yeah, you could've shot me before I would carry one of those artsy things with flowers on it. Now I know what to get you for Christmas. A plain, black umbrella."

She wanted to laugh at that, but that only made her start to tear up. Her crazy emotions must be causing all this weepy melodrama and such strange thoughts about Mike. She shrugged her shoulders, noticing how good his jacket felt on her. She'd never noticed his cologne before, but it was light and spicy. Subtle. If you didn't get close enough, you'd never know it was there.

Her wave good-night was a weak gesture, almost an afterthought, and she started up the stairs. He followed behind and her heart began to pound just a little. Maybe there was hope after all. She could invite him in, they could watch a movie, share a glass of Merlot, and maybe...

The keys to her apartment were magically where they belonged in her purse and she unlocked the door. He looked at her expectantly, and she moistened her lips.

A kiss? His eyes seemed so alive tonight, and she noticed green flecks shooting through them. His lashes were thicker than hers, the rat. She closed her eyes and leaned against the door, her pulse starting to race. He leaned in closer, pressing against her, and she ached for the taste of him, those firm lips brushing against her own.

His hands crept to her shoulders, slid underneath the jacket, and she fought back a gasp. His fingers were gentle, almost caressing, and a contented sigh escaped her.

His voice was warm against her ear and for a heart-stopping moment she felt his lips feather against her neck. "Hey, Carol?"

"Mmm?"

"I need my jacket back."

5

*On the fifth day of Christmas, my best friend gave to me—
five steamy dreams.*

"Hon, why don't you tell me about last night?"

Carol jerked out of her depressed stupor and glanced around the artfully decorated living room walls of her parents' home. Thank goodness her mother was in the kitchen.

How did she answer that question? Uh, yeah mom, had a great time. Discovered Mike, yes, the boy I've known almost all my life, made me hot. Yep, that's right. Hot. Steamy. Gooey. Sticky. And all I gave him was a medicinal woody.

Her mother would collapse on the spot.

She chewed on her nail. "It was okay. I need to get to work. It's nine o'clock and I'm already late. Just wanted to drop off this grant application."

"I hope it didn't take too much time. The Junior League appreciates all your help."

Yeah, right. Carol still believed in Santa Claus, too. "Anytime." She glanced at the kitchen door. "What are you doing in there?"

Meredith appeared, dressed in her Laura Ashley apron. "Making banana-nut bread. I have twenty loaves to make this year. Halfway done! Do you want to come over for dinner tonight?"

Carol's mom was the only woman in North America, not on Nickelodeon, who did her baking in a dress and heels. But how could you not love your mom, heels and all? "What're you having?"

"Veal picatta with asparagus tips. Your favorite."

Ugh. "Yum. Sorry, got to pass. I have to finish up a report for work."

"Have you bought something for Aunt Eleanor?"

"Some hand lotion and a new robe."

"Oh, she'll be so excited. She's losing her hearing, but still sharp as a tack."

Carol watched as her mom took off her apron and folded it neatly over the Chippendale chair before sitting down. "Now, tell me all about that Christmas Party. Did Mike behave? He didn't drink too much, or um, anything else, did he? He's so high-spirited."

"No, Mother. Don't worry. He was a perfect gentleman." Of all the nights, of all the years, why did he have to pick last night to be a gentleman? "There's nothing wrong with high-spirited."

"Well, no, not in a horse. But we like our men with substance, stability. Like Brock. He's such a nice, young man."

Carol fought back a yawn.

"Isn't it time you started to think about marriage and raising a family?"

"Men don't think permanency when they go out with me, Mom." Carol curled her feet up under her, and then noticed her mother staring with disapproval, eyebrows raised. Obediently, she put her feet back on the floor.

"Hon, don't sell yourself short. You're pretty and smart and look so nice when you take the time to fix yourself up. Now, don't be such a worrywart. In time you'll meet the right young man and settle down. If things don't pan out with Brock, Jolene Ellis has the best-looking son, Jackson. I've been dying to have y'all meet ever since I saw him at the Cancer Society Benefit. Nothing like a new beau to take your mind off the old one."

A new beau? She didn't need a new beau. "Don't marry me off yet. I'm young, got wild oats to sow."

June Cleaver leaned forward, shaking her finger. "Hon, you've got to be careful with oats. It only takes one little seed and then you'll be doing all the reaping that comes with that sowing. And in this day and age there's also," her voice dropped lower, "STDs."

"Mom, have you been reading *Cosmo* again? Where did you hear about STDs?"

"Sexually transmitted diseases. They're out there, everywhere. Never be too cautious. When you find your knight in shining armor, make sure he's wearing his armor, if you know what I mean."

"Mom, why now? I'm twenty-six years old. You didn't talk with me when I was thirteen and I had to have the school nurse explain the facts of life to me. Then you sent me off to college with a copy of the Life Cycle books. And mind you, they were thirty years old.''

''How did you know I was the one that packed those?''

''They had your name in them.''

''Well, I've done my best. My mother never had any talks with me. Just fed me to the wolves, uh, I mean your father. I only hope you find a nice man that will love you like your father loves me.''

''Mom, do you have some aspirin? I think I better take some for the road.''

''Of course dear.'' Her mother went upstairs and came down with two pills. ''Now, you think about what I said.''

Carol stood up to go and blew a kiss to her mother. ''Sure, Mom. Love you. Bye.''

Somebody new. Maybe her mom had the right idea. For Mike. If Mike got his mind off Linda, and safely involved in another relationship, then Carol could get her mind off Mike. Problem solved, no busted friendships and no hurt feelings. She just needed to find the right girl. She mentally ran through her list of friends at work and thought of one or two potential candidates. It would be easy. Mike would be a catch for any girl. She wouldn't let herself dwell on the sharp sting that seemed to hit right near her heart.

No, she just needed to move along so she could concentrate on Rock. After all, Rock, uh, Brock was just her kind of guy.

FIRST THING WHEN Carol got to work, she powered on her computer. The memory counted up and she went to get a diet cola. By the time she got back to her desk, she noticed the big blue screen of death. Fatal Exception. Seemed quite fitting. Had she backed up her spreadsheet? Yeah, she thought so. Wishing for a hammer, she punched the power button, ready to try one more time. After three more blue screens, she decided she needed professional help.

She lifted the phone, just about to call the help desk, when she spied Patricia, the IT manager, wandering by.

"Help!"

Patricia breezed into Carol's cube, her perfume trailing behind her and took over the driver's seat. "Here." She punched the power button. "Have you tried rebooting it?"

"That's how I got this."

Patricia checked the power cables. "Hmm, maybe the video memory got disconnected."

Carol was skeptical. "Can it really do that?"

Patricia nodded. "Oh, yes. Happens all the time."

The solution seemed obvious. "Well, connect it back."

"I'll get a tech. Last time I did it myself, I broke a nail."

Carol glanced at her own tortured nail stubs, and then sat on them. "Cool. I owe you one."

Patricia flashed a grin. "Find me a dream man, and we'll call it even."

Carol had a flash of inspiration. "Hey, what are you doing tomorrow?"

"Nothing. Why?"

"I've got somebody you should meet."

Patricia looked suitably intrigued. "Tell me more. Is he cute?"

Cute? Carol thought. Mike, cute? "No, can't say cute."

Patricia sighed hopefully. "Handsome, then?"

An image of Mike in a tux replayed in her head. "He can be when he tries."

"Sophisticated?"

Carol laughed. "No."

"Rich?"

Carol shook her head.

"And you think I should go out with him because?"

I have to get over the hormonal imbalance that's going to trash our friendship. "He's the best." Carol pushed the power button on her computer one more time. Just in case.

"So why aren't you going out with this paragon?"

Cowardice, fear of failure. "I've known him too long. There's no mystery." Carol would screw it all up, and then she'd be Mike-less. And that's one thing she definitely didn't want. "No zing." Except when he kissed her. She watched the familiar blue clouds come up on her computer screen. "Have you ever had such a good friend that you knew that a relationship would ruin it?"

Patricia just looked confused. "No." She pointed at the screen. "Wow, I fixed it."

"Yeah, guess you did." Why did she feel so depressed, then? Carol looked up at Patricia. "Well, what do you say? You game?"

"Sure, why not? Sounds like fun."

6

On the sixth day of Christmas, my best friend gave to me—six flambéed biceps.

"NOW TELL ME ONE more time why you believe this is a good idea." Mike stared at Carol, trying to understand the workings of the female mind. Two weeks ago, he could have quoted lines from her favorite movie, picked out the exact shade of green that was her favorite and known to duck immediately when she was using the spray hose to wash dishes. Now, hell, now he couldn't even figure out why she was so desperate to marry him off.

"Don't worry, it will be fun." Carol pulled a bottle of wine out of her refrigerator.

Mike took the opportunity to leer at her backside, tightly encased by a pair of blue jeans. He shook off the effects of lust and tried to remember what she had just said. Oh, yeah. The date from hell. "Famous last words. And I suppose she has a great personality?"

"Patricia is a lot of fun—"

Mike groaned.

And of course Carol ignored him. "And she's pretty. Just wait, you'll see. She and Brock should be here any minute. You need someone to take your mind off old what's-her-name. Want a glass of Merlot?"

"Got any beer in there?"

"No, sorry."

"Should have guessed. Give me a glass, then." Alcohol would take the edge off the ultimate humiliation. Carol, taking pity on him, trying to set him up with one of her friends. Of course, he'd brought this fiasco on himself. He was the one who dreamed up the dejected lover act. For two nights, ever since the Christmas party, he had been visited by the Ghost of Christmas How-Things-Ought-To-Be, teasing and pestering Mike with visions of Carol dancing in his head.

He picked up her remote control and began flipping through the channels.

Carol wrested the remote out of his hands. "Stop that. You don't have any reason to be nervous about Patricia. She's completely harmless."

Patricia? He wasn't nervous about her. It was Carol who terrified him. "I'm not nervous." He once again mentally recited the ten commandments of why it wasn't smart to be attracted to Carol. Number six was the most effective. *If thou sleep with thy best friend, thou shalt lose thy best friend forever.*

But what if he was wrong? He glanced up at Carol and noted the determined gleam in her eye, and the smug smile of accomplishment as she turned off the television.

He exhaled as the blank screen stared back at him, reminding him of exactly how good she was at pulling the plug.

Nah, he wasn't wrong. Once things went kaput, he would be eradicated from her life completely. He clenched his fist, welcoming the pressure as his fingers dug into his palm. Tonight he would concentrate on this Patricia person. In a way, Carol had the right idea. He did need a distraction. He needed a distraction from Carol.

The doorbell rang and she went to answer it. The voices of Brock and Patricia echoed from the four walls that masqueraded as a hallway. Patricia didn't sound too whiney. He wiped his hands on his jeans and stood up.

"Mike, this is Patricia, and you already know Brock."

Ah, so Carol hadn't lied about the good looks. And Patricia seemed to know it, too. Impeccably styled dark hair, big brown eyes and a mouth covered in red lipstick. She outstretched a hand, and Mike wondered if she expected him to kiss it. He took a chance and gave her his best damn-glad-to-meet-you handshake. As she situated herself on one of Carol's uncomfortable chairs, Mike took the rest of the inventory. Not bad. Her tight-fitting jumpsuit looked a little pretentious for his taste, but she did fill it out nicely.

Mike sat, noting that Brock placed himself next to Carol on the sofa and laid his arm around her. The toad. He turned his head and beamed at Patricia. "So, I understand you work with Carol?"

She batted her long eyelashes and flashed gleaming,

white teeth that must have cost a fortune. "Yes, but I'm the director of the information technology department."

Wow. Mike was instantly impressed. She didn't look the techie type. "That's a coincidence. I work in the computer business also. I'm a chip designer."

"I've always wanted to be a designer. What kind of chips?"

"Processors mainly. Where did you go to school?"

"Tech."

"Cal-Poly?"

"No, Texas."

Ah, a party girl. "IT director? Pretty impressive. You seem so young."

She unfurled her pearly whites one more time, and Mike got the impression she practiced that smile in the mirror. A lot. "Well, it's Daddy's idea, really. I wanted to learn about computers in school, but the classes were always full, so after I graduated, he decided to put me in charge of them for his company."

Mike closed his eyes, before turning to glare at Carol. "Carol, can I help you in the kitchen?"

Carol stared at him in confusion. "Uh, Mike, we were planning on going out to dinner this evening. I don't need any help."

"Oh yes, you do."

He stood up and held out a hand to Carol. She stared at it like it was going to bite her, which was probably wise. If witnesses hadn't been present, he would have strangled her. She neglected his hand, but did trot off to the kitchen.

"Carol, she's a bimbo! Granted, she's built, but still—"

"Shh. She can hear you."

"Where did you find her?"

"She's really nice, Mike. She's just a product of a privileged upbringing. Give her a chance. Once you get down to the real Patricia, you'll see that she's really…"

"Yes?"

"A real person." She gave him a look he had seen favored for stray kittens and the homeless. "Besides, you need to start seeing other people."

He ran a hand through his hair. Why did he let Carol get to him like this? She wanted him to see other women? Great. Not a problem. He managed to mutter through clenched teeth, "You know? You're absolutely right. I don't know what's come over me. Come on, let's go to dinner."

BY THE THIRD COURSE, Carol was ready to use her pepper spray on Patricia. The girl was hanging all over Mike. And the jerk was laughing, having a good time, obviously having forgotten all about Linda. And all about Carol, too.

The rat.

She smiled at Brock, needing something to soothe her downtrodden ego, but then noticed his eyes on Patricia's neckline. The woman must have stuck her breasts in a vise to get cleavage like that. At what point had Carol actually thought that this would be a good idea?

The waiter came forward, bearing a new bottle of wine for their table. Patricia didn't look like she needed anything more to drink. Probably a closet lush.

Carol took a bread stick she had hidden from the industriously clean waiter and tore it in half. After this evening, she was definitely going to dump that one-celled organism. What had she seen in him anyway? She eyed the perfectly cut designer shirt. Okay, his clothes were nice. She turned to look at Mike, noticing the trademark Levi's and the oxford shirt that looked like it hadn't been ironed. He took a time out from ogling Patricia and his gaze collided with hers.

She picked up her wine and gulped down the glass, feeling the warmth slide down her throat. It didn't help appease the ache that was building inside of her. Carol plunked her glass down on the table and stared back. An optical game of chicken. She sat there like an idiot, drowning in eyes that burned as blazingly hot as the cherries flambé. Desire ran through her, heating up places she was starting to be intimately acquainted with. Her knee began to shake uncontrollably, and she put a hand on the silverware as it began to rattle. She couldn't take this anymore and opened her mouth to speak.

"Patricia, I'm thinking about a trip to the little girl's room. Want to come?"

Patricia turned to Mike and pouted in a disgustingly fake manner. "Mikey, you'll miss me, won't you?"

Brock, always a master of the moment, piped up. "Of course we will."

Carol sidled closer to Brock and covered his hand with her own. He looked at her, startled, and she smiled seductively. When she felt his hand sidle up her thigh, she moved away. Can't let the guy get the wrong idea.

"Mikey?"

Carol eyed the knife on the table and looked at it longingly. Disgusted with herself, she realized it was way too dull to kill a brown-haired vixen.

Mike patted Patricia's hand like a pet poodle. "You girls go and have your fun."

Patricia followed Carol to the ladies' room and Carol pulled a tube of lipstick out of her purse and looked into the mirror. "You know, Brock sure has been eyeing you all evening."

Patricia laughed nervously. "Oh, he seems to be very devoted to you."

Carol shrugged. "Not really. We just have a good time together. More friends than anything."

"How nouveau. Doesn't friendship put a crimp on the romantic side of your relationship?"

"Nah, the romantic side is starting to fizzle anyway. Actually, I think you and Brock would make a really cute couple."

"You think?"

"Oh, yeah. We've been on the verge of going our separate ways. I don't think he'd be upset with me for telling you this. Girl, you ought to go for it."

"But what about Mike? He seems kind of dreamy. I get so turned on by those super-intelligent types."

"Mike?" Carol snorted for effect. "He's as dumb as a sack of hair. Go for Brock. Under that sleek, buffed exterior, he's sharp as a tack."

"I never would have guessed."

"No, neither would I. Y'all would be perfect. And you would look so great together. Trust me." Carol pouted, and started to apply her lipstick with a practiced hand. She watched the thoughtful spark in Patricia's eye snowball, and knew she had hit pay dirt. It was hard not to look pleased, but somehow she managed.

MIKE CLEARED HIS throat as he sat alone with Brock. After an evening of watching Carol and her date, Mike was ready to declare all-out war. At least he didn't have to worry about Carol's virtue. The way she had responded to him at the Christmas party spoke volumes. The girl wasn't getting any with the big lug. At least Carol had some taste. Brock was about as much fun as, well, a Rock.

"So, things starting to get chilly between you and Carol, huh?"

Brock looked up, confused. "No. Did she say something to you?"

Mike leaned forward. It really shouldn't be this easy. "Oh no. But then Carol always keeps these things bottled inside her." He picked up a matchbook and struck a match, twisting the wooden end between his fingers and watching the flame burn. "No, she just lets things build and build, until one day…"

"One day?"

Mike blew out the match. "Poof."

"Poof?"

Mike nodded. "Poof."

Brock shook his head. "What can I do?"

Mike reached out and struck his fist lightly against Brock's shoulder. Damn, the man had biceps of steel. Too bad his brain was going soft. "My friend, there's nothing to be done. Just enjoy it until she dumps you."

Brock's eyes opened wide. "I've never been dumped. Women don't let go of a man who drives a Beamer. It's not natural."

"You shouldn't have been dating Carol, then. She always dumps men." No lie there.

"I can't have that. I've got to get rid of her first. She was starting to bore me anyway. Getting a little wide in the thighs, too. I had just asked her to start running with me."

Carol jogging? Mike had to hide his laughter behind a napkin. When pigs fly. He had always thought she was a little too skinny, but Brock was on a roll, and Mike wasn't going to let up yet. "Yeah. A guy like you needs a woman who shares his passion for, uh, physical fitness. A woman with flair, style, two-percent body fat." Mike snapped his fingers. "You know, what about Patricia?"

That brought a frown to the big lug's face. "She's your date."

"Yeah, but did you see the hot looks she was throwing in your direction? I could feel the heat rolling off her every time she stared at you." Mike lit another match. "She's burning up for you. And, the best part? She's got hips like...hips like a...a...gazelle."

"She did look pretty hot."

"Dude, when the right woman comes along, you just gotta accept your fate."

Brock nodded obediently. "I think you're right. Would you mind if I asked her out?"

"Nah. Go ahead. Far be it from me to stand in the path of true love."

"Thanks."

"No problem, friend. Anything to help out."

First mission accomplished. Now on to the more challenging assignment. Get Carol out on a date without the assistance of a make-believe broken heart or wonder drug potency. Good old-fashioned honesty.

Mike swallowed hard as the girls approached the table. He had spent his life getting by on his brains and his charm. Now he was going to have to let his heart run the show.

Damn.

7

On the seventh day of Christmas, my best friend gave to me—seven pairs of sup-hose.

AT 5:03 P.M., Carol was down the steps of Creative Media, out the doors, and into the world of the living. Finally. Friday! The weekend. The campaign for Stoneware jeans was in place, and Carol's Christmas vacation was saved.

After last night's dinner-date disaster, she needed the rest. Patricia had avoided Carol all day. Not that they were great friends before, but well, what good was a friend if you couldn't pump her for information? She didn't know what had happened after Mike had walked Patricia to her car, and the suspense was just about killing her.

She looked up, and noticed a familiar silver BMW parked at the curb. Why was Brock here today? He hadn't told her he was coming to pick her up. He'd acted suspiciously cool last night after dinner. No "Night, sugar." No kiss. Not even a possessive touch. She'd been all ready with her "raging headache" excuse, and didn't even need it. Another relationship torpedoed. But he was here, so maybe things weren't so bad. Okay, but why the heck was he here?

The pageant rehearsal was tonight at Autumn Hills and hanging out with nursing home residents was not Brock's idea of a fun date. Besides, Mike had said he was driving her tonight anyway.

She started to walk over to Brock, just to say "hello, why are you here?" But then she noticed the way the broad shoulders slunk down into the seat, the gleaming blond strands bent low behind the dashboard. Nope, she was no idiot. It was the posture of a man who didn't want to be seen; unfortunately, the BROCK IT personalized license plates gave him away.

Not wanting to go where she wasn't wanted, Carol turned away and walked toward the parking lot, resigned to playing her usual game of find-the-car. She heard a happy yell from behind her, and turned back toward the building. Patricia, dressed in party clothes, teeth gleaming, was running down the steps. She saw Carol and then slowed. Carol put two and two together and got depressed. Apparently being dumped was never easy, even when you engineered the dumping yourself. She could get through this. With dignity, even.

Patricia slung her purse over her shoulder. "Hey, Carol."

"Hi, yourself, kiddo." She wiggled her nose.

"This is really awkward."

Carol waved her hand with far more enthusiasm than she felt. "Nah. Go on. Brock's waiting."

"You sure you don't mind?"

"Mind? No, not a bit. You crazy kids, go on. Have a good time."

Patricia knew a gift horse when she saw it, and ran. At the last minute, she turned around and waved, red fingernails flying like flags. "You're a pal, Carol."

"Don't give me too much credit." Carol scuffed her foot on the asphalt, and got dust on her new suede shoes. "Oh, okay, okay. I'm a brick, I'm a trooper. Now, shoo! Scoot!" The silver car tore away from the curb, wheels squealing. "Skedaddle," she whispered to herself.

Well, so much for her matchmaking efforts. She'd lost the Rock, and as for Mike...what was she going to do about Mike? He deserved somebody better than Patricia anyway. Somebody who didn't have a credit card where her heart should be. Somebody loyal, with scruples, and funny. Somebody who was pretty on a good day and sloppy on a bad one.

She wandered through the parking lot, and finally found her trusty mode of transportation. Honestly, she couldn't think of anyone to set Mike up with; she couldn't think of anyone she *wanted* to set Mike up with.

And that worried her. This sexual attraction thing was one bad itch and no way did she dare scratch it. She found her keys and got in her car. But it was a long time before she drove away.

CHRISTMAS LIGHTS LINED the city streets, the moon shone high, and the air was chilled. Mike thought that should have been a good enough reason to close the car windows, but Carol loved to ride with them down. Even in December.

The wind was turning Carol's hair into a mess, but she was oblivious, a contented smile playing on her lips. By the time they reached Autumn Hills, she would be thoroughly tousled. He kept his hands firmly on the steering wheel, even though the tumbled, blond curls were tempting. She spent a small fortune on hair stuff and would no doubt be screaming bloody murder if she took a moment to look in the mirror.

He grinned, couldn't help it. She tried so hard to live up to her mother's expectations of what a lady should be, but somehow never quite seemed to make it. At least in her mom's eyes. In Mike's eyes, she looked just fine. Obviously in Brock's eyes, too.

"So how's the Rock doing?"

She shrugged. "Don't know. He broke up with me."

Mike turned away, letting loose with a quiet "yes," before turning back. "Sorry."

"Don't be. I'm not too disappointed. What about Patricia? Did y'all two hit it off?"

Mike rolled his eyes. "No."

"Well, good because it seems Brock and Patricia are going out now."

A bit of guilt pricked at his conscious. "You're okay?"

Her sigh sounded relatively pain-free. "Swell. He was missing some… some…*je ne sais quoi,* anyway."

"That *quoi* you're trying to put your finger on is brains." Mike glanced sideways at Carol.

"That's a tacky thing to say," she said with a laugh.

"True, but tacky."

"You don't look too heartbroken."

"I was thinking of getting rid of him anyway."

"Getting a little rusty on the old lock-and-load routine?" The cars in front of them started slowing down.

"What's that supposed to mean?"

Whoops. "Forget I said anything. I'm just rambling." After checking his watch, he realized it was time for his let's-think-about-dating discussion. He had stalled long enough. A quick analysis indicated now would be ideal. They had twenty-two minutes before they needed to be at Autumn Hills, and that wasn't enough for a long, drawn-out talk. They were in a confined vehicle and neither one of them could ditch the conversation. And most importantly, if he waited much longer he would forget his lines and he didn't want to take a chance on forgetting any of the important parts.

"Carol, I've been thinking about our…um…situation."

That only earned him a confused stare. He really didn't want to ad-lib this. If he did, he'd probably screw it up. He held up a hand and hurried on. "Don't interrupt me. Just let me finish. I think—"

"But the traffic looks horrible. We'll never make it in

time if you don't take the tollway. The rehearsal is at seven." Carol pointed ahead to the long line of red tail-lights.

"And what's the worst thing that happens if we're late?"

She picked up her purse and pulled out her cellular phone.

"What are you doing?"

She lifted the phone to her ear. "If we're going to be late, I'm calling Aunt Eleanor. It's only polite."

"Carol, don't—"

"Aunt Eleanor? Hi, it's Carol."

After a few minutes Mike checked the time. 6:41. Carol was still on the phone, arguing about the commercialization of Christmas.

A few minutes later and they were still stuck in traffic. 6:43. Their debate had moved to whether it was politically correct for a Christmas program to include a menorah. At 6:50 they started on a discussion of the presidential candidates and Mike rolled up the windows out of spite. Enough was enough, damn it. The White House was not going to take priority over his love life. If he didn't allow her to get a word in, he could just about finish before they reached the nursing home. He had some duct tape in the trunk, however it was 6:51 and there wasn't time to stop. He reached over and took the phone away.

"El… Breaking up… Out of range…Bye."

He clicked it off and handed it back. Sometimes it took an engineer to set things right.

"That's a pretty high-handed thing to do, mister."

"I've got something important to say, and I'm feeling high-handed today. Now, as I was saying some twenty minutes ago, there's been a change in our re... relat...re...status as friends. We're both adults. Mature adults. Mature adults with sparks. I think there's a new dimension we could explore—"

Carol looked shocked. "Are you talking about sex?"

Mike winced. Obviously communication was lost in this discussion. "That's not the word I would have used."

She nodded in agreement. "I know what word you would have used, and I'm too much of a lady to say it."

Now it was time to start the ad-lib version. "I'm not taking an allergy medication, Carol. I lied to you the night of the Christmas party."

There it was. Illumination. Her lips formed that familiar little "o."

She ran a hand through her curls. "I see. What dimensions *are* you wanting to explore? You decided, after nearly twenty years, mind you, that now you want to sleep with me? Is this some sort of therapy to get over Linda?"

"I'm already over Linda."

"So!"

This didn't bode well for him. He sighed, feeling a lot like Charlie Brown.

She turned in her seat and faced him square on. "I suppose the whole pity-Mike routine was all made up, too?"

Yep, Lucy just jerked the football away, once again. But now was the time to come clean. He glanced over to make sure she had no weapons handy. "Well, yeah. She wasn't even there."

"Mike! You lied to me." Carol aimed her cell phone at him and shook it.

He felt like rubbing a hand over his eyes, but he was still driving. She sounded hurt. Angry, he could handle. Surprised, he could handle. Hurt, he was clueless. "Hold on for a minute. I had my reasons."

"I know about your reasons, buster," she said, punctuating each word with a poke from the rubber antenna.

"There's no reason to pull this holier-than-thou routine on me. You felt it, too."

"Felt what?" Her blue eyes widened innocently. A little too innocently.

"Electricity. Sparks. I had three classes in physics, two in thermodynamics and one in electromagnetic energy. And I aced them all. I know about these things." Mike stared at her, waiting for her response. She closed her eyes and turned away.

"It wasn't electricity," she muttered to her reflection in the window.

"Carol, I've known you too long, and you were never a good liar." Thank God for small favors.

She shrugged. "Maybe."

"Maybe you aren't a good liar?"

She began to rummage in her purse, grumbling. "No. Maybe there was a little electricity."

"Maybe? Babe, that was no 'maybe' when you kissed me." His body temperature spiked a few degrees just remembering what she felt like pressed against him.

She pulled out her calendar and started flipping pages. "It could have been hormones."

That didn't deserve a response.

Peering in the dim lights, she stared at the page for December, her lips pursed, a frown on her face.

Finally he broke down, and offered to help. At what, he had no idea. "What are you looking for? I can turn on the lights."

"I don't understand this. Maybe I'm just getting old."

This didn't sound like a discussion he needed to be a part of, so Mike stayed silent.

After a few moments of what looked to be intense meditation, she slammed the book closed and threw it in her purse. Sometimes women could be downright strange.

Carol began to ransack her purse once more before finding her sunglasses and putting them on. "All right. All right. Let's suppose you're right. Suppose I find that I respond to you physically."

"You're terrified, aren't you?"

Her black lenses coolly reflected the streetlamps rather than her response. Of course, the fingernail biting gave him a big hint. "No. I'm not scared."

"You aren't thinking about what your mom would say?"

"Of course not."

She looked up and he muttered a few choice words before taking away her sunglasses. And this time she didn't even argue.

"What do we do now?" she asked, this time meeting his gaze. He wished he had been wrong, but he saw the fear in her eyes.

"Now? We go out. This weekend. Think of it as an experiment," he replied in a tone reserved for small children and angry bosses. No need to panic the girl too much.

She sat silent, chewed on a nail, and his heart thudded painfully while he waited for her response.

Finally, she gave a quick nod. "Okay, there's a new restaurant that opened up that serves Southwestern cuisine."

He exhaled. Familiar territory at last, and no battle scars. "I was thinking about real food. Something with meat. Not those places that serve bite-size portions of citrus-flavored yak tongues to everybody."

"Sushi?" She took one look at his face and began to laugh. "Maybe not."

"How 'bout barbecue?" he asked.

"Forget about food. We could see a movie."

"Great. The new Bond flick just opened."

Carol turned up her nose. "What about the new Italian film about the farmers and their grain crop?"

"Subtitles? And wheat? That doesn't even make sense."

"Okay, bad idea. How about something a little lighter? Maybe that one with Julia Roberts?"

"That's a date flick, Carol."

"You're right. And this isn't a date, is it?" He watched as she began to chew on her fingernails.

He didn't like the direction that gorgeous brain was heading, and tried to cut her off at the pass. "Well, it might—"

"No." She held up the martyred finger and bobbed her head. "We are two mature adults who are deciding to pursue a physical relationship. Nothing more."

"That's not—"

"Let me finish. We can't even agree on a restaurant or movie. How could we possibly find enough in common to actually go out on a date?"

"We actually do—"

She smiled then. Teasing, female, sexy. "You're exactly right. We need to get this sex thing out of our system." Her hand began to roll in circles as she searched for the right words. "A good purging is all we need, and then everything will be back to normal. Tomorrow night. You can come over." She sat back in her seat, looking like she had found the cure for the common cold.

Amazing. He was thinking relationship-type thoughts and all she was thinking about was sex. And even more amazing, it bothered him.

But she was wrong if she thought they had nothing in common. They had more in common than she knew.

He just had to make her realize it.

And if he had to make love with her to do it?

Well, fine.

CAROL BLEW ON THE whistle she wore around her neck and hopped up on the makeshift stage, rather proud of her cool demeanor. "Okay, folks. Everybody quiet. We've got a lot of work to do tonight, but if everybody will just pay attention and follow instructions, we'll get through this." She gave an enthusiastic thumbs-up sign. "We've got teamwork, a good attitude and lots of smiles, and I know it's going to be a great show."

"Whoo, whoo, take it off baby!" The frail voice cut through the darkened silence.

Aunt Eleanor responded first. "Fred, behave yourself. Save some of that energy for later."

Carol coughed. "Uh, Aunt Eleanor, let's see if we can control Mr. Waring, hmm?"

The first act went up on stage, Mrs. Zidnicky on the piano and Mrs. Williams warbling a nightclub rendition of "The Christmas Song." Carol's gaze drifted across the room to where Mike stood in deep conversation with Aunt Eleanor. She sidled a little closer, trying to get near enough to hear without being noticed. She was ten feet away when Mike looked up, catching her in mid-sidle. She jerked her head back toward the stage and casually inched away from the twosome. After she had progressed a few more feet in the general direction of the stage, she leaned against the wall, folding her arms and crossing her ankles.

Nice. Composed. No one would ever sense the panic and turmoil that lurked under the surface and threatened to blow at any moment.

Had she actually agreed to make love—no, strike that, semantics were very important here—sleep with Mike? Tomorrow? She began to breathe in a Lamaze-type fashion. Easy, girl. Remember the plan. It's nothing more than sex. No need to get crazy. Mike had none of the requirements she needed in a man. Zero. Zilch. Nada. And think of the relationship aftermath. They'd be history. Four dates and he'd be out of her life. If his kiss could curl her toes into a figure eight, it didn't matter. If his smile was starting to haunt her dreams, it didn't matter. If she liked the way he argued with her, it didn't matter. If she wanted—

Shut up! She yelled at herself, stomping a foot for emphasis.

The singing stopped, the background chatter grew silent, and Carol looked up.

Seventeen pairs of eyes looked back. Uh-oh.

Aunt Eleanor broke the quiet. "Good God, girl. It's about time you found some gumption. But if you didn't like the singing, don't you think you could have been a little nicer about it?"

Williams and Zidnicky stood alone on stage, one about

to cry, the other apparently ready to lecture Carol on good manners.

Composed and nice may have won the battle, but unbalanced and overwrought were winning the war. Tears began to blur her vision, and she stammered an apology, but nothing intelligible emerged.

Never being a courageous person, she ran.

As her feet skidded over the tiles, she heard Mike's voice.

"Okay, folks. Carol has some issues with Santa that she's trying to work through right now. Give her a break. Let's just continue on, right from the top. Ladies, you were doing great…"

CAROL FOUND THE nearest empty room and closed the door, her back sliding down the wall. The tears that had threatened earlier started flowing in buckets. Her mother would be appalled at her behavior. Nothing like a good scene to upset Mom. She rubbed her eyes and came away with black mascara streaks on her hands.

The door clicked open, light flooding the room before it became dark once more. Warm arms wrapped around her, making her sob even harder. This shouldn't be so difficult. She could feel Mike's heartbeat underneath the soft cotton of his shirt. His chin rested on top of her head and he was wearing that killer cologne.

"Shh. Carol, honey, it's all right."

"No it's not. You don't understand." She rubbed her

cheek against him, probably spreading mascara all over his shirt.

"Why don't you tell me?"

"I can't. I don't even understand. You're my...if I...then...and you...and Mom..." She began to cry even harder.

"Carol, I don't know where you got the idea, but there's absolutely nothing going on between me and your mother. She's pretty and all, but she's just too old for me."

She hiccupped a laugh, then pounded against his chest, her hand lingering over the beat of his heart. "Everything is all messed up now. You messed everything up."

"I'm going to assume you're talking about the Christmas show."

"That's not what I meant."

"You know, I was afraid of that. I don't think I should be flattered." He began to stroke his hand through her hair. "If you want to change your mind, say the word."

"Oh." She wanted to change time. Go back to the way things were, but that was impossible. His arms tightened around her, and it frightened her even more that she didn't want to leave.

"Is that 'oh, yes' or 'oh, no'?" He pulled away from her. "Listen, stop the tears. You cry like that and my brain starts to shut down." He used his shirt to dab at her eyes. "Forget what we talked about earlier. If you're going to get this worked up about it, something is wrong."

Back to being friends? Have her skin burn every time she touched him? "No!"

"Nothing's wrong?"

She would get him out of her system. She had to. He wasn't right for her. They had been friends for too long. She'd mess up anything else. Didn't she always? One night would be plenty. Had to be. After that, poof. No problem. A whiff of cologne seduced her nose. She would just have to beat her olfactory senses into submission until after the deed had been done. "I'm not changing my mind."

"You sure?"

Sometimes it was worth it to live dangerously. This was a passing fancy. A phase. She had wild oats to sow, and who better to show her the ropes than Mr. Footloose and Fancy-Free. After the harvest, she would get back to her schedule for finding Mr. Right.

Her ready and willing hands worked their way under his shirt and her mouth began to mosey along his neck. "Positive."

He lowered his mouth to hers, and murmured against her lips. "I'm really glad."

His kiss was slow, drugging and she responded with reckless abandon. Sparks of desire fired in her stomach, and she whimpered when the pressure of his mouth changed. Urgent and insistent. Taking. She molded herself against him, passion overriding her senses. Tomorrow. She'd worry about everything else tomorrow.

Mike knew that somewhere, sometime, he was going

to pay for this, big time. But with Carol in his arms, her soft mouth laying into his, he couldn't be responsible for his actions. He had moved into overdrive and was desperate to touch her. Anywhere, everywhere. He just needed his hands on her.

He eased her down underneath him, the feel of the cold tile registering, reminding him that they were in a closet of cleaning supplies. In a nursing home. With many people waiting for their return. Her hips ground against him and he shuddered. Nobody would notice if they disappeared for a while.

Carol was burning up, acting on instincts she didn't know she had. This is what she had been waiting for. His weight was heavy and hard on her, but she wouldn't change a thing. Her hands kneaded the strong muscles in his back, dazzled by the feel of him. His hand edged between them, sliding underneath her skirt. Her heart rocketed as if she was about to explode. He reached the center between her thighs…

And stopped.

"We can't do this." His voice was low, tight, almost a snarl.

"I can do this," she snarled back. She rubbed her hips against him experimentally. "I think you can do this, too. Excuse me, I think this is a 'won't,' not a 'can't.'" She had no idea why he felt inclined to stop, but her oats were still tingling inside her, waiting for release.

"Can't, won't, whatever. Do you realize where we are?"

She blinked in the dim light. Then took note of the shelves lined with sheets, buckets and brooms. "And your point is?"

"I think we need to come out of the closet."

She wanted reality to stay firmly locked in the closet. Impromptu, spur of the moment, and seat of her pants were the new rules. "Mike?"

He raised his head at the husky tone of her voice. "What?"

She pulled him back down and placed light, teasing kisses on his neck. "You would never be caught dead driving a German car, right?"

A shudder ripped through him as she worked her way upward, her tongue performing miracles inside his ear.

"Not even when I'm fifty." He whispered his reply, incapable of much else. He was being much too easy, but she had him bewitched.

She slid her lips toward his mouth. "And you would never go with my parents to the opera?"

Getting back into the spirit of things, Mike abandoned his high principles. His hands remembered their earlier quest and he needed to hear that sexy whimper one more time. Maybe two. "Nope."

The sounds of heavy breathing echoed loudly, as if the oxygen supply was being quickly depleted in the confined space. "And you wouldn't know what to order from a wine list, right?"

Her kisses were driving him wild with need. His senses were overloaded, the control he'd always been so proud of, long gone. "Sweetheart, Mad Dog 20-20 is about as close as I get to grapes."

Carol felt his fingers thrust inside her and bit back a scream. Oh, my.

The door opened and Mike flew off her. Frantically, she put her skirt back in place. Carol sat up, staring at the light. The residents of Autumn Hills stared down at her.

Aunt Eleanor stood in front, wearing a big grin. "Lordy, lordy, what do we have here? You leave us stranded singing five choruses of 'Silent Night' and sneak off to get your jollies in the janitor's closet."

8

*On the eighth day of Christmas, my best girl gave to me—
eight flatbread crackers.*

THE LIGHTS WERE LOW, twenty-one votive candles flickering, and Johnny Mathis crooned Christmas carols in the
background. Carol grabbed the latest issue of *Cosmo*
from her coffee table and stashed it. Wouldn't want to
give all her secrets away. She surveyed the room before
adjusting the ebony and ecru velvet bows that adorned
her tabletop Christmas tree. Everything looked just right.
The perfect setting to cure the Mike problem.

She switched off the stereo, deciding she had had
enough of Johnny's crooning. The bows on her tree
looked crooked again and she fiddled, but they looked
pretty much the same as pre-fiddling. A candle dwindled
to nothing, and she panicked. She didn't have any more.
After ditching it in the trash, she looked around with a
critical eye. Twenty worked. Not as well as twenty-one,
but some things couldn't be helped.

With a last minute trip to the bathroom, she checked
her teeth for remnants from today's lunch and used one

last rinse of mouthwash. She looked in the mirror and smiled. Not bad.

In the bedroom, the sleigh bed loomed up like the creature from the black lagoon, and Carol felt a moment of panic ooze down her spine. She took a calming breath. No point in being such a sissy. After tonight, she would be over Mike. After all, she had to be. Ready to move on to pastures that were full of architects and lawyers. Maybe even a doctor. This hormonal tizzy she had worked herself into would be finished, kaput, ancient history. And she and Mike could go back to being friends.

She just needed a plan to keep everything in the right perspective. She picked up a notepad to make an agenda for the evening. Mike would arrive at seven. For ten minutes, they could converse politely. Next, she would offer him a beverage, perhaps even a light snack. A six-pack of his favorite beer sat chilling in the refrigerator. Then, at seven-fifteen, they would take a seat on the couch and watch forty-five minutes of TV. At eight o'clock, she would make her move. By eight-fifteen, they should be to first base, and she could huskily suggest they move to the bedroom. By eight forty-five, they should be ready to close the deal.

And by tomorrow morning, she would be ready to find the man of her dreams. She could picture him now, seated at her parent's dining room table, immaculate in his Armani suit, her mother beaming with pride. Laughing at one of Carol's jokes, he would wink, and then push the brown hair out of his eyes. Eyes that were brown, velvety soft and could burn right through her heart.

Oh, no.

The knock at the door intruded. Thank goodness for Mike. She couldn't afford to get carried away, as he was completely the wrong guy for her. Carol folded the paper and stuffed it into her pocket. Wiping her hands on her jeans, she walked over and opened the door.

And there he stood. Mike. He smiled, sending her blood pressure into orbit. He looked just the same as the ten thousand other times she'd seen him. Somehow, tonight her heart seemed to beat a little faster, and her stomach was determined to quiver like freshly made gelatin.

"Hey, Carol." He leaned over and kissed her on the cheek.

She shivered and closed her eyes for a moment. "It's not eight o'clock yet."

Mike frowned. "Was I supposed to be here at eight? I could have sworn you said seven."

"Well, yes. But it's only seven." She cleared her throat. "So. What have you been doing with your vacation?"

His dark brows drew together even further. "You know what I've been doing with my vacation. Helping you with this Christmas show. Have you been drinking?"

"No." She glanced at the clock on the mantel. 7:02. "In another eight minutes."

He nodded, still frowning. "Okay. Whatever you say."

She smiled her best, perky smile. "Got all your Christmas shopping done yet? Only four more shopping days."

"Most of it. All I have left is a few gift certificates. You?"

"Almost." She turned around. 7:08. "Did you see what the stock market did today? Whew!"

"Carol, eight points is not that big of a deal. It always calms down around Christmas time."

"Eight points is calm? Not in my book." She turned around. 7:10. Thank God! She walked into the kitchen, leaving Mike staring curiously at the clock. She hollered, "Want some beer? Maybe something to eat?"

"Sure," he hollered back.

She came back into the living room carrying a tray loaded with beer, brie and crackers.

"Why don't you have a seat?" she asked.

Mike started to sit down in the chair.

"No!"

He stopped, poised in midair, staring expectantly at her. "Is there a problem?"

She motioned toward the couch. "You need to sit here."

"Sorry, I didn't know we had assigned seats, Miss Martin."

He moved to the couch, and took a beer. She sat down next to him and patted her hands on her thighs. "Isn't this nice?" She picked up the remote control for the television. "TV?"

"Sure."

He took the remote and began to surf through the channels finally settling on PBS.

"You watch PBS?" she asked, truly amazed.

"Yeah. They have some great documentaries. The constant begging for money gets kind of annoying, but I usually send some anyway, hoping it'll shut them up. Hasn't worked yet, but I'll keep trying."

"That's very philanthropic of you. I didn't know that."

"There's a lot you don't know about me." He turned back to the television.

A familiar grunting filled the air, and for the first time, Carol realized what they were watching. The mating habits of the silver-backed gorillas. "Are you sure you want to watch this?"

"Yeah, it's kind of interesting. Reminds me of my family." He pointed to the screen. "Don't you think that looks like my dad? Listen, if you want to go out, maybe we could find a movie or something? There's a blues band playing downtown."

And ruin her schedule? No way. She smiled. "Oh, no. This is great. Maybe some other time. I just love these animal specials, don't you?"

He looked at her, frowning. "Sure."

Carol kept close tabs on the clock, while Mike seemed content to watch the gorillas. At 7:58, she faked a yawn, putting her arm along the back of the couch. She scooted closer, until their thighs touched. She leaned in, taking a whiff of his cologne, and shivered. Dangerous stuff. Could make a woman forget her plan. But not this one. The clock chimed eight and she moved in for the kill.

Closer. She inched her head toward the side of his neck.

Closer. Just a few more inches to go.

Closer. Her lips hovered just over his skin—

"Carol?" He turned and his chin connected with her nose.

"Ouch!" She rubbed her nose. No blood.

"What are you doing?"

He needed to ask? "I was trying to kiss you. It's eight o'clock."

He stared. "You turn into a pumpkin at nine, or something?"

Carol shook her head. "No, we just have to do this in an organized fashion."

"Are you sure you haven't been drinking, or are you like this with all the guys you go out with?"

"What's that supposed to mean?"

"This is a side of you I've never seen before."

"I'm just trying to be a good hostess."

"You're acting like your mother. It's kind of weird."

She brandished a finger at him. "Oh, that's good, bring my mother into this."

"Carol, you're the one I like. I really, really, really don't want to date your mother." He shuddered. "Geez. Why do I keep saying that?"

She looked at the clock. 8:13. Desperately trying to

maintain order, she threw herself into his arms. She made note of her target, closed her eyes and locked her lips onto his own.

She put everything she had in that kiss. *Everything.*

And he turned her away.

Very gently, he put her away from him. "Carol? I don't know what's going on here, and I know I'm going to hate myself for saying this, but I don't think this is a good idea. Maybe we try again. Go slow. Date. Like normal people do. I'll see you tomorrow. We can go to the park. That's neutral and public. How much trouble can we get in there?"

Normal, why normal? Better yet, what was normal for a guy who dated women with expiration dates and a girl who knew with an absolute certainty that he wasn't her kind of guy?

On the other hand, the sparks between them were driving her crazy, and he only wanted to prolong the torture. Days, weeks, maybe even months before she could get him out of her system. Each time she saw him, she got in a little deeper. Sinking into a quagmire of aphrodisia. This would never work. "No."

"Okay, we'll go somewhere else. I need to get out of here. You've got enough nervous tension to jump-start my car. That's not what I had in mind." He stood up to leave.

Leaving? He couldn't leave. Not yet. She had planned, prepared, scheduled tonight. And he wanted to leave? She watched as he headed toward the door. "You can't do this. It has to be tonight."

"What? What has gotten into you? First the time, now this?"

"Mike, you don't understand. I can't do 'normal' with you. What if I mess it up? How long before you're bored with me?"

"I would've been bored with you nineteen years ago if that was going to happen."

She noticed he left her "mess it up" question unanswered. "Okay, so what *do* you want? What is this?" She crossed her arms over her chest and began to rock back and forth, the room suddenly very cold. She searched his eyes, looking for answers, but he was giving nothing away.

"Well, whatever it is, it looks like you're going into shock." Finally, he closed his eyes, running a hand through his hair. "I don't know. Probably just a really, stupid idea."

The words were quiet, almost a whisper, but loud enough to kill any stupid ideas of her own. He turned and opened the door and she hugged her arms tightly to dull the ache in her heart.

"We have to do *something*. If we don't sleep together, how else do we get over it?"

He turned around and it frightened her to see so much fury in his eyes. "Carol, I'm sure that somewhere in that cartoon world head of yours, that is how things are supposed to be. But—and this is a big one—I don't want to make love and have someone 'get over' me. That's not what it's about.''

''Mike—''

''Carol, listen. You're my best friend. You know how much I lo…like you. It may be masochistic, but I do. But I'm seeing a side of you here that is—damn it, I hate it. You used to be normal. I like normal. I should've just kept my mouth shut.''

She ran to the door and stood in front of him. ''Mike, please. You can't leave.''

He moved her aside. ''Watch me.''

''If you go out that door, there's no turning back. It's goodbye lover, hello friend.''

''No, it's just goodbye Carol. Goodbye, Carol.''

He walked out the door, leaving her alone. She sat on the couch, watching the hands tick on her clock, wanting to throw it across the room. Gradually, numbness replaced the ache and she blew out the candles, returning the food to the kitchen.

That was that.

Things wouldn't have worked out between them anyway. Romance? She laughed. Nah. Noticing his beer, she grabbed the bottle and took one swallow, then another. She picked up the remote and watched the credits roll over the last of the silver-backed gorillas.

So he thought they shouldn't make love, that having his arms around her was a bad idea. Of course it was a bad idea. Stupid, wasn't that what he said? But right now she knew of nothing she wanted more in the world.

9

On the ninth day of Christmas, my true love gave to me—
nine nights, no necking.

MIKE WATCHED AS Eleanor eased back in her recliner, reaching for the bottle of Maalox and chugging a mouthful. The way his stomach was churning, he could really sympathize. He hadn't seen Carol since he walked out her door last night, and the thought of seeing her at tonight's rehearsal sent a sick combination of dread and anticipation plowing through his gut.

Eleanor patted her lean stomach. "Sorry, little gassy today." After putting the bottle back on the table, she looked at him and grinned, her eyes crinkling at the corners. "I see you took my advice. It does my heart good that y'all two finally clinched the deal." She winked. "So to speak."

"Don't expect to see wedding invitations anytime soon." If only she knew how far they'd come and gone in the span of a week. Mike had studied the situation in a keen, analytical manner, and had reached one inescapable conclusion. Keen analysis was useless when the subject in question was Carol.

Eleanor's face fell and she thumped a fist on the padded armrest. "Now, darn it, boy, don't tell me you messed it up."

Typical female. This must be where Carol got it from. "Tell me why it's always the male who allegedly messes things up? Has anybody really studied this? *New England Journal of Medicine? Harvard Business Review? Lifetime Network for Women?* I don't think so."

Eleanor humphed. "History tends to repeat itself."

"Well, write a new chapter. There's been a little hitch."

"Carol?"

He nodded. "Carol."

She sighed. "I've seen you tinkering with that car engine of yours 'til it purrs. What makes my niece so different?"

"I can get a ThunderJet engine to purr, I can even get Carol to purr, but her transmission keeps on shifting from forward to reverse, and I'm just getting dizzy." Mike held up his hands in a gesture of surrender. "What can I say? I was too easy for her. I should have been playing hard to get."

"Bull-honky! Go get her. Find some deserted corner of the nursing home and kiss her senseless. You got talent, we've all seen it. We need all the excitement we can get around here and you two are more fun than HBO." She stamped her foot. "No more dancing around. It's time to get on with it."

"It's a little more difficult than that." That was the

understatement of the year. Carol needed a good talking to, to help eliminate her mother complex, and after that... He smiled and got a little distracted.

"So what's the problem?" Eleanor's voice jerked him back to the present.

Mike cleared his throat and stored the fantasies away for later. "That's what she wants. She has this idea that if we...we...ah, consummate our relationship she can get over me. She's scared. Hell, I don't blame her. Scared the sh...ah, scared me pretty bad, too, at first." After one kiss, he'd been nervous. Two kisses, he'd been terrified. But after three kisses, well, then he just got determined. "I got over it."

"But Carol's a Martin. She's not a coward."

"Not a coward, just a little slow to get with the program. A normal mother wants their little girl to marry a doctor, Carol's wanted her to marry a prince."

"Meredith is going to stop by with those Junior League friends of hers to deliver Christmas baskets. I could put in a good word for you."

"Nope. This one's just between Carol and me."

"Hmm..." She steepled her fingertips. "Let's see, so she's hot to jump your noogies, pass you through like bad chicken, and then move on to some starched-shirt figment of her imagination?"

Mike nodded. "That pretty much sums it up."

Eleanor bobbed her head and pulled on her glasses. "You don't look too down and out for a man who just lost to some figment of her imagination."

He couldn't keep from smiling at that. *Like hell.* "Did I say I lost? I don't believe I said that. 'Lost' was your word, not mine."

She leaned in, so close he could see the tiny blue veins that ran below her eyes. "You love her, don't you?"

Mike swallowed. Hard. But he wasn't about to lie. "Yeah."

She sat back, satisfied. "So what are you going to do about it?"

"I'm going to take the one thing she wants—"

"Sex."

He flashed his most devilish grin. "And not let her have it."

Eleanor laughed. "Oh, that's good! Leave her hanging, desperate. Don't you let up till the girl's got her tongue hanging out. Then she'll come to her senses." Eleanor pointed to the inside of her hand. "You'll be serving her a four-course dinner right here between your life line and your love line."

"Huh?"

"Eating out of the palm of your hand, my boy. Try to pay attention."

"Yes, ma'am." There was something disheartening about getting advice on one's love life from a woman who was alive during the First World War, but then Eleanor was the Mata Hari of the Geritol generation. "Do you think it will work?"

Eleanor pounded a teasing hand against his shoulder.

"You are the modest one. It's brilliant. It takes a strong man to hold out to get the woman he loves."

Mike wished he had Eleanor's confidence. Just thinking of Carol in bed, his bed, made him hard as titanium. And his brain was operating at fifty-percent capacity due to extreme blood loss. "We'll see."

Footsteps echoed in the hallway and Eleanor pulled off her glasses and turned on the TV. "Here she comes. You'll do fine. Just confuse her my boy. Do what you've been doing all your life."

CAROL WALKED INTO Aunt Eleanor's room and stopped. Mike. No need for panic. She'd known he would be there, had sketched a rough outline of her speech, but her feet seemed to be dragging behind the rest of her.

She nodded politely, lifting her feet in a slow, methodical manner. Move. Just move. One foot at a time. As she shuffled carefully into the room, she heaved a sigh of relief. Now if the rest of her attempts went that well…

"Hello, Michael." Her aunt motioned her over and Carol bent down to kiss the wrinkled cheek.

She sat down, crossing her legs, and pasted a smile on her face. Eleanor stared at her expectantly, while Mike studiously avoided her gaze. She glanced at her hands, before folding them demurely in her lap.

"Nice weather we're having today. Got down to forty degrees last night," Aunt Eleanor said, aiming her remote at the TV and turning down the volume.

"Yeah, I heard we might even get below freezing for

Christmas Day." Carol glanced down at her palms, and breathed easier. No problems here.

Her eyes drifted to Mike, who looked disgustingly nonchalant and disgustingly sexy. She eyed the red flannel shirt he wore unbuttoned over a plain white T-shirt. She wore a getup like that and her mother would never let her hear the end of it. On Mike, it looked tasty. It definitely wasn't designer wear, probably nothing better than department-store stuff. But department-store stuff had never looked this good before.

Aunt Eleanor watched Carol and Mike like she would apple pie à la mode and rubbed her hands together. "Well, I can see you two kids have a lot to discuss. Why don't I wander off to the poker room and leave y'all to discuss the rehearsal."

After Aunt Eleanor left, Carol waited in silence. A quick peek at Mike showed nothing; he was watching the evening's news with a quiet intensity she had never seen before. Gathering her courage, she spoke. "Mike, we need to talk."

He replied without looking up. "Talking is not what you've got on your mind."

Wonderful. She coughed and stared at her hands. Not yet. No need to embarrass herself unless she was desperate.

"I'd like to have my friend back."

His head shot up. "You're rethinking the sex thing?"

She gave him a quick once-over. Thigh-hugging Levi's with grass-stained knees. Brown wavy hair with a careless five-dollar haircut that other men would pay big bucks for. Strong, work-roughened hands that could hold her so wonderfully. Rethink the sex thing? *As if.* "No."

He turned his attention back to the TV. "We're still friends."

Friends? This wasn't friendship. This was zero-degree etiquette. She began to chew on her nails, saw the damage she was inflicting, and sat on her hands. "I just need someone to wrestle with for the remote. And nobody else laughs at my stupid jokes. And I think my stereo is acting up again."

"Outsource, Carol. It's the wave of the future. And make sure you tell your stereo repairman that the right speaker needs a new crossover coil."

"I'm not calling a repairman." Carol sighed. Time for the big guns. She pulled her hands from underneath her, looked at her palms and stared at the smeared ink. She would remain calm. She had rehearsed this forty-seven times. Mike may have walked out on her, but bottom line—he was a guy. And *Cosmo* had told her step-by-step how to seduce the man she wanted.

She coughed delicately, lowered her voice to a scratchy whisper, and began to read. "I have needs. Wants. Desires. Like how my globelike *beasts*—breasts, that's breasts, ache to be free to fill your hands, your fingers loving, touching—" She raised her palms, angling for a better look. "Ah, yes, squeezing."

He jerked his head toward her, startled. His eyes held

a deer in the headlights kind of look and she could almost smell the fear. Good, she had him on the run now.

"Carol—"

She held up a hand, turning it to read the inside of her wrist, her heart pounding loudly inside her chest. She had memorized this yesterday, but now she couldn't even remember her name. "Don't interrupt."

His eyes grew even wider and he shook his head warningly. She smiled confidently and went on, enjoying her moment of power. She would have to read *Cosmo* more often.

"I want to curl my hand around the silky length," she stumbled for a moment, "no, that's silky strength of your love pump, each touch sending warm, wet drips—ah, drops—drops of desire flowing through my water mill."

"Carol—" His voice was more insistent this time.

"Don't stop me, Mike. It's time to get rid of my inhibitions. Be a woman of the new millennium. Time to tell the truth. I think about you at night. I fantasize about wrapping my thighs around you, your pulsing lance of love," she looked at the outside of her elbow and paused, "purloining? That can't be right. Parlaying! Yes, parlaying and thrusting inside of me." She watched in awe as a slow streak of red crept up his face. Well, this was progress. She'd never seen him blush.

"Carol Leigh Martin!"

The twenty-six short, wonderful years of her life flashed before her.

And all thoughts of parlaying and thrusting shriveled up and died.

She turned to face the door, and smiled weakly at Aunt Eleanor, her mother and three members of the Dallas Junior League. "Hello, Mom. Ladies. What a nice surprise. I guess you're here to watch the rehearsal tonight?"

"Rehearsal?" Her mother's voice was a near screech. "It seems the real show is in here, young lady."

Carol got up quickly and heard Mike rise just as fast. "Mom, it's not what you think—"

She stopped, the tickling sensation at the nape of her neck making her aware of Mike's presence behind her. A warm hand settled discreetly in the middle of her back.

"Mrs. Martin, I'm the—" Mike started.

Aunt Eleanor never let him finish, waving a hand in a magnificently feeble manner. "Now, Meredith. Don't jump to conclusions. I have Carol read to me sometimes. Got to keep up with my Fred. I had just left the room for a minute to go get some pain medication when I bumped into you in the hallway."

Carol watched the expressions chase across her mother's face, making her feel like a compulsive gambler playing the slots. Three sevens? A lonely cherry? She leaned back against the comfort of Mike's hand, and felt him knead gently in response.

Finally, her mother shook her head slowly from side to side. "I had no idea what you liked to read, Eleanor. I'll have to rethink that subscription to *National Highways* that I was going to get you for Christmas."

Aunt Eleanor smiled and turned to the other ladies who stood there, openmouthed. "Now, are you going to introduce these fine, upstanding pillars of the community to me?" She thrust out a hand. "Eleanor Martin. It's a pleasure to welcome you to Autumn Hills."

Carol watched in awe as her great-aunt moved into action. A five-star general could only wish to control his troops so well. The ladies were introduced to Mike, and Mrs. Ellis smiled in a smug, superior manner.

Meredith cast a glum look at the worn knees in Mike's jeans and shook her head. "Carol, Mrs. Ellis has a son that we're inviting to a holiday soiree. We need someone to round out the table, I'd like for you to be there." She wrinkled her nose. "He's such a nice boy and he has the loveliest modern art collection. Will you come?"

Carol sensed the social minefield her mother had laid out in front of her. The hand at her back had stopped the kneading. Her neck had stopped its tickling. And her mother stood there, waiting for an answer. The call of family loyalty or the sexual force field that emanated from Mike?

Carol opted for decision by procrastination. Her specialty. Performing the ritualistic Junior League nose wrinkle, she hedged. "Let me check my calendar and get back to you."

"I think we'll just go and talk for a minute," Aunt Eleanor said, who took advantage of the break in the conversation to shepherd the quartet out of the room. She poked her head back through the doorway. "Mike, be a dear and wait to see how the market did today. The Dow's on a hot streak. Can't wait to see how it finishes.''

"It's Sunday, Eleanor." Meredith smiled gently.

Aunt Eleanor favored Carol and Mike with a triumphant wink before she turned back to the Junior Leaguers, rubbing her eyes with a shaking head. "I'm just getting so old."

The clatter of high heels echoed down the hall and Carol finally gathered enough courage to turn and look at Mike. She wiped her brow. "Whew, that was a close one."

"I did try to warn you," he said. She melted some at the warmth in his eyes and the gentle smile.

"So you did. I guess I looked pretty stupid, huh?"

"Naw. Actually it was kind of cute." He picked up her arm, licked his thumb, and began to rub against the ink, the words fading with each stroke. "One suggestion though. Next time, cut the cue cards."

A sudden burst of hope shimmered inside her. "Does this mean you've changed your mind?" As soon as the words were out, she knew she had said the wrong thing. A curtain fell over his face, he dropped her hand, and his gaze grew hard.

"Carol, give it a rest, okay? I'm not changing my mind. Unless you've changed yours? I'm expecting more than a one-night stand."

A gauntlet. She looked down at the floor, half expecting to see a glove. She squared her shoulders and drew an imaginary line in the tile with her toe.

"I'm not giving up." She wanted her intentions firmly out in the open. No more lies between them.

"You know the price. You can try—"

"I will." She recognized the set of his jaw and sighed. How could he be so stubborn? She had met mules more easygoing than Mike when he was in a mood. But she knew how she could win.

A nice rational discussion was the best way to bring him over to her way of thinking. He didn't argue with facts. It was one of the things she loved about him. "Why did you lie to me about Linda being at the Christmas party?"

He met her eyes, and her heart gave a little cheer at the emotion that lurked there. "Things were changing between us. I didn't want to jeopardize our friendship."

"Aha!" She started to pace. *"You didn't want to jeopardize the friendship.* And so, you were willing to cast yourself in a cloak of deceit to scope out the situation. All the while, letting me twist in the wind like yesterday's laundry. Wearing my hormones on my arm, as it were."

He sank into a chair and squinted as if he was developing a bad headache. "What's your point?"

"I'm getting there. Don't jump ahead."

"I wouldn't even know how to make that leap."

"As I was saying, you chose to pursue a route that kept us from following the normal dating mores of society. *Because you were afraid.*" She pounded her fist on the TV for emphasis. "And yet, when I choose to do the same, I'm accused of living in a world of Looney Tunes." She bent over and got right in his face. "You've got a double standard, Mike. And it stinks."

He stood and stared right back at her. "It's not the same thing."

Oh, man, he had beautiful eyes. Soft and velvety brown. How had she missed that? She swallowed. "How are the situations different?"

"All I was doing was a little kissing on the dance floor. Just to make sure I wasn't having some weird dream. If the tests were conclusive, we would've gone on to the next step. Dating. Or at least that's what most normal people think the next step should be. You wanted to grab the whole enchilada and then throw everything away when you were done."

She took a small half step forward. "I knew what you were thinking on that dance floor. You wanted to taste that enchilada just as much as I did."

"Is that your way of asking if I want you?" He laughed, but it wasn't a pretty sound. "Carol, sometimes I hurt from wanting to make love to you. I imagine what your skin feels like beneath my hand. I remember how soft your lips were, and I lie awake, wanting to taste them again."

She lifted her face toward him, dying for his kiss. He leaned closer, his cologne teasing her nose.

"I want to hear your voice catch on my name. Hear your sighs against my ear."

Desperately she gasped for air, pressing her body to

his, savoring the hard planes of his chest against her cheek.

"I want to learn the rise of your body, the rhythm of your breathing when I sink inside you."

Her eyes drifted shut, dreams that she had locked away came tumbling out in startling clarity. She moaned weakly. "Please stop."

"Yeah. I guess you could say I want you." He drew a finger down her cheek and she turned her face into his hand.

She murmured his name and wrapped her arms around his waist.

"But Carol?"

She pressed closer, aching for him to just shut up and finish the job. "Hmm?"

He rubbed his chin against her hair for a moment, and then began to pull away.

A cold breeze descended down the length of her, replacing the hard warmth of his body. He looked at her for a moment, swearing, and then lowered his head for one lingering kiss.

She stood there, dazed, so close to falling, and he just turned away. She stared at his retreating back, willing him to return, but instead he left the room with one parting shot.

"I'm not cheap."

10

On the tenth day of Christmas, my true uh, friend gave
to me—ten tears a dropping.

EARLY THE NEXT MORNING, her mother called.

"Carol, have you heard a word I've said?"

*No. She was too busy having a very nice, very steamy
dream about Mike. Of course, her eyes were open, while
she was having this dream, which technically made it a
fantasy rather than a dream. There were other elements
in her dream—breakfast table conversation, evenings laz-
ing in front of the fireplace,—that made it more than just
a fantasy about—things better left unsaid. And if she was
having thoughts that were more than just sexual in nature, then didn't that mean that she was—*

"Yes, Mom." —*having feelings for Mike that—*

"Then answer my question. Was Eleanor covering for
you yesterday?"

"No, of course not, Mom." —*she really didn't have
any business having. Obviously his feelings for her
weren't well defined, either. He hadn't expressed his undying love and—*

"Well, why don't you want to go out with Jackson Ellis? He's perfect for you—"

—she certainly wasn't in love with Mike, was she? She loved him, of course. In a friendly, pals, buds, I really want to bear your children kind of way. "It's not that I don't want to go out with Jackson. It's just the Christmas show has been keeping me so busy, I really don't have much time for socializing right now."

"You certainly had time yesterday for Mike."

"We were just discussing the show, that's all." *She had loved him since he helped her pass seventh-grade algebra, which had been no small accomplishment. She probably could have passed on her own, but she really had hated those word problems, and Mike had been so good at them.*

"Carol, you know I can tell when you're lying to me, and if you're not telling the truth—"

"I know, Mom. Love you, too. Bye."

Carol hung up the phone, more confused than ever. No, she didn't need to think anymore. She needed to— go shopping. That always helped clear her head.

Twenty minutes later, she found herself at the mall. She pulled her Christmas list from her purse and looked over the four possibilities she had made for each member of her immediate family. A Christmas present for her dad was always the worst. From store to store she wandered, but nothing was getting checked off. This was certainly unproductive. Finally, she found herself parked in front of a pet store window. She was drawn to a puppy that had the most beautiful soft, velvety brown eyes. She went inside and poked a finger through the wire and rubbed his wet nose while he whined appreciatively.

"You're pretty cute and look kind of smart. What do you think? It's not like I don't care about him. Of course I do. But a relationship between us would never work. We're too different. The first time I took him to the opera, he would—"

The puppy barked loudly and lifted his leg.

Carol shook her head and moved on. "Exactly."

She stopped at a cage that contained a rabbit with earnest, intelligent brown eyes and a nose that twitched constantly.

"I could call you Bugs."

The nose twitched twice, which she interpreted as a "no."

"And what if things didn't work out? Two months of great sex, and then one morning we'd wake up, and not have anything more to talk about. What would I do then? I'd never have him back as a friend."

The nose twitched three times and the rabbit hopped in a circle.

"What do you know? I depend on Mike. He's been there for forever. I couldn't do without him."

The nose twitched one time, the ears wiggled, and the brown eyes seemed to condemn her for selfishness.

She moved on. "I don't know why I thought a rabbit would know diddly about relationships anyway."

The eyes of the last occupant on the row were black

and unemotional. Completely nonjudgmental. And when it swam up to the glass and opened its mouth with a little "o" of greeting, Carol knew she had a friend for life.

She drove home and christened the goldfish Pat since it looked vaguely genderless. After vacillating between beer or wine, she pulled the cheap beer from the refrigerator and sat on the couch, putting Pat on the coffee table for a mano to fish discussion.

"Okay, here's the deal. On the one hand, my mother has this plan for me. Marriage. To some society maverick. A doctor or lawyer. Now, up until today, that sounded pretty good. Couldn't you see that?"

Pat stared and made a little "o" with the mouth.

"Now, on the other hand, there's Mike. Whom I like, a lot. A whole lot. In fact—well, let's not delve any further into that subject."

Pat swam up to the glass and stared, wearing a look she interpreted as militant opposition.

Everybody was a critic. "Think what you like. The fact is, I don't think me and Mike would work out in the long run. I think the puppy agreed with me on this. And I can't lose my best friend. Heck, who am I kidding? He's my *only* friend I care about. But, I can't stop thinking about him. It's like I have the Mike Channel running in my head, twenty-four hours a day. All Mike, all the time."

Pat's gills bobbed approvingly.

"Maybe I should just go along with Mike. What if we did go out once? What would it hurt?" She grinned for a moment. "And if I change my mind about the date thing, maybe Mike will change his mind about—"

Pat stared with curiosity.

"You know."

Pat seemed to agree with her, and Carol picked up the phone to call. She stood for a moment.

"If you'd like to make a call, please hang up—"

Carol obeyed and pulled out a pad of paper, thinking she could jot down notes for the conversation. After ten minutes of staring at a blank page, she pulled out *Cosmo*.

After a few minutes of reading she still had no idea how to broach the date subject in a controlled manner, but she did have Ten Great Tips Guaranteed To Drive Your Man Wild.

Gathering her courage, she decided to take the bull by the horns, so to speak, and walked over to his door. She was just raising her hand to knock when Mike opened the door, an expression of surprise on his face.

"Carol? I was just leaving. What do you want?"

"I thought about what you said yesterday." His eyes narrowed immediately. "Do you have plans for tonight?" His eyes narrowed further. "I'm inviting you out on a date." *And possibly a steamy affair.* She looked up and began to drown a little in the velvet brown eyes that were currently staring at her with suspicion.

"A date?"

She didn't speak, only nodded in affirmation.

"What time?" More suspicion.

She began to feel like a defective engine block under his heavy scrutiny. "Eight?"

He nodded and she exhaled. "I'll pick you up at eight."

MIKE LEANED AGAINST the door and ran a hand through his hair. He was going somewhere. Where was he supposed to go? Pants. He should buy slacks. Christmas presents. Only three more shopping days left. That's where he was going. He still needed something for his dad. Damn. He could get him a gift certificate. Dad needed some new—new, what the hell did Dad need anyway?

He glanced down at his watch. Five hours. He had five hours to make himself respectable. And, oh yeah, he needed to get a gift certificate.

AT FIVE-THIRTY Carol started getting ready. She ransacked her closet to find something appropriate. Sexy, yet not too trashy. Finally, she dug up a kicky little leopard-print number that seemed to fit the occasion. Subdued clingy-ness. It didn't scream "I want to have sex with you," but it did have a low-level primal theme about it.

Mike showed up at her door ten minutes late. His eyes raked over her dress and his smile grew a little wider. "Nice dress."

Remembering *Cosmo* tip number one, she ran her gaze over his dress pants, liking the way the gray wool clung in all the right places. They must have been new, because her hormones would certainly have noticed this before. "Nice pants."

The smile she got was worth a ten-year subscription to *Cosmo*. Remembering their last discussion on eating places, she braced herself for an argument. "Where do you want to go?"

"What about the new steakhouse downtown?"

She nodded. Wow, this was getting easier.

The restaurant was dark, smoky, full of quiet laughter and clinking glasses. A place frequented by businessmen, politicians and cattle barons. A place where people went when they wanted something. Perfect.

The waiter arrived to take the drink order and intoned tonight's gastronomical litany, a delightful roast pork with tarragon sauce, perfect for the holidays. Light, yet jazzy.

Mike watched her, a speculative gleam in his eyes, and the hint of a smile playing on his lips. "We could get wine. What would you like for dinner?"

You. "Beef." It didn't seem like too much of a fib.

Mike nodded toward the waiter. "Let's have something red, ripe, with substance, but not too astringent. Maybe Cabernet Sauvignon, Opus One, '94?"

The waiter studied Mike with new appreciation. "Very good, sir." He scurried away and they were left alone.

This new persona was a credible impersonation of a worldly man-about-town. Scary. Appealing. She smiled. "I'm impressed."

He shrugged. "I can read."

She shook her head carelessly—another *Cosmo* move—and rested her chin on her fist. "So."

Mike studied her for a moment, trying to figure out her angle. She loved it when she could confuse him, 'cause it didn't happen often.

"So," he replied back.

"Here we are. On a date."

His brows drew together and his gaze locked on hers. Long moments passed, but she was unable to look away. The flickering candle on the table provided no competition for the raging inferno building inside her. His hand searched blindly on the table for a moment before he broke eye contact and looked around. "I think I need a drink."

She felt a thrill of victory, but then the waiter showed up with the wine to spoil the moment.

After a few more moments of heated glances, he spoke. "Why the change of heart? You seem much more, uh, certain tonight."

She laughed. She was feeling downright cocky. Of course, it might have something to do with the two beers she had consumed before he showed up. "You were right, Mike."

"I was?"

She remembered tip number four and licked her lips, watching his eyes follow the movement of her tongue. "Yeah. There's no reason we can't go out. It'll be a little adventure. I had a long talk with Pat this afternoon and—"

"Who's Pat?"

"A friend."

"Is this a he-Pat or a she-Pat?"

Carol hedged. "Jealous? You needn't be. Pat practices an alternative lifestyle and I really didn't want to pry. Anyway, I decided there was no reason to hold back any longer."

"Hold back what?"

"Our relationship." She let her mouth savor the *r*. The confused look was back on his face. She picked up his hand and began to trace the veins that ran along his wrist. He had such nice hands. Strong, capable. She could spend a lot of time with those hands. She threaded her fingers through his own.

A shadow loomed over the table, and Carol glanced up, annoyed the waiter would interrupt.

"Carol?"

"Mrs. Ellis?"

The exquisitely attired Junior League member looked at their entwined fingers and smiled knowingly. Obviously she hadn't forgotten the incident at the nursing home yesterday. Obviously she had as much trouble with Aunt Eleanor's explanation as Carol's mother did. Carol pulled her hand free and hid it under the table.

"I thought that was you." The socialite laid a protective hand on her shoulder. "And your friend." The older woman's voice grew chilly. "Hello, Mike. I hope I'm not intruding. You looked so—cozy."

Carol chose her words carefully. "No, no, just discussing the situation in the Middle East. Maybe someday there will finally be peace." She let out a long-suffering sigh. "But, enough about world politics." Carol waved what she hoped was a dismissing hand in the air. Her mom did that so well. "I hope we aren't interrupting anything. Maybe your dinner is getting cold?"

Mrs. Ellis shook her head carelessly, the artfully styled waves rolling impeccably. Carol bit back a few choice adjectives. "Oh, no. I just wanted to introduce you to my son, Jackson."

For the first time, Carol noticed the fashionable young man standing behind his mother. He came forward and smiled with genuine warmth. "Hello."

Mrs. Ellis continued on her roll. "Jackson, you and Carol have something in common."

"Really?" The man was young, handsome, oozing class and style. He was the epitome of what Carol's mother envisioned as a son-in-law, and about two weeks ago, he was the kind of guy that would have sent Carol salivating.

"Carol enjoys literature."

Carol shot a pleading look at Mike for help. But he only leaned back, steepling his fingers, taking sadistic pleasure in her discomfort.

The older woman turned to Carol and wrinkled her nose. "Jackson writes poetry. He's been published."

Jackson shrugged. "It's nothing really. Mainly haiku."

Carol smiled, feeling a stir of pity for this nice person who'd been sprung from the loins of a piranha. Jackson didn't stand a chance with her, but Carol's genetic makeup preordained a polite response. "I bet you're very good. Don't let your mother's talk fool you—I'm a firm believer in Cliffs Notes. I do like Dickens, though. And Emily Brontë was pretty cool in her day."

"How delightful," Mike ground out.

Jackson smiled at Carol, a nice, sparkling smile, while his mother scowled at Mike. "I was hoping you would go with me to the gala. I could bring some of my work with me and you could read it. See what you think."

"I don't think—" Mike started.

Carol never let him finish. "I don't know."

"Maybe some other time then? Unless you're," he glanced pointedly toward Mike, "involved."

Mike rested his chin on his fist and waited expectantly for her answer.

The restaurant suddenly seemed much smaller and Carol looked at Mike, then Mrs. Ellis, and finally Jackson. She could see her mother's pursed lips frowning in disapproval. Carol wrinkled her nose. "Well…" She looked at Mike, who wasn't giving one thing away.

"Well? I've heard a lot about you," Jackson prodded.

Mrs. Ellis smirked and Carol knew if she said anything about Mike, it would be back to her mom before they finished dessert. Everything was such a mess. She'd made it all such a mess and she had no idea how to clean it all up. She needed time, she needed a plan, she needed to stall. "I'm a little, uh, off men right now." She winced at the words, wanting to take them back. Why did she have to be such a social failure?

Jackson raised his brows and nodded. "Oh."

Mike threw his napkin and some bills on the table, stood up, and she cringed. "I hate to be the one to break up this little cotillion, but I have some things to do at home."

Mrs. Ellis looked in confusion at their table. "But you haven't eaten yet."

Mike pushed in his chair. "I believe I've had my fill."

He nodded politely at Mrs. Ellis and inclined his head half an inch at Jackson. He didn't look at Carol at all.

Carol smiled, shot Mrs. Ellis one last nose wrinkle and got up to leave, half running to keep up with Mike.

Why couldn't she do anything right? The last thing she wanted was to hurt him. "I did that badly."

"Yes."

"I'm sorry. I suppose you're angry," she attempted as he opened her car door.

He waited until she had climbed in and then slammed the door in reply. Carol winced. It took a lot of fury for Mike to slam a door Carol knew had taken him three months to restore.

They drove for several miles before she tried again. "Mike?"

He didn't answer and she chewed on her thumbnail. By the time they reached the complex, she had worked her way down to her pinky.

Surprisingly, he walked her to her door. "Would you

like to come in?" She didn't expect him to say "yes," but wasn't going to waste the opportunity. After all, they had gone out on a date. And a date was his price.

He rubbed his eyes. "What was the point of tonight?"

"Duh. This is what you wanted, remember?"

"Off men? Couldn't you have come up with a better lie than that?"

"No."

"What is it with you? Are you ashamed to be seen with me?"

Ashamed of him? He was the very best part of her life. "Of course not, I just need time. I have no idea what we're doing, and I just don't think it's very smart to advertise our relationship. Which by the way, I don't understand myself."

"Translated, that means you're afraid of what your mother would say."

Mike had always been quick. "Think of it like Romeo and Juliet. Star-crossed lovers whose families wouldn't approve. It'd be romantic."

"This is the twenty-first century, Carol. That just doesn't cut it anymore. I stopped worrying about what my mother wanted me to be when I was ten."

That was because his mother loved him for who he was. His family was proud of him. Most of all, she was terrified they wouldn't be friends anymore. She couldn't lose him. She laid a hand on his arm. "Mike, please."

He shook it off and turned to leave.

She tried again. "Don't go."

She heard him exhale and slowly count to three. "I'm calm. I'm going to remain calm and in control." He turned to face her. "Hand me your planner."

Okay, this was a new twist. But she would go with it. Carol reached in her purse and handed it to him. "What do you want with that?"

He flipped open the calendar to December 24 and wrote something on the page. "Christmas Eve. You have until Christmas Eve. Two days." He handed the book back to her.

Looking down, she saw the black scribbled words. *Mike's Christmas present.* Huh? "Is this some sort of reminder?"

He smiled tightly and took a few steps forward until she was stuck between the hard length of him and the hard length of the door frame. He planted his hands on either side of her head, trapping her there. Trapped? Right. She wiggled a little for effect, *Cosmo* tip number seven.

He lowered his head and murmured against her lips, "No, this is a reminder." It was a kiss meant for seduction, and there wasn't a body part on her that wasn't seduced. He was playing with her, teasing, kindling sparks that threatened to explode. His mouth tasted of aged wine, the intoxicating flavor making her head spin like a runaway carousel.

She opened her mouth, and murmured back, "Reminder for what?"

His tongue thrust inside, effectively shutting her up,

and she melted into him. She felt his hand work its way through her curls.

Her own hands, wanting a piece of the action, fast-forwarded to the back pockets of his slacks. She was going to love gray wool for the rest of her life. She flexed her fingers in a happy cat fashion, enjoying this newfound freedom to explore the anatomy of Mike.

He lifted his head and her lips protested the sudden withdrawal. She looked up to get a handle on the problem. He was breathing heavily and his eyes were dark, pupils dilated. She gave a silent cheer. This was definite progress.

"Carol, you're my Christmas present." He didn't smile, only watched her with an intensity that thrilled her.

Her stomach lurched to some hot, humid location as she contemplated the wealth of possibilities that statement implied. She grinned. Okay, she liked that plan. "Hot damn."

He put his fingers to her lips. "Uh, uh, uh. Not so fast, my little water mill. You have to choose. It's either me or all those other guys your mother thinks you should marry."

A decision. He wanted a decision from her. She coughed lightly. "Can you clarify, please?"

"You have to tell your mom about us."

That's what she thought he meant. A massive headache began to swell inside her brain. "What happens if I choose you?"

He leaned low and began to whisper all those happenings that he had planned for her. She closed her eyes and memorized every word. She would be replaying this for days. Maybe years.

"What happens if I don't?"

"Carol, I'll be honest with you. I can't go back to the way we were. I'm sure we'll still see each other, but..." He shrugged, the words hanging in the air. Life without Mike? She struggled for breath and the ache in her head plummeted to her heart. Even the moonlight seemed to dim.

"And in the meantime?" Hot, joyless tears threatened to overflow their ducts.

"For the next two days, we're just friends. Just like the good old days," he said, and she thought perhaps the good old days were a mite overrated.

"No kissing." He leaned down and kissed her lightly. She clung like glue, but he pulled his mouth away.

"No nibbling." His lips drove a hot trail up the side of her neck, ending to take a playful bite on her earlobe.

"No rubbing." He rocked his pelvis against hers and her center of gravity moved about eight inches below her waist. Oh, momma.

He stepped back a couple of steps, leaving her plastered against the door frame. The single outside lantern cast thin shadows on his face and she realized he was serious.

Dead serious.

An inept smile was all she could manage, and a few

undisciplined tears spilled over before she could wipe them away.

A muscle jerked in his jaw, but he didn't move toward her, instead he kept a rigid stance. "Say good night, Carol."

"Good night, Carol," she responded, her voice quivering. He turned and disappeared into the night, and she pressed herself further and further into the door frame until it hurt.

She scrubbed at her face, wiping away every trace of her tears. No point in crying. There were two days left. 48 hours. Two thousand, four hundred, and—three thousand minutes.

She buried her face in her hands and began to sob because three thousand minutes had never seemed so short.

11

On the eleventh day of Christmas, my true love gave to me—eleven dips of ice cream.

THE NEXT MORNING, the alarm clock went off twice before Carol got up and got dressed for work. Only half a day of work today, which was a good thing because her spirits were at a low ebb and she didn't want to think about work; didn't want to do anything, but create a new strategy for Mike, a new plan of attack. However, she was fresh out of ideas. She wanted to tell her mom, even picked up the phone once or twice, but the words wouldn't come. What was going on between her and Mike? Dating? Such a mild-mannered word to describe something so cataclysmic. She just felt drained.

To top it all off, when she showed up at her cube, an ominous note was waiting for her.

Carol,
    Need to see you immediately. Meet us in the 3rd floor conference room. Now.

                               MR.

Just great. This didn't bode well. She heard a pipe organ playing in the soundtrack of her life and she scanned over her e-mails to see if she could find a clue about the upcoming crisis, but none was to be found. Hmm. Finally, she straightened her skirt and coordinated sweater, and went to find the reason for the summons from her boss.

When she made it to the conference room, the first thing she noticed was the spread of food laid out on the table. There were bagels, pastries, breakfast tacos and all sorts of juices and cereals. She looked at Matilda, stunned. *A Christmas brunch?* Wow, it was the season for miracles. Now if only Mike... No, no, no.

Matilda coughed, more of a hacking sound, really, and then waved a hand in Carol's direction. Today, her dress was crimson stripes with a little set of jingle bells attached to the front. "Well, finally. Now, our little team is all here. I wanted to do something groundbreaking today in order to celebrate the Stoneware account. And here it is. Ta-da. Merry Christmas!"

Matilda lifted her glass of orange juice. "I'd like to propose a toast."

Obediently, everyone lifted their glasses, all looking just as confused as Carol. "To the best account team in the business."

Willard, never content to be a simple yes-man, bobbed his head at Matilda. "And to the best team leader in the business. We'd be nowhere without you, my liege."

"Nowhere," added Harold.

The brownnosers. Had they rehearsed this? Carol worked to keep the smile on her face. This was Christmas, after all.

"Ah, my faithful subjects." Matilda glanced over them all with pride. "You've all done so well, I'm giving you the rest of the day off."

Wow. Two extra hours of vacation. Carol was touched.

"I've brought Courtney's sketches for the new campaign. Thought you might like a little eye-candy while you're eating your Christmas candy." Matilda laughed at her own joke and taped the sketches up on the whiteboard.

Carol took a bite of her Danish, glanced up and nearly lost it. That was Mike up there on the board. Frantically, she looked over at Courtney. Did Courtney know Mike? Had Courtney mind-melded into Carol's brain? She rubbed her eyes and looked again. More closely this time. No, there were definite differences. Mike's hair was a little straighter than this guy's, and maybe a little shorter. Courtney had captured the mischief and the laughter that always sparkled in his eyes. This guy wasn't wearing a shirt. No, there was no white T-shirt to cover up those washboard abs. Washboard abs? Did Mike have washboard abs? Carol thought and then shook her head. No, his body was lean, his stomach flat and... She sighed, getting herself all aroused. What was she going to do?

"I know about that trick you pulled on me the other day."

Carol pulled herself from the fog of her mind and blinked, Mike disappearing, and Harold appearing. Darn.

"What trick?" Carol asked, annoyed at the interruption.

"With the powdered sugar. It wasn't very nice."

"Harold, I'm not a very nice person. You should have picked up on that by now. We've been working together for three years."

"I disagree. Why, when you wear those short skirts, you're really nice. Really, really nice." He looked up. "Will you look at that?"

The sprig of mistletoe hanging overhead might as well have been hemlock. Did he honestly believe she would kiss him? In front of witnesses? Ugh. "Sorry, bud. I think you've got the wrong victim." Carol started to move away, but before she made it to safety, he leaned in for the kill. He was quick all right, but not quick enough.

She lifted her cup of juice and poured it over his head. The liquid flew everywhere. With immense satisfaction, she watched as he spluttered, trails of orange wafting down his long, thin, outraged face, settling in his moustache. In the process, she had completely drenched herself, too, but it'd been worth it. Although, one important question remained. Could her orange-juice stained cashmere sweater be cleaned? For Harold's sake, she hoped so.

"Why did you do that?" he asked, wringing out his starched linen shirt.

So what if she ruined her sweater. It was Christmas,

times were changing, Carol was changing. She lifted her empty cup and winked at him. "Orange juice. It's not just for breakfast anymore. See ya, Harold. I think I'm going home."

MIKE HAD BEATEN himself up fifty times, cut himself shaving twice, and spent three and a half minutes debating with his toaster. Ultimatums were a risky proposition, and last night he had shot the moon. Carol had never handled pressure well, and he didn't want to cause a breakdown, but it was time for her to grow up. He just hoped that when she did stand on her own two feet, she wouldn't forget too many pieces of her old life.

Namely, him.

After analyzing the wisdom of knocking on her door less than sixteen hours after giving her the big "we're just friends" speech, he found himself doing it anyway, wondering if *ignavus* was really the Latin word for "wimp." On the other hand, he did say he was going to behave exactly like before. And *before* he would have fixed her stereo.

When there was no answer, he checked the doorknob—unlocked—and walked in. He was going to have to talk to her about that.

"Carol?" The front room looked empty and a little messy for her normal tidy nature. A diet cola can was lying on the coffee table, right next to an empty pint of ice cream. Half a bag of Oreos was almost hidden by a pillow on the couch. Three pens and an empty pad of paper looked as though they had been flung in the middle of the floor.

A small fish tank was perched on top of her bookshelf with a single goldfish swimming around. The fish was downright eerie, swimming back and forth as if it was sizing him up. He took a step back. Since when had Carol developed a thing for fish? He walked over to the tank and tapped on the glass. The fish made a little "o" with its mouth, looking a heck of a lot like Carol. It was true what they said about pets and their owners. He laughed and the fish seemed to understand.

A crash, followed by a string of colorful adjectives, came from the bedroom.

She was home.

"Mike?" she hollered.

What was she doing in there? Taking a shower? Kind of late for that. Mike was a visual kind of guy, and his visions were telling his good intentions to burn in hell. His feet followed the vision and accelerated in the direction of the bedroom.

No.

He stopped, mentally dressed Carol—maybe that sexy black dress she wore before. No. Baggy jeans and a sweatshirt. Or maybe not. He took a deep breath. "I got the coil for your speaker."

"You came to fix my stereo?"

For only the third time in five years. "Yeah. Where do you keep your tools?"

"Tools?"

"Is there an echo in here? You know, the ones I gave you last year."

"Look under the sink. I think I have a screwdriver." A little more muttering that he couldn't understand. "I'll be out in a minute."

He went to the kitchen and poked around under the sink, not finding anything resembling a toolbox, much less a screwdriver. Only a few bottles of cleaning goop, an old sponge and her trash can.

A trashcan overflowing with crumpled pieces of paper. He started to pick up the wayward wads, but then he noticed the writing. He froze, crouched under the dark sink, staring at those words.

Jump him.

His fingers twitched, poised above the paper, as he realized the impact that two little words could have.

He contemplated what she was doing to his normal logical nature. Here he was, actually thinking about going through her trash. He took the wad and placed it carefully on the top of the empty milk carton. Geez.

And all the little balls of paper came tumbling down, hiding between her cleaning supplies and the garbage disposal.

Oops.

Couldn't have that. He needed to pick them back up, and well, if they happened to open up, who's to say it's pathetic?

He rationalized away any trace of guilt. He was just a

neat and tidy kind of guy. He took the first piece of paper, smoothed it out and read.

P. Love to argue with him.

Well, well, well. He stared at the paper, wondering how wise it was to want to spend the rest of his life with someone who loved to argue with him. He shrugged. Challenges had always been fascinating.

He knew Carol. Pros and cons. He pushed aside a stack of sponges and made enough space for two piles. He put the paper in the she-loves-me pile and pulled out the next one.

C. Doesn't dress well.

Mike glanced down at the Levi's and white T-shirt. Obviously this went into the she-loves-me-not pile.

P. Great butt.

He grinned. She liked his butt? He remembered her hands the night before. He remembered her hands in the dark closet at Autumn Hills. He remembered her hands in Aunt Eleanor's room. Okay. She liked his butt. One more for the she-loves-me pile.

C. Mother.

That was pretty self-explanatory. Definitely the she-loves-me-not pile.

P. Cologne makes me want to jump him.

Damn, he forgot to put some on this morning. If he hurried, he could run over to his place... He jerked his head in the small confines and hit it on the garbage disposal. Stupid idea.

Another she-loves-me.

C. Doesn't like the arts.

She had scratched that out, so he wasn't sure what that meant. He moved her box of dishwasher detergent and made a third pile for unknowns.

P. When he kisses me, I want to jump him.

Was he the idiot who said "No kissing"? At least it went in the she-loves-me pile.

Ice cream.

He stared hard, but no matter how his eyes focused, it still didn't make sense. Carol loved ice cream. He liked it, too. Maybe she didn't know he liked ice cream? Maybe she had an ice cream fantasy and didn't think he would go for it? His hand wavered between "unknown" and "she-loves-me-not." Best to err on the side of caution. He put it in the she-loves-me-not pile. Besides, after he got through with her, that could definitely be changed to the she-loves-me pile.

P. When he touches me, I want to jump him.

Had he said "No touching?" He recited the ground rules he had laid out the night before. No kissing, no nibbling, no rubbing. Was touching in there? No, he didn't think so. And jumping him was becoming statistically significant. Things were looking up.

"Mike?"

Uh-oh. The suspect was on the move. He jerked up, forgetting where he was, and hit his head on the garbage disposal. "Hold on a minute. Did you know you have a leak in here?" As he shoved the papers back in the trash, he counted feverishly. Five P's. Three C's. One un-known. The results were in. She-loves-me wins.

The crowd goes wild.

"Can you fix it?"

"Of course." He sounded suitably insulted.

"Can you fix my mother, too?"

Her voice came from right behind him and he jerked, hitting his head on the garbage disposal. *Again.* Making sure to lower his head underneath the darned thing this time, he looked over his shoulder.

Legs. Bare. Long, silky. Hell. What were they talking about? Oh, her mother. All carnal thoughts withered away.

"If Sigmund Freud couldn't fix your mother, what makes you think I could?"

"Just checking."

A long silence and he gathered enough courage to look a little higher. Thighs. Bare. Great looking thighs. Hell. Okay, nibbling was out, but touching was still in.

"Will it take long?"

Oh, silly girl. "All night."

"Really?" She sounded disappointed. "Do you have to turn off the water?"

Slowly, her words rearranged themselves into some semblance of order and his brain came back online.

"Sorry." He angled his gaze higher, his neck protest-ing the awkward position. Robe. Terry cloth. Really, short robe. Hell.

She bent down behind him, smelling like soap, toothpaste and raspberries. "Where is it?"

He could lay her down, untie the robe one-handed, and they could spend the afternoon making love on her linoleum. "What?"

"The leak?"

He dragged his gaze away from the loosely tied knot at her waist and when he looked up, she was staring at him expectantly. He shook off any idea of burning it up on the linoleum. "Oh, I already fixed it." He stuck his head back under the sink. Much safer.

He felt her body nestle against his. There it was. The linoleum thoughts were back.

"Can you show me?"

Oh, God. He bumped his head on the garbage disposal for good measure.

"Uh, yeah." Steady, Mike. "Move back a minute and let me get out of here."

She instantly complied, the soft curves of her body moving away, and he called himself a moron. He backed out of the cabinet and stood up, drinking in what Carol looked like after a shower. A little bit sloppy, but very, very sexy. She smiled up at him and he wanted to wake up to that smile every day.

She was so beautiful. He closed his eyes for just a minute, but when he opened them again, she was still there, kneeling down next to her sink.

He stood still for a minute, unable to move, unable to do anything but stare into those big, blue eyes.

The leak. She wanted to see the leak. What leak? He shook his head. Oh, yeah. He crouched down behind her and pointed to some dark corner where her cleaning stuff had spilled. "Right over here." His cheek brushed against her damp hair, and he breathed in the simple fragrance of her shampoo. His lips moved involuntarily, ready to find the little place below her ear that could make her moan.

No. Kissing was out. Nibbling was out. Touching was the only loophole he had. Touching. Think, touching.

He trailed one hand over her hip, then flirted with the bottom of her robe. She wriggled back, her rear end settling right between his legs. He closed his eyes, torn between agony and ecstasy. He groaned and she turned her head.

"Mike?" Her voice was husky, her cheeks flushed.

His hands were halfway to his fly before he noticed the victory dance going on in her eyes.

The little minx.

He stood up and dusted his hands on his jeans, ignoring the way he was fixing to bust the seams. "Well, enough of that. Why don't you put some clothes on? It'll only take me a few minutes to replace the coil in your speaker and then—hey, I know…let's go get some ice cream."

THE ICE-CREAM place in the mall was crowded, full of kids, parents and a swarm of last-minute Christmas shoppers. Sometimes Carol wanted the snow and cold weather that rarely happened in Texas, but there were perks to a warm climate. Ice cream in December was one of them.

As they sat at the small glass-topped table, Carol watched Mike over the top of her cone. It was scary how easily he read her mind. She had stayed up last night finishing her tub of coffee ice cream, trying to outline what to tell her mother about Mike. And the only thing she managed to make was her grocery list.

Which she had promptly lost.

She took another lick. "I didn't know you liked ice cream. Well, at least I haven't seen you eat it in years."

Mike shrugged. "I love ice cream. Adore it. In fact, you know what? I don't think I have enough of it in my life. How do you feel about it?"

"It's good."

"Good? Or great? I mean, do you ever wonder what it is that makes it so, uh, fascinating?"

"What is this? You got some kind of thing about ice cream?"

"No, no. Unless you do? Do you?" He waved his hand. "Some people see ice cream in ah, sexual light. If you have that kind of vision, I applaud you for your, um, imaginative nature."

So Mike liked to get kinky with ice cream? Wow, he was much more creative than she ever gave him credit for. She began to smile at the possibilities.

"This is certainly a side of you I've never seen before. But it sounds," she took a lick and marvelled at the way his eyes followed her movements, "pretty fun."

She swirled her tongue around the sides of the cone, and he met her gaze. She did see him swallow once, but his eyes remained locked on hers.

Finally, he moved his chair until their thighs barely touched and smiled. "Do you like sundaes? There's something about a woman in whipped cream that can be—fascinating." Intently, he studied her chest and she broke out in a sweat, her nipples hardening at the same time. Had she really thought she could keep up?

She fanned herself and turned around to look at the other patrons. "My, it's sure getting warm in here. And look at that those kids over there. Aren't they cute? Ice cream dripping everywhere."

He leaned back in his chair and crossed his arms over his chest. "Wimp."

Wimp? She took a long, lingering lick of her ice cream, teasing and taunting. His eyes were no longer laughing. Wimp, indeed.

He moved in closer to her. "You know I'll make you pay for this."

Hypnotized by the gold flecks in his eyes, she worked to find her voice. "Name the time, name the place. I'll be there," said a voice that sounded dazed and more than a little unsteady. Unable to withstand any more torture, she concentrated on finishing her ice cream.

He stood up and took the remains of his raspberry sherbet to throw away. When he sat down again, he picked up her hands. "Carol, you are one lethal lady. I never suspected that."

She had never suspected that herself, and it did wonders for her self-esteem, but for now, she was still stuck on the idea of this payback thing. "We could leave right away."

Slowly he shook his head. "Don't think so."

Disappointment settled over her. She needed his arms around her again with an ache that bordered on desperation. "Talk to my mom?"

He nodded.

She stood up and pushed in her chair, watching him do the same. She could conquer the world when he was beside her, surely it would be an easy thing to have a shoot-out with her mom. She'd been so sure she would mess everything up, but not anymore. No, sir. When she was thinking of Mike, she could handle anything. And since she was always thinking of him nowadays... "Well, come on then," she said aloud. To herself she added, "I've got a speech to write."

AFTER TWO HOURS of doing nothing but wasting paper, she had learned one thing. Pat was absolutely no help at writing speeches. Carol paced back and forth and the useless fish still swam from side to side.

"Okay, let's go over the salient points one more time. First, I'm not going out with Jackson."

Pat swam around in circles, leaping in and out of the plastic diving bell.

Carol went over and sprinkled some fish food into the tank. "Second, I'm going to see Mike. Talk to him when-

ever I want. Decide if he looks better *avec* or *sans* Levi's.
I've got my money on *sans* Levi's and *avec* nothing
else.'' Pat concentrated on the food, not nearly as excited
about Mike's Levi's as Carol.

She sighed. Fish did not understand the art of blue
jeans. That's what happened when you dived around all
day wearing nothing but scales.

''Okay, what about this one? I could invite him over
for Christmas dinner. Mom needs to get used to the idea
of us being a couple.''

A couple. She could make dinner for him all the time,
not just when she wanted to check out a new recipe. They
could even move in together. Oh, no. What if he didn't
want couple-hood with her? He really hadn't mentioned
much about the future.

Surely he wasn't just playing with her. She stuck a
fingernail in her mouth and nibbled. She had always
wanted marriage, maybe kids, and a husband who looked
and acted just like Mike. What did he want? He had told
her he wanted seven kids when they were in junior high.
Seven? She looked around at the small apartment. They
would need more space.

Mike had never been one for long relationships. Come
to think of it, she didn't seem to be either. With a rather
brilliant flash of behavioral insight, she knew why all the
men she dated had never seemed quite right.

They weren't Mike.

She watched Pat gobble the food and realized how
desperately she wanted a future with him. ''I've got to

think positive thoughts about this. Mike must care something about me, don't you think? He wouldn't have put up with me all these years if he didn't. And as for Mom, well, she's just going to have to get over it. Dad's reasonable. Maybe he can help me win her over.''

Carol called her mom and asked her to meet her for a really late lunch. That would give her another two hours to come up with something. Anything.

She picked up her pen, determined not to procrastinate any more, and began to list all the points she needed to cover with her mom.

She got to number ten, and became distracted with thoughts of whipped cream. She turned to a fresh sheet and started another grocery list.

WHEN SHE ARRIVED at the tea room, Carol opened her planner and checked the notes she had made earlier. With everything in place, she was armed and ready for The Talk, otherwise known as WWIII.

She looked up, saw her mother already seated and waving, and smiled. Clicking the book shut, she strode confidently toward the table and sat. No problems here.

Her mother air-kissed her and pulled her into a hug.

"Hello, hon. How are you doing?" Her mom waved a hand, indicating the blue silk suit Carol had chosen specially for the occasion. "You look lovely today. That blue matches your eyes just so. And what did you do to your hair? *Très chic.*"

Carol touched her hair, still sticky from the jar of hair

gel she had used to tame it. "Thanks, Mom. I've been trying to update my image recently."

"And may I say that it's about time? My little girl is finally growing up."

Her mom would always see her as a little girl, wanting to protect and shelter her. Unfortunately, Carol had done little to disabuse her of that notion. What a wimp. She created a mental image of Mike to sustain her nerve. He didn't want a little girl and to be honest, Pat was right. She didn't want to spend the rest of her life being something that she wasn't.

After the waitress had come and given them coffee, Carol cleared her throat and discreetly pulled her planner in her lap, flipping it open to her notes.

"Mom, we need to talk."

"Of course, dear." Her mom's gaze wandered around the room, and she wrinkled her nose, waving elegantly at some of her friends.

Carol coughed and her mom turned and graced her with a genuine smile. "I'm sorry, that was rude of me. You were saying?"

"I *am* growing up, Mom. I think we should have had this discussion about ten years ago, but I've been a little slow."

"What discussion is that?"

"My life. I'm capable of making my own decisions, deciding what is best for me."

"Of course. But hon, you need to make the right decisions, not the wrong ones. Take Jackson, for example.

With a good man, you'll be set for life. Two kids, three living areas and a Jag in the garage. One wrong decision and you'll be stuck with three divorces and visitation on the weekends. Look at Kitty Constantine. She's been in therapy for ten years and there's no end in sight."

Carol wanted to roll her eyes, but that wouldn't score any points in the I'm-not-a-little-girl debate. All this ping-ponging between her mom and Mike was going to put her in therapy anyway. "I need to make my own mistakes. If it's a bad decision, so be it."

"Carol, I just want what's best for you." Her mom waved a hand around the tastefully furnished room. A wave that encompassed the crystal stemware, the antiques scattered here and there, as well as the Persian rugs laid out on the floor. It was a room that smelled of money. "You're accustomed to the accoutrements that come along with your life."

Charity events, fine wines, opera and panty hose. Nope. Not for her. She lifted her chin. "I didn't come here to discuss the Dallas social scene. I have some specific items that I would like to bring up."

Her mom humored her with a smile.

Carol looked at point number one. "I really don't want to go out with Jackson. I know you and Mrs. Ellis are sold on this idea, but I just don't see it happening." She raised her head to see the impact this would have on her mom.

Meredith looked disappointed and Carol realized she would be seeing a lot more of that disappointment in the future. But she'd survived it before, she'd survive it again. "Oh, but you two are just perfect. And you must admit, he's a very handsome fellow."

"Okay, I'll give you that. He is easy on the eyes, but I don't think he's my type." He didn't have those brown eyes that sparkled and smiled all the time.

"Of course he's your type, hon. Remember when you used to play with your dolls? You told me exactly what you wanted your husband to be like." Meredith Martin was in her native environment in a tea room and she smiled with the confidence of someone on home turf.

"Mom, I was eight years old then. I've become more multifaceted, more adventurous." The kind of adventures that involved ice cream and whipped cream and Mike. Oh, my.

"I think Jackson could be adventurous with the right encouragement." Her mom said that with a frown, as if she was having trouble with that image.

"Yes, I'm sure he could. But I don't want to provide that encouragement."

"Now, hon. Can't you just do this one thing for me? You know I don't ask much, and it would do me so proud to see you and Jackson together at the charity gala. It's for a good cause."

"No."

"Now Carol, calm down. I don't know what's come over you lately. If that Mike is behind this, I swear—"

"Mike has nothing to do with this." Okay, he had everything to do with this, but now certainly wasn't the time to bring it up. She remembered her notes and glanced down at point number two. "I'm twenty-six years old and it's time I started deciding who I date." Her mother's frown grew darker. "I'll be twenty-seven in June." And darker. "And I need to, you know, make my own decisions." Even darker.

Her mother twirled her spoon in her coffee for several long moments before replying. "Carol, your father and I tried to make sure that everything you've needed, you've had. If you and Mike were to become involved, you're condemning yourself to an existence that you've never known." She looked up, her eyes full of love and concern. "You're just not that strong, honey."

"Mom, that's not fair. You have no idea what kind of feelings I have for Mike." Carol heard the sound of her heart being ripped in two.

Her mom speared her with a glance. "What kind of feelings are those?"

Carol swallowed. "He's my friend. I think about him, want to talk to him all the time. I think I'm falling in love, Mom." She expected a crash of cymbals, a flourish of trumpets, a burst of fireworks, but instead she was filled with a sense of peace.

"Carol, when you love someone you know with an absolute certainty. It's not a feeling you can mistake. Don't commit yourself until you know for sure."

Carol was amazed that her mom seemed to be calm, rational, even listening. She owed it to her mother to reciprocate in kind. "So what do you think I should do?"

"Go out with Mike, but at least go with Jackson to the gala. Do this for your mother."

She wasn't ready to give her mother an answer and she glanced down at point number three. This one should go much easier. "I like beer now."

Her mother frowned, her brows knitted together. "I think that's fine, after all, this is Texas. But I fail to see how this is germane to our conversation."

"It's important to me." Important to take the victories where she could.

"Of course, hon. You need to feel independent. Now, do say you'll go with Jackson to the gala. We can all go together." Her mother wrinkled her nose. "It'll be fun."

"No."

"Carol, I know our relationship hasn't been an easy one, but you have so much potential. Look at you, look at what you've started to make of yourself. You graduated from college, found yourself a good job. You're on your way, hon." For the first time Carol heard pride in her voice.

"I've tried, Mom. I really have."

"And it shows." Her mother picked up her cup and took an elegant sip. "Have you and Mike talked about a future?"

"Not yet."

Meredith nodded. "Has he told you how he feels?"

"Well, no." A cramp started in her stomach.

"You don't even know what he wants, do you? And

you're supposed to sit around twiddling your thumbs while he makes up his mind?''

"Mike isn't like that." She didn't know exactly where things would end up between them, but she would trust Mike with her life. And her heart.

"That saying, 'don't put your eggs in one basket' was invented for a reason. Look, just go out with Jackson once. Do this for me. After that, I won't say another word about him or anyone else, especially Mike."

"Nothing bad about him, ever again?''

"Of course."

Carol sighed and picked up her pen. "Just tell me when it is.''

CAROL RIPPED OFF the blue silk suit and stared at Pat. "Okay, shoot me. You might as well, 'cause I know Mike's going to." She poured some fish food into the tank.

Pat swam to the surface and began to eat with tail-twitching excitement.

"How could I have agreed to go on this date with Jackson? Is there some sort of mother-mind-control that goes on? Some gene that's inherited at birth that enables them to always, *always,* make you do their bidding?"

Pat swam up and down. The fish version of "Yes."

"I've got four choices here." She took out a piece of paper and began to write. "One. Tell Mom no." Pat gave her that you're-a-moron look. "Okay, you're right, I failed that one. Maybe I could write an anonymous letter?''

Pat stared and Carol sighed.

''Yeah, I didn't think so either. Two. Tell Mike I need more time. Nope, that's out. I haven't lasted twelve hours. This morning he was here, puttering around, fixing this, fixing that, and every time, there's some reason that he needs to touch me. And then I just go crazy.''

Pat seemed to quirk a gill.

''I know, I tried that. But he caught on before things got out of hand. I almost had him, though.''

That garnered an ''o'' of appreciation.

''You know, Pat, I was crazy if I thought that one night of mad passion was going to get him out of my system. I mean, none of these stiff-necked, pretty boys is going to make me laugh like he does, and I just can't imagine Jackson Ellis looking quite so good in blue jeans. And heck, who knows me any better than Mike?''

Pat stared.

''I know. Nobody.''

She looked down at the paper and saw two disgustingly awful choices. ''But there is a third. I could not mention to Mike about the date. One date. What could it hurt? Anyway, you should have seen Mom. She seemed so sincere. She's never looked at me like that before. With pride.''

Pat glared accusingly.

''All right, I might tell him eventually and I could manage to keep Mike away from Mom for a while. And this way I could be with him. After all, he asked me to tell Mom about us. I did that. So, I'm not really doing anything wrong. Right?'' It sounded pretty good to her.

She closed her book, trying to ignore the way Pat was swimming in disapproval.

''Fine. Just be a Goody Two-shoes. You don't have to like it. All you have to do is keep your mouth shut.''

The contrary fish made an ''o'' of protest.

THAT NIGHT AT rehearsal, things went amazingly well. Everyone knew their lines, the Widow Chandler maintained an unhappy distance from Mike, and Aunt Eleanor was on her best behavior. Fred too.

As the last carols were being sung, Carol walked over to Mike, smoothing her festive Christmas-motif skirt and sweater. ''I need to talk to you.''

He looked at her with suspicion. ''Why?''

''I talked to Mom today.''

Suspicion turned to shock. ''I figured you would wait until tomorrow. You know, put if off until the last minute.''

She heard the implied ''like normal'' and ignored it. ''Surprised you, didn't I?''

''Sorry, I shouldn't have underestimated you.'' He gave her a soft smile. ''I'm proud of what you did, though. Are you okay?'' He laid a hand on her cheek.

A moment of guilt simmered in her blood.

''Mother will get over it eventually.'' After a suitable

cooling down period. After Carol went to the gala. After Carol ditched Jackson. "Can you take me home?"

"Sure. There's only a few things left to do here, and then we'll head on out."

He turned back toward the stage and she laid a hand on his arm. "Mike?"

He turned to face her. "Hmm?"

She stared at him a moment and sighed. No wonder women kept throwing themselves at him, he really was breathtaking. And for tonight he was hers. She didn't try to analyze why her heart began to race. Instead she just accepted the way things were destined to be and smiled. "Thanks."

"For what?" His dark brows drew together.

"For being there."

He stepped a little closer, and guilt transformed into something that sent her pulse pounding. "You should know by now that I'll always be there for you."

Hadn't he proven that time and time again? She closed her eyes, savoring the memories she had built up over the years. He'd been there when Garrett had broken her heart in tenth grade. He'd visited her every day when she'd had her appendix removed. And in eighth grade... When her lashes drifted open, she smiled. "There was that one time you finked on me for not doing my homework...."

His mouth twitched in a lazy smile. "You deserved it, always putting stuff off until the last minute. Besides in the long run it was good for you."

The challenge was there in his eyes, and she rose to the occasion, just like they both knew she would. Excitement flared in her brain, her stomach, finally settling between her thighs. Did he have any idea how turned on she got from arguing with him? "I suppose you think you know what's good for me?"

"Naw, but you know what?" He stepped closer, tilted her chin, and his eyes went dark with promise. "I'm going to have a hell of a time finding out."

Yeah. He knew. She wilted, and he caught her to him. "Carol?"

Incapable of any major linguistic efforts, Carol just looked at him.

"Why don't you go get your stuff together? I think I'm in a hurry to get home."

CAROL DIDN'T THINK a supersonic jet would have got them home fast enough, but Mike did a pretty fair imitation with the Thunderbird. He didn't touch her and for some reason that seemed to only make her more crazy.

When he walked her up the stairs, she felt his presence, her neck tingling, the back of her knees shaking, even her elbows getting a little flushed. By the time they reached her door, she was a mess.

She fumbled a little with her keys, but finally managed to correctly unlock the dead bolt.

They both moved inside and she shut the door.

Alone. At last.

No relatives, no Autumn Hills residents, no Junior Leaguers.

"Carol, are you sure about this?" He didn't smile, his gaze intent on her.

She studied him, the dark velvet of his eyes, the smooth line of his jaw, the ridge that sat in the middle of his nose.

Sure? She wasn't sure what the hit toy of the next Christmas season would be, couldn't decide where she wanted to be in five years, and didn't know if she was Republican or Democrat. But there was one fact she could absolutely, positively count on.

In the next three seconds she was going to start kissing Mike, and she wasn't going to stop. Ever. Five years. Ten years. Yep, fifty years later, she was still going to be kissing him. Her mother could have a fit and it really didn't matter.

Not anymore.

She crossed the room and pulled an ecru bow from her little Christmas tree, stuck it on her head, and smiled.

"Merry Christmas, Mike."

Mike exhaled slowly. He had never seen a woman as beautiful as Carol was tonight. He went to her, bent his head and captured her lips, wanting this kiss to go on forever. He was hungry to taste her, hungry to have her. A moan escaped from the back of her throat and threatened the last vestiges of his control.

He pulled her closer, and she wiggled her fingers between them and began undoing the buttons on his shirt.

She was almost to the end, when the last button refused to give way. He heard her murmur against his lips and in the face of her vicious yank, the button went flying across the room.

He laughed against her mouth, but his sense of humor collapsed when she rubbed back and forth against him, her hands buried in his back pockets, keeping their bodies locked together.

His fingers trembled as he untied the tiny bows that kept her sweater together. One by one, the ribbons gave way, until with a sigh of accomplishment, he slid the sweater off her shoulders.

She stood there, so still, looking up at him, that silly white bow perched on her hair. His heart slammed in his chest. She was softer and silkier than in his dreams, and he felt himself drowning in the deep blue of her eyes.

He swung her up in his arms and carried her to the bedroom.

Carol was sure this was heaven. Nothing she had ever experienced had prepared her for the inevitability of being in his arms. Burying her face in Mike's neck, she caressed and teased, tasting the moist flesh. He eased her back against the pillows and followed, his mouth finding her own for one hot, greedy kiss.

Her fingers grasped his loosened shirt, eager for the feel of his skin against her own. She sat up, cast the shirt over the side of the bed, and then started working furiously to discover the rest of him.

Mike's fingers were much more efficient than her own,

but what she lacked in skill, she made up for in speed. And after a few giggles and a lot of heavy breathing, she began to explore him for real.

His chest was powerful and hard, created to fit together against her own. His arms were strong, potent, the muscles tight and supple under her hands. She shivered with delight as she traced the ridges and hollows of his body.

The strong arms braced on either side of her and he lowered that powerful chest until she was inlaid between the softness of the pillows and the overwhelming hardness of Mike. A shock of pleasure pulsed through her as his flesh met her own.

And then things got serious.

His fingers trailed over her throat, skimming over her nipples, his caress blazing a trail of flames in its wake. The safety of her world came crashing down around her, destroyed by the wicked power of his touch and the raging ache that vibrated low in her belly.

He drew his mouth in a maddeningly slow path from her cheek to her breasts, which swelled one cup size just at the touch of his tongue. She couldn't stop the moan that escaped when his lips followed the curve of her stomach and her fingers frantically buried themselves in his hair.

He went lower, sending her blood reeling, her back arching, her voice whimpering for relief. Coils of pleasure began to build, and helplessly she felt herself being sucked into a vortex of pressure.

She had to take him, had to possess this piece of him

she had never known before. Desperately needy, she bucked against him, impatient for release. Her hands pulled him upward and she murmured her plea in his ear.

She wanted him now, she wanted him tomorrow, she wanted him forever.

He grew still, but only for a heartbeat.

With quiet purpose, he took a foil packet and sheathed himself.

Then, his hands slid underneath her and he lifted her hips. In the dim moonlight his eyes flashed. She saw the question there. One last time he was asking. One last time she could walk away.

Her voice caught, trembling with need. "Mike. Please."

He buried himself inside her, and her world began to spin. She began to move, matching his rhythm and following mindlessly.

His face blurred, her eyes losing focus. She was only aware of the sound of their gulping breaths, the touch of his skin, hot, damp, against her own.

He took her with him, further and further into dark recesses she never had known before. With a final gasp of air, she fell, her body shuddering and convulsing.

Her head dropped back into the pillows and he collapsed weakly, burying his face against her neck.

For long moments, they laid there together, silent and unmoving, the hot, musky smell of their lovemaking heavy in the air.

She felt his lips press lightly against her neck, the touch cool and tender.

A kiss that touched her heart.

She stared at the ceiling, guilt blossoming anew. For years she had played at meek and mild, always giving in to the wishes of her mother. This time would be different. Mike had offered her his strength, and before she had always looked away, leaning on him instead. But now it was her turn. No date with Jackson. Not going to happen. Not ever. She smiled and began to hum the theme from *Rocky.*

"Carol?" His voice was low, raspy, and exhausted.

"Hmm?"

"Are you sure?"

Of course she was sure. She mentally pictured herself running up the steps, shadowboxing the world. Her mom wouldn't stand a chance. Mike was going to be hers forever and ever. "Absolutely."

He raised up on his forearms, and she felt him begin to move inside her.

"Okay, champ."

Happily, she gave him her body. Quietly, she gave him her heart.

12

On the twelfth day of Christmas, my true love gave to me—two hearts a drumming.

CAROL AWOKE SLOWLY to see the sunlight streaming in through her bedroom balcony window. She stretched her arm, but the sound of a knock at the door interrupted a most pleasant dream.

Her fingers found shoulders that were much broader than any teddy bear she had ever owned.

No dream. Definitely not a dream. Dreams didn't make her blood heat.

She jerked upright, realized she had no clothes and clutched the covers to her chest.

The sudden movement disturbed Mike, who opened a sleepy eye to glare at her. "Go back to—" He stopped when the knocking started again and sat up.

Her mouth grew dry at the sight of all that hard, masculine flesh gleaming in the morning sun and she forgot all about the door.

Until she heard it open.

"Carol? Are you home, hon?"

Disaster.

Mike grinned. "Come closer and we can really shock her."

She beat at his chest, letting her fingers linger for just a second longer until she remembered her impending doom. She needed a plan.

The plan was easy. Get rid of her mom. ASAP.

"Wait just a minute. I'll be right out." She pitched her voice to a whisper. "I need to get dressed."

Mike lifted his hands. "Sweetheart, don't let me stop you."

He was going to be no help at all. "Fine." She took a deep breath, threw back the covers, and stalked over to the coat rack where she kept her robe. Glancing in the mirror, she caught a glimpse of Mike watching her. Their eyes locked and she shrugged on her robe a little bit slower than necessary.

"Hey." Mike motioned her over and pulled her down on the bed. "Just in case I don't survive." His lips met hers in what started as a quick kiss and then exploded into a full-blown bonfire of passion. With more regret than sense, she pulled away.

He smiled. "I'm not moving from this spot. Hurry up."

She tightened her robe and left the room.

Her mom looked immaculate as usual, but let out an exaggerated sigh at Carol's short, scruffy robe.

Carol straightened her shoulders and met her mom's gaze. She wouldn't let her ruin her morning. Absolutely nothing could ruin the best day of her life, but she really did need to get rid of Mom.

She glanced at the clock on the mantel and dropped her jaw. "Nine o'clock? I'm late!" She started to push her mom toward the door. "Gotta run."

Her mom dug the heels to her pink suede pumps into the carpet. "Hold it a moment. This will only take a minute."

"Mom, I really have to—"

"I had some shopping to finish up and I stopped by to see if you wanted to come along."

She kept shoving, but her mom didn't budge. "No can do. Got places to go, people to see."

"But you're going to need a new dress—"

"For the nursing home tonight? Nah, I've got lots of things to wear." She took hold of her mom's arm and pulled. "It was really nice of you to visit."

"No, no. The gala. I want you to look nice for the gala. A little bird told me that Jackson's favorite color is green. Maybe we could find something in a soft mint? Or what about an emerald velvet? That would look so pretty with your hair."

Carol pulled harder, but to no avail.

"Mom, I really, really—"

Her mom jerked her arm free. "Carol, what is wrong with you?" She looked at Carol with suspicion and noted the sweater lying in the middle of the floor.

Carol quickly picked it up and shrugged. "I'm such a slob."

"Carol, is there something going on here I should know about?" And with that intuitive radar that every mother has, she honed in quickly on the real situation. "Is Mike here?"

Carol stared at the closed door to her bedroom, stared at her mom and made up her mind. "Yes, he is. I don't need a new dress because I'm not going with Jackson. And now if you don't mind, I think I'd like a little privacy. Is that a problem?"

Her mom opened her mouth to say something and then shut it quickly. Her eyes promised dire consequences and Carol knew she hadn't heard the end of it. "We'll talk about this later, young lady."

She closed the door after her mom, and dusted her hands, sure the conversation wasn't over yet. Still, it felt good. Pat was swimming in approval and Carol punched a couple of times in the air.

Now she just had to take care of Mike. Heat washed over her as she contemplated the many options available. She grinned, feeling pretty sure of herself. Her hands worked the knot at her waist and the robe fell to the floor. Wouldn't be needing that.

She walked into the bedroom and stared in confusion at the empty room. The wind caught the curtains and she noticed the open balcony door for the first time. She shivered in the cool breeze and slowly rubbed her arms.

It took only a quick inventory to realize that the only clothes scattered about the room were her own.

Mike had left.

She started to pick up her clothes, ready to go after him, needing to explain.

A piece of paper fluttered to the floor and she picked it up. Underneath the program she had made up for tonight's show, Mike had scrawled two words.

Don't bother.

She mechanically wrapped herself up in the sheet. This was one problem she couldn't rely on Mike to fix. Once again she had messed things up. She rubbed the soft material against her cheek, the scent of Mike mingling with the scent of their lovemaking.

She walked to the other room and sat down in front of Pat's bowl.

Why hadn't she just told Mike the truth, or at least dealt with her mom yesterday the way she had planned? If she had, her heart wouldn't feel so heavy and her arms wouldn't be so cold. And her eyes wouldn't be blinking so desperately.

Pat just stared, not saying a word. Carol hugged the sheet tightly and started to cry.

She messed up the best thing in her life. Now he was gone.

MIKE LAUNCHED HIMSELF into his car and slammed the door. Hard. Firing the ignition, he ground the pedal into the floor, and pealed out of the parking lot. He had to get away. And nowhere in Texas was far enough.

Deceitful, two-timing, lying— he stopped, reining in his thoughts.

Carol was nothing more than herself. She wouldn't want to go with the social dipstick, but she'd do it anyway.

He had found the woman he wanted, the woman he loved, and the piece of her she offered wasn't enough. He would not be cast off to some backroom affair while she went about her life.

Pounding on the steering wheel didn't help. The thing he wanted to hit most was himself.

Why did he think she could change? He should have pulled off his rose-colored glasses a long time ago. Maybe it was the way she sparkled lately and smiled at the drop of a hat. She had been happier than he'd seen her in a long time, and he thought it was because of him.

Stupid. Foolish. He'd been an idiot.

And now he was just an idiot that hurt.

By THE TIME Carol got to the nursing home that evening, she was way beyond misery. She was furious. His car had been missing all day, she'd been left talking to his answering machine, and the operator at his paging service knew her by name. At least she knew he would be there for the show. When Mike committed to anything but women, he was there 'til the end.

Why now? She was in the middle of a radical personality change and he'd walked out when she was in midmodification. Maybe she should've told him about Jackson, or maybe she should've been firmer with her mom. She blew out a breath. Okay, she wasn't there yet, but these kinds of changes come after years of thoughtful introspection, not one night of great—extraordinarily great, to be honest—sex.

She sighed. There was no time for consultations with a specialist, the man she needed to consult with was Mike. Who was she kidding? Consult? She needed his arms around her, needed to see his smile, needed to touch him again.

The biggest obstacle to kissing him again was Mother. Carol had stood up to her this morning, told her Mike was there—in the bedroom no less. At least now her mom knew her little girl had already grown up. She rolled her shoulders. Yeah, this taking-control-of-her-life stuff was getting easier.

The second biggest obstacle to touching him again was Mike, and this time he was going to listen to her in person.

She stalked to Aunt Eleanor's room and flung open the door. Of course they were there. Together. Just sitting, shooting the breeze like absolutely nothing was wrong. He had come in, stripped away all the tokens and trinkets of her world, until nothing remained but him—and she wasn't going to give him up without a fight.

"Aunt Eleanor, I need to talk to Mike."

Her great-aunt raised her brows. "My, my. Look what the wind blew in—hurricane Carol. And I'd say all that raging fury is headed straight for you, my boy." She got up and walked out, laughing all the way.

Carol didn't see any humor in this situation and turned

her attention to Mike. His eyes seemed a little less bright and his magical mouth was stamped in a hard line rather than the careless grin she loved. Had she done that to him?

She stood in front of his chair and looked down. "You're going to listen to me."

He shot her a bland look. "Shoot."

"First off, I'm sorry. Second, I don't want to go to that stupid thing with Jackson Ellis."

His lips curled into a forced smile and a tremor flowed down her spine. "I know. That's what makes this whole thing such crap."

"Mom means well, she just wants what's best for me."

He walked over to the window and looked out. "And I suppose I'm not it? Maybe your mom is right."

He spoke in a quiet tone and for the first time she saw vulnerability in the square of his shoulders, the tense angle of his jaw.

She walked to him, raising a hand to comfort, but her fingers trembled and fell helplessly back to her side. "That's not true."

"I'm not in the same league with the Brocks and Jacksons of the world."

"No, you're in a league all your own. I'm just beginning to realize how lucky I am to have you in my life, and I'm sorry I haven't clued in before. Clueless, that's me. I did learn something though. I don't want what my mother wants for me. You probably figured that out a long time ago.''

"I thought I did, but now I'm not so sure." He turned around and faced her then. He studied her for a moment before raking a hand through his hair. "So why?"

Why was this so difficult for him to understand? They could usually communicate without words, and now it seemed like words weren't helping at all. "This one you haven't figured out?" She laughed, more at herself than anything. "Slipping today, huh?"

She ground a palm against her forehead and continued. "I know my mother loves me, but I never was good enough. That day, when I talked to her—really talked—I started to think that maybe she was changing her mind. She told me she'd respect my decision if I went to this thing with Jackson. It'd be *my* decision. She told me she'd lay off you, Mike. She promised." She swallowed, her throat going dry. "This from my mom. I thought, maybe… I guess I was wrong."

He stared at her coldly. "So you'd go out with this dork just to make some brownie points for Mommie dearest?"

"I want her to be proud of me. Why can't you see how important that is to me?"

"If she asked you to go to bed with him, would you have done that, too?"

Something inside her burst and she raged at him, "How dare you ask me that after what happened between us last night." She'd been trying so hard to win his respect and for some reason, his lack of faith hurt more than anything else. Her vision started to blur with tears, but she wiped them away, determined to follow this through. Finally she found her voice. "You know better, Mike. Of everybody in the world, you know better."

He threw up his hands, like he was giving up. On her. "How am I supposed to know? Don't you think you should have at least asked me first?"

"And what? Then you'd give me permission?"

"Like hell. I don't want you going out with anybody else."

"Oh you're Mr. High-and-Mighty, telling me what to do. Well, move over buddy 'cause I already have one mother and that's more than enough." The words were coming out of her mouth fast and furious.

"One mother that runs all over you."

"At least Mom's got an excuse, what's yours?"

He winced. "Geez, Carol, how could you? I love you."

Love?

Her heart pumped in response and she sank into a chair, her legs unable to hold her anymore. A smile twitched at the corners of her lips and all the anger melted away. Love, what a magical word. Not "loved," but present tense. If he could love her now, after all she'd done... Well, there was hope yet. "Say that again."

"No."

Her smile turned into a grin. Trust Mike to always say

the right thing. That was one of the millions of reasons she loved him.

She stood and took a quick look at her watch. Twenty minutes to show time. Her mistakes needed fixing and nobody else was going to do it for her. She pressed a quick kiss against his cheek. "Sorry about the lipstick. You'll have to get used to it. I've got to go. There's not much time." She grinned and waved. She knew exactly what to do. "Trust me."

MIKE TRIED TO concentrate on the show, he really did, but his gaze kept sliding to Carol. While Mr. Golivanni was belting out "O Christmas Tree" on his accordion, Carol had her head down, scribbling away in her planner. Mike knew what she was writing—Speech to Mom, the Sequel. In other circumstances, he would've been exhilarated, but Carol was sporting a new look tonight. A warrior goddess attitude that was scary. Arousing, but scary. Carol, with her normal, demure programming could still be a recipe for disaster when she applied herself. And tonight, with that devil-may-care gleam in her eye, she was a wild card.

As the final chorus of "We Wish You a Merry Christmas" ended, she mounted the stairs two at a time and climbed up on the stage. Clasped tightly in her hand were several sheets of paper.

She waved at him, a shy wiggle of her fingers that reminded him of the first time he saw her in second grade. Droopy knee socks with hair ribbons to match. He'd been a goner right from that moment.

She squared her shoulders and Mike closed his eyes. Surely the speech was just for Mom. She wouldn't recite the whole thing to the residents of Autumn Hills and all their respective families.

He watched as Carol took a deep breath and smiled at the audience. Lifting the paper in front of her face, she coughed and the pages shook ominously.

On the other hand, who could really tell with Carol? Mike began to pray. "Dear God, I promise to be more tolerant and accepting of people. I will never attempt to help change another human being even if it is for the better—"

"Ladies and gentleman, thank you all for coming out tonight. So often at Christmas we take for granted our families and the ones we love."

She cleared her throat.

Mike prayed harder. "I swear I'll never cuss again. Just don't let her do anything crazy here. I'm going to take care of her—"

"The holidays are a time for togetherness. To realize just how lucky we are to have—" Carol stopped, lowered the pages, and began to chew on her bottom lip.

She wadded up the sheets of paper, glanced over at her mother, and tossed them over her shoulder. Mike, sensing he had just dodged a bullet, heaved a silent, "Thank you."

But then she started up again. "Mom, I have something to say."

Mike swallowed with difficulty and began to inch toward the door.

Carol leveled a finger toward him in a Salem witch-hunt manner. "You. Don't move."

He stopped in his tracks, frozen as the spotlight speared him.

Oblivious to all the people staring transfixed, Carol shook her finger. "You missed this once, darn it. You will not miss it again."

Mike obeyed and the spotlight zoomed back to Carol.

"Mom, I love Mike. No doubts, no uncertainties, not even a quiver of vacillation. I'm going to marry him and I can't very well have you fixing me up with other guys when I'm engaged. So, to summarize, I'm not going to go out with Jackson, or anybody else. I've found my guy and I'm keeping him."

Everything else blurred around him as a giant vacuum began to siphon all the oxygen from his body. He pinched himself, but the pain didn't register.

She loved him.

Carol seemed to clue in on her surroundings and she looked down, scuffing her foot against the floorboards. "Um, there's refreshments in the cafeteria. Good night everyone and Merry Christmas!"

The room exploded with applause and Carol peeked up then, nervously doing a half wave from her waist.

A smile tickled the corner of his mouth and then began

to grow. Carol's sense of timing had always sucked, but she somehow managed to come through.

Eleanor shuffled over and clapped him on the back. "Congratulations, my boy! You didn't tell me you'd popped the question."

"I haven't. I mean, I was going to eventually…"

Eleanor's laughter cut him off. "Beat you to the punch? Oh, she's a Martin all right. Knows what she wants and grabs it with both hands. Just think of what Christmas dinners are going to be like now."

Mike recoiled and closed his eyes to block out the vision. "Dam…dagnabbit."

She pointed to where Carol and her mother were embroiled in an animated discussion. "You better go bail her out. But before you do, remember one thing about your new mother-in-law." She put on her glasses and looked up at him. "Whatever she's done, she's done out of love. And over time she'll see what you and Carol mean to each other."

Mike glanced over at Meredith Martin, but just at that instant Carol turned toward him, and he couldn't help but smile. She grinned back, and for a few moments they both stared at each other across the room.

Mrs. Martin shook her finger at her daughter, effectively eliminating any magical moments. Mike took a deep breath and mentally rolled up his sleeves. With a spring in his step, and the Mormon Tabernacle Choir playing in his heart, he went to rescue the woman he figured he was going to have to marry after all.

He walked over and didn't think Carol had noticed as she continued her argument with her mother, but her hand tucked into his as if it belonged. He squeezed gently. "Excuse me. I hate to interrupt, but I think there's a paper plate emergency that Carol needs to tend to right now."

Meredith Martin turned on him, her eyes narrowed. "This is all your fault."

"Now, Mrs. Martin. Should I call you Mom? Or Meredith?" Her eyes flashed fire. "We'll stick with Mrs. Martin for now. I'll do everything I can to make her happy. You really have raised an extraordinary daughter."

That seemed to subdue her somewhat. "Thank you," she said with a gracious nod. "But don't think I won't be watching you—"

"Meredith," Carol's father interrupted. "Behave. Don't know how you could have missed it. She's been in love with the boy forever. Now that everybody else has, I think it's time you woke up and smelled the bacon." He smiled and extended a hand to Mike. "Welcome to the family, son." He gestured toward his wife. "Just hang in there and you'll do fine."

Aunt Eleanor grabbed Mike's arm, with Fred Waring close behind her. "Told you, my boy. You should've listened to me earlier. I may be old, but I'm always right." She turned to Fred, beaming with pride. "Ain't that right, Fred?" When he didn't respond, she punched him in the arm. "Fred!" She leaned closer to Carol, sighing. "Now if those little blue pills could get his synapses firing as well."

IT WAS ALMOST midnight before Mike drove Carol home. She rambled during the drive, but he didn't seem to mind her chatter. The car heater was running, not that she needed any warmth. When they got to her apartment, he followed her inside. "I need to talk to you about this marriage thing."

Her heart dipped precariously until she saw the mischievous sparkle in his eyes. Mischief and something else that was creating havoc for her respiratory system. She took a step closer, her senses humming. "You don't want to marry me? You said you loved me. My hearing is very good. I heard that."

He grabbed her hand and intertwined their fingers, pulling her toward him. "I do love you. I'm always going to love you. You're stuck with me."

"So what's the problem? I know there's no ex that has permanently spoiled you for marriage. Your parents are still together—no nasty divorce skeletons to adorn your closet. No childhood scars to mar what I consider a perfect physical physique by the way. You're absolutely healthy and mentally sound."

"Thank you, Dr. Martin. I just think we need to go out on a date first."

She frowned, confused that his normal elephantine memory seemed to be going. "We have been on a date. We went out on a date just the other night. That counts."

He shook his head and moved a few inches closer. "That was a crappy date. Crappy dates don't count."

Her eyes narrowed, her blood pumped faster. She had facts on this one to back her up. "Of course they count. We did a survey for some magazine." She pulled her hands free and poked him in the chest. "Seventy-five percent of all marriages are based on at least one crappy—wait a minute. Are you deliberately trying to start something here?"

Mike had never mastered the art of looking innocent. "No way," he said, eyeing her mouth with studious concentration.

Hot flashes prickled her skin, but she planted her hands on her hips as a last-ditch attempt at control. "You're lying to me. I can always tell when you're lying to me."

He reached out, trailing a line from her throat to her heart, and shrugged. "I like to argue with you. It gets my blood stirring."

Mike moved forward until their personal spaces merged, letting her feel his stirred blood. Her corpuscles did a little stirring of their own. She wrapped her arms around his neck, then rubbed against him in a shameless fashion.

He began to nuzzle at her neck, his warm breath sending a shiver through her. "I'm getting a little hungry here."

Carol sighed and tilted her head to the side as his lips found that special spot right below her ear. "I've got some stuff in the fridge.'' Her hands stowed away in the back pockets of his jeans.

"That's not exactly what I had in mind," he murmured, sliding his mouth over to find her lips.

Carol kissed him, all the while backing him toward the kitchen. When she came up for air, she smiled with delight. Either his IQ was scaling down, or hers was climbing. "Hey Einstein, you should see what I have in mind."

The lightbulb flashed and he laughed. Very masculine, very sexy, very Mike.

His hands roamed over her and she wiggled with appreciation. *Cosmo* would be proud. She took his hand and led him into the kitchen.

With a grand flourish, she opened the refrigerator door, removed the can of whipped cream, and smiled. "Voilà!"

Mike looked at her and started to laugh. "You are wicked, Carol Martin." He took the can and removed the cap. "But I like it."

He grinned with evil intent and sprayed her.

He was going to pay for that. "Wait a minute. This was intended for uncensored decorative purposes, not a food fight."

"Oops. My trigger finger must have slipped. This sweater is going to have to go." Her sweater was gone in less than five seconds. Carol counted.

She wasn't going to be the only one wearing whipped cream. She retaliated by giving his pants the artistic design signature they called for. "Oh my. Look at that, will you? What a mess. Here, let me help you clean it up." Her fingers began to work at the buttons and when they didn't come apart as fast as she liked, she bent down to finish cleaning up her mess.

"Carol? Carol! What the... Oh, yeah."

IT WAS A LONG TIME later before Mike gained full function of his senses. The linoleum was sticky against his back, but with Carol splayed on top of him, he was actually more comfortable than he'd ever been in his life. They were going to need a shower later. She rose up, her body glowing pale under the kitchen lights. With appraising eyes, he noted the bits of whipped cream that still clung to her. Maybe a bath. He felt his body stir, and he ran a light finger between her breasts. But then he looked at her, really looked, and stopped.

Her hair was a mess, her smile lopsided, but her eyes... He forgot to breathe. The stars were there. Finally. And more love than he ever dreamed about. He sat up, gave her a gentle kiss, just as the clock struck midnight.

She grinned. "Merry Christmas, Mike."

"You're not wearing your bow." He wasn't the least bit sorry.

"You got your present." She pressed a warm kiss against his neck. "I hope you liked it."

There was a teasing tone in her voice that worried him. He took her face in his hands and tilted her chin. This was too important. "You're the most beautiful woman I know, and don't get me wrong, the sex is mind-boggling, but I love *you*, Carol. I want you to be my wife, my lover, and my best friend. Always. *That's* what I wanted for Christmas."

Carol felt the tears well in her eyes. She blinked them away. "Don't let me mess this up, Mike."

He smiled and kissed her, long and slow. "You're not going to mess this up. Besides, even if you did, it wouldn't matter. I'll still be here."

He sounded so sure, so absolutely certain. "Promise?"

He crossed his chest. "I swear."

"Your faith in me is the best present I've ever had. Do you know how much I love you?"

He pulled her down to the linoleum, his eyes full of every Christmas yet to be. "Show me."